M. J. Engh is the author of several short [illegible] and the novel *A Win*[illegible]k on a historical nove[illegible]

By the same author

A Wind From Bukhara

M. J. ENGH

Wheel of the Winds

GRAFTON BOOKS
A Division of the Collins Publishing Group

LONDON GLASGOW
TORONTO SYDNEY AUCKLAND

Grafton Books
A Division of the Collins Publishing Group
8 Grafton Street, London W1X 3LA

A Grafton UK Paperback Original 1989

ISBN 0-586-20614-0

Printed and bound in Great Britain by
Collins, Glasgow

Set in Plantin

To the memory of
Lysander McDog,
the original of Broz

The First Turn

It must be a very long river – so you would think, looking at it from here. You would think so because here it was broad and deep, and flowed with a powerful current, and yet here the land was not steep. The river must have come a long way already, gathering water and force from many streams and many heights. But how much farther it flowed before it poured into what sea, you would have no way of knowing.

So you would think, and watch, and turn away again, to pace your creaking floor and finger your cold walls and always turn back at last to the window. Deep, *you would know by the size of the largest ships that moved along it;* powerful, *by the speed with which they swept downstream, swinging in toward the curve of the bank and away, as though they ran on wheels set on an underwater track; and so broad that the forest on the other side – or what you would suppose to be forest – loomed low as the thick moss on your windowsill.*

Downstream – which you might call east, to have some other frame of reference than the river – you would catch glimpses of the town or city stretched along the far bank at that forest's edge: bright roofs or plazas, as if a giant hand had scattered fish scales amid the moss, a glint of movement. Somewhere out there, somewhere far downstream or beyond that unknown sea, was the equipment you must use. But how much time you had to find it would be still unclear, and how long your ship would wait beyond the flat gray clouds that roofed this sky, and how far downstream your journey lay. East, *you might call it for the light that came from that direction. But not a true east; for though it brightened and dimmed as the clouds changed, the light never rose, never sank; the night would never follow. So you would turn, and pace again, and stoop to test the crevices between the planks, and come again to the window. And watch the ships move downstream. Always and only downstream.*

1

Journeys of the Warden of Sollet Castle

There was one of the little coastal ships that plied from Beng to Rotl, and back again, which people called the *Mouse,* and its captain they called the Woman Without a God, because she had once incautiously answered 'None' when somebody asked her which god she looked to for protection. She had an old black dog with a gray muzzle, that had been with her as long as most people remembered, and so some would laugh and say the dog was her god, or what she had instead of one. But she made a fair living with her *Mouse,* carrying passengers and light cargo along the Coast, and there were more than a few people, in Beng or Rotl or on the waters of the Soll, who were neither afraid nor ashamed to call her friend.

One of these was the Warden of Sollet Castle, who every year rode down the Sollet in one of the river ships to Beng, disembarking with considerable pomp, and after his business there always sought the *Mouse* to carry him to Rotl. The two of them would sit on deck, or in the little crowded cabin, with the black dog asleep between their feet, and talk over the year's happenings and what they thought of them; and the Warden would bring out all the news of upriver (which indeed she had heard many times over from the shippers) and the Captain would give him all the news of the Coast (which indeed he had been hearing for two weeks past in Beng). And they would laugh and drink a little ale and speak of growing older, but each of them would find that the other seemed no older at all. And after three weeks in Rotl (for he had family there) the Warden would retrace his journey to Beng; but this time there would be less, and less sociable, talk on board the *Mouse* – there being less news for them to hash over, and the Warden having his mind bent forward on the tedious journey upriver by canal and road, and the Captain's eyes always occupied with the business of her vessel.

It was on the talkative leg of one of these shuttle voyages that the Warden brought out the news of his prisoner. This was a rare plum of a happening, and the Captain had been waiting with interest for him to mention it. 'Now, Repnomar,' (this was the Captain's name) 'you'll never guess what's come to me from upstream,' the Warden said proudly, and paused for her guesses.

'Bad weather, I suppose, but that wouldn't make you grin like a beaver,' said the Captain.

'Bad weather on the Sollet is no news,' said the Warden, grinning wider. 'Though there was that flood that brought us down the raft-load of White People – '

'Shut up and have some more ale and out with it,' said Repnomar, a little illogically but with no loss of meaning.

'It's not so different from that time. Let's see, five years ago was that?'

'More like six or seven. What did you get this time, a raft of pink people?'

'Just one, just one,' said the Warden with relish. He had a deep, chuckling laugh that did the heart good.

Here the Captain excused herself to swear at some of her sailors concerning a matter of leeway, and the black dog (whose name was Broz) joined in with a dutiful growl; though indeed, in good weather, this coasting voyage was so routine a business that all hands could have done their share of it blindfold, curses and growls included. 'Now, Lethgro,' said the Captain, leaning back again (for the *Mouse* was so small that she had not even left her seat by the taffrail to deliver her cursing), 'now, Lethgro, get it out and get it over. What kind of savage have the waters washed down to Sollet Castle?'

And Lethgro the Warden – with a little more urging, to bring out the full savor – told her how the Sollet shippers had delivered to him a man unlike any ever known to have been seen between the Mountains and the Soll. It was clear that he had been driven out from his own place, wherever that was; and his own name, though he tried hard to teach it to them, was so uncouth in sound, and required such uncomfortable and unseemly twistings of the mouth to pronounce, that the Warden and his people soon gave it up and called him simply the Exile. He seemed well enough satisfied with that.

Indeed he was a pert little person, cheerful and uncomplaining so far as his own affairs went, but full of question and suggestion for all else. It was hard, what with his size and his clumsy speech (for he knew little or nothing of any familiar language, and talked in scraps and guesses) and the utter innocence and ignorance of some of his questions – it was hard not to think of him as a child. He asked, for instance, why ships always went downstream (as if a ship could float against the current), and why the light never moved across the sky (to which the Warden had replied, 'For the same reason, I suppose, that Sollet Castle doesn't get up and walk to Beng and back again,' having his journey on his mind).

All things seemed strange to the Exile: the packtrains of sheep moving slowly up the road with their loads of basketry and grain, the great lografts sweeping down-Sollet between the lumber ships, unpainted wood stark white against the dull pink of the muddy river, the hunters with their dogs. He delighted to watch the half-grown pups scrambling up trees with excited yips and jumping clumsily down again, and the river birds dipping and skimming over the waves. The Warden fancied sometimes that the strangeness of the Exile's view (in which the commonest things, it seemed, looked wondrous) was somehow due to the strangeness of his eyes. These were small and pale, but with great pupils that were as round as crow's eggs and had the unsettling property of changing size.

However it was, the little man was a source of much interest in Sollet Castle. He wanted to know all its ins and outs and turnings, which was natural enough in a prisoner looking for escape, but in him seemed so guileless that the Warden was hard put not to tell him more than was proper. Then, too, misshapen though he was, it was a deformity more to raise kindly laughter than disgust, at any rate after the first blink. Hunched and scrunched, and limping on his bandy legs, he was like a great good-natured toad who had recently learned wisdom and decided to be a man.

So he had paced limpingly up and down his cell, brighteyed and patient, and gazed hourlong from its window, his thick chin on the sill, and most often dined with the Warden and entertained him with his questions. Once it had been made clear to him that he must be kept there till the Warden could consult in Beng and in Rotl, he raised no further objections and showed no sign of resentment; only asking, from time to time, questions that showed a keen interest in what the results of that consultation might be. These the Warden did not like to answer, since the chances were that (unless far more information should be forthcoming than seemed likely) the Exile would be imprisoned in Sollet Castle till he died, or perhaps be done away with at once, to save the upkeep. 'For after all, Repnomar,' said the Warden. 'The only thing clear is that there's a nation of crippled dwarves somewhere up the Sollet; and if he's not here as a spy, he'll be looking for help to make his way back to the place he was chased out of; and either way leads to war and troubles.' For Warden Lethgro was a peaceful man.

'There you have it again,' said Repnomar earnestly, with the solid joy of one confirmed in an old argument. 'Doesn't this prove to you, Lethgro, that there are nations far upstream, and even beyond the Mountains?'

'Far upstream, I don't argue with you,' answered the Warden, chuckling. 'I've seen too much come down the Sollet. Beyond the Mountains, how could that be? As well say beyond the clouds. And you know as sure as I do that water runs downhill. The whole Sollet and all its streams flow from the Mountains. How could there be any river beyond them? And how could there be a nation without a river?'

'I'm glad to hear you admit that water runs downhill,' said the Captain, veering to a tack still more congenial to her than the Mountain one. 'You grant, then, that the Current across the Soll must lead to some outlet?'

'Maybe to a leak in the bottom, like the current in a leaky ale-can,' said the Warden unpropitiously. 'If there is a bottom. Or maybe it goes round and round, like the rings of a whirlpool.'

'And slopes you down to drowning in the middle?' Repnomar cried. 'You're a cheerful friend to have on board a boat!' She rose and stretched herself, and old Broz thumped his tail, tipped with white hairs like a dipped paintbrush. 'Your stories make me restless, Lethgro. One of these days I'm going to try it.'

'It's the length of your legs that makes you restless,' said the Warden, grumping a little into his ale. 'You worry me with your nonsense, Rep. I like to feel I'm sailing with a prudent captain, not a harebrained daredevil.'

'Well, stay on land, if you're afraid of ever getting your feet wet,' said Repnomar rudely. 'There's a road from Beng to Rotl, and from Rotl to Beng.'

The Warden groaned, for the prospect of the journey upriver from Beng to Sollet Castle always weighed on him, and he preferred not to contemplate another on the top of it. He did not much enjoy plodding through the hills of the Middle Sollet country, breathing the dust raised by the laden packsheep; but still worse, in his opinion was to sit idle on the deck of a canal boat, slowly hauled through the dead level of the Lower Sollet, where as far as the eye could see there was nothing but the rich purple of ripening grain brushed and dimpled by the wind.

By now they had moved almost out of sight of land, only a gleam of cliffs showing on the horizon; for the winds of the year had risen early (as everyone agreed), and already there was such an offshore breeze along the Coast that the little *Mouse* was carried far out, and would have to tack patiently back to Rotl. This was nothing, of course, to what she would feel at the height of the season; and *that* was nothing – so the Warden would tell the Captain – to thc great winds that boomed down the Sollet, lifting trees like straws and roofs like handkerchiefs; but the Captain would always reply with some scorn that there was a world of difference between a river and the open Soll, regardless of the speed of the wind.

'You know there's no vessel I'd rather sail on than the *Mouse*,' the Warden began soothingly, and paused as the Captain, who had been about to sit down again, straightened herself and squinted high into the wind. 'What is it?' he asked somewhat anxiously; for in his judgement what came on the wind was usually trouble.

'Crow,' Repnomar replied in brief; and she waved her long right arm in a slow arc overhead, and stood there, squinting and waving, while Warden Lethgro peered here and there in the blank sky and chanced at last on a sailing fleck of black. Presently the crow came coasting in, landed in a ruffle of feathers on the rigging, preened itself while

Repnomar swore, and then flapped and hopped downward by stages and came pacing across the narrow deck with the dignity of a town councilor, while all the crew gave it room and the Captain waited, for shipcrows are spirited and touchy birds and must have their due.

'What's the news?' Lethgro asked the Captain, as she stooped and lifted the bird and undid the rolled message from its leg. *The bad news,* was the thought in his mind, but he schooled his tongue to turn away the omen.

'Whatever it is, it's for you,' the Captain answered, and handed it to him. It was well known that Warden Lethgro always traveled on the *Mouse*, and thus natural that any word for him that reached the message station at Beng harbor would be entrusted to one of Captain Repnomar's crows.

Now the Warden groaned aloud as he read, and Repnomar blinked her eyes in sympathy, for in fact she had taken the gist of the message before she passed it to him. 'Well,' he said resignedly, handing it back to her to read with more leisure, 'they'll have had the news in Rotl too. I must make my report and take my disgrace. And then there's work to do.'

'Where will you search for him?' the Captain asked, for the news was nothing less than the escape of the Exile from Sollet Castle, not long after the Warden began his journey downriver; and the Warden answered gloomily, 'Well, if he can fly, I suppose we must search everywhere the wind goes.'

Now, it was true in a way that the Exile had flown from his high window in Sollet Castle, as a buzzard flies with tilting wings that seem to do no work at all; but this did not prove – so the Warden was to argue patiently and long in Rotl, and again with less patience in Beng – this did not prove that he stood high in the favour of some outlandish god, still less that he was such a god himself, but only that he was a small, light man and that the Sollet winds were strong. 'Which till now,' the Warden added with exasperation, 'no one has ever doubted.'

'The question, Warden Lethgro,' said one of the councilors severely, 'is why, if you knew these things, you gave him an unbarred window and cloth enough to make his wing, or his sail, or his kite, as you choose to call it from one moment to the next.'

'There are no bars,' said Lethgro, 'on Sollet Castle windows, and no prisoner has ever escaped before.'

'Which would seem to be a miracle,' observed another councilor drily.

'Under that window,' went on Lethgro, when he had champed his jaws together hard and relaxed them again with some difficulty, 'runs a parapet always patrolled by my best guards.'

'Whom you stationed there, it seems, to gaze at this devil while he flew over their heads and down the Sollet,' remarked one councilor, while another murmured to her neighbor, 'Those are his *best* guards, mind you.'

'They shot at him,' said Lethgro, 'and it's certain that arrows pierced his kite-sail – '

'Or wing-kite,' interrupted a gray-bearded councilor who had sat silent till now, and laughed mightily.

' – And possible that one at least struck him. He may be wounded. Indeed, he may be dead.'

'And the cloth, Warden Lethgro,' pursued the first councilor; 'why did he have so much cloth?'

'It was coverings from his bed,' answered Lethgro. 'He was always cold, and needed more bedclothes than an ordinary man.'

'And he complained so pitifully that you had mercy on him and gave him more than a prisoner's just due?'

'He complained not at all, but I saw that he was cold,' said Lethgro, and cursed himself at once for a fool and an honest man; for the councilor who had mocked at his guards said again to her neighbor, 'A very helpful Warden to his *prisoners*.'

But the upshot of all the talking was that Lethgro was perhaps not to be degraded of his post if he could bring back the Exile, or at any rate his head, and if no war with unknown nations, or visitation of unknown gods, resulted. 'And that "perhaps",' said Lethgro morosely, when he sat again with Repnomar by the *Mouse*'s rail, 'is the worst word in a bad lot.'

'"Perhaps not" is better than "certainly",' said Repnomar, to whom chance was like weather, a thing to be used and impossible to escape or do without.

The Warden sighed deeply. 'And then too,' he said, 'it was no easy thing he did. First manhandling that wing, or kite – '

'Sail, I would call it,' said Repnomar, who had heard much of it by this time.

' – Onto the window ledge, with the guards always passing just below; and then diving into the air, not knowing surely if the thing would carry him past the parapet, or let him crash on the road below, and likeliest anyway to fall into the Sollet, or be riddled with arrows, or at best be caught in the branches of some tree.'

'Either he knew well what he could do with his sail,' said the Captain, 'or he wanted his freedom very badly.' And added after a moment's thought, 'Likely both.'

The Warden sighed and said nothing. The truth was that he felt betrayed by the Exile, toward whom he had had no feelings but friendly ones; and yet deprived of the satisfaction of blaming him, for a prisoner who sees a way out has surely no obligation to stay imprisoned. Also, though Lethgro had defended his guards to the councils of Beng and Rotl, he felt in his heart that they could have done better, and this weighed upon him sadly. He felt, too, that every hour spent in talk would be held against him as an hour wasted, and yet there was nothing more profitable to be done, unless there was profit in rushing up and down the Sollet, which he doubted. He had already set every man and woman he could muster or borrow to combing the woods and shorelines for any trace of the Exile, squads of searchers working down both banks from Sollet Castle to meet others working up from Beng. Rewards had been offered in Beng and Rotl, as upriver at Castle Wharf, and inspectors waited at every landing to greet every river ship. So that the Warden told himself he had a right to sit for an hour in Beng harbor, while the *Mouse* waited for a new cargo, and talk to Repnomar, who for all her arguing did not reproach him for things not much his fault.

They were alone on board, and indeed alone at the pier; for it was a festival time (which put the Warden into a still gloomier frame of mind), so that there would be no loading for some hours, and Repnomar (having no taste for this particular festival) had chosen to stay on guard while all her crew joined the celebration, and the captains of the two smaller vessels moored at this pier, trusting her to keep good watch (for the *Mouse* lay between them) had likewise gone off with their whole crews. All the waterfront was quiet, so far as human sounds went, with only the peaceful noises of wind and water, birds going about their business, and the occasional yap of a dog; but from inland, deep in the city, they could hear the cries and music of festival.

'It's a good time,' said Repnomar, seeing that the Warden had no wish to speak further of the Exile at present, 'for pilferers and sneak thieves.'

Just then Broz set up the furious barking he reserved for those he took to be pirates, more urgent and threatening than his sneak-thief bark. The Captain sprang up to investigate, and the Warden followed, glad enough to have other troubles than his own to look to. It was not on board the *Mouse* that this trouble lay, but on the vessel moored at her landward side, a taller, lengthier ship, with a prayer against pirates painted along its bulwarks in green. Someone was in the act of climbing over these bulwarks, prayer and all, and in spite of Broz's objections. Repnomar hailed this intruder with a bellow that seemed to transfix him like an arrowshaft, for he jerked hard and hung quivering for a moment; but instead of falling back into the water, he heaved himself up onto the deck with one last effort.

By that time the Captain was already on the pier, and Broz, considering his duty nearly done, had subsided into a low growling; but Warden Lethgro had not moved from the *Mouse*'s rail, which he clenched with a violent hand. His face was dark with anger and his back stiff with dignity, and when a tuft of the intruder's hair appeared above the gunwale, he uttered a bellow that put Repnomar's to shame. 'Come here!' was what he shouted in his wrath.

Repnomar paused for a scant moment, with her foot on her neighbor's gangplank. At first sight she had taken the intruder for some thieving or frolicking child of the town; but neither Broz nor the Warden would have raised such an outcry for such a cause. So she went on assured in mind, and as soon as she caught sight of the dodging figure among the ropes and barrels she shouted out, 'The Warden is your only friend!' and the Warden chimed in with another 'Come here!' (not so loud this time but no less firm) and Broz with a throatier growl.

He came out then from his cover and stood before her, most forlorn to look at, bedraggled as he was, and ugly, and limping. But he nodded his head and essayed a smile, though his strange face under his tangled hair showed pinched and wild. The Captain gripped him by the arm and led him back to her ship, where she had to shout Broz into silence, and stood him like a naughty child before the Warden. When she let go his arm, he reeled, and sank wet and senseless to the deck, and 'Poor Exile,' said the Warden; 'there's blood on his shirt.'

2

Occupational Hazards of an Inspector for the Council of Beng

When the festival was over, and the waterfront had begun to stir again with sailors and traders and wharf people, they were still arguing on board the *Mouse*. The Exile lay open-eyed and silent in the Captain's cabin, his hands and feet well bound and his wound well salved and bandaged, while the Captain and the Warden paced the deck outside, and frowned in at him now and again, and waved their hands in each other's faces and debated the question that was life or death for him. 'For,' said the Warden, 'the order is out to kill him at will (though that's not the order I gave *my* people), since he lacked patience to wait for judgement. And if he's judged now, while the Councils are hot against him and against me, his life will be as short as his stature. No, I'll take him upriver in secret. I can hire a canal boat and crew it with my own people, which will get us as far as the forest country – and from there on we can camp in the woods. And when his wound has healed, and the councilors have seen there's no war afoot because of him – ' ('How do you know that?' demanded Repnomar) ' – I'll send the news downstream that he's been found; and all can be done in calm and reason.'

'But there's no point in it,' the Captain said, not for the first time. 'If you mean to report him found, why not do it now – ' ('I've just told you,' said Lethgro) ' – instead of making yourself his accomplice? If the Councils are hot against you now, think what they'll be if you're found hiding him – you who were charged to hold him in the first place – '

'And let him go while my back was turned – I know,'

said the Warden gloomily. 'But who's to find that I'm hiding him?'

'Who?' cried Repnomar. 'Are you utterly mad, Lethgro? A hundred of your people will know of it, and likely all seven of my crew, for you'd have to bundle him out of here somehow – '

'Not a hundred, nor half that,' Lethgro objected. 'And if you'll drop us quietly up the Coast a little way – '

Here the captain of the ship to landward of the *Mouse* hailed Repnomar to ask if all had been quiet. 'Quiet enough,' she answered, after a moment. 'Once I thought I saw some wharf child lurking about, but I was wrong.' And she and Lethgro lowered their voices and took their argument to the other side of the cabin, where presently she called out to the captain of the third vessel that all was well, and greeted her crew as they came merrily, and staggering a little, on board.

Being here on the lee side of the cabin, they leaned against it cozily enough, while the Warden told the Captain that now she had no choice to speak of but to land him and the Exile at some unfrequented spot an hour or so along the Coast and let them make their own way thereafter, and the Captain assuring the Warden that she knew her choices better than he and that she did not mean to be a party to his foolishness, nor for that matter allow him to commit it.

They were still at it when an inspector came onto the pier, supplied against objections with a certificate from the Council of Beng and a platoon of soldiers. Being on the wrong side of the cabin, they never noticed her till she had finished her inspection of the ship with the green prayer and stepped unceremoniously on board the *Mouse*. But at this, one of the crew, who was a little soberer than some, ran aft to warn the Captain, while others tried to discourage the inspector from advancing. For indeed all the *Mouse*'s crew were well aware, from the tone of the discussion beside the cabin, that something was afoot, though they might not have rightly guessed what.

Now the Captain and the Warden looked at each other hard, though not long, there being little time, and as though there were only one thought between them they turned and strode to the starboard bow, where the narrowness of the *Mouse*'s gangplank more than the arguments of the crew was holding back the inspector's people.

'What's this all about?' the Captain demanded threateningly, while the inspector did likewise in very nearly the same words and at the same moment. And when the inspector made it clear that she came to search for the Exile, on grounds of a report that he had been sighted near the waterfront, Repnomar, who had been crowding her all the while toward the head of the gangplank, suddenly pushed her down it and stooped and heaved the end of the gangplank into the Soll, while the crew joined in with a good will, some casting loose the mooring lines and shoving the *Mouse* free with poles, while others ran to set the sail for the offshore wind, and all without an order given.

Three or four of the inspector's guards had been dumped with her on the gangplank, and the others mostly blinded by the splash, so that the sail had caught the wind before the first missiles struck the deck – arrows and a spear – and the *Mouse*, yawing wildly, scraped past the third ship at the pier and plunged headlong and staggering toward the open Soll. But very soon the Captain had her ship under control, and they were running straight before the wind, past the breakwater at the harbor mouth, with a good lead on whoever might follow.

'What have you done now, Repnomar?' the Warden asked bitterly, and Repnomar answered, 'You had your chance to tell her you'd taken him already, and you said nothing. What was I to do?' And the Warden sighed and blinked his eyes, and laughed at last, there being little else for it.

Presently they were out of sight of Beng, and no sign of pursuit yet, which did not surprise the Captain. 'For,' she said, 'when they've wrung the Soll-water out of that inspector, she'll have to go back to the Council for another certificate to commandeer a ship with – for I know there's no Council ship in Beng harbor right now – and then find the ship, and argue with the captain, and then with the crew, and pray to all the gods the Council will be counting on to find us for them, and by that time we'll be past finding.'

Meanwhile the Warden had gone back to the cabin and undone the Exile's bonds, considering it not likely he would fly from the *Mouse* in mid-Soll as he had flown from Sollet Castle. The Exile had thanked him cheerfully and sat up bright-eyed and asked no questions for the present, seeming to understand enough from the roll of the *Mouse* under him and the singing of the rigging; and when Warden Lethgro looked in on him again a little later, he was lying flat again on Repnomar's bunk, his eyes closed and one crooked hand clasped over his chest where his wound was.

By this time Lethgro had found a new cause of uneasiness; for the Captain, once out of sight of land and with no pursuing sail in view, had begun to cast her course first left, then right, sweeping a broad zigzag across the Soll's face, and keeping always a keen eye on the waves. 'What are you up to, Repnomar?' he demanded at last, for just then he had seen a flush of satisfaction leap in her face, and a setting of her lips that, he suspected, boded ill.

'There's no better time to try it than now,' said the Captain, and Lethgro groaned.

'It's not your fantasy of the Soll Current you're talking about, is it?' he asked, hoping perhaps to undo with words what was already done in fact.

'Does it *feel* like fantasy?' cried the Captain, who could never understand that not all feet and hands and ears could read the various throbbings and workings and sighings of the *Mouse* as hers did. And when Lethgro asked, to be quite sure of the depth of trouble, 'You mean we're already in the Current?' she jerked her head for 'yes' so vehemently that her hair flew against the wind.

'I don't deny the Current,' Lethgro said with feeling. 'But it's fantasy and foolishness to suppose it could carry us anywhere but sooner or later to the bottom of the Soll.'

'If there is a bottom,' the Captain added mockingly.

'I knew you were hasty and headstrong, Repnomar,' said the Warden; 'but I thought you had better care for your crew and your ship (I don't speak of your passengers) than to set sail into uncharted waters on a moment's notice, without a plan, without supplies. Chances are we'll starve before we drown, if pirates or a storm don't finish us first.'

Repnomar laughed, a sound which to Lethgro's ears had a hard ring to it. 'Plans we'll make as we go,' she said. 'And the *Mouse* is never without supplies, unless at the end of a longer voyage than any I've made yet. We have enough to feed us all till Windfall, if we're a little careful. Now,' she added more kindly, 'think, Lethgro. All the Coast both ways from Beng will be full of inspectors and troops and councilors, and all the coastal boats and the Sollet shippers looking for us. I might, by good luck, find a spot to land you; but where would you be then, except in trouble and surrounded?'

'That may be true *now*,' said the Warden bitterly, 'since you've wasted so much time.' But, 'We had to get clear,' said Repnomar; 'and by then it was already too late.'

So Warden Lethgro, when he had paced a turn around the deck and looked into the cabin once more (where the Exile slept, breathing hoarsely through his open mouth), settled himself beside the Captain where she sat at the tiller, saying as cheerfully as he could manage, 'Well, then, Repnomar, what kind of a plan can we contrive?'

And Repnomar said briskly, but with a deep crease between her brows as she squinted round at the blank circle of the horizon, midmost of which the *Mouse* seemed to sit like the one dry chip in a world of uneasy water, 'We'll sail to the other side of the Soll, what else?'

3
Sailing

The Warden of Sollet Castle was hungry, but he had no appetite. He lay uncomfortably (for he was a large man) on a bunk in the hold, and everywhere he looked in the half darkness of under-hatches he saw empty spaces around him, that might have been filled with food and were not. It was true that the Captain kept her little ship well stocked as if she stood always in expectation of such encounters as the one with the inspector at the pier in Beng, and laid in new foodstuffs at every landing before she looked for paying cargo; but it was just as true that the *Mouse* was not stocked (if any ship could be) for a voyage across the Soll. There was no particular likelihood, so far as the Warden knew, that the Soll *had* another side. Every hour's sailing, with the wind on their stern and the Current rushing them headlong, took them a distance from the Coast that three or four hours might not suffice to struggle back across. The Captain had claimed from the beginning that they had food enough to last them till Windfall, and it seemed now (the Warden thought with a pang) that she had been more than right; for the wind was already failing, and the weather had turned rainy, though it should have been weeks yet before the Rains, and many weeks till Windfall. But who knew how the seasons might be perverted in this wilderness of waves? And if the winds of the year fell indeed, what hope would there be for the poor *Mouse*, becalmed in mid-Soll under the blazing light?

For they ran always and always into the light. It glowed now not so much ahead of them as above, and the Warden groaned to notice how clearly he could see now even under hatches. There was one spot in the sky from which the light seemed to pour as from a lamp, making the clouds there too bright to look at. Also, the Warden noted, the air was warmer here in mid-Soll, and growing warmer still as they fled down the dying wind. It was true that the Exile blossomed in this warmth, and seemed for the first time comfortable in his clothes, for all the trouble of his wound and of a wrenched ankle that made his hobbling gait more awkward even than before; but the Warden was accustomed to the pleasant coolness of the Middle Sollet forests, and this ever-growing heat was like an ever-heavier weight that pressed upon his skin.

'Why,' he had asked the Captain, 'if you're determined to cut water that's never felt a plank before, why not at least follow the Coast? You can come to the end of the world that way as surely as this, and in the meantime we'd have food and supplies within reach, and coves where we could lie up in case of storms.'

'And pirates, and shoals and rocks I don't know the marks of,' the Captain had answered, 'and the Councils' people dogging us afloat and ashore. A sure way to put your neck in a noose, Lethgro, or your head well salted in a bag beside the Exile's, for the Councils to make much of. Not to mention,' she added, 'mine.' And went on at length concerning the foolishness of his idea, so that Lethgro suspected sadly that she was uneasy in her own mind about this wild voyage and had spent much time beating down the arguments that arose there.

All these things had taken away the Warden's appetite, so that though he was always hungry he ate little and with no pleasure. Soll water, too, had a sharp taste he had never liked, and he fancied it did not quench thirst as well as the snow-fed streams that ran into the Sollet; but Repnomar told him this was nonsense. The Exile had refused at first to drink of it, when he saw it hauled up in buckets over the

Mouse's side; but, there being nothing else to drink, he came to it soon enough, and seemed surprised (as so much else surprised him) that it was water indeed and not poison.

It was an arrow of the Warden's guards that had struck him in his flight from Sollet Castle, and his ankle, as well as they could make out from his clumsy speech, had buckled under him when he came down awkwardly among the trees. Clearly it had been a hard journey for him since, and Lethgro thought it must have been in desperation that he decided to stow away on board one of the coastal boats at Beng. But with food enough and rest enough and Repnomar's salves, and now with the warm air that he seemed to bask and bathe in, his wound was healing at last (though he still drew his breath with a harsh whistle) and the swelling of his ankle had melted away. Whether he understood at all what sort of voyage they were embarked on because of him, there was no knowing.

And having run through all these thoughts again and come to no happier conclusion than before, the Warden rose cramped and unrested and hungry from his bunk, and made his way on deck where he could stretch and not be tormented by the sight of the empty spaces in the hold, though indeed there was enough to torment him here too – the shoreless swell of the Soll spreading beyond sight whichever way he turned, with a squall of rain off the right bow; and the hot, unwholesome light raining down from overhead, so that he bowed unwillingly under it and pulled his hat low over his eyes.

The Captain was in the cabin, showing maps to the Exile. Lethgro went in to them, glad of a chance to speak to her out of the crew's hearing, for it was of the crew he wanted to speak, this being another item that troubled him. Broz moved himself from where he lay at the Exile's feet (not as in affection but as ready to set his teeth in him if the need arose) and came to stand at the Warden's side, for he liked old friends best. The Captain had out her great map of the whole Coast, and was showing the Exile (who throughout his escape, it seemed, had had little enough idea where he was) how Beng and Rotl lay both on the right side of the Sollet, Beng just at its mouth and Rotl downcoast, while on the left bank and up the Coast from there the towns were smaller and more scattered; and when the Warden entered she looked up challengingly, ready to answer when he should ask again why she had not taken them up that empty shore. But instead he asked sharply, 'What do you mean to do, Repnomar, when your crew refuse to sail farther?'

'Put them under hatches and sail on,' she said darkly, 'if it comes to that, Lethgro. But it won't come to that. We've sailed too far already to turn back.'

The Warden clamped his mouth shut, so as to say nothing. This was what he had most feared to hear her admit; but, supposing it to be true (and he believed it very surely), he saw no good to any of them in quarreling over what was too late to change. He moved a heap of charts to make room for himself (for the Captain's bunk was the only seat in the cabin, and served sometimes to eke out her chart table as well) and sat down heavily, and Broz laid his gray muzzle on his knee. 'Well,' the Warden said.

And she answered, 'I've never seen this kind of weather at this time of year any more than you have – but I didn't expect the middle of the Soll to be the same as the Coast. And if Windfall comes before the Rains out here – well, we have the Current.' She saw the look in the Warden's eyes, and laughed. 'I'm not a fool, Lethgro, though you may think otherwise. If the Current ever slacked, I would have turned back then and there, and struck land somewhere far upcoast from the Sollet, where we might have a chance of landing unseen. But it hasn't slacked. It's stronger watch by watch and hour by hour; and that means we're coming to the Outlet.'

'Where?' the Warden asked skeptically, and gestured toward the cabin window, where the Soll showed unbroken as the sky, without change or end.

'We're not there yet,' the Captain said testily; 'I grant that.'

'And what good will it be to come there,' added Lethgro, 'if it's as starved skeletons we come?'

'We won't starve – not with the fish we've been catching,' Repnomar began. But just here a shout was raised on deck, and she leaped up, with her face flushing, and cried out, 'You hear that, Lethgro? A sail to leeward! It can't be from the Coast – good or bad, it's from the far side of the Soll!'

4
Meeting

Downwind of them it was, but running into the wind, slantwise across their course. 'See that,' said the Captain to the Warden, where they stood watching in the *Mouse*'s bow. 'The Current must veer to starboard here, for if it ran straight they'd be cutting across it now, and it would be setting them back; but see how they come on.'

'I see,' answered the Warden, 'all too well. I hope you've weapons on board.'

'We've no cause to think – ' began the Captain, and broke off, for the lookout cried out then for another sail, to starboard. 'Held back for a little by the Current,' said the Captain, nodding calmly; but she gave orders to run up the red flag, which all along the Coast was the signal of distress, and in the meantime to break out pikes and swords and what bows and arrows they had.

'I suppose,' said the Warden, 'you have your reasons for not turning out of harm's way.'

'Sooner or later we have to meet the people of these waters,' Repnomar said reasonably. 'We've still no cause to think it's anything worse than curiosity that drives them on so fast – it can't be every day they see a sail coming over the Soll from this direction – but if we run from them at the first sight, what can they think but that we're an enemy? Besides, they know these winds and waters, Lethgro, and I don't.'

'Well, give me a bow, then,' said the Warden with a sigh. 'For I don't suppose you've many expert archers in your crew.'

'Young Flitten is good enough,' said Repnomar, but she

looked somewhat grim, and had the best bow brought quickly to the Warden, to try the feel of.

Now the *Mouse* ran straight on – as if, the Warden thought, into a pair of open jaws; for the first sail was tacking back toward their port side, and presently, as Repnomar had predicted, the Current bore to the right, carrying them toward the second sail, that turned to meet them. The wind, at that critical time, had lapsed into a veering and gusty breeze, and the Captain gave order to shorten sail, letting the Current carry them. Lethgro said nothing, but he finished bending his bow and began studying his arrows, sorting them by the straightness of their shafts and the evenness of their feathering.

'There!' Repnomar cried out suddenly. 'There's the land!' Lethgro peered, and the Exile beside him, and all the crew took their eyes off the sails closing in on them to follow the Captain's pointing arm. Just when the Warden was ready to confess he saw nothing, it came to him that he had been seeing it for some time past – a line of heavier color where the pale clouds ahead met the glistening Soll. 'Low. Very Low,' the Captain said, almost in awe; for the Coast she had sailed up and down all these years past was high and rocky, with dark pinnacles and bright cliffs that stood out clear to ships far offshore. 'If it comes to that,' she said presently, 'we'll run straight to land there, where there's a kind of point. But I want to stick with the Current as long as we can.' And she gave command for the oars to be got ready, since the wind was no longer to be relied on.

All this time the Exile had stood silent, except for the rasp of his breath, his quick eyes going from Lethgro to Repnomar, from sail to sail, and from the dim land to the red flag at the masthead. Now he plucked the Warden's sleeve and began to ask the meaning of these things, and the Warden explained as best he could.

'And the red flag,' put in the Captain impatiently, to

finish the story, 'is to tell them we mean them no harm, and need their help.' And the sail to starboard being almost within bowshot, she set one foot on the rail and sprang up, holding by a rope that throbbed at that moment in a gust of wind. She waved her right arm and hailed them loudly, hallooing in every language she knew a word of, for who could say what outlandish tongue might be spoken on the far side of the Soll? Then she jumped down, saying to the Warden, 'Do you see that? See how their sail slacked? That was no trick of the wind, though it's tricky enough here. They've cut into the Current, trusting to have enough way on them to hold against it till we come up with them. Look! Look at that sail!' And for all the hazard they stood in, she laughed with pure delight, for these alien ships were rigged in a way she had never seen or heard of, and schooned against the gusts like gulls.

Here the Exile asked leave to carry a pike; and the Captain and the Warden, after one glance exchanged, both nodded, and the pike was brought to him, though indeed it was hard to see how he would manage it, the weapon being twice as long as he was tall.

Now the Captain gave order to slack the ropes so that the *Mouse*'s sail no longer caught the wind, but fluttered uselessly, swinging one way or another with every gust; and the Current bore them steadily down on the near ship, that stood almost motionless on the water. Gaudy scraps of color flapped on a pole or mast in the bow, and beside it on a raised perch a figure waved other banners, green and orange, with both hands – signals, plainly, but what they signified none knew on board the *Mouse*. All stood tense and waiting now, for they were well within bowshot, and drawing nearer and nearer they gazed steadily into dark faces that gazed steadily back, and tried to make out there some trace of promise or threat. The Warden held an arrow nocked to the bowstring, but with the bow lowered at his side, and the archers of the crew did likewise. No weapons showed on board the strange ship, but there were many people on deck, all watching and waiting – many more, Lethgro thought grimly, than would be needed to sail such a vessel. For though this ship was longer than the *Mouse*, it was narrower and lower, and so in all perhaps not quite as large. No one moved on either ship, except one sailor twitching a paddle on the far side of the stranger vessel. They were so close now that the two crews might have reached across the gap and touched each other's hands, if this had been the time for handclasps. The Exile gripped his pike stoutly with both hands, and stood back from the side to give himself room. Repnomar had taken up a short sword and Broz beside her growled low in his throat, as one well acquainted with the ways of pirates. Now all the *Mouse*'s crew commended themselves to one god or another, and reflected briefly on the unwisdom of shipping with a godless captain, though in most times Repnomar's luck was good. There was a light jolt and a long scrape, and the two ships were floating side to side.

At the first touch, all had come alive on both decks. Like a breaking wave, the strangers flung themselves at the *Mouse*'s side. Lethgro jerked up his bow and let fly his arrow point-blank, but there was no room for archery here, and though some of the crew had a little more time, being farther from the onslaught, none had leisure for a second arrow. Those who were able dropped their bows and snatched up swords or pikes; the rest fought with their knives and their hands. Broz leaped to it like a devil, and the first cry was a scream from the man he struck. Repnomar's face was like iron, and she swung her short sword with a long arm. But the Exile, rushing forward, had planted his pike point in the *Mouse*'s deck and vaulted over the side into the stranger ship.

Lethgro, much occupied with three men who were trying

to bear him down, nevertheless heard Repnomar shouting something about the sail; and managing a glance in that direction, he saw one of the crew laboring to haul it round into the wind, that for the moment held strong toward shore. This seemed to him something more pleasant in itself than fighting hand to hand, and perhaps more profitable. With a giant effort he got free, heaving one stranger bodily overboard and disposing of the others he did not well know how, and strode across the deck through the hubbub to join the sailor on the rope. Another, with a two-handed sword, was holding back the strangers who might have put a stop to the business. So they got the sail well into the wind and made fast there, and the *Mouse* began to swing away from the other ship and shudder along its side.

Now was a strange time on board the *Mouse*. Three of her crew lay helpless (whether dead or wounded none had time to inquire); with the Captain and the Warden, and without the Exile, that left six able to work or fight, and there were more than twice that many strangers already on board, and more climbing the gunwales, and the second ship bearing down on them fast from the other side. Nevertheless these six felt their hearts leap when the sail caught the wind, as if all were well now. Repnomar with a pike reversed was shoving the *Mouse* away from the stranger ship, and between shoves beating at various hands that clung to the gunwales; and as the *Mouse* floated clear she gave a whoop of joy, and two or three of the crew picked up the cry and redoubled it. Lethgro, who was not quite in a mood for whooping, yet smiled as he made havoc behind the mast with a swung pike, tumbling down with the same stroke pirates and empty kegs that had not yet received their cargo when the *Mouse* left Beng so hastily.

But Broz should be counted the seventh of the *Mouse*'s fighters, for he alone had cornered four pirates against the taffrail, and held them there with a great racket of barking.

Repnomar, her face shining now with triumph, sprang onto a crate behind her dog and shouted to them to jump into the Soll and leave her ship, pointing to the water and making jabbing motions with the pike to help them understand. Indeed they understood so well that first one and then all four crawled or vaulted or dived over the rail and struck out for their own ship. And as Broz turned in a fury of snarls to look for others, they began to drop off from the *Mouse* like ripe fruit from a wind-tossed tree, the crew and Lethgro helping them with a good will.

Now they ran out the oars, two on each side, and the Captain herself let out more sail, and the *Mouse* began to pick up headway fast. The stranger ship would be forced to trim sail and veer a full half-circle before it could follow, aside from the matter of picking up its people from the water. But it was still close enough for shooting, and now a hail of arrows struck the *Mouse*. The second ship, too, had closed the gap so well that a few arrows came from that direction, but still fell short. The Captain hurried to her tiller, crying out to the crew not to shoot back but to look to their work and their wounds. Indeed, they and their arrows were too few to do more than exasperate the pirates – 'If,' as Repnomar put it to herself, '*pirates* is the right word for them.' She steered with the wind across the Current, heading for that point of flat gray land; not that she had much hope of safety there, but that she had no hope at all of outsailing these strange ships on the long haul. And in spite of their momentary triumph, it was clear that they would have no chance in a pitched battle.

Now, however, peering through the screen of matting that a sailor had set up to shield her from arrows, the Captain caught her breath and swore in wonderment. The ship that had grappled them, barely underway in pursuit, had luffed its sail and turned away from them again. She could see the signaler furiously waving multicolored banners. And the other ship, that had been not quite within bowshot, answered with flags of green and dropped farther behind.

So it was observed but unpursued that they came to land. Captain Repnomar's luck held good, for the wind did not die until they were almost out of the Current, and after that the rowing was easy. One of the stranger ships hung steadily offshore – following a little, as wanting to keep them well in sight but stay otherwise as far off as possible – while the other flitted away up the low coast, contrary to the direction the Current had taken. This last pleased the Captain. 'For,' she said, 'we'll move down the coast till we find the Outlet. But first we'll land and let them think we're going ashore.'

The Warden, who had been lending a hand at one of the oars, wiped his face and squinted in the blazing light, trying to make out features on that low smudge of land. 'And wait till the other ship's brought more pirates to take us?' he said.

'Wait till this one has left us too, I hope,' said Repnomar. 'They could have taken us already, Lethgro, if they had their hearts in it – you know that. Why they didn't, it may be we can find out from these passengers.' For they had three wounded pirates still on board, the Warden having said that they were too much hurt to throw overboard, and the Captain that they could be useful. Two of the *Mouse*'s crew were badly lamed with wounds, and one (it was that young Flitten the Captain had praised as an archer) dying of a knife thrust, though for the most part the pirates had fought bare-handed, a curious thing enough. So that between tending the wounded and handling the ship there was work for all hands able to do it.

When they had rowed close inshore the Captain loosed her crows, for the place was not welcoming to look at. The point of land they had aimed for was not a ridge of solid rock, as such points were likely to be on the Coast they had come from, with shelter on one side or both and grassy uplands at its back; it was no more than a jutting sandbar, puddled with slimy pools, and all the coast to left and right of it dunes and pools, all blurred and humming with swarms of gnats or midges. So they moved slowly downcoast, rowing and making what use they could of the light and shifting breezes, in the direction that the Captain said would lead them to the Soll's outlet (which the Warden was now more inclined to believe in, having seen that the Soll had at least another side). And the pirate ship, hanging farther offshore, seemed to follow.

'It has a bad look to it,' the Captain said soberly, studying the shore. 'There are no birds.'

The crows seemed to be of her opinion, for they flew left and right, inland and back, and one by one returned to the *Mouse*'s rigging and sat sullen there, having seen nothing to their liking. Only one circled and circled, and then came cawing over the *Mouse*'s bow and circled back again; and the Captain, with her eyes squeezed almost shut against the glare of light on sand and water, had the last scrap of sail taken in and followed her crow gingerly through a maze of sandbars into the mouth of a creek where they could anchor conveniently and the midges were fewer. 'And we'll have a clear way out,' the Captain said a little later, 'behind that long bar with the bit of scrub on it. So we could be in a worse fix, Lethgro.'

They had paced the dunes in a sad drizzle of rain, seeing little but sand and water. They had rigged a lean-to of matting and built a fire to keep away the midges, considering that they were already watched and had no need to hide themselves. They had stowed Flitten's body under a thick layer of sand, to keep the midges off it, and shared out his belongings among the crew. The wounded were sleeping under mats on the *Mouse*'s deck, for below-hatches the heat was too great for sleeping. They had posted lookouts, and they waited, gazing at each other ruefully across the embers; and at last the Warden shook his head and laughed and said, 'Well, Rep,' and the Captain shook her head and laughed (though grimly, for her mind was on Flitten in the sand) and said nothing. 'We might have done better,' Lethgro added, 'if we'd set the Exile on a plank, with a bag of nuts for provision, and pushed him out of Beng harbor into the Current.' But Repnomar would not allow this, and said they had done well because they had crossed the Soll. 'And much glory it will get us,' said Lethgro. And so in time they slept, not yet understanding why the people who knew this coast saw fit to shun it.

5

Curiosities of the Low Coast

There were no birds, except the *Mouse*'s crows; and these, in the way of shipcrows, preferred their boxes against the cabin side and their perches in the rigging to anything the land could offer. There were no birds, and in the creek where they were anchored few fish or other water creatures, and the land itself so bare that they must bring fuel from the ship to build their fire. Left and right, and as far inland as they could see, there was only the barren sand and the scummy pools and the swarms of midges, little soft flying things like the fluff of blooming trees, that seemed never to bite or sting but got into the nostrils and the eyes and the mouth. 'I think,' said the Warden, stirring up the embers to make them smoke, 'they've smelled us out.'

Indeed, the midges seemed to be gathering to the creek mouth, where before they had been few enough. The remains of some ill-tasting fish that the sailors had caught in the creek and made their meal of were furred all over now with ashy-colored wings; and inland and along the shore, the dunes in the hot light seemed to shift and smoke and change color, as the midges came crawling and fluttering along the sand, or flying in hazy swarms that drifted and floated on the breezes and yet somehow trended always toward the creek mouth.

'Well,' said the Captain, 'it's too hot anyhow to be sitting by a fire.' And she got up, calling all hands to come back to the *Mouse*.

But one of the sailors, who had been on lookout at the top of a high dune a little inland from their fire, came running and stumbling, with her hands busy about her face, making a choking cry that sent a chill down the spines of all that heard it. And though the Warden, who was nearest, ran forward to meet her, with the Captain hard at his heels, she had fallen on the sand before they reached her. Then it was Captain and Warden who stumbled as they ran, dragging the drooping sailor between them, and threw their arms across their faces to try to breathe through their sleeves. One of the other sailors had wit enough to fling his own shirt on the dying fire, so that it sent up a great puff of angry smoke, and in the smoke they drew breath, and beat the choked sailor on the back and scooped and scraped midges out of her mouth and nostrils with their fingers, so that she gasped and breathed again. At the same time, the Captain, looking up, saw one of the shipcrows that had come down from the rigging to eat midges suddenly stagger in midair and fall flapping to the sand. So she cried out to shut up the crows and lift anchor and get the *Mouse* under way, and with their hands to their noses they all waded into the creek and were helped on deck, where they found the wounded pirates praying ardently to Broz, who cared little enough for their worship.

It was hard times for a while then on board the *Mouse*; for with what wind there was against them, and the creek current too feeble to help much, and little room for the oars, they had to pole the ship to the more open water behind the long sandbar Repnomar had marked, and with every minute passing, the midges swarmed thicker. All had to be done at once – the ship poled, oars run out, fires built on deck, a way found through the tangle of sandbars – and all with a short crew and everyone fighting for breath. Yet all was done, and done in time, and they rowed out into the open Soll, where breezes and the smoke of their fires soon cleared away the midges. 'And,' said Repnomar, shading her eyes against the light and gazing offshore, 'we're back to where we were, for there's our pirate waiting for us.'

Indeed the stranger ship still hung offshore, and seemed now to be moving in the *Mouse*'s direction. 'Well, Rep,' said the Warden; and Repnomar answered briskly, 'We'll head for the Outlet.'

Now for almost a week of watches by the Captain's count (although she was willing to admit that things on board the *Mouse* had been upset by these late happenings, and the hourglass not turned, so that altogether three or four hours, or even as much as a watch, might have fallen out of the reckoning), they sailed along the Low Coast. They called it that, for lack of a better name, in mark of difference from the Coast they had known on the other side of the Soll. Bit by bit the look of the land changed, growing less sandy and more rocky and earthy, but still barren, with no life they could see except a sort of low gray scrub in places. Now food was very short (for the fishing here was nothing like what it had been in the Current) and tempers shorter, what with the death of Flitten and the abandoning of his body, and the pains and complaints of the wounded, and the troublesome presence of the prisoners (for though Repnomar got some good out of them by setting them to the oars, they had to be always watched and understood nothing said to them and yet must have their share of what food there was) and the unending light and heat and the fitful breezes that fell sometimes to a dead calm, and the dreary course they ran between that hostile shore and that hostile ship.

For watch by watch the other ship kept pace with them, sometimes barely in sight, sometimes so near they could see the faces of people on deck, till one watch when Repnomar was startled out of her sleep by a sailor bringing word that another sail had been sighted, coming from the other direction to meet them. Now they expected the worst, and made ready to defend themselves, the Captain looking out a spot on the coast to run to and steering closer inshore. The three wounded pirates were bound and stowed securely; but the two wounded sailors of the *Mouse*'s own crew, being now well enough to fight, were given weapons and set beside the rail where they might be useful.

'Both at once,' said the Warden, and nocked his arrow. Indeed the two ships seemed bent on coming together before they turned against the *Mouse*. The first ship especially, which had followed them so long, was flying down the wind (though it was only a skittering breeze) with a speed that made the Captain swear in admiration, and closing fast with the second. 'We can't outsail *that*,' she said regretfully, 'not if our lives depended on it.' ('"If"!' muttered the Warden.) 'And we can't fight both at once. We'll have to go inshore, and trust to the midges to hold them off. Unless Broz – ' But here she cut herself short with a cry, and all the crew began to yelp and chatter and shade their eyes for better staring.

The two ships had met, and now drifted aimlessly like two fighting dogs that tumble down a hillside, clawing each other's bellies. Repnomar whistled low, and said to the Warden, 'One has grappled the other'; and added after a little, 'At that rate, they'll be among the midges before they settle their difference.'

But in this she was wrong, though indeed the *Mouse* had rowed past unmolested and left them well astern before they broke apart. Almost within arrowshot of the land, first one ship then the other trimmed its sails and turned, the one heading opposite the Current and away from the *Mouse*, while the other seemed bent on putting as much distance as it could between itself and the other vessel.

'Did you see those people, Lethgro?' the Captain asked thoughtfully; for they had passed close enough to the fight to see that it was a fight indeed, and even to make out faces on board both ships. And when Lethgro said yes, she asked again, 'Have you noticed anything peculiar about the Low Coasters – every one of them we've seen?'

Now, Lethgro felt that there were several noticeable peculiarities of these people, and began to name them, as their piratical way of life (preying upon each other as well as upon strangers), their methods of fighting, their style of signals, their sailing rig, their uncouth language, and their curious awe of dogs, or at least of Broz, to whom their prisoners now offered prayers at the beginning of every watch. But Repnomar brushed these aside, saying, 'Haven't you noticed their faces? All bearded.' And Lethgro, thinking back, concluded that this was so. They had not seen a woman in any Low Coast crew.

They puzzled over this curiosity, trying to guess what it might mean, and the Captain said with a laugh that perhaps Low Coasters were like the folk of Perra (for in that remote district the custom was such that women and men did different work and even wore different clothing, as if they belonged to different nations, so that all along the Coast the joke ran that Perrans could not tell women from men without their clothes). But just then the lookout shouted for land to starboard, and all the crew scrambled for the rigging or the side to catch a sight of it, for till now there had been nothing in that direction but the open Soll. The Captain grasped the tiller, calling out orders, and the *Mouse* turned briskly toward the new land.

'What is it, Repnomar?' asked the Warden. 'Don't we have trouble enough to satisfy you, without seeking out more of it?' But she answered that they had not crossed the Soll and come so far only to turn their backs on every new thing.

'And besides, Lethgro,' she added after a time, 'we'll be in worse trouble yet if we don't find fresh food soon.' And since Lethgro knew this to be true, he nodded and made no more objection.

Now they had come into the Current again (which they had been inshore of, to avoid the Low Coast ships), and the new land, ahead and still to their right, grew clearer with every breath. At first it looked no more inviting than what they had already seen of the Low Coast. But, 'There are birds!' cried the Captain. 'And there's green on that slope. We'll have a good dinner if we don't meet more pirates first.' And at this moment the lookout shouted for more land dead ahead.

Indeed they had come, as they soon found, to a line of headlands or islands that seemed to stretch along the far side of the Current, opposite the Low Coast; so that for a time the Captain was in high excitement, believing they were in the Outlet. But when they left the Current and rowed in among them, they found they were islands indeed, and tiny islands at that, and the open Soll beyond them. Still, they were happy enough to anchor in the lee of one of them and go ashore, where they found birds' eggs, and small game, and bushes full of berries, and made a feast. But the Warden, who did not like the eager looks and chatter of the prisoners, insisted that they be put under hatches, bound and even gagged to keep them from calling out; and this proved wise. For one of the *Mouse*'s crew, who had been foraging for berries on the upper slopes, came down at a gallop, crying out that there were ships everywhere. In sober truth he had sighted three on the waters among the islands, and one anchored on the other side of this very island, so that likely enough some of its people were on shore and apt to come upon them at any moment. The ships, he said, were not like those they had fought and run from, but broader built and slower – a word that heartened the Captain.

'And most likely they're a different folk altogether,' she told the Warden, when she had given orders to gather up all the food they could in haste and make ready to sail at short notice; 'and maybe friendlier to strangers. I'm willing to hail one of these ships, once we're under way and close to the Current.' And while Lethgro tried to dissuade her from this, one of the sailors came running up with a hatful of eggs and a finger to her lips, and led them to a thicket from which they could see, not ten yards distant, a ragged person on the shore who seemed to be fashioning a raft out of brushwood and driftwood. The Captain whistled softly to herself. But the Warden burst forth from the thicket and thundered down the shore, half-choked between rage and laughter; for it was the Exile.

6
The Dreeg

About the middle of the next watch, the clouds thinned, and the heat and dazzle were such that three fights broke out on board the *Mouse* in little more than an hour. They had rigged the spare mainsail in front of the cabin to make shade on deck, but it gave them little enough relief; for not everyone could lounge there at once (this was the occasion of some of the fighting) and the reflected glare that blazed up from the Soll was almost as bad as what blazed down from the sky.

Now some were for laying in what food they could and turning back toward Beng, though it meant rowing or beating upwind all the way; but the Captain said there was nothing for it but to push on to the Outlet. To this, some objected that the farther they had come the hotter it had grown, and was likely to do so forever; but the Captain said that when they had reached the Outlet they could get out from under this burning region of the sky and find a more temperate country on the other side; and the Exile agreed.

He had come back very docilely to the *Mouse* (indeed he seemed glad to see the Warden again), though he gave no good reason for his leap into the pirate ship, only saying, when questioned, that he had thought it was worth a try; and they were glad to have him, for it seemed that in the week he lived among the Low Coast people he had learned a good deal. He told them that both sorts of ship they had seen belonged to the same folk; only the swift sailers were fishing and fighting ships, which the men worked, and the slower ships, which seemed to stay close among the islands, were full of women and children. The Exile's opinion, so far as they could make it out, was that these people lived their lives on shipboard; that the whole occupation of the men was to catch fish and steal each other's catches on the open Soll, but that they lived together peacefully enough among the islands. Of one thing he was sure, that they feared the Low Coast very greatly – though, not having seen the midges, he did not know why. It seemed he had hoped to reach that coast on the raft he was building, and continue his journey on foot.

'You can thank your gods, if you have any,' said the Warden, 'that we found you first.'

The Captain had questioned him eagerly about the Outlet, but he seemed to have heard nothing of it. At her urging, he questioned their prisoners, for he had learned a little of their language; but either it was too little, or they knew of no outlet from the Soll. All he could get from them was that they feared the Low Coast because of something they called Blaajan (which he took to mean the midges, now he had heard of them) and they feared the Current too, because of something they called Dreeg. But when the Captain asserted that this Dreeg would be the Outlet, the Exile disagreed, saying that from the way they spoke of it, he took this Dreeg to be a sort of god, and a very ferocious one. So the Captain had the prisoners gagged again, and left them bound on the shore of the island, though not bound so tightly that they might not work themselves free in a few hours; and the *Mouse* set sail again into the Current. And it was a little while after this that the clouds thinned and the fights broke out.

The wounded sailors, though still complaining, were well enough to be put back to work, and the Captain set them to drawing buckets of Soll water and pouring it over their shipmates; and the Exile helped them, marveling at how quickly their wounds had healed (which both of them took amiss, asserting they were not nearly healed yet). So they sailed on, for the most part half-naked, cooled enough by the water and the puffs of wind to do their work, but not to be in better temper. Still the barren shore of the Low Coast lay on their left, with now and then a glimpse of an island on the right. They saw no more sails. And now the Low Coast itself seemed to fall away, as the Current swept them farther offshore, back again into the open Soll. On board the *Mouse* unhappiness grew, some of the sailors grim and silent, some speaking openly of seizing the ship and heading back to the last island they had passed. But the Captain promised they would not go utterly out of sight of land without first turning back for more supplies, and kept her eyes glued to thc horizon, swearing she could still make out the Low Coast there. And in a little while the Current swerved once more, flowing now almost straight shoreward. But there was no shore. The Low Coast seemed to have vanished.

Now even those of the crew who had spoken most fiercely for returning to an island were silent, for they hoped that Repnomar's luck was proving good again. When presently a shore came into sight again on the left, it was high and forested; and a little later it was Warden Lethgro himself (for all others' eyes were following that shore) who sighted another long, dark line on the right. And Repnomar, her joy too great for much noise or movement, clasped his hand gravely and said in a hushed voice, 'We're in the Outlet.'

'From the look of it, we could be back on the Sollet,' said Lethgro, and at the thought found himself shaken by a great shuddering sigh. But after all it was not so much like the Sollet, what with the burning light that blistered their skins, and what with the closing-in of the shores. For the river (as they had to call it now) ran ever swifter and narrower, between steep banks that were sometimes forested to the water's edge and sometimes bare cliffs of yellow rock. The Captain's brow was creased with frowning; for there was no wind at all, and the current of the Dreeg (as she had begun to call the river itself) was strong, so that it seemed to her she had little control of her own ship. Thus they raced on, till a little beach showed ahead at the foot of the wooded slope of the left bank; and with much slamming of the rudder and throwing of draglines they brought the *Mouse* to rest there, running her slantwise up onto the beach. She struck with a rasping shock, so that the mast and all the rigging pitched forward and nearly buckled, and for the next three turns of the hourglass the Captain had all the crew and the Exile busy testing and tightening and caulking. But there was no grave damage.

Toward the end of those three hours the Warden came back very well pleased from the woods where he had gone with Broz to hunt for food. His belt was hung with small game the size of young rabbits, and he carried on his shoulders a bigger beast something like a wild pig, so that when he had unloaded himself he sat down puffing and panting, but content. Indeed the woods were full of game, and he had lost only one arrow, broken in the pig's side when it ran through the brush. So they built a fire on the beach and ate well, and hung the rest of their meat in a tree at the water's edge. And the Warden and the Exile chatted comfortably, as they had used to do in Sollet Castle. The Exile said that in his own country (which he had long forgotten, but remembered better now) there were animals much like dogs, but of many shapes and sizes, none of them given to climbing trees. Likewise there were (he thought) birds similar to crows, but not so clever and useful; and creatures like sheep, but without fleece and so large that people could ride on their backs; and so with many other creatures. But where his country was, he could not or would not say.

Now those whose turn it was to sleep stretched themselves on the gravelly sand, and all the others pursued what pleasure they liked, some in the shallows of the river, some in the shadows of the woods. For it was cooler here in the canyon of the Dreeg, with a new wind springing up (though it came perversely from straight downstream), and the woods were rich with flowers and vines and fruits that none of them knew, and there was no one but felt their luck had turned for the better. Only, by kind of silent agreement, the Captain and the Warden kept close watch on the Exile. For though they had no warrant now to hold him prisoner, being beyond all law or concern of the Sacred League of Beng and Rotl, yet they did not intend to lose him again if they could help it, since he was a useful person close at hand and an unsettling one at large.

'I don't doubt,' said the Captain, as these three sat on the river side of the *Mouse*'s bow, with their backs against her hull, 'that this Dreeg will carry us wherever we choose to go. It must flow again into the Soll – ' (here the Warden grunted) ' – or into another Soll, or into some greater river that will bring us back to the Soll at last.' For she was one of those who held that the world was round.

Here the Warden objected that only the Sollet flowed into the Soll, and the Sollet flowed from the Mountains. But, 'How do you or I know what flows into the Soll?' answered the Captain. 'Upcoast or downcoast, past Perra and the desert country – ' and here broke off, for Broz beside her was bristling and growling, and now he leaped up and raced around the bow, just when a shout rose from the other side of the *Mouse*, and worse noises like a great dog mumbling its meat.

It was a dog indeed to look at, or something like a dog, but when it reared itself to claw at the game in the tree it was taller than Lethgro, and its chest broader than any human's. The sailors were busy around it with shouting and waving of sticks, and Broz with snarling and barking, but it paid them little heed, only rolling up its black lips to show its muzzleful of great teeth, that looked well made for stabbing and ripping. When it sank down onto all fours it was yet chest high to the sailor who stood before it, and it snarled at him, its heavy head slung low and tilting to the side, so that he sprang backward and brandished his stick more for protection than in threat. The Captain had shouted to break out pikes (for the thing seemed too huge to fight, if it came to fighting, with any lesser weapon); but before this could be done, the beast, which till then had moved its shaggy bulk with a stately slowness, suddenly whirled and struck down another sailor with its forepaw. All of them (except the two who were fetching pikes from the *Mouse*) recoiled for a second at that blow and then plunged forward, some silent and some howling like beasts themselves, and Broz among the first. The monster seemed about to give back, and two or three of them seized the fallen sailor to drag him away; but it rolled forward again, as a great wave rolls, and plucked down neatly one of these sailors with its paw and began to bite at her head and shoulders.

Now for a time the noises on that beach were hideous to hear, with the ravening of the beast and the crying of the sailor in its jaws and the shrieks and snarling all around. Broz flung himself again and again at the monster's very head, distracting it a little from its work; and others beat at it with sticks and tried to poke it in the eyes, and the Warden (cursing the prudence that had made them put out their campfire) struck a light and would have kindled a firebrand to use against it. But by then the pikes were brought, and with four hands on a pike they charged at the beast, driving the blades in through its thick fur; and it half reared, and struggled, and struck at the pikes, and then gave way before them, retreating in short runs, turning to snarl and threaten, and then running again, till it was hidden in the woods. Broz followed it for a time, and came back snuffing and sneezing with his anger. By then they had built fires along the forest edge of the beach and were tending the wounded sailor (for he who had been struck down first had no hurts worth mentioning). The Captain's face was very stark; for though she was skillful enough with salves and splints and bandages such as every captain has need of, she was no surgeon, and the wounds were not light ones.

When all had been done that could be, the Captain took counsel of the Warden. 'It's not as if we had a choice,' she said. 'We can only go on.'

'But how far, Rep?' Warden Lethgro asked gloomily. 'That's the question.'

'It's a question we don't have to answer yet,' Repnomar replied with almost equal gloom, for her sailor's wounds on top of Flitten's death had cast her down, and she seemed to see her crew dissolving in blood before her eyes. Still, she shrugged her shoulders and went on more sturdily, 'At least we can agree to get out of this place and find a safer one. But first we'll lay in supplies.'

'Like the game I hung in the tree?' Lethgro demanded sourly. 'Who'll go hunting or picking in the forest now?'

But she answered, 'We'll get the *Mouse* afloat first, and we'll go four or five together and well armed. We need food, Lethgro, and it's here for the taking. How do we know what we'll find downriver?'

So the *Mouse* was dragged off the beach and anchored in the shallows, and the wounded sailor made as comfortable as might be in the Captain's own bunk, and one of the other crew set to watch over her, and another to stand guard on the beach, and all the rest of them set out well armed to gather whatever food they found. But this was not before the crew, who had taken their own counsel, built a small altar of branches and sand and stones and made what peace they could contrive there with the wild gods of this country.

They saw no more monsters in the woods, though now

and again they heard noises that made them start; but neither did they see much game. So they came back at last well laden with fruit and nuts and green stuff but with little enough meat, and were glad to find that the sailors on guard had passed their time with catching fish. So they weighed anchor and moved out into the current. 'And now,' said the Captain, 'we'll see where the Dreeg takes us.'

7
Of the Running Downhill of Water

Deeper and deeper into a forest land that called to them with unknown voices, the *Mouse* drove on downstream. The canyon walls began to fall away, sinking into broad forested hills as the river widened. They saw no sign of human life, but twice they saw great doglike shapes on the shore, and once heard a strange roaring. The opinion of the crew was that these monsters were what the Low Coasters called Dreeg, and had best be prudently worshipped, from a good distance; but the Captain stuck to it that Dreeg was the river itself. 'And if not,' she said, 'I'll call it so anyhow; for a river must have a name.'

Watch by watch they drifted onward, stopping twice or three times to send a hunting party ashore, after what the crew hoped were proper rites. And perhaps they were, for the hunters found game without going far and without seeing unwholesome beasts. Watch by watch the wounded sailor in the Captain's bunk raved as her hurts festered, and then sank into a drooling weakness that was painful to see. Now the Exile showed himself a good nurse, tending the sailor very patiently, though there were those in the crew who held it unwise and unsuitable for an outlander to care for one of the *Mouse*'s own people. But, 'We're all outlanders here,' said the Captain. 'We'd best stick together.' Nevertheless the sailor died, and they went ashore to bury her, digging a very deep grave because of monsters, and dragging a log over it; for all agreed that it was unseemly for alien beasts to eat human flesh.

It was after this burial that Warden Lethgro first complained of two uncanny things that had been troubling him for some time past. 'I can't understand,' he told Repnomar, 'why the light is in the wrong place.' (This was the first of the things that troubled him.) 'We've traveled under it and are on the other side now. But I don't understand the wind.' And indeed all the crew were afflicted with the same trouble, and more keenly than the Warden. For till this voyage their lives had been spent steering by light and wind, that were to them as secure almost as the Mountains and the Sollet to Lethgro; and now the light had changed sides in the sky, so that shadows fell the wrong way, and the wind had risen from the wrong point, dead ahead. So that with light astern and wind on the bow they all felt in their bones that they had somehow turned and were heading back for Beng, though at least the wiser of them knew this could not be.

'On the far side of the light,' Repnomar said cheerfully, 'it may be everything sails on the opposite tack.' Indeed she seemed not at all oppressed by so much strangeness, but glad of it and eager for it, so that Lethgro many times looked at her and blinked his eyes in dismay. Broz seemed in two minds about the matter, sometimes gamboling like a puppy, or standing hourlong a-quiver in the bow as he snuffed in and snorted out the strange scents, but other times creeping forlornly into the Captain's cabin, as the last safe place in a changed world, and (if she was there) pressing his head hard against her leg. The crew, too, could not agree either to despair or to rejoice, but kept the *Mouse* all alive with their quarrelings and imaginings. Only the Exile seemed quiet in his mind, taking what came as it came, all things alike without complaint and with equal wonder.

'I feel sometimes,' the Warden said plaintively to Repnomar, 'like a father teaching a toddling baby to talk.' For he spent much time now in conversation with the Exile, questioning him and instructing him and trying to make out first meaning and then truth in his talk. But the Exile's answers were still strange ones, for he claimed he did not remember being driven out from his own place, nor how he had come to the Upper Sollet, where the foresters had found him blinking and gaping. At the same time, he claimed to know things (or at least had strong opinions about them) that it seemed impossible for any human to know. Thus he said that the winds of the world flowed like two great rivers running down from opposite heights till they met in that region of squalls and calms and veering breezes along the Low Coast. And he said with assurance that both of those great winds turned like a waterwheel, scooping up water as they skimmed over Soll or over marshes, lifting that water and carrying it backward through the upper air to the heights from which they had come, and spilling it there each year as the Rains.

'There's no reason, of course,' Lethgro said to Repnomar privately, 'to believe him.'

'And not much more to think he lies,' she retorted.

'None but common sense,' the Warden said with some asperity, for it seemed to him that all this matter of the Exile served to encourage in Repnomar a wild and hazardous spirit. It was clear, too, in Lethgro's opinion, that if the Exile told some truth he did not tell it all. His bright eyes seemed always searching, and he listened to the talk of the crew, as to the Warden's conversation, with the quiet eagerness of those who hope to hear answers to questions they dare not ask. Too, he never claimed that he could not remember where his own place was, but only that he did not know how to get there – a nice distinction of words, but one that Lethgro believed the Exile well able to make now.

So in uncertainty and discontent, and against a rising wind – shifting at first but steadying watch by watch – they rode down the Dreeg. 'It's no river to compare with the

Sollet,' Lethgro said at last, when he had studied the matter fairly.

'It's half a mile wide,' exclaimed Repnomar, as if that answered him; for she had not been up-Sollet from Beng harbor for many years, so that the Dreeg seemed to her a great river indeed.

Lethgro looked kindly on her, as pitying her ignorance, and explained that half a mile was not wide for a river, and that width, in any case, was a lesser thing than depth. 'This is as shallow as a snow stream,' he added slightingly.

Here the Exile, moved perhaps by the word *snow*, remarked that it had grown colder.

'Not quite so hot, at least,' said the Captain. It was true that the heat no longer oppressed them on board the *Mouse*, and not all of this was because of the wind, for even under hatches it was cooler now. Likewise, now that they no longer faced into the burning light, their eyes were eased. So that all, except perhaps the Exile, had some cause for better cheer. The crew and the Captain were much occupied with learning the handling of a ship on a river (a ship not built for it, at that); and though all complained of it bitterly, and spoke with scorn of this means of travel, and swore to an unusual degree, it was clear to the Warden that they were glad of the occupation and pleased with their new skills.

For himself, the Warden felt like one blindfolded and whirled round and round on a log that floated from eddy to eddy. All sense of direction seemed to have gone from him, leaving only a queasy and groping unsteadiness, and whenever he rose from sleep he hurried first of all to search out the direction of the light. But that too was harder at every trial, for they were farther from it now and the clouds were thicker, so that there was no longer one bright point from which all light seemed to flow, but only a brighter side of the sky and a duller side. As for the wind, it was sometimes on the port bow, sometimes the starboard, and sometimes even abeam; but it was not easy to know if the wind had turned, or the river, or it might be both.

'Be glad it's not strong enough to drive us upcurrent,' said Repnomar. 'We'd have a hard time beating against it between river banks.'

It was in Lethgro's mind to ask why they *should* beat against it, and where she supposed they were going, and why they should go there; but he said nothing. Indeed he saw nothing for it but to sail on, unless they should haul out the *Mouse* and cut down trees and settle between the forest and the river, living by fishing and hunting and what fruits and salads they could gather or grow, with perhaps a strong stockade against monsters; and this (though in fact there was much to say for it) he did not like to mention, for it seemed to him altogether too final. And who, if he did not come back, would be Warden of Sollet Castle? The League could not leave that important post unfilled for long. So that the only answer he made to Repnomar was, at last, 'We're making good time.'

She had hoisted sail again (for she understood winds better than river currents) and was working this breeze for all it was worth, heading now slantwise downstream on a broad reach and in hope of doing better still, for a little ahead the river curved away from the wind, so that the *Mouse* should be able to run straight on into the curve without turning, and have the wind then (unless it changed suddenly) almost on her beam.

Here the Exile came up to report brightly on the state of his laundry, for he had taken to doing washing for all on board, and to check on a nestful of fledging crows in one of the boxes. But the Captain broke in on his chatter, asking harshly, 'Do you hear anything?'

They had come into the bend of the river, their straight course cutting close to the inside bank; and as the new stretch opened before them, a tangle of whiteness showed on the dark water, as if a great pure-white net had been flung across the river, bank to bank, and floated now on its surface, here spread loose, there heaped and wrinkled. Broz paced stiff-legged toward the bow, his ears slanted forward; a noise like a storm wind rose from the white-laced water; the Captain gripped the tiller with both hands, shouting an order to swing the sail full into the wind and keep it there, and the *Mouse*, jerked thus sideways against the current and her old course, turned her head, staggered for a moment, and plunged toward the near bank.

It was lucky (as the Captain explained later to the Warden and the Exile) that they were already so close inshore; otherwise they would have been swept into the rapids before the *Mouse* had enough headway to resist the current, which was stronger farther out. This, when she first explained it, seemed like some comfort; but the longer the Warden considered their situation, the less he was comforted.

They sat, like three crows on a spar, along a fallen log, from which Repnomar now and again jumped up for a few words with the crew. The *Mouse* had been hauled out and lay canted on her side, while the sailors labored outside and in to mend her battered hull. 'And we're lucky,' Repnomar said again, 'to have taken no worse damage on these rocks. If she'd been really staved in, we'd have had to wait for her to dry out before we could even begin to patch the hole. A week, at least.' And she shook her head at the thought, for a whole week of ten watches spent on shore was, in Repnomar's opinion, a week half lived, at best.

'And how long as it is?' asked Lethgro. His right hand steadied the staff of a pike that stood grounded at his knee, and from time to time he glanced at the woods behind them.

Repnomar squinted thoughtfully at her ship. 'The middle

of next watch before she's sound enough,' she said. 'And then we'll be rigging rollers and cutting a path through the brush and some trees will have to come down too, before we can drag her past the rapids and get her afloat again . . . say two watches and a half altogether. A little less if we push it hard.'

'Time enough,' said Lethgro, and he stood up, saying to the Exile, 'Shall we take a walk downstream?' And the Exile popped up eagerly.

'What do you think you're doing?' the Captain protested. 'I can use you here.' But, 'What's the point, Repnomar,' the Warden said, 'of dragging your ship past these rapids if there are worse below? We'll scout ahead, and be back before the end of next watch. And remember there's no use moving the *Mouse* till we get back.'

The Captain objected that she would do with her own ship what she chose and when she chose. But in fact she saw that it was a good plan, and only bettered it by making them take a shipcrow with them. 'For the crow,' she said, 'can fly faster and straighter than you can hike upstream, and so you can scout almost twice as far before you turn back. Or if the Dreeg is fit for a ship all the way, then don't turn back at all, but send word by the crow what landmark you'll wait beside, and we'll pick you up when we get there.'

No one spoke of monsters, but the Captain had already kindled a fire beside the *Mouse*, and they set out well provided, with a pike for each, and bow and arrows for the Warden, and live coals in a jar, and the crow. They tramped along as fast as might be with this baggage and the Exile's short legs, the Warden telling himself (though not the Exile, for whom he felt some distrust) that there were worse places to grow old and die than along the Dreeg. Indeed they had come into a country of pleasant coolness, so that the Exile pulled the neck of his shirt close about his throat, and Lethgro sighed for pure homesickness.

When at last the crow came cawing and hooting over the treetops (not well pleased with all this forested country, nor with the unnatural slant of the spar on which it lit) the Captain was pacing restlessly along the bank. The *Mouse* had been ready to float for more than an hour, and every minute of that time had chafed the Captain, for the portage past the rapids would be a slow business, and she wanted to get on with it. So that now in her impatience she called the crow down with little ceremony, a mistake she repented of at once, for the bird only clutched its perch and cawed angrily; and to climb for it, while that mood was on it, would be to lose it for an hour. The sailors exchanged looks concerning this, for the Captain's temper, though it was familiar to all of them had seldom been known to interfere with the *Mouse*'s business; and for the most part they took it as an omen of worse things to come.

But when the crow came down at last and the Captain read its message, it was all good news (granting that it was good for them to travel onward). The Dreeg ran clear for as far as the Warden and the Exile had gone, and they would build a fire and wait where a leaning tree slanted over the water from a high rock on the left bank. They said nothing of monsters. So the Captain, swearing violently and saying that they had wasted two hours and were four hands short when they needed every finger, gave order for the portage to begin. And with much labor and the use of rollers they heaved and dragged the *Mouse* along the path they had cleared, past the rocks and the foam and the roaring, and the smooth ledges where the water poured shining but only thumb-deep, and all the while the crows circled around them in angry spirals, uttering cries of outrage.

Now they rested for a little; but as soon as the Captain

herself had got back most of her breath and could stand without swaying, they went to work on the business of easing the *Mouse* back into the water, and checking for leaks, and getting under way again. And one of the kedge anchors with which they were working the ship off from the bank caught fast in a crevice of the rocky bottom and had to be abandoned, and this too looked like an omen to some. But the Captain, hearing the word, gave them such a tongue-lashing that it was some time before any dared mention omens again on board the *Mouse*.

They knew where their scouts were waiting even before they saw the landmark, for a tall feather of smoke rose from the left bank. Repnomar drew her breath through her teeth in a slow whistle, and said clearly, 'Monsters,' which made some of the sailors frown and blink their eyes. But she was right, for before the *Mouse* had well dropped anchor the Warden and the Exile were wading out to meet her, looking back over their shoulders as they came. 'And if you'd waited on shore till we lost way,' the Captain told them, when they had been hauled on board and were drying themselves in the cabin, 'you'd have been less likely to be run down and plowed under. Stopping a ship under way isn't like stopping one of your plodding sheep-carts.'

'Well, you didn't run us down and plow us under,' the Warden answered shortly, rubbing his legs with a towel while Broz sniffed at them.

'And if you've seen beasts,' said Repnomar (for she would not say 'monsters' to their face and thus encourage them in their fears), 'why didn't you send word by the crow?'

But the Warden said with dignity, 'Could you have come faster if we had?' And when she had granted that they could not, he added with still more dignity, 'The shorter the message it carries, the faster a crow flies.'

It had been a different sort of beast this time, and

perhaps a worse sort. They had not been long out of sight of the rapids when the Exile first glimpsed something in the branches of a tree, and since then they had seldom been alone. For a long time they had not known if it was a single beast following them, or more than one, but at last they had seen two at once, and after that three and even four. Sometimes the creatures ran on the ground, but more often they were in the trees. Very silent they were, the size of a half-grown child or of the Exile. The only sound that came from them was the ripping sound of claws as they sprang up a treetrunk (much like a forest dog, though faster and higher). But when the Warden threatened them with his pike and shouted, they would draw back their lips from their fangs in noiseless snarls, and crouch and clutch in the branches, never giving back and always creeping closer again when he turned.

Once they had picked their landmark, and scouted farther till they judged their time had run out, and loosed the crow and turned back to the landmark to wait for the *Mouse*, they heard a screeching ahead of them that made the Exile drop his pike for an instant and scramble to pick it up again in great haste, and a piglike creature like the one the Warden had shot farther upstream came crashing through the underbrush, with a furious thing clutched onto its back, clawing its sides and crunching its thick neck in its jaws, till a little way past them the pig went down in its blood, and the beast began to worry and mouth it and dig out its entrails. So they hurried on a little, and stopped to light torches from the coals in their jar, and with these back to the landmark, where they built a good fire. They were both weary, but they agreed that neither should sleep, for the tree beasts seemed not much troubled by fires; and though for a time they saw none, and heard from downstream what sounded like several of the beasts fighting over the pig (a devilish racket enough), soon the movements in the trees began again, and little by little the beasts closed in around them.

Sleek-furred and long-armed and patterned with leafy spots, they moved like shadows in the forest, and now they began to utter soft endless cries, a sort of horrible crooning, and now one would drop to the ground and run forward a little way, and another flash up to the very top of a towering tree and leap to the next; so that the Warden and the Exile were starting and staring this way and that, backed against their fire and aiming their weapons uncertainly. But the *Mouse* had come. 'And very welcome,' the Warden said heartily.

So they voyaged on, all of them a little cheered – the Warden and the Exile because they no longer had that unwholesome crooning in their ears, the Captain and crew because they were learning to handle their ship between banks. 'And every river,' the Captain said again, 'runs sooner or later into the Soll.'

By now the crows had resigned themselves to this strange manner of travel, and taken to their old ways of flying around the masthead, an omen which the sailors found still more heartening. But in this they were too sanguine, though indeed the crows soon showed themselves useful; for two of them, ranging ahead and high aloft, suddenly turned back with such an outburst of squawking that Repnomar, who was not then at the tiller, shouted to turn inshore and hold the drag anchor ready, and sent a lookout scrambling up the mast. But this time the *Mouse* was solidly in midstream, far from both banks and well in the grip of the current, so that she was swept helplessly along.

They heard it before they saw it – a low thunder that was like a pounding within the skull – and what they saw from the *Mouse*'s deck appeared to be simply the edge of the world, for the river and its banks came to an end and nothing showed beyond. Only a little wooded island rose in the middle of the river, at the very verge of that emptiness, and blocked the view there. But the lookout cried out 'Reef!' which was the likest thing that came to his mind; and the Exile, in great excitement, exclaimed that they must make fast to something, either shore or bottom, or else be carried over the edge and smashed to pieces. And at that the Captain, wasting no time in talk, had all anchors dropped, and was tying a line to a pike when one of them, dragging on the rocky bottom, caught fast enough to stop the *Mouse* dead, so that the ship jerked, and swung, and throbbed. And though within a few moments that strained anchor cable broke, by then the Warden had hurled the pike into the nearest land, which was the island before them, a great throw and a lucky one, for it stuck firm; and by gathering in that line and trimming the sail and throwing kedge anchors they were able to work their way into the easier water above the tail of the island (for the current split above it and swept past on both sides).

By this time the crash of the falling water was so loud in their ears that they talked more in signs than in words, and none of the crew dared look to see how close they floated to utter destruction, thinking it better to die in hope than to know and despair. They had lost all but one of their anchors in that short voyage on the lip of nothing, so that now three or four sailors must leap into the water with mooring lines and carry them ashore, swimming and wading, where they moored the *Mouse* securely, bow and stern, to the stoutest trees their lines could reach.

All the sleepers had been waked by this hubbub, and now some took turns climbing the mast to see over the world's edge, if they could, and all the others went ashore, bracing themselves cautiously by the mooring lines, to see it from whatever vantage the island offered. Lethgro and the Exile were among these, and in a little while they were lying on their bellies at the rocky head of the island, peering straight down. For the island perched on the very lip of a great cliff, and on both sides the broad waters of the Dreeg plunged a thousand feet and shattered into spray.

8
Crows and Choughs

'There are times,' Repnomar said sternly, 'when you're caught between a squall and a reef; but those are not the times, Lethgro, to sit down and put your head in a sack.'

This was unjust in Lethgro's opinion. It was true that he had been sitting, first on one shore of the island and then the other; but so far from putting his head in a sack, he had been measuring with his eye the distance to each river bank, and calculating the possibility of reaching it with an arrow and a light line. And having come back to the *Mouse* in great gloom (for the calculations were not good) and wet to the waist from wading in the shallows, he was not pleased with this sort of greeting.

They could talk well enough under hatches, where the noise of the waterfall was muffled. This was almost the only spot that Broz could bear at all, for he was in grave agitation, trembling and snuffling and whining, and no more able to rest than if he had been adrift on a floating log that spun under his feet. He lay now half leaning against Repnomar's ankles for a few minutes at a time, and then rose and went to Lethgro, and lay there, and again to Repnomar, and sometimes to the Exile, for in his trouble he had made friends with all who might give him any comfort.

The Warden, too, felt inclined to cherish what comfort there was, and not to quarrel; so that all he answered to the Captain was, 'It's too far to either bank for getting a line across.'

Repnomar chewed on this for a little and then said, 'If

worse comes to worst, we can lower somebody down the cliff with a line and a float.'

'To somehow come out of that cauldron down there still breathing, and then swim across the current?' Lethgro said skeptically. 'That will be a long line, Repnomar, and a strong swimmer. And then, I suppose, to climb back up the cliff by land, dragging that mile of line and never getting it hung on the wrong side of a tree or a rock, and pull us off with it.'

But the Captain said shortly, 'When you think of a better plan, tell me about it,' and Lethgro fell silent.

Here the Exile, as trying to cheer them, reported that he had been over the island with an eye toward provisions, and that there was no need for them to go hungry. For there were many birds, of different sizes, and many of them nesting; and there were bushes that bore nuts, and succulent herbs which he did not doubt they could grow more of if they chose to make a garden; and with fish from the river, he supposed they could live on the island forever. But at that word, Repnomar gave him so grim a look that he cleared his throat, and began to stroke Broz busily, and said no more.

But Broz, hoping perhaps that things were better outside than he remembered, went whining to the hatchway; and with one accord they all went silently on deck, and from there ashore in the ship's boat. Broz, like one half frantic, began to dig under a fallen log (for the island was well wooded, though the trees were small) and the others went slowly, and each one walking a little apart, to the cliff's edge.

There were birds indeed – birds in the trees, quick and busy but all silent, as not choosing to try their voices against the voice of the Dreeg, and water birds that soared and plunged and scooped lightly at the water, catching fish as they were swept over the edge of the falls; and at the very margin, a flock of red-feathered birds, bright and fresh in the mist of the cataract, that seemed to find their sport there, for they strutted at the cliff's edge like acrobats before a turn, and then peered over and suddenly plunged as if they had never known the use of wings, and a moment later would rise and tumble in the air, playing with the crazy drafts and breezes that boiled along the waterfall's face. If you leaned over the edge – or, better, lay flat and hung your head over it – you could see that these bright tumbling creatures nested in the crevices of the cliff, where the island thrust its rocky head between curtains of water; so that their very fledglings, when they were ready to fly, must at the first trial ride those wild airs upward to a safe landing, or else fall to destruction in the churning water and blind mist below.

Here, in the very roar and tumult of the falls, there was no hope of talk; and each of the three, like the two or three sailors who already lay or stood there, was as if alone in a desert place. Captain Repnomar, watching the birds, thought to herself that they were like the choughs that nested and sported on the cliffs of the Coast between Beng and Rotl; and she felt with a terrible pang that anything would be better than to have come so far and go no farther. Warden Lethgro, seeing how those same birds plunged and soared, sailing sometimes far out across the river and wafted sometimes high above the falls, felt his own heart plunge like a dropped stone, and turned his eyes cautiously to view the Exile. Indeed the Exile lay very quiet at the cliff's edge, but his ugly face was all intent and his eyes bright as wet stones.

Now Broz came through the woods with a little beast like a rat in his jaws, and Repnomar made much of him and followed him back to the log where he had dug it out. In a little while the Exile, looking up, caught the Warden's eye on him, and at once put on a different face. But the Warden came and squatted beside him and began tossing leaves out from the cliff's edge, where some of them caught an updraft and flew and fluttered for a long time, but more were swept headlong into the mist by the downdraft of the falling water; so that the Exile smiled sheepishly enough, and they both rose and went back together to seek the quiet of the *Mouse*'s hold for conversation. On the way they fell in with the Captain, who was blinking her eyes sadly, and Broz, who seemed to have lost his head, for he was barking at nothing.

When they were all under hatches again, Broz barked a few times more and then lay down at Repnomar's feet and went to sleep. 'Poor dog,' said Repnomar, not using his name so as not to rouse him. 'He can't hear himself bark out there, and that's enough to drive him crazy. We've got to find a way off this rock.'

Lethgro looked hard at the Exile, but the Exile smiled blandly and said nothing. And the Captain added, 'I thought for a little that if all else failed, we might be able to dig down and tunnel under the river bed. But it's all rock, with a little dirt on top like caulking.'

It saddened Lethgro to hear Repnomar talk of such a scheme, which was wild even for her. She must be, he thought, nearly as desperate as Broz. And he looked again at the Exile.

But the Exile began to defend the island, saying that its thin skin of soil was enough to feed them well, if they made good use of it, and that with the stone they could build thick-walled houses to shut out the noise, and that with the strong wind from downstream he had no doubt that so skilled a captain as Repnomar would find a way to reach the bank.

To all this the Captain listened impatiently. Indeed she sat still only for fear of waking Broz, for she thought he needed whatever ease he could find. But when the Exile began to praise her ship-handling she could bear it no longer, for flattery angered her as much as insult, and she doubted whether the Exile knew enough of ship-handling to praise it rightly. So she leaped up, only taking care not to strike Broz with her foot, and went on deck to find some useful work for the crew and to think about ways of leaving this island.

'Well, Exile,' said the Warden, when she had gone, 'do you think you can do it?' And when the Exile would have turned to him an innocent face, as not knowing what he meant, he added, 'If you can fly from Sollet Castle, why not from the top of a waterfall?' So that the Exile had to confess that this had been in his thoughts when he looked over the cliff. But the winds, he said, had been much better at Sollet Castle, and the flight much less dangerous.

'Then why are you so keen for it?' the Warden asked sternly.

The Exile protested that he was not keen for it at all, and would be content to live on the island and help build the stone houses and plant the garden. But Lethgro kept at it patiently, and got it out of him at last that he believed the Dreeg led to a place he knew, and that all his hope and endeavor was to come there. As for his lack of candor, he said (and maintained it sturdily) that he did not want to lead others into danger, and it would be truly better for them to stay on the island and hope for stronger winds from downstream; but for himself, he would push on by whatever means came to his hand.

Now the Warden found himself in two minds at least. On the one hand, he doubted that even Repnomar could work miracles with the wind; and if their only hope of ever leaving the island was to spread wings and fly, then they had best use the skills of the Exile, who alone knew the art of it. But again, even the Exile hesitated before this flight, and to Lethgro's eyes it seemed as sure a road to destruction as sailing against the current on the precipice's lip. Also, it was harder and harder for him to see the good of going forward. So far, all their journeying had brought them always from one peril to a worse; and if they were coming to the Exile's country, what welcome could they expect there? Since they had kept him prisoner and yet saved him from arrest, they were certain to be in trouble with both his friends and his enemies. And if they could build houses proof against the thunder of the falls, the Warden thought he could live out what years remained to him as comfortably on this island as in some beast-besieged clearing in a barbarous forest somewhere downstream. But then again, not all were of his disposition, and he had no doubt that Repnomar would rather die in a crazy plunge from that tumultuous height than resign herself to keeping a garden on this rocky clod.

But while the Warden stewed in this uncertainty, the Exile, as trying to clinch his argument, remarked that they had no need to follow him, since his cause was not theirs. At that, Lethgro slapped his hand on his knee, startling Broz awake, and rose up in considerable heat; for it came flooding home to him that the Exile's cause (whatever it might be) was indeed theirs, since this whole mad voyage had no other origin. 'You'll tell the Captain,' he said, taking the Exile hard by the shoulder, 'all that you think and plan and know. And if you fly from this cliff, you'll take us with you. It was for you we sailed out of Beng harbor into nowhere; and you won't desert us now!'

Once they had come to it indeed, the Exile put aside his coyness and explained to them very eagerly how a sail could carry a rider through the air as well as a ship along the water. For, as Repnomar said at once, 'All you need to do is add up and down on your port and starboard and head and stern.' Or, as Lethgro put it, 'It's easier to sink.' He felt more alone now while the three of them talked and worked busily together, than ever before on this voyage; for the Captain and the Exile were like two strangers in a foreign place who suddenly find that they speak the same language, and the Warden (whose word before now had carried weight even in the Council of Beng) saw himself reduced to asking always 'Why?' like a dull student, and doing what he was told without understanding.

The problem here, as the Exile strove to explain, was the contrary of what it had been at Sollet Castle. There, he had launched himself downwind on a powerful gale, and the danger was that he had no more control of his course than the *Mouse* caught on the current of the Dreeg. Here there was a headwind, which was good for flying, but the strands of the wind were muddled and tangled, and its force half broken, by the wild air around the waterfall. The steadiest part of this wind was the downdraft that swept along the surface of the falls into the smash and tumble of broken water below; and that was sheer and sure destruction. But as if to make amends for that (or, thought Lethgro, as if to tempt them into destruction's reach) there was a contrary updraft that rose from the river a little way downstream and blew upward and backward toward the falls. Now and then (for they spent much time now at the precipice, watching the birds) they would see a chough plunge down the face of the falling water, into the very welter of the spray, and through the spray, showing muted crimson in the white haze, sailing then with spread wings just above the rush of the river, till it rose suddenly without a wingbeat and drifted backward, and then tumbled in the air, and with a few quick flaps came to land again on the island. So that the Exile's plan and hope was to catch that breeze and ride it upward till they met the headwind blowing from the lower reaches of the Dreeg, and then steer away from the falls for the bank downstream, as a ship sails close to a contrary wind. For he said that the wind, pushing and lifting, would save them from falling into the Dreeg; and because they would be facing it, not drifting with it, they could steer with their sails, as a ship close hauled to the wind steers better than running before the fairest breeze in the world.

This was well enough, and the *Mouse*'s spare sails would do better service than the bedclothes of Sollet Castle; but it was clear to any eye that a few at most could take that road. The Exile weighed no more than a child, yet plainly he himself, for all his experience, had no certainty of reaching that distant bank. For all the others, certainty would be even further off, they being heavier and not skilled in such a means of traveling. 'And besides,' said the Captain, 'there's the *Mouse*. As things stand now, we can't get her off; and I won't leave her without a crew.'

'Who do you expect to steal her, Rep?' said Lethgro. But the Captain answered impatiently, 'The river may rise, or the river may fall. There may be storms. A ship without a crew is no more than a piece of expensive driftwood. And I won't have all my sails cut up, either.'

The fact was that she had seen the looks of the crew and heard their talk, and knew that not more than one or two of them would willingly step off the edge of a precipice above a frothing river, and those few only if they were dared or shamed into it. So that, while what she said was true, there was more truth beyond, and she was glad enough to have sound reasons not to risk her sailors' lives against their wills and in so chancy a business.

Thus almost without argument it was settled that the Exile, the Warden, and the Captain would undertake this thing, while all the crew would stay with the *Mouse*. And the Captain named the head of the second watch, who was called Anscrop, to command both crew and ship in her absence. But when she said that Broz must come with them, the Exile was unhappy and answered at first that a frightened dog would struggle in the harness and spoil all; but when he saw that the Captain was set on this, he gave up arguing and went to work with a will, measuring and hefting Broz (whom he could scarcely lift) and tying for him a harness of padded rope.

Now that these things were decided, all (except Broz) were easier in their minds. The crew began at once to dig out rock for their house-building, using wedges and mallets to crack it along its seams and growing merry over this unusual manner of construction; while the others began to cut and stitch (for the Captain said that none should touch a sail whose life was not to depend on it). And even as they cut and stitched, they watched the birds, for they had laid out their sail loft at the edge of the cliff. Now the Exile and the Captain, following with their eyes the plunging and the rising of the choughs, began to speak of a pattern in the winds; and the Warden was constrained to believe them, though, so far as he saw, it was a pattern of chaos.

'Don't look so glum, Lethgro,' said the Captain. 'It's a matter of picking our time, that's all. You want the breeze to be coming up just when you're coming down. That and jumping far enough to miss the downdraft.' To which the Exile added some words about eddies and flow.

'And Broz, I suppose,' said Lethgro, 'is a good judge of flow and eddies, and knows how to jump past the downdraft with half a topsail fastened to his back.' Broz, indeed, was in such a state by now that he hardly ate of the fish the sailors gave him, and lay for hours gnawing at his paws in distress. But the Captain maintained that he would fly as well as any of them, saying she would launch him into the air with her own hands before she jumped, and tow his sail with a rope tied to her own harness. 'And you needn't worry, Lethgro,' she added with a laugh. 'We may not be able to dance in the air like these choughs, but we can plod along like crows.' For no one had ever called shipcrows graceful in flight.

In fact, for all his grumbling, Lethgro was glad enough to have work in hand, and the time coming on when this thing would be finished, one way or another. What that other way might be, he saw no need to dwell on. The Warden of Sollet Castle had taken his stand, and he would not sidle away from the consequences.

It was the Exile who now seemed to hesitate before this leap. He was forever making trial of the air, tossing leaves and branches and weighted scraps of sailcloth over the cliff and watching them till they fell – some swiftly, some slow – into the boiling mist and were snatched downstream. Lethgro did not find this a cheering sight; but the Exile held to it that one advantage they had here, compared to his flight from Sollet Castle, was the chance to try the air before they leaped into it, and he meant to make the most of that chance, shaping their sails as these tests taught him. As for his toys falling into the river (which without exception they did), he held that this was only because they had no one to guide their flight, as a derelict ship will founder for lack of sailors to trim its sails and turn its helm. But when, finding they had cloth to spare for it, he stitched a trial sail almost as wide as the one he meant for himself, and weighted it with a log as long as he and half as heavy, and watched it splash into the Dreeg not a hundred yards downstream, he grew very quiet and said no more about the utility of tests.

Now they had finished their sails and were studying how to control them; and the Exile again put aside his silence and had much to say about this, telling them how to turn, how to rise, how to stall as a ship's sail stalls when it faces too hard into the wind, and all by pulling the ropes of their harnesses this way and that and by swaying their bodies in the air. But all this, as he never ceased to remind them, hung on their first leap taking them far enough out from the cliff to catch the updraft.

'Well, the worst that can happen,' said Repnomar, cutting him off in the midst of one of these reminders, 'is that we have to swim for it. So we might as well get under way.' Certainly this was not the worst that could happen, as the thunder of the water on the rocks told them with every heartbeat; and swim for that far bank, with that mass of sail dragging at your back, was a task for a god, and not every god at that. But as they all knew these things, there was no need to mention them. So Lethgro nodded, and the Exile, and they came up from the hold where they had been talking, and shouted their good-byes to Anscrop and the others, and rowed ashore from the *Mouse* one last time, taking each a crow with them and Broz at their knees, and walked through the booming of the waterfall to the precipice's edge. And all the crew trooped after them with sober faces.

Now they tucked their crows into their shirts and fitted themselves into their harnesses, and Repnomar with some difficulty got his harness fastened onto Broz, and they stood at the edge of the cliff, all the others watching the Exile, and he watching the bright birds; for he was to give the signal. Repnomar had gathered Broz in her arms, and stood with her toes over the brink, ready to fling him as far out as she could. He was trembling like a taut rope in a high wind, and the Captain's face was all lined with trouble, but her hands were steady on him.

Along the face of the waterfall, and past the mist and spume of its crashing, the choughs sank and rose and drifted like flying flowers; and the Exile watched motionless. It sat hard with the Captain at that moment not to make her own judgement of the wind; but she kept her eyes firm on the Exile, knowing that in this matter of flying he outwent her as far as she did him on board a ship. Lethgro leaned forward, to harden himself against the deep emptiness below him and the riot of water at the bottom. Then the Exile flung his arm up wildly, and with the same motion sprang. Repnomar heaved Broz and his sail with a great sweep of her arms, so that she staggered for a moment at the cliff's edge, and lost time in regaining her footing before she could leap herself. Lethgro had jumped as the Exile's arm went up, so that he did not see her, and he got a kind of benefit from this, for the panic he felt as he hurtled through the air was little for himself and more for Repnomar. He had time to think that if he struck the water feet first he might not be stunned by the shock of it, and there would be some hope of getting loose from his harness before it dragged him under forever; and then his sail caught the wind.

He was not falling now, but floating, though indeed floating downward swiftly enough, and he hung in the ropes of his harness like a baby in a swing. At once he pulled a rope and tried to tilt his body as the Exile had taught them, to guide his flight toward the left bank. But it was too soon, for his sail had not yet steadied and filled, and all he managed was to spill what air he had caught, so that in an instant he was falling again like a stone. This time he set his teeth and pulled carefully on the rope that should bring the sail back into the wind; and again it caught, and he took a great breath of thankfulness as his harness dug into his shoulders. Now he waited (though it was pain of heart to wait, for the river seemed to be rushing up to meet and drown him) till he thought the sail must be well steadied, and began his turn; and the sail followed his bidding, and carried him slanting downward toward the left bank. His leap had brought him so far from the cliff that the others (if they were in the air at all) were behind him, and his sail cut off all sight of them; and the roar of the waterfall killed all other sound and all sense of hearing, so that he floated in loneliness.

For the Captain, after the first stomach-clenching moment, it was as if the world opened all around her like a broad reach of calm water, and she felt she had been born to fly. Broz's sail was close ahead on her left and likely to be run down by her (for the old dog's struggles, though they had not yet capsized the sail, had slowed it); but she pulled her harness ropes and slid smoothly past, and shortly felt the tug as she took Broz and his sail in tow. She could see Lethgro's sail ahead of her, and the Exile's, farthest from the bank and soaring high, so that she laughed for pleasure. Now, if the wind from downstream held steady . . .

Lethgro was close to the bank when the wind failed him, but still far enough to very readily drown, and as the sail collapsed above him he struggled in mid-fall to free himself from the harness; for in that instant he knew very surely that he would rather trust to his own limbs in the water than to that dead wing in the air. He was half loose from it when he struck, but it came down on his head and all around him, muffling him in its heavy folds, so that perhaps nothing saved him then but his weight and the speed with which he hit the water; for he went down like a flung stone, while the sail floated for a little on the churned surface; and underwater, as the current tugged him along, he tore free from the last ropes and struck out downstream, and so came up gasping for his life but clear of the sail.

Now, half turning in the water, he saw a strange sight; for Repnomar was flying like a gull that sails and swoops behind a ship, and Broz and his smaller sail were close beside her. In that quick view Lethgro did not see the Exile; but he did not look long, being hard pressed with his own concerns, and some hundred yards downstream he came to shore at last, and lay for a time with his legs still in the water, not finding strength just then to drag them farther. Indeed he was so weary from that struggle with the Dreeg that when he heard the Captain's voice hailing him fiercely, he thought at first he was asleep and dreaming. But when she cried out again, 'Help me, Lethgro!' (not as in fear but as in great indignation) it came to him that he was awake and that they were past the waterfall, for he heard her clearly; and then the meaning of her words reached his mind, and he scrambled somehow upright and turned to find what help he was needed for.

Repnomar knelt on the bank upstream from him, busy, it seemed, with her sail, and only looking up to yell at him again and wave him toward her. So the Warden broke into a plodding run, for he was sodden and heavy with river water. But she finished her business and came at a faster run and dragging a length of rope to meet him halfway, and Broz from the tumble of sailcloth set up a yelping and howling of pure fright that was like a child crying.

'Hold the rope,' the Captain said shortly, though she was even then tying one end of it to the back of her belt. And while Lethgro was getting the rope into his hands, she kicked off her shoes and dived into the Dreeg.

He saw then what he was to do, and what the Captain was doing. Downstream of them – almost even with where he had come ashore – a sail was caught on a rock or on some drowned tree. It might have been his own sail, except for a dark bobbing thing that hung at its edge like a fishnet's float. The Warden twisted the end of the rope around his hands and held hard.

Repnomar was a strong swimmer, and for all the rush of the current and the drag of the rope she seemed likely to reach that snagged sailwreck before the river swept her past. Reach it, at least, if the length of her tether allowed. She had cut loose the longest rope from her sail, and tied a shorter one to it for more length, but together they were not quite enough. Lethgro eased his way downstream to keep even with her; but though this gave her the full benefit of what rope there was, it could not make it longer. So that he had no choice (unless he was to let her go or pull her up short, and neither of these things he was willing to do) but to slide and stumble down the bank into water knee-deep at the first step and waist-deep by the third, and there dig in his feet and lean against the current while Repnomar, her knife in her hand, fought the sail and the tugging water and the Exile's dead weight.

Then there was the matter of landing them, like two great fish on a single hook, Repnomar gripping the Exile hard and letting herself ride with the current while the Warden struggled hastily up the bank again (not to be jerked off his feet in the water and so all three lost together), and then leading them in with the rope, Repnomar swimming now with slow backstrokes. But as soon as they were come into the shallows, and Lethgro had run downstream to help drag the Exile up the bank, Repnomar staggered to her feet and headed back toward the waterfall at a stumbling run. And when Lethgro shouted out to know where she was going, she answered over her shoulder, 'Broz!' and went on, leaving him to find out whether it was a live man or a corpse they had pulled from the Dreeg.

9

Of the Definition of Land and Water

They camped on the river shore, near the spot where the Exile had been hauled out, for no better reason than that they were too tired to go farther. Lethgro had spent a weary time squeezing water out of the Exile's lungs; and though he had never been overly disturbed by the general run of omens, he had taken it hard when the first thing he found was a great lump on the Exile's chest, and that lump the Exile's crow, dead and drowned inside his shirt. Lethgro's own crow had somehow disappeared, and – cast back in his mind as he would – he could not remember when or how. Still he worked on drearily, with that dead thing beside him and what seemed another dead thing under his hands, till at last the Exile began to twitch and gasp. Then Lethgro sat back on his haunches and watched the blubbery breath come and go, and the ashy face (that had been like some horrible fish seined up from Soll bottom) begin to take on something of human color again. He himself was not a much more cheerful sight, still sodden as he was and smeared with mud and weeds from scrambling on the bank, disheveled too and pale with weariness. So that the Exile, when his eyes opened upon this apparition squatting at his side, started violently and lost his breath again for a moment. And the Warden, who was well pleased not to have the disposing of his remains to face, laughed and clapped him on the arm, saying, 'I think neither of us will be thirsty for river water for a while.' And the Exile smiled feebly.

By this time Repnomar had come back with Broz, who capered strangely around her, whining and almost laughing in his joy to be down from midair and free of his sail and out of the roar of the waterfall, yet still trembling with the backwash of those horrors. And Repnomar, though in his gambols he bumped against her knees and got between her feet and almost tripped her, would not so much as speak harshly to him, but contented herself with swearing mildly and softly. She had meant to bring her sail downstream with her, considering that there was always some use to be made of good sailcloth; but in her weariness she had dragged it only a little way and left it lying. Nevertheless, she brought a good omen; for Lethgro's crow had neither drowned nor flown back to the *Mouse*, but come to join Repnomar's on the river bank where she had left it with Broz, and the two crows rode now on her two shoulders, complaining whenever Broz made her stumble.

So they made a fire, for the Exile was chilled through and shaking very miserably, and dried their clothes a few pieces at a time, and rested. Here they were still in sight of the waterfall, and when the Exile was strong enough they stood all three in a row by the fire and waved their arms, so that Anscrop and the rest of the *Mouse*'s crew could see them from the island and know they were all living. And they found shellfish in the river's shallows, and slept a little, two at a time.

But when they were all awake and stirring again it was a different story, for they found themselves full of excitement and congratulation. They talked of nothing except their flight, but they talked a great deal of that, comparing and arguing with such vigor that scarcely a sentence was finished without interruption. The Exile was sure that he knew now how he could have made the sails better for this flight, and the Captain was sure that her towing of Broz's sail had made them both fly better, and the Warden (who on this point spoke from good experience) was sure that the harnesses should be made for easier escape. All these matters required them to study the two sails that were left to them, and for a while they ranged up and down the shore, dragging the sails this way and that, trying the harnesses, and drawing lines and arrows in the mud of the bank, while Broz and the two crows watched without approval.

But at last they packed up Broz's sail (as being the less cumbersome) to carry with them, and left Repnomar's folded and stowed under brushwood, and set off downstream at a comfortable pace, waving farewell toward the island, in case any of the *Mouse*'s crew were watching.

Journeying like this, they followed the watch plan of land travelers, which to the Captain's thinking was a poor way of arranging the time, though while they were on foot she could offer no better. So they would travel for a watch (only pausing to rest or eat) and sleep for a watch, taking it each in turn to stand guard till all had had their sleep, and then travel on for another watch. The Captain's thought was on building a raft, or some such vessel, to carry them down the river. But here luck was against them, for downstream from the waterfall there was no more forest, but open grassland sparsely dotted with trees, and these for the most part gnarled and twisted. The Exile viewed this new country with some surprise, saying that the lowland was like a highland and the other way about; and Lethgro and Repnomar looked at him curiously, considering that if they were coming to a place he knew, it was odd that the country should be strange to him.

Still the Captain held that they might have contrived a raft, if they had only had proper tools to cut what trees there were; but they had none, for the Exile had insisted that they carry no dead weight beyond their clothes and the Warden's bow and arrows and some few small things in their pockets. 'But if we don't have axes,' the Captain added, 'we have crows. We can send word for the crew to cut logs and toss them over to us.' And she had to be persuaded by studying the current that there was no way they could catch such logs if they were thrown. So in the end she resigned herself to walking, though she kept a keen watch for anything that might serve to carry them on water.

For a time the river still ran swiftly; but when they had waked twice and slept twice and were in their third watch of walking, the Warden remarked, 'We'll be coming to reedbeds soon.' And when they asked him how he could know, he said this country was like the Lower Sollet, where the great river broadens in the flat floodland and flows slowly through many channels. And indeed he was right, for the Dreeg too widened and slowed, and broke into winding streams, and tall reeds grew on the wet flats and in the broad shallows of the river. 'Now,' said the Captain, folding her arms and planting her feet solidly, 'we've gone far enough with this nonsense. You can splat and puddle in the mud if you like it; but I'm building a boat here and now, for Broz and me.'

'Building it of what?' said Lethgro. 'Mud, or reeds?' For one seemed to him no likelier than the other. So that at first he thought she was joking when she said with a smile, 'Reeds.'

But it was reeds she meant, and reeds she began to gather. And indeed they all saw quickly the sense of it, for the reeds were thick and stout, and so buoyant that they shot up like arrows from a bow if you tried to hold them underwater. 'And you can bend them however you like,' the Captain said happily, for she was well pleased to think of having a vessel under her feet again, if it was only a scrap of a raft plaited of rivergrass. 'And we can weave them together, or tie them with smaller stuff. And I told you we were right to bring a sail!'

So they camped on the mud flats, and labored among the

reeds for the rest of that watch, and the next, and into the third, taking it now in turn for two to work while one slept, a system the Captain found more seemly. It was not altogether child's play; for the largest reeds, that grew higher than Lethgro's head, were too tough to cut with their knives, however much they honed them. But this, as the Captain said, was all to the good, for it meant that their craft would be sturdy; and all but the very toughest could be broken easily enough at the knot you found by groping down a little way into the soft mud. And by trying every kind of grass and weed that grew thereabouts, they learned to use a sort of long-stemmed sedge for their cordage, which was thin and pliant and yet tough almost as rope. With this they bound armfuls of reeds together into bundles, and wove the bundles together with other reeds, till they had a raft broad enough to hold them all in some comfort and yet so light that the Exile could carry it alone, though awkwardly. When they had set it on the water and climbed aboard one by one, it settled low but still floated securely.

'It's not a Sollet cargo ship,' the Captain said at last, when she had tried and tested everything twice or three times, 'and it's not the *Mouse*; but it floats.' It did more than float, for they had set certain reed bundles upright and hung Broz's sail between them – a clumsy contrivance, but by shifting the sail from one bundle to another the Captain was able to make some use of the wind, so that they were not all at the mercy of the current.

Now for a while they voyaged easily between flat banks that were forested with the great reeds, and past long islands flat too and reed-crowded like the shore; and banks and islands and raft alike were half awash in the quiet river. It had begun to rain; but this, as Lethgro observed, was no surprise, since it was high time for the Rains to begin. The light was well behind them now, and the air cool, and the wind gentle, rippling the dark face of the Dreeg and soughing in the reeds; and there was little for them to do but fish and talk under the shelter of a reed mat which the Exile had woven. 'And we've come a long way,' the Warden said, 'and lost two lives and a few lesser things, not to know yet what we're journeying for.'

Now the Exile, when it was pointed out to him clearly that this remark had to do with him, fell into despondency, telling them that the death of those two sailors was a grief and a reproach to him, and hoping earnestly that he would bring them into no more trouble. To which Repnomar replied testily, 'Tell us where you're bringing us, and we'll tell you if it's trouble.' And Lethgro seconded her in this.

But what the Exile now told them, with all signs of frankness, was not well calculated to produce either belief or ease of mind. For he claimed to have come from nowhere in the world, but from another world entirely, beyond the sky, and pointed out its direction to them (though of that, he admitted, he was not quite sure); and he believed (or said so) that he had been sent here for a purpose, and that precious things had been left for his use somewhere ahead of them, and now not far ahead, and that it was to seek these things that he journeyed so eagerly. But he seemed very cloudy in his mind as to what that purpose might be. For, as he explained it, all he knew was that he had waked on a riverbank, as ignorant as a baby of himself and his whereabouts, but feeling everything he saw about him foreign and somehow wrong, the very clothes on his back outlandish to him. Making his way along the river, he had come to a logging station, where the loggers had seen fit to detain him and hand him over to the next ship (for it was the Upper Sollet he had waked beside), and the shippers on their way downstream had handed him over, as was due, to the Warden. Bit by bit some knowledge of himself had come to him, but none of this world, so that he understood that it was indeed new to him, and he to it. But how he had come to where he first found himself, or what he was to do in this world, he could not yet say. (Or, thought the Warden, would not.) It was when he remembered the precious things left for his use that he had determined to escape from Sollet Castle. But when the Warden asked him how he knew where these things were, he was hard put to answer, seeming not to find words for his meaning, though for all else he had been voluble enough. At last he said that he remembered knowing that these things had been left in the darkness – close to the edge of the darkness; and that was all he could tell them.

'It's what I've always thought of gods,' said Repnomar, with a laugh. 'They have all they can handle taking care of themselves, let alone anybody else.' The Exile protested that he was no god, only an outlander; but Repnomar scoffed at this, saying that persons from other worlds could hardly be human. But the Exile, confessing readily enough that he was not human, yet stuck to it that neither was he a god, and said that there were many worlds beyond the sky, each with a sky of its own and many with their own peoples; which incomprehensible talk only seemed to confirm the likelihood that he was either a god or a liar.

Now the light was far down in the sky behind them, and all was in shadow from the tall reeds they mazed among. The sighing of the wind and the whispering of the rain made a quiet music that was melancholy to hear; but the tallness and closeness of the reeds protected them for the most part from wind and rain alike, so much so that the sail hung almost useless. The Exile, though he shivered somewhat with the coolness and the wet, kept a cheerful face; and Broz, who found this life not too different from rainy times on board the *Mouse*, dozed placidly under the awning mat. But the tempers of the others were wearing thinner, as they still voyaged and still no way opened out of the reed beds. The current had grown so weak that they had to pole themselves along with stout reeds, that were not stout enough but broke again and again.

'Why not admit it, Repnomar,' said the Warden, 'that we don't even know if we're on a river any longer?'

'There's still a current,' said the Captain, leaning to her work as she poled. 'And water still runs downhill. Besides, we have the crows.' For as the reeds closed in and the river raveled out into a skein of intertangling channels, she had begun to send out the crows.

'Yes, and look at them,' said Lethgro, and the Captain grunted. Indeed one crow sat hunched and muttering on the Captain's own shoulder, balancing itself with a bad grace against her movements and flicking its head to throw off the raindrops, while the other circled aimlessly in the drizzle above them, returning always to croak its displeasure and then fly off again. So that the Warden, though not expert in the ways of shipcrows, felt confident that the crows were of his opinion.

'You see the kind of channels we have here, Lethgro,' the Captain said obstinately. 'These crows grew up on the Coast and the open Soll. You can't expect them to like this river, nor to see where the water runs between the reeds. I don't doubt that it all looks like land to them. But they'll tell us when we're coming to open water.'

'What makes you think we'll ever come to open water?' said Lethgro.

This was badly timed; for, the Captain's poling reed breaking at that moment, she lurched and almost fell, upsetting her crow, which dug its claws into her shoulder and squawked in indignation. So that, when she had smashed the broken reed against the side of the raft and sworn at it and the crow, it was somewhat testily that she turned to the Warden and answered, 'Water flows into water. This is a *river*, Lethgro, and it's on its way to the Soll, or – '

But here she stopped, and stood looking with grave displeasure at the wall of reeds that loomed dark green and blank before them, for the last thrust of the poles had brought them around a turning of their sluggish channel.

'Or what, Rep?' the Warden asked heavily, when they had all gazed as long as they could well bear (for the Exile, whose watch it was to sleep, had waked when the raft ceased to move).

'Or something *like* the Soll,' Repnomar finished through her teeth, and giving him such a look that he thought best not to pursue this question. 'Water flows into water.

'Only,' she added more temperately, 'it may be very shallow water. And full of reeds.'

Lethgro sat down thoughtfully, resting his poling reed across his knees. He had believed heretofore that both land and water could be traveled, this by ship (or, if need be, other vessel) and that by foot; but what were they to make of this shallow Soll of reeds where neither vessel nor foot could pass? 'Though if it comes to that,' he said aloud, 'we could wade it.'

The Captain looked at him with revulsion, and even the Exile seemed saddened by this idea. But the Warden stood up again, measuring himself against his poling reed. 'It's not more than waist deep,' he said. 'And we're wet already with the rain.'

The Exile pointed out that waist deep for some meant chin deep for others; but the Captain, though the notion of walking *through* water rather than sailing over it was to her uncouth and unseemly, said only, 'I'll send up the crows again. There's no point in wading ourselves into deep water.' With which the Exile heartily agreed.

So the crows, squawking resentfully, were flung upward, and took the air with angry wingbeats, for they had formed their opinion of the country already, and saw no need to confirm it. Nevertheless, they circled off, rising high to see as far as might be (for Repnomar would have no crows on her ship that did not know their business) and in due time returned and paced sulky and aggrieved around the Captain where she sat by the raft's edge, so that it was clear they had seen nothing of interest.

'Remember it was your idea, Lethgro,' the Captain said somewhat grimly, and she swung her legs over the edge and slid into the water, so that the raft bobbed and shook, and Broz whined uncertainly. An expression of grave distaste spread across her face, and she added, 'I hope those are good boots you're wearing.'

Indeed the bottom of this Reed Soll, as the Captain chose now to call it, was blanketed thickly with ooze, so that they waded through water above and much below. As the Warden had predicted, it came little more than waist high for him and the Captain; but the Exile, when he had lowered himself into it with a shrug and a grimace, was constrained to keep his chin lifted and his mouth shut. Broz swam behind the Captain till he grew tired, after which she and the Warden took it in turns to carry him.

'Not that he couldn't swim it,' the Captain observed, 'if it were clear water. It's these cursed reeds that wear him out.'

'Not only him,' said the Warden, who at that moment was carrying Broz, hung dripping around his shoulders like a heavy scarf. And the Exile grunted.

Indeed the worst of their wading was neither water nor ooze, but the reeds that grew here thick as grass blades on the prairies of the Lower Sollet. They went in single file, the Captain first now (since it was Lethgro's turn to carry Broz), spreading the reeds aside and trampling them down as she plowed a slow way through, and the Exile last, where the trodden reeds gave him somewhat higher footing through the muck, like a springy carpet full of loops and tangles. He had said very little for some time, not choosing to open his mouth to the mucky water they stirred up, but now he declared that they were almost there; and Repnomar agreed with this, saying somewhat darkly, 'One way or another, we're coming to the end.'

It seemed to Lethgro that the reeds grew ever taller; but it was hard to be sure of that, for they showed uncouthly tall in any case, looking straight up at them thus and into the rain, and (worse yet) there was no light worth mentioning at all now, only a blackness of reeds and water and a grayness of sky. But taller or shorter, it was certain that the reeds here were more slender, and flattened like narrow swordblades; so that the going was easier in one way (for the grassy blades bent or broke with no more resistance than the rottenest wood) but harder in another, for they were like swordblades in the nature of their edges also.

They went on doggedly now, and with few words, and the Warden took care to break as many reeds as he well might in their passage, so that if the time came to turn back they would find a clear trail to follow. Indeed it was not easy to know whether or not they kept a straight course in this slicing darkness. Only, as Repnomar remarked, so long as things changed, however slowly, they could be sure they were making progress.

And it was true that things were slowly changing. Not only were the reeds of a different shape, but they grew now more sparsely; and as the Exile remarked, the rain had stopped, though the wind was stronger. There was a difference, too, in the feel of the muck about their feet, stickier but not so deep. And when the Exile offered to take his turn at last in carrying Broz, it was clear that the water itself was shallower, for he had his arms above the surface. The crows had long since fallen silent, hunched now on one shoulder, now on another.

'Look,' Repnomar said suddenly. 'Ahead and up.' And for a time they all stood all three staring. What reeds still grew here were thin and scattered, and they had a clear view of what hung softly shining, low in the black sky ahead. 'What do you make of it?' the Captain asked, and there was an unaccustomed tinge of awe in her voice.

Lethgro, after a moment, cleared his throat and answered, 'It's not the Soll we're coming to, Rep. It's the Mountains.'

10
Walking

'It's land, I suppose,' the Captain said reflectively. 'But I wouldn't moor a boat to it.'

'If you had no other choice – ' Lethgro began, but the Captain interrupted, saying, 'There's always a choice, if you look for it.'

What they sat on, though indeed it was land enough for sitting, was not much more, being spongy watery stuff like fleeces of sodden wool. Yet it seemed to serve as shore to that mucky Reed Soll behind them, and their legs were tired with the wading. So they had chosen to sit, as soon as sitting was possible, searching no farther for solid ground; and they sat now and gazed at the glowing peaks before them. The Captain, who had never seen a mountain till now, was hard put to understand how the summits could shine out like lamps while all the lower slopes were dark and unseen, till the Exile declared that they were like distant ships, whose rigging you may see while their hulls are still hidden; but on that word she jumped up, saying, 'Then let's move on, for it will be a long journey on foot,' and the Warden had to remind her, with something like a groan, that they had not waded that muck-field to seek the Mountains, but the Exile's precious things.

These, however, they seemed not likely to find at once. The Exile – who, it appeared, had counted on somehow recognizing the place as soon as they came into darkness – confessed that all hereabouts was as unfamiliar to him as to the others. The Warden was for searching left and right along the shore (such as the shore was) till they found the place; but the Exile seemed now uncertain in his mind, looking often toward the lit peaks, and at last declared that he had been slightly mistaken, and the precious things were waiting at the other edge of the darkness.

'*What* other edge?' the Warden said ungraciously, for he did not much like the sound of this remark. But the Captain, who had sat down again when it appeared they were going nowhere for the time, now turned quickly to the Exile, asking, 'How far?' as if it seemed reasonable to her that darkness should have edges like a pancake.

At this the Exile began to speak apologetically of the shape of the world, declaring that it was round like an apple ('It's what I've always said,' said Repnomar) and added that as all things balance, so the world was half light and half dark.

'By which you mean,' Repnomar asked after a minute's thought, 'that your things are halfway around the world from here?' And Lethgro shuddered inwardly, for he thought her voice had a dangerous ring to it, part angry and part eager. And the Exile answered yes.

'Well,' Repnomar said with decision, and once more leaping up, so that the spongy bank quivered under them, 'the longer we sit here, the hungrier we'll be before we get there.'

The Warden took her firmly by the arm, reaching up for a good grasp. 'Hold still for a while, Repnomar,' he said. 'It was your mad steering out of Beng harbor that started us on this miserable voyage. But we're on land now, or what passes for land in this godforsaken country, so get your hand off the tiller.'

'Where would you steer us to, Lethgro?' the Captain demanded impatiently. And he answered without much hesitation, 'Upstream, if you can call it that.'

Repnomar snorted. 'Wade through the muck, pole ourselves through the marsh, sail against the current till we come to the falls – for what, Lethgro? You want us to climb that cliff and wave good-bye to the *Mouse* and my crew again, and build a new ship, and sail upstream like rain falling upward, and fight through the midges and the pirates, and row ourselves across the Soll (for we'll be long past Windfall, and no current that way to carry us), and hand ourselves over to Beng Council?'

'Better a journey on water you can see than on land you can't,' Lethgro said. 'And better journeying to a place you know is there, than searching in the dark for a place that's always on the far side of something else.'

Repnomar would have answered; but now it was the Exile who sprang up (clumsily enough), saying that all this was needless, and thanking them very courteously for their kindness to him. And with no more words he turned away and trudged off into the darkness.

Broz rose with a whine, and the Captain lunged forward to stop the Exile by what means she might; but it was the Warden who settled matters, standing up with an angry snort and shouting out that if they were all crazy enough to do this thing, they should at least find food before they started. So the Captain laughed, and the Exile turned back sheepishly, protesting many times that there was no need for them to come with him; but the Warden only grunted. He was angry with himself for ever beginning this journey, which was like a path with no end and no room to turn around in; for certainly the captain's talk of what it would be like to go back was true enough, and certainly it would have been a hard thing to see the Exile walk off alone into the darkness half a world wide. 'But,' said Lethgro, as he scooped little shellfish out of the oozy mud with his fingers, 'it will be more miracle than I've ever seen if we live to see the light again.'

Shellfish, it seemed likely, would be what they lived on, together with certain little bulbs from the roots of the sword-reeds. They found no fish in the mucky waters they had last waded through; and though they heard rustles in the reeds, and the crows found small things enough creeping in the mosses of the bank, neither Broz nor the others could raise any game – 'or,' said Lethgro, 'catch it if we raised it.' So they filled their pockets with the little shells (no bigger, mostly, than Lethgro's thumbnail) and the fleshy bulbs, and the Exile filled a flask he had brought all the way from the *Mouse*, straining marsh water into it through a corner of his shirt. For, as he said, they did not know when they would come to water again; and Repnomar thought this so prudent that she filled the little bailer that dangled always at her belt. But the Warden was more troubled by their lack of fuel, either for heat or for light, so that in the end he gathered a great bundle of dead reeds and spongy mosses, and slung this from one shoulder, keeping his bow and quiver handy on the other. 'And Broz could carry a load, too,' he told the Captain. 'We've carried *him* far enough.'

'Broz is no sheep to carry freight,' the Captain retorted. 'And if we raise game, he'd better be free to chase it, without a pile of sticks on his back.' So they set out, with the bright peaks before them, and all around the darkness of a ship's hold with all hatches sealed, and the ground like wet sponges under their feet.

This was slow going at first. But presently the Captain took the lead, leaning forward into the wind, and the journey went more swiftly. For the Captain, quite against her expectation, found this quaggy navigation in the dark so much to her liking that before long she had laid bets with the others that they would reach the lit peaks within twenty watches, 'though we waste ten of them sleeping. For,' she said, 'it can't be longer than the way from Beng to Sollet Castle.'

This the Warden disputed. 'You're too used to judging the distance of a sail on open water, Rep, where you have a good idea of the size of what you're looking at. Those peaks might be a thousand feet high or ten thousand – and the taller they are, the farther they are. And even if your guess is right, I've wasted sixteen watches between Beng and Sollet Castle many a time – and that was by canal and trodden road, that didn't sink and squelch underfoot, and in the light. So I'll take your bet, and your money too, if we ever come again where we can spend it.'

'Wasted is right,' said Repnomar. 'That's the pace of the Sollet traders ambling along with their laden sheep, and those so-called boats on the canal, that are no more than wool carts set afloat. On your own, Lethgro, with hunger to swell your sails, you could have done it in half the time. As for this boggy ground, it's now worse than a dinghy on choppy water; and you've said yourself' (as indeed he had) 'that it will get firmer as the land rises. And as for the dark – '

Here she stumbled and swore, giving Lethgro time to put in morosely, 'As for the light, we'll find it on the other side of the world, if we get there, but that doesn't help us see our feet on this side.'

'Even in the dark, you can see a little,' the Captain persisted (though in fact she could not see her hand before her face, for she did not like to admit that this darkness was deeper than the familiar darkness of under-hatches). 'And if we were blind as oysters, we still have Broz's nose and our own ears to pilot us, and the wind and that landmark to steer by.' Here she pointed toward the glowing peaks, not caring that no one saw her gesture. 'So don't toddle along like a baby, Lethgro. Stretch your legs! What is it you're afraid you'll bump into – a tree, or a stone wall?'

'It's more what we're likely to *fall* into worries me,' Lethgro answered. 'You can stride along as you like, Repnomar; but it's the rest of us who'll be hauling you out if you step into a pit, or a river, or quicksand. And if it's a cliff you step off the edge of, there'll be no hauling.'

'I'll yell as I go down,' Repnomar said unrepentantly, 'so you can back away when you hear me.' But the Exile was much of the Warden's opinion, and suggested by way of pleasing all (at least in part) that they rope themselves together as mountaineers sometimes do. And this is what they did, the Captain insisting only that Broz must not be roped. 'For,' she said, 'he's the one of us least likely to fall off the edge of anything – having four feet and a good nose – and he can't go after game if he's tied to us.' So they fastened themselves together like a line of floats along the edge of a net, using the rope from Repnomar's sail (which she had carried in a coil on her shoulder), and went on again. The Captain still led, but now the Warden went last, to have the most weight at the end of the line in case of trouble; and Broz snuffed and rummaged around them, seeming to turn up creatures now and then that led him on short dashes in the dark, but never getting his teeth into his quarry.

It was a strange feeling to walk thus blindly into the dark, and not least so for the Captain, however boldly she strode along. Indeed, every stride for her was like the leap from the waterfall, a plunge into unknown space. But she said nothing of this, thinking that someone must be first on the rope, and that it would be a slow journey if the leader shrank from every shadow in a country where all was shadow. She believed, too, that the Exile could still see even in this blackness (for she had heard him muttering agreement when she spoke of seeing a little in the dark) and would give warning if they came close to any serious obstacle.

Certainly there were urgent reasons to cover ground as fast as might be. In all her life the Captain had never lacked for water, but she had heard tales of travelers strayed in the dry plains of Perra, maddened and dead for want of it, and this within no more than a dozen watches. How much drink it would take to save them from the same end, she did not know; but the Exile's flask and the little bailer she cherished in her hand, swearing between her teeth when any drop splashed out, seemed small defense against the dark width of the world.

And not dark merely. The warmth seemed to have vanished with the light, and the wind sang cold in their ears. The Captain's mouth shaped into a hard line as she thought of the watches to come when they must contrive to sleep somehow. Fuel they had, on the Warden's shoulder, but still damp and too little to squander, whether for heat or light. And what food they might find, in this sightless desolation, was beyond the Captain's guess. For all these reasons, she thought it well to move as fast as they might, and swung her legs in a long stride that compelled the Exile to jog along behind her like a puppy pulled on a leash. But with every step she took, her muscles braced against whatever her foot might come down upon. Sometimes it was a pool of icy water, sometimes a hard ledge of stone that jarred her leg to the hip, but most often it was a spongy wetness that sank unwholesomely beneath her tread. She walked with one hand stretched out before her, while the other steadied the bailer full of water against her waist; for, despite her mocking of Lethgro, her mind's eye conjured up trees and stone walls in plenty, and worse imaginings. Meanwhile, her bodily eyes saw nothing, turn them where she would, except the far peaks, glowing between the dark above and the dark below like the rough teeth of some great god that gaped for them.

Gods, it seemed, were on all their minds, Broz perhaps excepted. The Warden muttered prayers as he went, naming every god known or hoped to care for travelers; and after a time the Exile, hurrying his trot to get a little closer to the Captain, asked her if it was thought that gods lived in darkness or perhaps in light. To which the Captain replied shortly that in her experience they lived in empty heads and the pockets of priests, both of which were dark enough. But she kept her eyes on the lit peaks.

It was traveling like this, with eyes lifted and arm outstretched and feet finding their own way, that she came crack against some obstruction in the dark, and for a little while could not so much as mutter an oath, but stood silent and rocking a little on her legs. So that the others crowded into her before they were well aware of trouble, and then fell to questioning her anxiously, and the Captain answered, through her teeth, 'Knocked my knee against one of those stone walls, Lethgro.' And when they felt it out with their hands, it was stone indeed, though whether to call it a wall was less easily settled.

'Stone like this didn't cut and set itself,' the Captain argued. She sat now on top of it (for it stood less than waist high), rubbing her knee tenderly. 'There are people in this country, and that means food and drink.'

'Or *were* people once,' the Warden answered; 'if this is cut stone indeed, which from the feel of it I doubt. If this was ever a wall, it's long since a ruin. Your people may have died out a thousand years ago, Rep.' He spoke with some assurance, for he had been born in Rotl, where stone walls were not uncommon, and knew that one reason stone was so prized as a building material was that (besides being expensive and hard to come by) it lasted forever.

But the Captain maintained that whatever it was she sat on, it had been built by human hands, for it was made of smooth upright columns set close together, each as thick as the *Mouse*'s mainmast and neatly squared. 'Or six-sided,' the Warden said, running his hand thoughtfully along the rock face.

'The more sides, the more work it took,' said the Captain. 'Do those angles feel like accidents to you, Lethgro?'

Lethgro blinked his eyes uncertainly – a useless motion in the dark. If this were a wall, it would be a very strange one, filled to the top as it was on the far side with solid earth or rock. 'It might be a terrace wall,' he said dubiously, peering up into the blackness ahead in the questionable hope of seeing the lights of some fort or castle there. For in such a country, he thought, what welcome would a fort give to strangers out of the dark?

Here the Exile, who had been feeling his way along the row of columns, returned saying that he knew these stones. But when the Captain had jumped up in excitement and sat down again, cursing the pain in her knee, and the Warden had clapped him on the back, asking eagerly how far they were from his precious things, it transpired that they had been misled by the Exile's clumsy speech. Indeed, he meant no more than that he had seen such stones in his own world; worse, that he knew them to be an accident of nature and built by no hand at all. For, as he explained it, all this rock must once have been hot and flowing like melted wax; and as it cooled, these columns had shaped themselves, as frost crystals form out of cooling air, or arrowheads of ice along the edges of a freezing pool. And when the Captain asked him where was the heat that could melt rock, he answered that in this world he did not know, but that in many worlds such heat lurked underground, melting great beds of rock and spewing it forth in fountains and streams, so that it hardened sometimes into mountains that opened now and then to spew again.

The Warden said that in all his years at Sollet Castle he had never heard of such, though strange things enough and stranger tales came down from the Mountains. Nevertheless all their eyes rose again to the peaks before them, as if those shining rocks were strange sponges that soaked up all the light of the world and must now soak up the beams of their eyesight. And they shivered in the cold wind, so that the Captain said brusquely that they had best move on, unless they wanted to sit till they turned to frost crystals themselves.

So they roped again and clambered over the little wall and pushed on, the ground hard now and drier, being mostly bare rock so far as they could tell. The Captain was glad enough that the others could not see how she walked, for the pain in her knee, though it did not slow her down much, constrained her to a clumsy and uncaptainly limp.

When at last they stopped to camp, they were all bone-weary, and yet the peaks seemed no nearer than when they had first caught sight of them. 'Nevertheless we've come a long way,' said the Warden, 'both forward and up.' For the ground had risen always, sometimes at a steady slope, sometimes in giant stairsteps or rock, faced with those angled columns that had so puzzled them at first. In places these were so tall that they had been hard put to manage a way up them, the Captain scrambling sometimes onto the Warden's shoulders before she could find the top, and poor Broz roped after all in a rude harness and hauled up like so much cargo. And the wind whistled and shrilled down those vast steps, buffeting them as they climbed. At the foot of such walls there would be many loose stones and sometimes whole columns lying flat – cracked away and fallen from the rock face, so the Exile said.

Now the Warden spread his fuel out to dry as well as it might, and with much difficulty got a little fire burning in the corner between two rocks, so that they were able to roast some of their shellfish and make a scanty meal – all the scantier because the Captain insisted that Broz must have his share. Certainly the question of food now loomed large before them, and one by one they cast hard looks at the crows. These had taken the journey quietly enough, clutched one on the Captain's shoulder and one on the Exile's, and now scavenged uneasily around the campfire, picking at the empty shells and scratching through the Warden's fuel for edibles. But for the time, at least, all bellies had their bit, and the water was shared out so sparingly that the Exile's flask was untouched and a little remained even in the Captain's bailer, though she had to cover it with a rock to keep Broz from finishing it. They had good hope, besides, of finding a stream or spring or pool, for in many places the rocks were damp. 'And it's too bad,' the Captain said, 'that the crows can't see to scout for us.'

'It will be a long time,' said the Warden, 'before we have use for their eyes again.' He was thinking that Broz, for what game he had roused, might as well have carried a load of fuel and food; but he thought also that there was no point in quarreling now, and indeed no way of saying that the Captain had been wrong, for if Broz had caught so much as a rabbit it would have been a great thing for all of them.

Now one of the crows, as if knowing that it stood in strange danger, snuggled itself close against the Exile, so that presently he took it up and stowed it inside his shirt, saying that thus they could warm each other. Certainly there was need of what warmth they might find, and their fire too little to do more than ease their cold hands and feet for a time. In the end they slept huddled in its ashes – humans, Exile, dog and crows together – the Captain taking the first turn on guard with Broz across her legs.

There was not much talk among them when at last they stretched themselves and gathered their gear and set out, glad to be under way again, and munching the raw marsh-bulbs as they walked; for it was clear enough that what hope they had lay all in pushing onward. None of them had slept long or well, what with the darkness and the cold, and they were thirsty now and hungry and sadly chilled; but as they walked they grew warmer and thereby cheerier. The Captain, who had started out with her teeth clenched tight, finding it almost more than she could do to bend her stiff and swollen knee, rejoiced in the walking that limbered it, and pressed the pace, faster and still faster.

What they sought now was water. Food, as the Captain remarked, they could do without for many watches, if need were. 'And keep your greedy eyes off my crows,' she added, though it was too dark for looking, and though she herself had eyed them hungrily enough at the campfire.

So they went listening, their ears pricked for sounds of running water, but all they heard was their own laboring breath and the rush of the wind and the thump and clatter of their shoes and the clicking of Broz's claws on the stones. Now and again one would quickly stoop and feel for dampness, but what they felt now was frost. How long they could have kept this pace they never knew; they had held it perhaps for an hour when a cry from the Captain stopped them short.

'What now, Rep?' the Warden panted (for the way had been uphill and the pace brisker than he liked).

'Not a wall this time, Lethgro,' she said drily. 'But it's for you to answer, not me. Come put your hand on this. Is it a mountain?'

11
Climbing

It was some hours after they began the ascent before they had leisure to talk again, except for certain desperate shouts in the dark. It was not a matter of climbing so much as of scrambling; for what Repnomar had struck upon this time was a steep slope not of solid ground or stone but of loose rubble, like a pile of chips at the edge of a lumber yard. Scouting left and right along it, they found no change, nor feeling as high as they could reach. The Warden lit a sheaf of reeds and handed it up to Repnomar on his shoulders; but even with this they could see no top to the pile, and the wind soon put out their torch. The Captain would have sent the crows up to find what lay above; but they did not well understand this task and had no liking for it, and only flapped complainingly about in the dark.

'Well,' said the Warden, staring up into the darkness, 'we've known all along that if we want to reach the peaks, we must climb sooner or later.'

After some trial and much discussion, they agreed that the safest way was to climb side by side (though with considerable space between them) and not roped; for any move on that rubble heap was apt to start a cascade of stones downward, so that none wished to climb behind another; and where there was no sure hold, one climber who slipped could drag down all on the rope. Still, as the Exile observed cheerfully, they faced a much lesser danger here than at the cliff of the Dreeg, for here the fall was not sheer but only a rough slide to the bottom, so that whoever fell could hope to scramble up again. To which Lethgro added sourly, 'Depending on which bones are broken.'

For Broz it was a different matter. He could scramble well enough, 'but perhaps not on this steep a slope,' said Repnomar. (For Broz, being a plains dog, was not of the climbing breed.) 'And I'll take no chances of losing him.' So Broz once more was knotted into a harness, which he bore patiently enough, and the other end of the rope fastened around the Captain's waist, for she would have no one else charged with Broz's safety.

Meanwhile the Exile had offered to carry the Warden's bundle of fuel; and when the Warden assured him that there was no need of this, he had urged his offer so eagerly that at last the Warden realized that he wanted the bundle to cover his back with. Indeed the Exile, though he did not complain, clearly suffered much from the cold; and when, in passing the fuel, their fingers touched, Lethgro found that the Exile's hands were wrapped in scraps of cloth. 'Torn from his shirt tail, most likely,' the Warden thought; but he said nothing, not knowing any comfort to offer, and only helped arrange the fuel to cover the Exile's back as thoroughly as might be.

So at last they began to climb, not knowing what lay above, nor whether they would ever scramble high enough to find out. The rocks gave little purchase to hand or foot; for if you gripped too hard, you dislodged the very stone you gripped at and your weight came suddenly upon another, that was all too apt to give way and roll beneath it, so that (unless sheer luck or desperate skill preserved you) you were likely to find yourself scrambling on the face of a rolling avalanche. Within the first half hour of climbing they had each taken at least one such a devil's slide, though luckily no bones were broken. The Warden was no longer troubled by the cold, being hot with a kind of anger, against the stones or the dark or perhaps his own helplessness. For it was a pitiful thing to be sprawled like a blind lizard on this gravel heap, every inch upward won by a weary groping struggle and likely to be undone in a moment, and the Warden of Sollet Castle was unaccustomed to such indignity. Nevertheless he clambered on without complaint, and took his slides with as good grace as might be, burying his face in his shoulder to save his eyes and teeth, for the stones were mostly as big as a fist and far harder, and some of them bigger than Lethgro's head.

Presently the Exile called out from somewhere above that he had found water, forgetting in his excitement the right names of things, for indeed what he had found was ice. This they all had to deal with soon enough, and found it both good and bad. They were glad to ease their thirst, sucking at the ice-crusted rocks they crawled over or breaking off bits of ice and popping them into their mouths like dainties at a banquet; also the going was easier, in a way, the stones being held together by the ice and less likely to shift and tumble. But it was slippery going, harder than ever to find purchase on, and the ice wet their stiff fingers and panting faces, making them colder yet. Also the wind streamed down their backs like an icy river, fluttering their clothes and scattering bits of their fuel. They went ever more carefully; for the higher they climbed the less they liked the notion of an avalanche that might sweep them to the very bottom, gathering stones all the way.

It was on the ice that Repnomar first paused to give Broz a rest. The old dog had climbed gallantly so far, but it was a hard thing for him, and he whined and wheezed as he went, and trembled hard. The Captain had managed to keep him close to her most often, helping him along with one hand when she could; but there were times when he slid to the end of his rope, yelping with dismay. Twice he had pulled her down with him; and once she had been the first to slip, and dragged him after her. Now, finding her feet steadier than heretofore on two ice-glued rocks, she worked Broz up to her and braced him against the slope with her arm and shoulder, so that at last he could ease the trembling of his taut limbs and take some warmth from her, and she from him.

That was their first rest. Five more times they rested, on icy stones or dry, and all the while the crows – who, by all reason, had least to complain of – fretted wretchedly around them, flying now up and now down, clawing and pecking at their shoulders, trying to ride their backs, and in every way troubling and hindering them; for shipcrows could make nothing of this climb in blindness, and did not like to find their Captain and her companions thus spraggling on the side of a rubble pile.

So that they all were ready to curse crows forever, when suddenly one that had flown upward began to call steadily from above, and the Captain said, drawing a great breath through her teeth, 'It's found the top.' At once the other crow left off pestering the Exile and flew upward, and a moment later joined the first in glad and strident chorus.

They crawled now still more cautiously, each one feeling that at all costs they must not now lose what they had so painfully won, and it seemed a long age before the Warden called out that he had come to the end of the loose stones. His voice was somewhat strained.

Indeed he had not the heart to tell the others what he had found, thinking that they would learn soon enough. For the loose stones ended at the foot of a sheer wall of angled columns.

12
Things Seen in Darkness

'One thing's certain,' the Captain said; 'there's no hope found where there's no hope looked for.'

They had leveled a narrow space at the top of the heap, working carefully first with their feet, then with their hands, so that after a time they were able to sit with their backs against the cliff face and their legs outstretched down thc slope. Here the wind left them alone, except for an occasional gust; but they could hear it whining and howling above them. This was the first real rest, for any of them except Broz, since the climb began, and even this was uneasy enough, perched as they were on the topmost edge of that unsteady pile. It was hard sitting, too, and devilishly lumpy, but it was so welcome to them that there were tears of pleasure in the Warden's eyes, though little enough pleasure in his mind.

They sat side by side, the Exile in the middle and Broz lying across their thighs, so as to have the most good from each other. The voices of the crows still came querulously down to them. 'And it's not far,' Repnomar persisted. 'I still think I could reach it from your shoulders, Lethgro.'

'We've tried that,' said the Warden, and repressed a shudder. Indeed it had been an uncertain few minutes, himself pressed hard against the cliff and trying to balance while the Exile helped Repnomar to scramble up him, and feeling the stones shift now and again under his feet. 'And after all you didn't reach it,' he added.

'No,' the Captain said reflectively. 'But we could pile the stones higher – '

'Not without glue,' the Warden interrupted.

' – Or search along the cliff till we find a better place,' she went on, and Lethgro nodded in the dark, for he thought that this was what they must do indeed, little as he liked the idea.

'And besides,' Repnomar added without warning, and stirring so that Broz jerked uneasily on her legs, 'the rock's not smooth. These columns have crevices between them, and it's a safe bet they have cracks across them, too. All you ever need to climb straight up is a fingerhold and a toehold. Are we going to sit here till we freeze, or are we going to try it?' And she moved as if to stand up again, discomfiting Broz and rousing the Exile to protest that they should lay their plan before they acted on it.

Yet it seemed clear that the Captain was right, as they all shortly agreed. For unless the rubble heap they perched upon had cracked and fallen stone by stone from the cliffs above, how had it come to be? And if all these had cracked loose, it was only sensible to suppose that more were in the way of cracking, and the fabric of that cliff above them must be webbed with fissures.

So when they had talked enough, and picked a few bites of food out of their pockets, and cold and hunger were goading them to movement, with some trouble the Warden lit a fire on the stones beside him, and made a torch of reeds and mosses, and fixed that to the end of his bow. But although he raised it as far as his arm could reach, and they all stretched and craned, peering upward by that uncertain light, they could not see surely where the cliff top was that the crows had found. 'If it *is* the top,' said Lethgro; 'for it might be only a ledge.' But the Captain would not have her crows doubted, saying that though this dark country was strange to them, they still knew a harbor from a sandbar.

The crows themselves were much excited by the torch-light, and flew around the Warden's contrivance with loud cries, so that he swore at them ungraciously, forgetting his usual patience. In the end, laying aside the torch, he bound moss to an arrowhead and set it afire and shot it upward, kneeling on the teetering rocks with his elbow braced against the cliff and shooting almost straight up along its face, so that they all hunched their heads a little between their shoulders in fear of the arrow's return. But it sprang upward, scattering its sparks through the blackness, and disappeared from their sight. Lethgro groaned, and reached for another arrow, for he thought that the wind or the speed of its own flight had put out the fire; but before he had finished binding moss to the second arrowhead, Repnomar cried out that she saw light above them. Indeed the flames, that had been almost snuffed out, now burned up again brightly, and they saw the glow of them where the arrow had landed above their heads. Lethgro rose to his feet carefully.

'Well, Rep, we'd have had to pile stones pretty high before you could have reached it from my shoulders,' he said.

But Repnomar answered in excitement, 'It's no more than a mast's height. If we can't climb that, Lethgro, we should have stayed in Beng harbor!'

Warden Lethgro made no answer to this, though he very heartily believed that they should have stayed in Beng harbor, but silently stowed his arrow, and his bow, and his fuel (on the Exile's back), and made ready to climb. By now the little light above them had burned out, leaving the darkness blacker than before. But now they knew how far they had to go, and were ready for it, and without more talk they began to feel along the rock wall for holds.

These they were some time in finding. There were cracks indeed across the stone columns, but few wide enough or deep enough to put a fingertip into, still less the toe of a boot. What served to start them up at last was only the staggered line of the cliff face, some columns standing farther out and some set back into the body of the cliff; so that, bracing his feet and hands against two that stood out a little way and within close reach of each other, the Exile was able to work his way up between them to a good foothold where one of the columns was broken off short, just beyond Lethgro's reach.

'Can you feel the top?' Repnomar shouted up to him. And when he answered no, she was all for calling him down and taking his place herself. But the Exile, painstakingly groping along the rock face, found another foothold, sideways and a little upward from the first, and above that such good handholds that he was able to climb straight up, till a chunk of rock broke loose in his grasp and he came near falling, a thing that shook them all badly. For the broken rock and the sound of his scrabbling and gasping came down through the dark to the others, and they spread their arms in hopes to catch him as he fell. But he managed to stop himself, taking only some scrapes and bruises; and after resting for a time (if it could be called rest, clutched insecurely to those tiny crevices in that sheer wall of rock) he began to climb again. And no more than a few minutes later they heard the jubilation of the crows, and then the Exile's shout that he was on the top.

It was simple enough after that for the Exile to let down the rope and, first, to haul up Broz, grunting and yelping (for this seemed to him the worst journey of all he had made yet), and then to play up Repnomar, she half-climbing and half-leaning on the rope, and the two of them together to play up Lethgro in the same manner, who was the heaviest of the lot.

Now they rested, building a little fire to warm themselves, swallowing their last scraps of food, and talking cheerfully as they searched for fuel, while Broz frolicked about their legs; for in spite of darkness and cold and hunger they were all inclined to celebrate after winning up that cliff. But they found neither fuel nor food, and in a little they put out what was left of the fire, to save what fuel they might, and their talk died away into silence. A strange silence it seemed, for there was nothing in it but silence itself and the wind and their own breathing. To the Captain, who these long years past had never been out of the sound of Soll water, and seldom out of earshot of her *Mouse* and her crew, it was as if a great blankness had swallowed up the foundations of the world, and nothing remained on which to stand or float. And the Warden was in little better case, for his ears strained always to catch some rustle of life, the murmur of leaves or the whisper and gurgle of running water, plash of fish or call of birds, stir of creatures in the woods and grasses, or the tread and voices of his people about the castle, crackle of fires and creak of floors; and it was a grief to him to hear the beating of blood in his own ears.

Now Broz nuzzled against the Captain, and his stomach rumbled emptily. Whereupon she sprang up, saying that now they had climbed the mountain (for she did not see fit to mention the lit peaks that still stood high above them) they were in no danger unless they determined to sit still and starve. 'And we can make good time now,' she said, 'till we come to water and better time after that.' Lethgro, who knew more of mountains, sighed deeply; but he said nothing, not liking to lessen any hope there was among them, and they started off again at a brisk pace, rubbing their hands together against the cold.

As the Warden had thought, their climbing was not done. The land was level enough for a little way, but soon it began to rise, sometimes in smooth and rounded slopes, sometimes in broken terraces and stairsteps, and again in anthill piles of loose rubble like the first they had climbed; and all, always and everywhere, was bare stone, without a fistful of earth to cover it, still less any growing thing. And when again they built a fire at one of their resting stops, that came ever more often, the Exile's face by its light showed sick as if with grief.

Yet a little while later, coming to the top of a crag, they found the darkness lightened so that they could make out each other's shapes; and, turning, they saw far behind them a red light as of forests burning, and the clouds afire with it, so that all the horizon flamed and glowed. And the Exile said in a choked voice that they had climbed so high they could see the edge of the light. But what troubled him, as they found by much questioning, was not that they were so high, but rather that they were still so near.

Indeed it was not cheerful to think that they had half a world to cross in the darkness, being already at the end of their food and water, and no sign of more to be found. 'But,' Repnomar said impatiently, and shaking the Exile's arm to be sure of his attention, 'you thought you could do it alone; and if one can do it, four can do it better.' (For she considered Broz to be as useful a companion as any.) 'All that remains is for you to tell us how.'

But the Exile replied that he had no hope of crossing that desolation of darkness and coming alive to its farther edge, and that in his opinion four would be merely four times quicker to die from lack of food, unless in desperation they chose to feed on each other (a notion at which he shuddered in disgust). And when the Warden demanded to know why, in the name of any or all gods, they were yet journeying, he added hastily that he had good hope of the mountain peaks before them; for those peaks, standing in light, had their own edge of darkness, and it was there that he believed his precious things to be.

To which the Warden answered heartily, 'Damn your precious things! Will there be food and drink there?' And the Exile answered yes. 'Then let's go on,' the Warden said in a voice like a growl, and turning abruptly on his heel. And without more talk they all followed.

Once only they stopped to look back to where the clouds burned now dull purple and scarlet on the horizon, and the Exile had to be pulled away at last from his staring; for, as he explained it to them, in his own world such sights were momentary, coming and going swiftly about dinnertime. 'And I suppose,' said the Warden, 'that the mountains also rise and sink while you have breakfast.' To which the Exile, with some diffidence and clearing his throat once or twice, replied that in most worlds of his acquaintance darkness and light were not fixed in their own places, but moved steadily forward, as a river flows.

'Flowing to where?' the Captain asked. And the Exile answered shyly, as one without much hope of being believed, that they flowed round and round those worlds, coming every three or four watches (as human watches went) back to where they had begun. But the Captain said that this was nonsense.

Indeed they had all grown irritable, and perhaps a little lightheaded; and when, at the next pause, they looked back and saw only darkness, the Captain burst into raucous laughter, saying, 'Well, we've sunk the light!' Lethgro felt in his heart that it was folly to speak words of such ill omen aloud, and it was silently that he made his own farewell to light forever.

All sense of time seemed to have left them with the sense of sight (for the shining summits above were like things dreamed of rather than things seen), and they had no notion how long they had trudged and clambered, on hands and knees as often as on their feet, when Broz saved them. This he did with a short bark of joy, and thrusting his muzzle into Repnomar's hand; and Repnomar, straightening from a crouch, cried in a hoarse voice, 'He's found water!'

What Broz had found was more than water, though they

did not realize this at first. He led them to a frozen pool, thickly iced at the edges but with a runnel of liquid water through the middle, and there they drank deep and refilled the Exile's flask, which had long been empty. It was the Warden who, his boot breaking through the ice, lifted a chunk of it in his fingers and cried out that there was something growing on it.

'Under it, you mean, Lethgro,' the Captain muttered a minute later, as they all three, on their knees around the pool, pried and pounded at the ice. And Lethgro said, 'We need light for this,' and fell to striking a fire.

In some places it was no more than a frothy slime on the underside of the ice; but in others it was a mat of mosslike stuff, gray and unwholesome to look at in the firelight, and infested with soft sluglike things that shrank and stretched and oozed between the fingers. Disagreement arose at once.

'This is no time to be squeamish,' the Captain insisted. 'Any muck's worth eating, when it comes to eat or starve.'

'It hasn't come to that yet,' the Warden answered somewhat snappishly. 'There's still a chance for the Exile to show us he knows how to speak the truth.'

To this remark the Exile could not well object, only maintaining that while he was sure there would be good supplies of food with his precious things, he could not be quite sure how near those things were. Still, he too was against eating of the stuff they had found – not, he said, from squeamishness, but from fear that it might prove poisonous. His idea, therefore, was to carry a supply of the gray muck with them (slugs and all, for they were the only meat that offered), hoping to reach his precious things before they were obliged to eat it; or, if they thought that too long a wait, at least to let the crows sample such unpromising food before they ate of it themselves.

This, in truth, it was too late to decide on, for the crows were already pecking and scratching at the overturned slabs of ice, eating the slugs with all signs of relish and nibbling at the moss. So they built up the fire and rested and warmed themselves, watching the crows a little uneasily. But the crows, so far from giving any sign of distress, were altogether happier than they had been for many watches past, taking much pleasure in the fire and the food. 'And I've watched their feasting long enough,' said the Captain. 'The rest of you can sit hungry as long as you like, but I'm ready for a bowl of slug stew.' And she set to filling her bailer with slugs and water and a fistful of slimy moss for flavoring.

It was unsavory enough, and Lethgro had to turn away from the light of the fire before he could bring himself to choke down his share; but once down it warmed his belly, and went some way toward filling it. So that they started on again warmed within and without, and freshly supplied with a flask full of water and a bailer full of stew. Their very eyes felt rested, by the firelight and the sight of each other and of their own hands, so that they went back to their groping in the dark with better courage. And though, as they journeyed, the Warden was taken by one strange pang after another as the unaccustomed food worked in his belly, and the thought of it in his mind, still he was glad on the whole that they had eaten it and were likely to eat of it again; especially as the Exile now began to say that it was likely his precious things were not on this side of the peaks, but rather just beyond them.

As it turned out, they had come into a land of plenty, or what seemed like plenty after the desolation they had struggled through so far. It was rough and rising ground, but still walkable; and what gladdened their hearts was that it was laced with little streams and pools, and on the pools ice, and under the ice all that muck of moss and crawling things, which was to them now like a banquet spread. Still more, the very stones they traveled over were crusted here and there with a thin growth of something, like flaking layers of paint, and sometimes padded with bristly mosses; and in little hollows of the rock the Warden rubbed between his fingers what felt like soil, a sweet thing to touch after so many miles of barren stone.

These things excited them all, but they excited the Exile beyond reason. For he said that on his world nothing could live without light, unless by feeding on the things that lived by light, so that at bottom it was light that fed all things living; but here, it seemed, life grew out of darkness. And he talked at length of little live things, doubtless too tiny to see, that could make nourishment in the dark out of rock and water, and so feed such larger game as slugs and make soil for mosses and the like. He was forever stooping to pluck and scrape bits of whatever he took to be live stuff from the ground, and pocketing them proudly. The Warden, too, did his share of gathering; for where the spiky moss grew thick he plucked it by handfuls, to restock his bundle of fuel, for they had burned almost all in their celebration at the first ice pool. And the crows came down from perching on their shoulders and busied themselves; for they found small game, some as big as crickets, in the mosses and in the patches of soil. But Broz, for all his searching, found nothing larger.

When they camped at the end of that watch (though indeed they kept but ragged account of time in the darkness, and no longer knew or very much cared how many real hours had passed) the Warden spent his time on guard in scouring all the rocks about for more mosses; and when the Captain woke she heard strange rustlings in the dark, and upon her asking, 'What are you doing, Lethgro?' he answered, 'Padding my shirt.' Indeed he had already stuffed the toes and bottoms of his boots with dry moss, sadly cramping his feet, and was now cramming wads of it into his sleeves and close against his chest. 'And you'll do the same, Rep, if you take my advice,' he said. 'And the Exile most of all, for the cold is hardest for him to bear.'

It was the streams that had put this idea into the Warden's head, for they reminded him of the snow streams that fed the Upper Sollet, and he thought that if these streams too were fed by snow, it would be snow that made white those peaks to which they climbed; and thinking thus, he remembered that the mountaineers around the headwaters of the Sollet padded their garments with sheep's wool against the cold. This spiky moss was a poor substitute for soft fleece; but, as the Warden said, 'Logs will keep out the wind as well as marble; and who eats slugs might as well wear moss.' So for a time they busied themselves with this, plucking the moss and shaking out of it as much of its livestock as they could before they wadded it into their clothes; and when they went on they kept up their harvesting, stooping whenever their feet struck a mossy place, and calling out to each other when they found good patches.

They were so busy with this reaping that they scarcely noticed how close they had come to the light of the peaks. A feeling of triumph had been on them since that meal by the ice pool, as if their way thereafter must be easy and all their troubles sure of solution. So that they were ill prepared when Repnomar, stopping dead in her tracks, cried out suddenly that the peaks were gone.

Indeed, those beacons, that had begun to seem within their reach, had vanished utterly. Before them as behind, the world was solid darkness.

13

Of the Preciousness of Things

Later – when they had got back strength enough to argue – they discussed whether that watch had been the longest of their journeying so far, and came to no agreement, having no means but the weariness of their muscles and the fogginess of their minds by which to measure the time since their last sleep.

'But I'll grant you your bet, Repnomar,' said the Warden. 'For if it's been more than twenty watches I couldn't prove it; and in any case, we've outrun my expectation by coming here alive at all.'

They were settled at ease on a ledge of bare rock, out of the wind and taking their pleasure in the light. At their backs rose a cliff smooth and hollowed like the inside of a bowl, so that it arched a sort of lip or roof over their heads, hiding the white snow peaks above them. Below their ledge, a long white slope stretched downward into darkness. 'And if the crust on that snow had been thinner,' Repnomar said thoughtfully, 'I might not have won that bet, Lethgro.'

It was the Exile who had first realized what had wiped out the peaks from that black prospect (for indeed his eyes served better in the dark than those of ordinary humans, and he could make out shapes where all was one blind blank to the others); but they would all have known it soon enough, for walking straight into the cold breath of the wind they came against the foot of whatever tall barrier it was that had cut off their view of the peaks. Repnomar laid her hand on it, and swore briefly, and tried her knife on its surface, and swore again, not so much in anger as in admiration. 'Taste a bite of this, Lethgro,' she said, putting a cold chip of something into his hand. 'Is this what you make mountains out of?' And Lethgro answered, 'Not Sollet Mountains.' For this time the cliff that blocked their way was not rock, but ice.

'Well, for my money,' said Repnomar, 'a mountain of ice is worth two of rock; for we can make our own toeholds where we want them.' And she went on hacking at it with her knife.

Here the Exile remarked that it was not truly a mountain, but a kind of river. At this Repnomar could not repress a snort of laughter. 'And better a river of ice than of rock, if it comes to that,' she said. 'But I hope the next one will be water.'

They had not discussed this question of ice rivers much, nor any other, being too occupied with the business of cutting holds for themselves in the wall of ice, and after that with climbing. It was not all so easy as the Captain would have it, for the ice was sometimes hard almost as rock itself, sometimes flawed and brittle; and they came to the top at last panting and trembling, whether with cold or with strain, and dragging Broz bodily behind them at the end of the rope.

'But it *is* the top,' the Captain said, when she had got her breath back, and was rubbing Broz's limbs to comfort and warm him; 'for there are our landmarks.'

Between climbing and walking, they had come a long way; and the peaks, no longer hidden by that bulwark of ice on whose top they now sprawled easily, stood like white towers above them, almost within their reach. The Exile drew a slow breath and stood up, saying stolidly that it was time to move on (though indeed they had not rested), and the Warden followed. The truth was that freezing now seemed a likelier death than any other, and to keep moving their only hope of keeping warm. For not all the Warden's stuffing of moss sufficed to keep out the wind that gnawed at them now, not strong but icy; and besides, a good deal of that stuffing had fallen out in the rough climb. So they plodded on, their hands jammed into their sleeves for warmth and the crows sailing out of sight on the wind above them.

The crows, it soon appeared, were lucky. 'If this is a river,' the Captain said sourly, 'that was the waterfall where we found it first, and this part must be the rapids.' For they had come now upon a stretch of ice that was rough with great lumps and split with cracks and pitted with holes of a size to catch feet and wrench ankles; and all this shrouded over with dry snow. And the Exile warned them that there might be worse cracks and pits, apt for breaking more than ankles. So they struggled on, stumbling often, till sheer weariness constrained them to rest for a little, and then on again, sometimes refreshing themselves (to call it that) with frozen chunks of their stew chipped off by Repnomar's knife. Once the Exile, tugging at Lethgro's moss-padded sleeve, asked meekly what were the chances of lighting a fire; and Lethgro without hesitation lifted the bundle from the little man's back and set about it, for he thought that the Exile was not one to beg a favor unless out of desperate need.

It was only a poor fire they managed on the ice, for the hotter it burned, the faster the ice melted and soaked it. But with constant care (and, as the Exile mournfully observed, the waste of considerable fuel) it sufficed to thaw the Exile's hands and face, which were near turning to ice themselves; and though this clearly brought tears of pain to his eyes, he made out that they were tears of relief, and rubbed them away quickly before they could freeze. Here too they thawed the dregs of the stew, and finished it (Broz licking out the bailer) and drank water warmed in the soggy embers. And after this they went on very silently, thinking each their own thoughts.

So that the others, Broz included, all jerked with surprise when the Exile spoke suddenly, saying in a hoarse voice that they had arrived.

This, as it turned out, was somewhat hastily spoken. But the Exile held to it that the dark had lightened, claiming that he could now see passably well, and attempting to prove it by foretelling humps and holes in the ice before they reached them, which he did with some success. 'But be that as it may,' said Repnomar, 'we can all see what we're about to come to.'

Very strange it looked to her, though she strove to liken it to sights she had seen often enough – a fogbank on the Soll, the white cliffs of the Coast, clouds to windward of a passing storm. It was like all these, indeed, but more unlike, because it rose out of darkness – a pale, far-stretching sheet of light that climbed even higher, whiter, clearer, to where it leaped in striped and jagged pinnacles against the black sky.

'It's a field of snow, Repnomar, not a storm on the Soll,' the Warden said curiously, for he wondered to see her stand hesitating. He himself had tramped such snowfields on the skirts of the Sollet Mountains.

In her heart, Repnomar might have preferred a storm on the Soll just then; for glad as she was to be coming into the light once more, and eager for a sight of those elusive things of the Exile, yet she was very weary, and so much strangeness had taken a toll even on her. So that she only muttered something about sinking in snow as well as in water, and put her head down and strode forward.

She was almost right. The snow, as they came out of darkness into a growing pallor of light, lay ever thicker, hiding crevices and fissures and hobbling their cold and weary legs, that moved now like so many ungainly planks and poles. Snow blew into their faces, filled their shoes, found its way down their collars. It was Broz, floundering off to one side in his search for footing, who found a better path and called the others' notice to it with sharp yaps. Here, by some trick of the ground, the light fell brighter, which was a comfort to them; but a greater comfort was the crust of hardened snow that bore up considerable weight before it cracked and gave way beneath a plunging foot. Broz and the Exile traveled at ease here, or what seemed like ease to the others, who went most uneasily and with many sudden oaths, yet better than before. The slope was steep here, too, and the wind perhaps more keen; so that with one thing and another they paid little heed to the scene around them, till the Exile (who was now first on the rope) called out eagerly and pointed. And looking up, they saw that they were coming among the very peaks, where stone stood bare out of the whiteness.

It was on one of these outcrops above the ice river that they lay now, gazing back over their trail and rubbing their cold limbs. The Warden, when he had breathed a little, set about his fire-making. 'And this will be the last,' he said warningly, 'till we find more fuel – unless you want me to burn my bow and arrows, or the moss we've stuffed into our clothes.'

'Well, we won't need fire for cooking,' said the Captain, 'for there's nothing to cook.' And they both fell silent and looked pointedly at the Exile.

Now the Exile cleared this throat with some embarrassment, and suggested that while the others rested here, out of the wind, he should go on into the shadows beyond and find his precious things, which doubtless were close at hand. But at this the Warden heaved himself stiffly to his feet, declaring that he would go with the Exile if there was any going; and the Captain stretched out a long arm to bar their path and said that there was no need to go anywhere till they were warmed and rested, and then they would all go together. 'And you might as well tell us first,' she added, looking fiercely at the Exile, 'what it is you have to hide.'

The Exile protested this vehemently, insisting that he hid nothing, and twisting up his ugly face in such contortions of earnestness and dismay that in the end they could not help laughing at him and turning the line of talk elsewhere.

But when they had rested and warmed themselves, and their fire had burnt out to the last wisp of moss, the Warden rose again and put the rope into the Exile's hand, saying, 'You first,' and they roped themselves and started in line toward the farther darkness.

This was not such hard going as they had feared, for the river of ice they had followed seemed to be the outpouring of a lake of ice, that spilled between two peaks close by the ledge where they had rested. So for the most part they traveled by walking, not climbing, and were glad of this; for they all were more than a little weak and stiff and privately in dread of falls, and not eager to hoist Broz's weight at the end of a rope. The light still lay pleasantly upon their backs as they passed between the shoulders of the two peaks; but now the Exile turned them a little to the right, into the shadow of one of those pinnacles, where the way ran gently downward, the snow here so well crusted that they walked as if on solid ground, but overlaid with newer snow that blew in sudden gusts around them. But the Captain said that the wind was falling, and they took some comfort in this.

Certainly the Exile went now as if he knew his road, and hurrying their pace in spite of his short legs. Yet the Warden followed with no great hope in his heart, and still less faith; for he thought it likelier that the Exile was planning some sudden escape than that they were coming at last to those unknown treasures that seemed always to vanish from before them. So that he was not well prepared when the Exile stopped short and scooped with his hands into a mound of drifted snow that showed as a paleness in the dark, and then straightened sharply and turned to them, saying almost sheepishly that here were his precious things.

Precious they might be to him, but it was hard to know what good they were to any other. What the snow had hidden was a string of great shells or pods, like bird's eggs or the covering of certain seeds, the smallest of them as big as Broz, and one so large that three or four people might have crawled into it if it had been empty. 'And I hope that some of that,' said Lethgro, as the Exile pulled one packet after another from an opening in this pod, 'is the food and drink you promised us.'

'Let him be, Lethgro,' the Captain said sharply. 'I don't doubt he's as hungry as you are.' And in fact she had forgotten her own hunger in her eagerness to uncover these new things. Lethgro was by no means certain that so small a person as the Exile could hold a hunger to match his own; but he schooled himself to patience for a time, and even helped the Exile bring out his ungainly and misshapen treasures (not one of which resembled any useful or comely object known to the Warden) and set them on the ice. The Exile seemed to be in haste now, moving nervously and muttering to himself as he unpacked this litter of strange objects; and when, to the startlement of the others, he struck a light that brightened all the scene like the dazzle they had passed through in mid-Soll, they saw that his face was drawn with some anxiety.

Now the Captain was much excited, exclaiming that with this light of the Exile's they could cross the whole dark side of the world and see what they were crossing. But the Exile, making no answer to this, fingered his torch so that the light narrowed into a single beam, and set it to shine only on his unpacking. It seemed to Lethgro, too, that he took care to set it where the bulk of the pods would hide it from any eyes there might have been (supposing such a thing to be possible) in the darkness beyond the peaks. He was just beginning to ask what this meant – for he found it disquieting to consider – when the Exile brought out a new packet with some flourish, declaring that it held food.

Then for some time they were busy with happier matters, though indeed it was a strange sort of victuals, such as would never have been called food (so the Warden reflected) in Sollet Castle. 'But it's no worse than stewed slugs and moss,' the Captain said judiciously, when she had chewed down three or four mouthfuls; and the Exile seemed to be in bliss for thc time, his eyes glazed over with a look of fond satisfaction each time he swallowed. But as soon as he was a little strengthened by the joy of eating, he popped up eagerly to open another of his packets, unfolding it into a many-legged device that seemed to do nothing and yet must have contained a blazing fire in its belly, for a great swell of heat went out from it, warming their hands and faces and melting the snow a yard around. But as with the torch, so with this curious stove; the Exile twirled certain of its legs or spines, and the heat ceased to beat on the snow and ice, and only poured upward, spreading a little, so that they could warm themselves over it. And it gave no light at all.

Now they began to talk of moving to a spot sheltered from blowing snow, where the Exile promised to show them all his things, and there discuss what to do next. But the warmth and the food began to act on them like some sleepy drug, and when the Exile unfolded what seemed at first to be a handkerchief but opened into a sheet that could have covered the broadest bed in Sollet Castle, and laid it out on the ice, saying it would do for a place to rest, they all stretched themselves on it and agreed that this was as good a camp as they needed (for indeed they had been hard pressed). And without more discussion they settled to sleep, the Exile taking the first turn to stay on guard, for he said he had work to do.

The sheet of stuff they lay on, thin as it was, kept out the cold of the ice, and the Exile fiddled at his stove till its heat fell full upon them; so that there was nothing to trouble their ease except the fitful wind scattering snowflakes on them from time to time, that melted at once and wet their faces and clothes. They slept where they lay, like fallen logs, unmoving for a long while. And indeed they might have slept longer if the Exile's notion of comfort had not been so extreme, for in time the heat from his stove set the Captain to tossing restlessly, and she woke with a start, demanding in irritation why she had not been roused to take her turn on guard. But she got no answer, for the Warden still slept, and the Exile and all his pods were gone.

14
Quicksilver

'At least he doesn't mean for us to starve,' Lethgro observed somewhat wistfully. The truth was that he did not find it easy to harden himself against the Exile, despite all the disappointments and troubles he had brought them, and looked still for reasons to think kindly of him.

The Captain snorted. 'I grant you he's not a devil,' she said, and wrenched another mouthful from the square of stuff she was gnawing at. 'He left us food, he left us the sheet, he left us the stove, and he left us the light. But you can't deny that he left us; and the question is, why?' She chewed thoughtfully for a minute, and added, 'For that matter, how?'

'He's flown before,' said the Warden. 'Maybe he found a way to fly again.'

For the curious thing was that the Exile, in all that sweep of snow around them, had left no track. 'He might have gone back the way we came, and trodden in our footprints,' said the Warden, shining the Exile's torch along the trail, 'but he couldn't have carried those pods on his shoulders.'

Indeed the mystery would have been far less without the pods to account for. Lethgro, who had rolled one of the larger ones half over to help the Exile get at the next, knew that they were heavy. And even if the Exile had contrived to drag or roll them, they would have left a track like a beaten road through the snow.

'And there's no wind,' said the Captain. For the wind had fallen, and fallen utterly; and in the pale silence a nightmare sense came over her that in this country Windfall was like death (whereas in all reasonable countries it was only like a sleep, stirred always with little movements and breaths). And she thought that those who trusted in one or another god had this advantage, that they knew always where to address their complaints.

But she sprang up and began to scan the heights and slopes around them, looking for a spot from which the Exile might have flown, pods and all. 'And who knows,' she said, 'what sort of sails he might have unpacked? If he has a stove that burns without fuel, why not a sail that flies without wind?'

Lethgro sighed, and turned up his collar. He was not cold yet, but he expected to be. 'Come on, Rep,' he said. 'It's time we were going.'

Repnomar looked at him in surprise. 'Which way do you think he's gone?'

'Straight up, for all I know,' said the Warden. 'What difference does it make? He's found what he came for, and we have the wherewithal now to make our way home again – if we don't sit here till we've wasted it all. Besides,' he added brusquely, seeing her about to object, 'there may be others than we that can see a light in the dark.' And he told her what he had thought of the Exile's shielding of the torch.

This (he later reflected) he should have known better than to do. The Captain took it as a strong argument for following the Exile (supposing they could decide which way he had gone). For, as she said, the Exile had stood by them stoutly on more occasions than one; and if he was going now to face his enemies – 'or, it may be, monsters,' she added – he was likely to need help.

'If he wanted help he could have asked for it,' the Warden said hotly; for he felt the time had come to take a stand against the Captain's foolishness. 'And I think, Repnomar, it's not so much the Exile's safety that tempts you into the dark, as your own wild curiosity. You'd risk all our lives for a sight of some outlandish nation of ice people.' And Broz whined softly, as if this talk made him uneasy.

This was striking close to home, and the Captain immediately changed her tack. 'If you see a road hereabouts without a risk on it, point it out to me, Lethgro. And what's wrong with learning something new? There may be more harm in *not* knowing what's out there.' (Here she gestured roundly at the dark.) 'For who can say what trouble's brewing there, that may blow all the way to the Coast? And if you talk of going home, remember that you're in no good standing with the League, and your best hope of keeping your head on your shoulders is to bring the Exile back with you.'

Lethgro bit his lip (being in the shadows where Repnomar could not see his face), for there was something in what she said. 'Whatever trouble's out there,' he said, 'remember that he chose to meet it alone. Also he has his precious things now – ' ('Unless it was somebody else that carried them off,' put in Repnomar), ' – and we've seen a little of what they can do. But all your arguments sink on one rock, Repnomar, and there it is!' And this time it was the Warden who waved his arm at the surrounding darkness. 'It's true we have food for a time, such as it is, and light and heat; but if there's any truth at all in what the Exile's told us, to say nothing of what we've seen with our own eyes (or rather haven't seen), there's half a world out there of darkness and desolation. If we travel to the end of our provisions and are still in the dark, it's too late then to decide on turning back.'

'You're right,' Repnomar said promptly, somewhat to the Warden's surprise; and she sat down on the sheet beside Broz and began spreading out the food the Exile had left them. And when the Warden asked what she was doing, she answered, 'Counting our rations. We'll save half of this, and a little more, to get us back to the light if need be; and we can safely go on till we finish the rest of it.'

Now, 'safely' was not the word the Warden would have chosen; but after a minute he sat down beside her, taking the stove in his hands and working with the legs and spines of it. 'For,' he said, 'we'll need to know how to use this thing.' And the Captain smiled in satisfaction.

This stove the Warden found not difficult to control, within certain limits. By thrusting in or pulling out the legs of one side or another (all of which stayed strangely cool, however hot the stove) he could send the heat in any direction, and by twisting those legs he could make that heat greater or less. But it worried him that he could not, with all his pushing and pulling and twisting, find a way to put out the fire altogether. 'And whatever fuel it burns,' he said glumly, and rubbing his hand in the snow (for he had burned it), 'it can't last forever.'

'Well, turn it as low as you can,' said the Captain (for she had concluded that this twisting of stove legs was like setting the wick of a lamp). 'It will keep us warm as we travel.' She had packed up the rations and folded the sheet, laying it over Broz's back and fastening it around him with her belt, so that it made a kind of coat for him. The stove was a more awkward thing to carry but the Warden contrived to sling it from one shoulder with his own belt, and with bow and quiver on the other he stood ready to travel. 'And which way, Rep?' he asked morosely. 'Shall we close our eyes and spin around to choose a path, the way children do in their games?'

But she answered, 'What are shipcrows for?' And she sent the crows up into the darkness, signaling to them with the torch to show them what they were to look for. At first they were for turning back to the snow peaks, where there was most light, and Repnomar was hard put to explain her meaning to them. Yet she did so very patiently, saying to

Lethgro, 'He wouldn't be such a fool as to leave us this torch if he didn't have another one for himself.'

'And if they don't see anything,' she added after a time, and looking fiercely at the Warden, whom she fancied to be showing signs of restlessness, 'we're no worse off than we were before.'

To this the Warden objected, saying that if the Exile and his torch were beyond the crows' finding, it was not likely that anyone without wings would do better. 'And it would be blind foolishness, Rep, to start off into the dark at random.'

'You were ready to do it a little while ago,' said the Captain. 'It's late in the game to lose your nerve, Lethgro.'

This made the Warden snort with indignation, for he had not struggled through the perils of half a world to be taunted for cowardice, and he was tired of holding his temper and his tongue. 'And it's a little early for you to be losing your head,' he answered. 'If your idea of the torch makes sense at all – and I think it does – let's not throw it away before it's had fair trial. He needed sleep as much as we did – or more, it may be, having those pods to deal with. Chances are he's asleep now; and if we start out in the wrong direction (and any direction is likely to be the wrong one), we'll be that much farther behind. Wait a few hours, and try the crows again.' And he unslung the stove and set about making himself comfortable.

This was good advice, as the Captain could not deny; but it vexed her to sit idle. Also she still had hope that the crows would return with news of a light, and told the Warden curtly that he had better be ready to pack up the stove again at short notice. But when presently the crows came in cheerless and newsless, she stood up impatiently, saying that she and Broz would do a little hunting while the Warden sat and burned fuel. To this the Warden made no objection, but offered his bow and arrows, which she refused. For, as she said, she was no archer; 'and the truth is, Lethgro, and we both know it, that any game there may be in this country is likely to find you here in camp as I am to find it out there.' And with these inauspicious words she wandered off into the dark, and Broz at her heels, leaving the Warden and the crows to their own devices.

Lethgro watched her go uneasily. Since that wild flight from the cliff of the Dreeg, their little party had never been separated till now, and he felt himself sadly alone, for the crows were poor company enough. 'Though better than none,' he said aloud, with a sudden shiver, and one of the crows answered him with a disconsolate squawk. He was not so foolish as to think that Captain Repnomar would lose her way in the dark; still, he would have been better satisfied if she had taken a light with her.

As it turned out, he had more cause than he knew to worry. But it was some time before he learned that, and the first news was passably good; for very shortly the Captain and Broz came back, without game indeed but in much excitement. 'There are beasts out there,' the Captain declared, 'for Broz smelled them and I heard them; and that means this country isn't such a wasteland as it looks. There's food to be had!'

'Yes, if we could catch it,' Lethgro answered grumpily (though in truth he was mightily relieved, first by their return and second by their news), and he put aside the stove, with which he had been tinkering to pass the time.

'Not just the beasts,' said Repnomar, 'but whatever the beasts feed on, for I don't suppose they live on snow any more than we do. We don't need to starve, Lethgro, even if our rations run out.'

Now the Warden's heart, which had risen warmly at sight of her, sank with a thump, and he began to object strongly; for he saw where her thought was tending, and he had no wish to die in the icy darkness, so far from the

Sollet, chasing after an outlander who wanted no more of them. And with some argument he got a promise from the Captain to abide by their plan, and turn back toward the light before they had eaten half their rations. 'Only,' she said, 'if we find other food, we'll eat that first, and so the rations will go further. But we haven't set our course yet.' And she sent the crows up again to search for the Exile's torchlight.

This, too, brought good news of a sort, for presently they heard one of the crows returning with loud cries, who swooped above them and arrowed off again into the darkness, calling for them to follow. This they did, the other crow soon joining its fellow, and both of them impatient at the slowness of foot travelers. But in a little, Repnomar called down the crows and made them ride on her shoulders. 'For,' she said, 'we know our course now, and there's no need to shout our whereabouts to all the world.' And indeed, though the Captain had taught her crows well, she had never been able to teach them silence.

The course the crows had set for them led downhill, into a deeper darkness than any they had known yet and, for a while, into deeper snow. The Captain went first, shining the torchbeam on the snow just ahead of her, and now and then swinging it side to side to look for better footing – in hopes, too, of seeing tracks, whether of the Exile or of some beast. Broz foundered behind her, sniffing the cold air and snorting hopefully, for he knew by the Captain's bearing that they were on a trail, though of whom or of what he did not know; and the Warden, loaded with such supplies as remained to them, brought up the rear.

One thing most clear in all this darkness was that this was not the path the Exile had followed; and if he was now somewhere straight in front of them, it seemed to the Captain that one of two things must be true: either he had gone roundabout, by some longer but easier road, 'or,' she said aloud, 'he flew.' And when the Warden from behind asked her what she was muttering, she repeated all her thought to him; and he said soberly, 'Yes. He flew.'

Indeed all other theories foundered on the matter of the pods. Those must have risen straight up from where they lay, and doubtless the Exile had risen with them. 'Only this time,' the Warden added moodily, 'there's nothing for it but admit, Rep, that some god must have had a hand in it – or else some giant bird. For with all the sails in the world, a man couldn't have done it.' And he tramped for a while in silence, considering which would be worse to meet in this unhallowed country, the giant bird or that outlandish god. But presently the Captain's casting-about of the torch-beam caught a long ridge of ice where the snow lay thin, and here they paused while she sent up the crows again and made sure of their course; and for some two hours, at the Warden's guess, they followed first the ridge and then the rocky flank of a peak above the ice.

It was here that Broz, who had been snuffling at the snow from time to time, suddenly began to dig in a frenzy, raising a cloud of flying snow around him. So they stopped and watched in hope; and Broz, when he had plowed a trench longer than himself, made a last plunge and yank, and dragged out a little beast the size of a young mole but more like a fish in color, and flapping like a fish in his jaws. The Captain raised a discordant cheer, and the Warden dropped on his knees and patted Broz warmly on the back. 'And where there's one beast,' the Captain observed, 'there are more, and what they feed on besides.' And while Broz killed and ate his snowfish, growling proprietorially at the crows that came to peck at the scraps of it, she began to dig the snow in her turn, working backward from where Broz had begun his trenching. Lethgro watched for a minute and then bent to help her, saying, 'Not so rough, Rep; go gentle,' for he saw that she meant to trace out the snowfish's burrow. So they worked for a time, and presently Broz joined them at it, leaving the last morsels of his prey to the crows, for in truth he had not found it savory eating.

'It's more a land beast than a fish, Lethgro,' said the Captain. 'What do you say it feeds on?'

'I'd tell you better if I'd had a chance to look at its jaws,' answered Lethgro. 'Maybe worms and the like. Maybe roots and bulbs, I'd say, if this were soil we were digging through and not snow. Go easy, Rep; there may be a nest of them.' It was not that Lethgro was jealous of Broz for his kill; but the Exile's rations had not set well with his stomach, and his mouth watered now, swallow as he might, at the thought of fresh meat.

Here Repnomar whistled sharply through her teeth, and tightened her hand around something in the snow. 'What is it?' Lethgro asked quickly, and she shook her head. The truth was that her fingers were too numb to tell her much about what she had hold of, only that it was long and thin, and she yanked hard to bring it out into the light of the Exile's torch. But in the same moment she gave a yelp of pain that brought Broz's head up anxiously, and said between her teeth, 'Get a bit of rope around this thing, Lethgro, and help me pull it out. But be careful how you touch it.'

Lethgro brought the beam of the torch to bear on the Captain's hands in the snow. 'It looks like a root,' he said, and there was surprise in his voice, he having expected something worse.

'Root it may be, but it bit me,' the Captain said doggedly. 'Look, here's a leg. Tie your rope under that and it ought to hold.'

'It's a branch, not a leg,' said the Warden; but he eyed the thing warily as he knotted the rope around it, all the more so as he thought he saw certain buds or nodes or tubers scattered down its length stir restively. Yet when they hauled on the rope the thing came up lifelessly enough, with a slow ripping like a root being pulled out of soil. The Captain sat back on her heels.

'It's as long as an anchor cable,' she said. 'But it looks more like a strand of kelp with the leaves stripped off.' She blew out her lips in a long whistle, but the sound was strangely faint, and Broz and the Warden looked at her questioningly. So that they were watching when she passed a hand over her brow and muttered, like one in puzzlement, 'The blasted landkelp bit me,' and sagged sideways into the snow.

Lethgro caught her before she was quite down, and so held her propped against his knee while he got the Exile's sheet off Broz's back and half spread behind her, and then eased her down upon it. Now for a time the world looked very bleak to him, squatted on that dark mountainside with rock above and ice below, no help to call on but one old dog and a pair of ill-tempered crows and whatever unwholesome gods might have cognizance of this far country, while the Captain's breath came slow and shallow beside him, and that thing lay stretched on the snow within reach of his hand, like a great warty snake, opening and closing its knobs. Nevertheless he wasted no time, setting both stove and torch to shine on the Captain, and soon found the little wound on her hand, for it was already dark and swollen. He did what he could, opening it with his knifepoint and sucking at it to draw out whatever poison the thing had put into her, though indeed he had little hope of this, since the poison was at work already. Broz would have tried his teeth on the landkelp, but Lethgro called him sternly back from it, and he came and lay beside the Captain with his head on her stomach, turning up his eyes to the Warden from time to time, for he was troubled by the strangeness of her sleep; and the crows sat hunched at the sheet's edge, muttering to each other as crows will do; and the Warden watched.

His thoughts were so bleak, and he so deeply sunk in them, that he fairly jerked with startlement when Repnomar's eyes opened and she said grumblingly but very clearly, 'Why didn't you wake me for my turn on guard?' And for the next little while he had much to do to explain to her where she was and what had happened, for she was groggy in her mind, and all the matter of the landkelp, and indeed of the Exile's disappearance and their searching for him, seemed to have gone from her memory.

Otherwise she was well enough, though a little dizzy when she first tried to stand. As soon as this had passed, or somewhat sooner, she was hot to examine the landkelp, and this they did very carefully, turning and prodding it with the Warden's arrows, till the Captain snorted impatiently and grasped it with both hands, saying, 'There's no harm in it if you keep away from its mouths. Here, Lethgro, you wanted to see the jaws on that snowfish – ' (for memory was coming back to her in flaws and gusts); 'take a look at these instead, and tell me what you make of it.' She was teasing open one of the knots or bulbs with her knifepoint.

The Warden peered close, and clicked his tongue in surprise. 'Well, it's the first time,' he said, 'I've ever seen a root that eats worms.'

Certainly it was like a root, no thicker anywhere than two of the Warden's fingers pressed together, and tapering to a wispy tip like a root's end; branches, too, along its side as a root may have, but none of these longer than Broz's foreleg, and every branch tipped with one of those same unwholesome knobs that studded the main length, looking like harmless buds but opening to show each a sac like the craw of some small toothless beast, with a sting in the middle. And indeed some of these, like the one Repnomar had first opened, held the half-digested remnants of little colorless worms. Stretched out in the snow, the thing was twice the Warden's height in length, and might well have been longer, for the thicker end was broken, or more rightly torn, showing a raw edge and a fringe of snapped hairs.

'Not a root, but a trunk,' the Warden decided. 'This is where its roots went down into whatever's below. What do you say, Repnomar?'

'Kelp,' Repnomar answered with assurance. 'But call it a tree if you like, Lethgro.' For she felt that (landlubberly terminology aside) he had come round to her judgement. 'Whatever it is, it might make pretty good rope, once you got those jaws off.' And it was only by reminding her of the time they had lost already, and of how far ahead the Exile might be, that Lethgro persuaded her to put away the knife with which she was picking at it and send up the crows.

These, however, returned quickly and with eager cries, setting them a course well to starboard of their former one and almost straight across the ice river. Here the snow was no deeper than a few fingers' breadth, so that they could see crevices and hummocks before their feet found them, and they pushed ahead briskly. Only Broz was restless, sniffing the air and trotting off now this way, now that. But they still saw no tracks, and the Captain had good hope that they were traveling a shorter course than the Exile and so would cut him off. 'Except that we can't cut him off while he's flying,' the Warden added. And he looked up into the blackness of the sky that hung like solid hopelessness above their torchlight.

And it was just here, looking up into nothing and leaned a little forward as he finished a stride, that he felt himself grasped and jerked by both ankles at once, so that he toppled helplessly; and flinging out his arms to catch himself, he was worse caught instead, for something grabbed and tightened on his right forearm, and suddenly he was face down in a tangle of snow and ropes, half stunned by the fall and with his gear poking into him in various uncomfortable places. He had seen Repnomar go down in the same instant, and just in front of his head Broz was lunging and heaving, caught too by all four legs. Repnomar had kept her grip on the torch, and now she flared the beam wide, so that they lay in a pool of light, and at its edges flashes of silver-gray that sprang and flitted. But before they could make out anything clearly they were all tumbled together, like fish in a net, and dragged with much bumping across the ice.

This did not last long, for which they were grateful. Lethgro, finding that he still had some control over his left arm, shoved aside Broz's rump and said into the Captain's shoulderblade, 'Can you see them?' To which the Captain answered, 'Shh!'

Indeed, being on the top side of the bundle, she saw well enough; and she thought that except for Broz's desperate panting in her ear and Lethgro's muttering at her back, she would be able to hear, too. And she wanted to hear, for they were talking now.

Clustered near the edge of the light, some of them still gripping the cords that tightened the net, they cheeped and whistled and flashed their gestures like spurts of molten silver, swerving and dancing. The Captain's breath came hard from her lungs, for she had not thought to see that glint and swiftness except in the Soll and its creatures. She knew, too, and it was strange to think of, that these sounds were like the sounds that she and Broz had heard when they went hunting in the dark. 'Well,' she told herself, 'we would have eaten one of them if we'd had the chance; it's fair enough if they want to eat us.'

Certainly the three of them (not to count the crows, who had fluttered up from the Captain's shoulders when the meshes tightened around her feet, and so escaped) should feed a good many of these creatures, if they were meat-eaters. None of them was bigger than Broz, and all more slimly built, something like coneys in their shape and movements, but furred all over in that glistening silver-gray, and with great saucer ears that swiveled suddenly this way and that, and long dog-whiskers, and the bigger part of their faces filled by their huge deep-blue eyes. Now, it seemed to the Captain that eyes meant light to see by, and she thought it was poor luck indeed if they were to be butchered and eaten by the very folk that might have shown them the way out of darkness.

Here Broz gave an outraged yelp; for the Warden was struggling to draw his knife, in hopes to cut some of the meshes, and with his twisting, the tip of his bow had poked Broz in a tender spot. At this, some few of their captors came forward, dropping onto all fours to run across the snow, while others pulled the meshes still tighter. The Captain held grimly to her torch, thinking to flash it in their eyes and dazzle them, or perhaps to smash a head with it, though in fact she could barely move either hand. But they did not so much as blink at the light; and stopping a few feet off, they whipped each one a slender rod from behind their shoulders, and blew them like so many whistles, and the Captain felt something sting her cheek.

When she awoke this time, as before, it was to see the Warden gazing glumly down at her. 'Well, Rep,' he said, 'how do you like your Quicksilver People? Or have you forgotten everything again?'

Indeed she had forgotten much, but this time it came back more swiftly, just as the poison had acted more swiftly, and she sat up in a rush, saying, 'Where are we? Where's Broz?'

'In an ice cave,' he answered. 'Right beside you, still asleep.'

On this she would have sprung up, but found her ankles tied together, and she began to swear at the Warden for not having unbound her, and to work at the knots with her fingers (for their hands were free). The Warden chuckled gloomily.

'You're a better sailor than I am, Repnomar, and maybe you can manage it,' he said; 'but I've been working at those knots for the better part of an hour. And they've taken our knives.'

The Captain held to it that any knot ever tied could be untied, but she put the problem aside for the moment and turned to Broz, stirring now and whining in his sleep. The Warden had spread the sheet and laid them on it, folding a corner over Broz against the cold; for though the Quicksilver People had left them the torch, they had taken the stove. Broz's hind legs too were bound together, and this proved to be a lucky thing, for no sooner was he well awake than he lunged at the Captain, catching the arm that she flung up in startlement and almost crushing the bones of her wrist in his jaws before the Warden could get him loose. Whereupon he turned on the Warden, snapping and ravening, so that both Warden and Captain dragged themselves hastily away, and with a shaking hand the Captain took up the torch to use as a weapon if need should be. 'He'll remember us,' she said hoarsely. 'Let's hope it's soon.'

15
Knots and Nooses

It was a weary time later – none of them knew how long – when Broz, with a puzzled whine, dropped his chin onto the Captain's knee and fell asleep. The Captain and the Warden met each other's eyes and drew a long breath, for all in all it had been a wearisome watch. Lethgro, with some caution, undid the belt he had fastened with considerable effort not long before, looped through the cords that bound Broz's hind legs. The moss he had stuffed his clothes with against the cold had proved useful for another purpose during that operation, and though he was ragged enough now, with tufts of moss everywhere raveling out through the gashes, he had not bled, or not to mention. The Captain had fared somewhat worse. Her own belt had gone to loop the old dog's nose in a makeshift muzzle, and for that success she had paid with a torn right hand, and come near to paying with an eye, for Broz at close quarters was no light antagonist. Lethgro had been for noosing it around his neck, as being easier to do and a surer means of quieting him; but the Captain would have no harm done to her dog, even by her own hand ('so long as I can help it,' as she had added), and thought a noose around the neck all too easy to tighten too hard or too long. So it had been touch and go, the Warden yanking at Broz from behind and the Captain teasing him with the looped belt in front, till they got him passably well muzzled and pinned.

'And all this would have been easier,' the Captain said, searching for a clean spot on her shirt to wrap her hand in, 'if we'd had a proper rope to work with.' She looked at the

Warden and her face relaxed into a grin. 'I've seen scare-crows in the beanfields below Rotl that looked better than you, Lethgro.'

'And why shouldn't they?' answered Lethgro, with another sigh. 'They're in a better place, and with better prospects. Answer me this, Repnomar: Why *did* they take our rope, and our stove, and nothing else but our knives? And why have they left us here alone all this time, sealed up like fish in a frozen pond?' It was on his tongue to ask, *Are they ever coming back?* but he did not.

'Well, since they didn't take our food, we can eat while we wonder,' said Repnomar. But with one bad hand and one bad wrist, and a trickle of blood into the corner of her eye, she was clumsy at getting out the food, and the Warden had to bandage her wounds as well as he could, and share out the rations. It was not quite true that the Quicksilver People (to call them that for lack of another name) had taken nothing but rope and knives and stove; they had taken the Warden's bowstring too, and even the spare bowstring coiled at the bottom of his quiver; but they had left his arrows, and with the point of one of these he cut mouthfuls for the Captain's easier eating.

'If we had the stove,' he observed ruefully, 'we could melt a way out.'

Even untied, neither of them could have stood upright here. The cave or tunnel in which they lay was so low that when Lethgro straightened himself on hands and knees his head almost touched the roof. It was wide enough – perhaps twice the Captain's height – and half again as long. It made Repnomar think of the underwater caves in the cliffs below Rotl, walls and floor and roof smooth, stony, curving, uneasy with shifting colors in the strange half-light of under-Soll; except that these were not stones but naked ice, and the light the steady light of the Exile's torch. Yet there was an underwater feel about this place, everything somehow slowed and muffled by that low, glossy roof hung looping and ponderous so close above their hunched shoulders, so that she felt unreasonably that her ears and lungs would burst from the long pressure on them.

For there was no way out. At one end there was an opening of sorts, wide enough for the Warden to have crawled through without trouble if it had not been closed with a tight-meshed net of stout cords. 'And somehow they've made it fast all around the edges,' said the Captain, when she had hitched herself across the floor to inspect it.

'Frozen into the ice,' said the Warden – gloomily enough, for this seemed to him an unduly permanent manner of closing a door.

'We have your arrows,' Repnomar said briskly. '(And that's a good question, Lethgro, why they left them to us.) What are we waiting for?' So they took each an arrow and began to saw at the cords. But the cutting edges of the arrowheads were small, and this work dulled them, for the cords were very tough. 'And I don't want to blunt them all,' Lethgro said grimly. 'We may have other use for them.'

'Another good question,' said Repnomar, ignoring this, 'is what they make this cordage out of. And still another is how the devil they tie these knots.' She had gone back to working at the rope that bound her ankles, prying the knots with her arrow point – not an easy business with her wounds, but easier than sawing at the entrance net.

The Warden gave a grunt of satisfaction, for one of the cords had just given way. But in cutting one cord he had blunted two arrowheads, and it was clear that the cords were too many and the arrows too few. But he said nothing, and took another arrow, thinking it better to work than to despair.

So they went on with it, sawing and prying, no sound in

that dead-ended tunnel but their steady breath, and the faint rasp of arrowhead on cord, and now and again the Captain's muttered curses or the Warden's muttered prayer, and Broz whining in his sleep; till at last Repnomar's head sank onto her raised knees as she worked, and her eyes closed; for her poisoned doze had more wearied than refreshed her, and they were all in sad need of sleep. Seeing this, the Warden labored to keep his own eyes open, and to force some opening through that wall of strings, now sawing at the meshes, now chipping at the ice about their roots, and sometimes (more to rouse himself than in hope of doing good) throwing his shoulder against it with what force he could muster in that awkward space. And a kind of dull hope began to glow in him, like a fire banked with ashes, for with these various assaults the net began to loosen.

He had got so far and no further when without warning something stung his cheek. For the moment he was too stupid with weariness to take note of it; but an instant later there was a little twinge in the hand with which he was sawing at a mesh, and looking down he saw a dainty sliver of bone that hung by its barbed points from the heel of his palm. Then he understood, and knocked it loose, and flung himself with a bellow headlong at the net; but it held, and he jerked back from it again and crouched with an arrow grasped in each hand, ready to stab with them as long as he could stay awake to do it.

The Captain had roused at that outraged bellow; but after her first start of waking, she lay still, seeing how the wind stood and thinking by playing dead to be spared another of those little darts that washed the mind so blank. But she reckoned without the cautiousness of the Quicksilver People. There was a flicker of motion on the other side of the net, and then the darts were flying. She threw her arms around her head, trying to shield her bare skin where she could, and indeed most of the darts buried themselves harmlessly in her clothing; but some struck home, in scalp or neck or hand, and as she slapped them away her brain spun drunkenly, and she heard the heavy thud of the Warden falling sideways onto the ice.

It might be, the Captain reflected later, that you could get used to the poison, as you could get used to sleeping in the dark. This time, she had no sooner begun to come to herself than she remembered all that had happened before the darts had struck – strangely, it was true, like things remembered from a dream – and indeed it was as if she had not quite slept, for she recollected dimly a crowding of little bodies around her, small paws that turned her and lifted her head, the touch of a cord at her throat. So that she supposed hopefully that on the fourth or fifth trial she might be able to stay awake entirely.

This, however, was small consolation at present. One thing she could not remember was when the light had gone out. Another was how they had come outside again. Outside they clearly were, for she felt loose snow beneath her and chill air and a sense of openness all around. She found herself half-squatted on all fours, like a crouching beast, and the darkness around her prickled with little movements – rustle of snow, faint click that might be claw on ice, sudden glints that were like polished jewels flashing up out of ooze as a current washes them, but that were in fact (it came to her suddenly) eyes catching a light from behind her – and close at hand she heard harsh breathings that she trusted were from Broz and the Warden. She turned her head and saw light indeed, that came through a hole which must be the cave mouth, fringed as it seemed with a heavy lacework of netting that stood black against the glow.

But she had little time to see and none to reflect; for as she turned, something grasped at her throat, tugging and tightening, and before she could draw breath she was sprawled headlong and choking, with her face in the snow. And it was now she learned, as she strove to get her hands to her neck and pluck away what strangled her, that her wrists were shackled by a length of rope to her ankles.

Indeed, as Repnomar remarked later to the Warden, she might never have drawn breath again (for it took a moment to realize that if she could not get her hands to her neck, she could still get her neck to her hands, and in that moment the darkness was closing down on her brain) except for the stretchiness of the cordage. For as soon as the pull on the other end slackened, which it quickly did, the tightened noose around her throat relaxed, and with a great heave of her lungs she breathed again.

'And I might have got the nooses off then and there, Lethgro,' the Captain insisted, 'if – '

'If they hadn't known what they were doing,' Lethgro interrupted. 'Don't you see, Rep, we're not the first beasts they've herded.'

'Or hunted,' Repnomar agreed readily enough. For it was clear that the Quicksilver People could handle a rope with a skill she would have admired in a sailor. 'Do you think they mean to eat us, or breed us?'

'Either way,' said Lethgro, 'let's hope they decide to fatten us up for it.'

It gave them some pleasure to talk as they traveled, and any pleasure was welcome, for the going was hard enough. They shambled four-footed like beasts indeed (though no beast, the Warden reflected, could have been so awkward), going sometimes on hands and knees, sometimes on hands and feet, and again rising to walk two-footed, but not as humans walk, for the short ropes kept their hands bobbing below their knees and their backs arched steeply. Broz had an easier time of it, being already accustomed to traveling on all fours, and being besides not hobbled; but he was sadly puzzled to find his Captain and the Warden at his own height, and much distressed by the nooses around his neck.

For they were each harnessed not with a single noose but with two, the lines held apparently by keepers on opposite sides; and this arrangement they had all quickly learned to bear with a show of patience. The Quicksilver People played their captives like hooked fish, keeping the lines just tight enough to urge them forward, so long as they made no struggle. But if one of them turned restive, trying to hold back or (as the Captain learned by experiment) to lunge forward, then instantly a noose yanked tight; and that fierce pinch on the windpipe was marvelously effective at quelling any such tendency to roam.

It seemed clear, too, that the Quicksilver People could see in the dark; for, however surreptitiously the Warden or the Captain might move, there was always that horrible yank just as a head was coming near a hand. So that very soon they gave it up and determined to wait for better opportunity.

Traveling doubled over like this, they made only poor time; but the Quicksilvers seemed to be in no hurry, never urging them to greater speed so long as they kept moving at all. How many there were, managing the ropes or carrying the gear or circling around them in the dark, they could not tell, except that, as the Warden said wryly, 'It's the whole pack.'

So it seemed. All around them flowed a musical conversation of whistles and chirps. Now and again a little furry hand suddenly patted one or another of them on back or side, startling Broz sometimes to a yelp, and then was gone. Sometimes even, for a moment, they saw flitting glints of silver-gray as the torchbeam swung into their sight and swung away again.

For the torch was still with them, or rather behind them, its beam jouncing so capriciously through all directions that the Captain concluded it must be slung loose from some furry neck or shoulder. 'And that makes no sense,' she added in a tone of complaint (for this cramped and uncomfortable style of travel had put her in poor temper). 'Why should they bring it at all if they make no use of it?'

But the Warden answered, 'If they can see in the dark, what use do they have for a torch?' and after a minute's thought the Captain agreed with this, saying, 'It may be they don't even notice the light.' And after another minute added, 'That's why they left us the torch at first and took your bowstrings. They took what they understood. And most certainly they understood cordage.'

'And knives,' Lethgro said somewhat ominously. 'They took our knives, remember.' He ruminated for a moment. 'But by that principle, Rep, which I trust is sound, they don't understand arrows. If I could get my bowstring back – and my hands free – '

Indeed he still had his quiver on his shoulder, though nearly empty now, for to his sorrow some of the arrows had slid out during the handling the Quicksilver People had given him, and where these were now he did not know; but (as Repnomar reported to him after a glimpse in the swinging torchbeam) only two were left in the quiver.

'And since they took the stove,' the Warden went on, easing himself down to hands and knees again (for he had been shuffling along on his feet while he pinched and pummeled his hands to warm them) 'they must understand warmth. And if we ever stop to rest, I hope we'll get some of it.'

The Captain gave him no answer. She was pursing her lips to a whistle – not one of her private whistles of surprise or consideration, but a high, loud signal whistle that brought an answering whine from Broz and set off a sudden tumult in the Quicksilver troop. All headway stopped; their birdlike voices came clustering swiftly around the Captain, their quick paws and hard little shoulders nudging her away from Broz and the Warden. But after a few minutes the pressing circle of bodies loosened, the chorused pipings died away to the scattered calls that had milled around them through all the journey so far, and the Captain swallowed gratefully, for she had spent these minutes in expectation of a tightening noose.

Now the ropes tugged gently, and they all moved forward. 'What was that about, Repnomar?' the Warden asked presently (in a low voice, not wanting to draw more attention), and the Captain answered, 'Crows,' adding after a little, 'Chances are they're following the light already. But it doesn't hurt to make it even likelier.'

Here Lethgro felt one of his nooses urging him sidelong away from the Captain, and he followed docilely, wondering what good shipcrows were likely to be to them here but not disposed to argue, either with the Captain or the rope.

'Sooner or later we'll have to stop,' the Captain said loudly (not knowing how far away from her the Warden might be now in the dark). 'And with a little luck – ' Here, however, the feel of the rope at her neck warned her, and she broke off.

As it happened, the halt came soon. The torch's waving beam flashed slantwise back and forth across a swelling mound of white, so that the Warden grunted in pain of soul, foreseeing what it would be like to scramble thus hobbled through deep snow; but at the foot of the snowbank they drew up, and there was a great bustle of movement and twittering voices all around. The Captain and the Warden squatted close together, and Broz leaned trembling against their knees. Those who held their tethers kept their heads well up with a steady, gentle pulling, but let them huddle together as closely as they liked, so that they might have worked at leisure on the knots that hobbled wrists to ankles, if their hands had not been now too stiff with cold to do more than fumble. The Quicksilver People seemed to be busy at something; but, since the torchbeam now pointed steadily into the emptiness behind them, they had no glimpse of what the business was.

'They're spreading out,' the Warden said presently, and added low, 'Now what are you up to, Rep?'

For the Captain, with certain careful contortions, had managed to fish a stub of clay pencil from her pocket, and a shred of paper, and was trying to write. This, in the darkness and with near-frozen fingers, was no easy thing; but she stuck to it, twisting her clumsy hands between her shoes to wake some feeling in them, and warming them against her belly. She did not answer the Warden, except with a busy grunt; but in a few minutes she lifted her face and split the air with a long, keen whistle.

This time both nooses tightened on her throat at once, pinching off the whistle in an unwholesome cluck that raised hackles on Broz's neck and the Warden's. But this time the Warden, lunging upward on his toes, contrived to get two fingers of one hand between her neck and the ropes, and so eased the pressure on her windpipe. So that when one of the crows came flapping over their heads, calling irritably as it searched for its Captain in the dark, she had voice to croak out her whereabouts.

'It was a fool thing, Rep,' the Warden told her later. 'They could have stopped you with one of their darts, or strangled us both to death, and caught the crow, too.'

'Better steer into the storm than be driven onto the rocks,' said Repnomar. 'And they didn't stop me.'

Indeed the Quicksilver People, though they clustered around the Captain as before (and though this time the Warden was dragged away from her with some violence to his neck), made no attempt to interfere as she spat on her scrap of paper and clamped it around the crow's leg, nor when she flung the bird upward as best she might – a pitiful jerk of her fettered hands – crying out to it to find the Exile. For the Warden, it was a strange business in the dark, the crow never seen but only heard by its cries and its wing-beats, the red agony at his throat, the press and twitter of Quicksilvers around him, and Broz's growls of fear and fury. But after what seemed a time of agitated conversation, both he and the Captain were hustled a little way to one side and thrust like sacks of cargo against a wall that was not so hard as ice, and Broz dumped with a yelp beside them. It was here, when they found themselves left in peace for the time being, that the Warden called Repnomar's doing a fool thing, and she gave him her answer.

Fool thing or no, it was nothing to make Lethgro think less well of the Captain. Indeed any chance of rescue, however tiny, seemed worth a bit of strangling. But he could not hide from himself how small a chance it was. It was not likely, to begin with, that the crow had understood instructions so unexpected and given in such unseemly haste. It was not likely, if it had understood, that it would find the Exile. It was not likely, if it did find him, that he would find the message still clinging to its leg – or, if it was there, be able to read it. And beyond all other 'ifs' there was the Exile himself. At this point in his thoughts, the Warden heaved a sigh that pained his battered throat.

He placed more hope, though still little enough, in their own efforts; and so, he judged, did Repnomar, for she said no more of crows or Exile. Instead, 'While we're in here,' she said, 'maybe we can contrive to eat.'

For it was clear that they were in some shelter, where little outside sound could reach them; and huddling together so, they began to feel warmer, or at least less frozen. The nooses were still at their necks, and at least a few Quicksilvers close by, for they heard their sweet chirps and now and then a whisper of movement. They knew, too, which way the entrance lay, for a dim ghost of light told them that the torch still burned outside it.

'I'll lay it on your knee,' the Warden said.

'Don't forget Broz,' she answered.

Indeed eating was no simple matter, though they still had some of the Exile's rations in their pockets. The Quicksilver People seemed to care little enough what movements they made, so long as no hand came near any neck; so that Lethgro was able to pull a chunk of food from his pocket and set it on Repnomar's knee, and another chunk for Broz, after which it was up to them to mouth it as best they could. Broz, having the use of his paws, had the easiest time of it; for the stuff was tough and chewy, and required holding if you meant to bite off a mouthful. In the end, Repnomar managed hers by squeezing it between her raised knees and gnawing at it, and Lethgro did the same.

'And there are good things about the cold,' Repnomar said cheerfully. 'We don't have to crouch on our bellies to lap up water.' And she twisted her head and took a bite out of the wall behind them.

For by now they had concluded that the shelter where they lay, or rather squatted, was a cave scooped into the side of the snowbank they had seen earlier. At least it was floored and walled and roofed with snow, and this not tightly packed, for now and then their motions dislodged showers of it. The Warden kept his eyes fixed on the opening, meaning to know which way to crawl if the whole bank collapsed upon them. The faint torchlight still hung there, unmoving now, as if whoever carried it had settled to sleep (or perhaps to guard duty) or laid it aside. This, too, interested the Warden, for he thought that if they did somehow contrive an escape, they would need that torch afterward.

And if an escape was to be contrived, this seemed as likely a time as any. Crouched here together in the dark, they had, it appeared, all leisure to work at the knots that bound them and to talk between themselves. The heat of their own bodies – capped and held in here by thick walls of fleecy snow – slowly thawed their numbed hands and faces and made a pool of pleasant warmth (or what seemed like warmth after their long freezing); so that Broz stopped shivering and fell asleep with a blissful sigh, and their fingers could once more feel out the knots and pick at them.

'I think I'm getting the hang of it,' the Captain murmured. And the Warden answered, 'Best loosen them one by one before you cast off any. Remember they can see.'

Working thus with all the care they could manage and shielding each other's busy hands from the sight of the Quicksilver People (or so they hoped), they might at last have managed the untying of those knots – though whether they could have gotten further is another question. But the warmth and the quiet and the food in their bellies closed in upon their weary bodies and minds as powerfully as the working of any poisoned dart; and in a little while they were slumbering as peacefully as Broz, leaned together like half-empty sacks and all three snoring gently.

16
Of the Nature of Exiles

When the light burst in on them and the nooses pulled at their necks, they were so unready that they all jerked like wet sticks tossed into a blaze, and the Warden let out a grunt of pain (for his throat was sore inside and out). The torch, they saw (once they had their wits about them) rode in a little net hung from the neck of one of the Quicksilvers; and it was strange to see its beam bobbing sometimes straight into the creature's face without rousing so much as a blink – so that, 'They may see in the dark,' the Captain said, 'but they're blind in the light.'

'I wish they were blind *in* the light,' the Warden said morosely; for he felt he could undertake to get hold of that torch somehow, if only it would be a weapon in his hand once he had it. 'And we missed our chance with the knots, Rep.'

'It's not all so bad,' the Captain answered, with what struck Lethgro as unseemly good cheer. 'Likely we wouldn't have gotten far, as tired as we were then. And now we know we can do it. I've got one knot so loose I can cast it off in half a minute.'

This was somewhat optimistically spoken, seeing that in fact she was no more than halfway through the intricacies of that knot; but the warm sleep had heartened the Captain mightily, though she would have been gladder still if they had been given time to eat again. But before she could get what was left of their food out of her pocket, they were led out into the open once more – an uncomfortable process enough, for their backs and limbs were sadly strained and sore from the four-footed walking. Once the beam of the torch caught the Warden full, and Repnomar, seeing him, could not withhold a great guffaw of laughter. 'There may be strange beasts in this country, Lethgro,' she said, 'but I've seen none stranger than you, with your tail in the air and your back humped like a wharf rat.'

This the Warden felt to be unfair, since they were both in the same pickle, and one no lovelier than the other. But he said nothing, to save his sore throat, and hobbled on with what dignity he might.

But he did not hobble far, for they were stopped against a place of trampled snow in front of the cave. Here the swing of the torchbeam picked out range after range of quicksilver, so that the whole troop seemed to be gathered here, and all in motion. 'What are they doing?' Repnomar muttered. And the Warden croaked (having no more of a voice left to him), 'They've been hunting.'

Indeed there were strange beasts in this country. Some of the Quicksilvers were busy around the bodies (dead or stunned) of several creatures almost the size of sheep but with splayed feet and great scoop-shaped underjaws like shovels. Others were coiling lengths of what looked like rope. ('Landkelp,' said the Captain. 'But I think they've stripped the jaws off it.') They could make out no more certainly, for the light was too fitful, swinging for the most part upward into the dark beneath the clouds; but they caught glimpses of Quicksilvers filling their little nets with what might be smaller game, or busily stowing gear. A sharp breeze gusted around them, veering and lulling and starting up again. Broz sniffed hungrily.

'And it's kind of them,' the Captain observed, watching the torchbeam swing across the sky, 'to do our signaling for us.'

It was true that the other crow might still be following them, or that the first might be returning, with or without a message from the Exile, or even (for hope could make anything seem possible) that the Exile himself might be flying somewhere in the dark above, searching for them; but it seemed at least as likely to the Warden that other beasts, or other people, might see that beacon and attack the Quicksilvers unawares. Which, he reflected, might be bad and might be good, if only to give them a chance of slipping their nooses in the confusion. Though, for that matter, they might as easily find themselves dragged both ways by their two keepers, and so strangled to death.

Thinking these things, and following the sway of the torchbeam with his eyes in hope of glimpsing his knife or his bowstrings, he was startled by the grip of paws, and a rope drawn across his chest and over his shoulder. At the same time the Captain jerked out an oath, and Broz a strangled growl. But when it was done, and the Captain muttering surlily that she had never thought to carry baggage like a packtrain sheep, Lethgro found a laugh of sorts rasping through his battered throat; for there was little else he could do, and surely it was droll enough for the Warden of Sollet Castle to be loaded with bloody chunks of some dead and outlandish beast, and led by the neck like an unreliable dog, all by a pack of little furry things that saw in the dark.

Baggage beasts they clearly were now, all three of them. The Warden had a moment of dismay when he thought his quiver was being taken from him; but instead, it was only stuffed full of something and dropped back to its place on his shoulder – balanced now by a butchered beast's ham slung at his other shoulder. Broz and the Captain each had a share; and after the first resentment, not one of them was altogether sorry, for the loads were not too heavy and the warm meat gave them, for the time, some help against the cold. Only it was hard for Broz to bear the smell of so much juicy eating tied to his own back, and he not able to get a tooth into it.

Repnomar was indignant over this, saying that the Quicksilver People were beasts indeed if they lacked the decency to throw a scrap of meat to a hungry dog. But once he was loaded, they did exactly that, giving him (it seemed) the leavings of their butchering, though these were scant enough, and offering the Captain and the Warden bits of raw hide to gnaw on. 'I don't suppose they mean it as an insult,' the Captain observed philosophically. 'And it's something to work the jaws with.' But presently they began to travel again, and something else drew her attention.

'Have I lost my bearings in the dark, Lethgro?' she asked thoughtfully. 'Or are we going back the way we came?'

Certainly it was hard, with no light and no wind (except the occasional veering and unsteady breeze) to manage even an inkling of direction. The bouncing torch picked out few landmarks, and those not good ones – a snowdrift, a stretch of rock. The Warden found nothing to go by but the ground underfoot (or underhand) and some sense of which ways they had been turned and herded since they left the snow cave; but all in all, he agreed with the Captain. He would have been hard put to say whether he was glad or sorry. It was true that they were likely moving away from the Exile and whatever help he might offer; and though that hope was slender enough, it was a thread worth clutching in this extremity. But it was also true that every mile farther into darkness was a mile farther away from light, and the Warden felt to the innermost marrow of his bones that light was their only safety; for in this waste of frozen darkness they were like drops of water on a hot pan in the fire, that live for a little by skittering this way and that, consuming their own substance, and then disappear. So that it was better, in a way, to be heading toward the light again. 'But not,' the Warden added to himself, 'if the next stop is the slaughterhouse.' For the thought had forced itself upon him that when they put down their burdens they themselves might well be converted into the same form.

Trudging thus painfully on all fours, and thinking of the light as of a thing like childhood, gone forever and half forgotten, he was ill prepared when in an instant all the scene around was lit up as brightly as if he stood on the highest terrace of Sollet Castle. In his surprise he stumbled and half fell, bringing the nooses tight around his throat, and for a moment he half imagined that it was death that had burst so dazzlingly upon him. Yet in another minute he was plodding onward, his eyes easy now with the light, and nothing changed, it seemed, except that now all was visible. For the first time he saw the Captain shuffling on hands and knees beside him, a great side of meat, with the hide still on, lashed to her back. The Captain's drawn face was radiant with growing comprehension, and she met his eye with a silent and conspiratorial grimace.

For it was plain that the Quicksilver People noticed nothing. Now that they could see them clearly, it was stranger than ever to be among these small busy persons. Under the brightness of that light, their movements flowed like quicksilver indeed – ripples and shudders of brilliance, long gleams of racing gray. They moved seemingly without order, some dashing helter-skelter for a time, and again sitting pensively while others passed them, some pattering sedately at a steady pace, some moving together like schooling fish, turn for turn and leap for leap. Twos and threes of them would suddenly confront each other, in play or consultation, and then break apart, while others were always sunk in some private thought or trance, with pursed mouths and great ears canted forward, as if they harkened intently to their own silent whistling. Most of them wore nets on back or shoulder, variously loaded with game or gear, and the thick fur behind their heads bristled with what the Warden made out at last to be blowpipes and the tips of darts. Young ones (to judge from their size and their merriment) skittered and danced among their elders, or rode their backs, and now and then – a thing surprising enough at first sight – a grown beast would tuck a little one into its chest, as lightly as pocketing a piece of string. 'Look at that, Lethgro,' the Captain said admiringly. 'They can open a flap of skin – two flaps, it is – to make a place for their nestlings.'

The Warden had noticed another use for those flaps, though he did not understand its meaning; for two Quicksilvers, facing each other at a little distance, had risen high on their hind legs and opened their chests like humans baring their bosoms in prayer. But he said nothing, thinking it frivolous of the Captain to be thus attending to minor matters when their lives balanced on a knife edge.

Their place in all this churning and quiet hubbub was the very center. Their keepers trotted beside them, the ends of their leash ropes gripped sometimes in a furry paw, sometimes between firm little teeth. This duty, it seemed, was not popular – that, or else too popular altogether. Again and again one of the leash-holders would hand a rope to a passerby and dash away, kicking up heels and wriggling sides and shoulders till silver seemed to fly like water drops, while the new keeper settled promptly into the steady jog of a jailor, and all so smoothly done that (the Warden realized) these trades might well have been going on without his notice through all their journeying. There were not always two keepers for each prisoner, either; for sometimes a single Quicksilver, running between Captain and Warden, held a leash on each side.

Nevertheless, the keepers watched their charges keenly; and it came to Repnomar with a prickling of uneasiness that they were watching now more closely from moment to moment, as if they saw and wondered at some change. 'Try to look blind, Lethgro,' she said urgently. 'They may not see the light themselves, but they can't help seeing that something's given sight to us.' And the Warden nodded grimly, thinking to himself that it would have to give them more than sight if they were to get any good from it. He had been praying earnestly (in case it was some god that had shed this light upon them) that the nooses would fall away from their necks, for he could think of no lesser gift that would be of much help to them.

All this time, the light kept pace with them. It was a broad circle that spanned the whole Quicksilver troop, and seemed meant to do so, for it widened and shrank as their dashings and interlacings spread them apart or drew them together. Where the light came from was hard to say, especially for persons walking doubled over and with two nooses each around their necks, who were furthermore trying to appear blind; but the Captain concluded that it must come from overhead, and 'If it's not the Exile's doing,' she asked rhetorically, 'whose is it?'

Lethgro only blinked his eyes, for he feared sadly the answer to that question. It seemed likely to him that there were many possibilities, few of them good. In the meantime, however, he was gathering himself to fight, thinking that after all he was as big as four or five of these people put together, and that if the nooses were the root of his captivity, it behooved him to take the nooses off. He thought that by quickness, and a willingness to endure a little more throat-pinching, he should be able to get his fingers under the nooses before they tightened too much; and after that it would be a question of brute force and persistence and getting clear before the darts took effect – for without doubt he would be a pincushion within minutes. Of success he had no hope worth mentioning; but whether the light was friend or enemy, it called for action.

One stroke of luck came to him, great or small, for just then a stout-set little Quicksilver, running between his righthand keeper and the Captain's lefthand one, took the leash from each. The Warden waited only till the relieved guards had danced away out of easy reach. Then he ducked his head and reached for his neck, at the same time plunging to the left.

So, too, did the Captain, a second later. In that second, Lethgro had got the fingers of one hand under his righthand noose and the fingers of the other under both, and was ripping with all his strength, while he charged in a furious hobble toward the guard on his left. Sudden uproar swirled through the troop, as a silvery whirlpool might form in river shallows. Like a hurt beast, Lethgro lunged and snarled, and Broz on his left answered with a roar of barking that was cut off short. The air seethed with whistling that seemed to cut and twist the ear. Somehow Repnomar by main force had reached and clutched the guard who held the two leashes, dragging the other behind her; but there she fell. Lethgro felt the one noose go slack, and tore it off. He had the other over his chin (taking some of his beard with it), though the lefthand guard still pranced beyond his reach, when suddenly the Quicksilvers were struck by a new trouble, and the whistles shrilled beyond hearing.

To the Captain – the knuckles of her right hand buried in her own throat by the pinch of a noose, and her left clenched in a death grip on her keeper's fuzzy arm – it was as if the world reeled for an instant, like a ship turning through the eye of the wind, and stood away on a new tack. The arm in her grasp (so small that she had pinned wrist to upper arm in a single handful) jerked and stiffened, the creature's head hunched, both nooses slacked at once; she drew breath in a tearing gasp and ripped one of them loose, getting thus her right arm free again – expecting all the while (for the moment seemed to stretch without end) the prickle of darts or the yank of the second noose. But the darts did not come. All around her the Quicksilver People stumbled and cowered, some racing into the darkness like rabbits into their holes, some milling blindly, some crouching with paws to eyes. As for the second noose, she had that off before she had well thought about it, and clearly before the keeper she grasped had thought to pull it tight. Then it was what to do next, while everything called for action. Already some of the Quicksilvers had brought blowguns to their mouths, though they seemed still to stagger in uncertainty, not sure which way to shoot. Lethgro was rising, like some outraged sea beast shaking off a wave thick with seaweed, from under three or four of the troop that had somehow tangled with him. But poor Broz twitched voicelessly between two taut ropes, as his keepers pulled opposite ways, and it was toward him that Repnomar flung herself with a wild yell.

That yell was perhaps a mistake, for it gave the blowguns a target, though not a steady one. On the other hand, one of Broz's keepers bolted in panic, letting that rope fall slack, so that Broz got his feet under him with a scramble and his breath back in a harsh gasp. But before the Captain had reached him, or any clear current broken free from that whirlpool of confusion, a blast of wind struck them that scattered Quicksilvers like dry sticks and brought Captain and Warden alike to their knees.

'Climb!' the Warden sang out above the wind – an order that made little sense at the moment to Repnomar, who, suddenly finding that she still carried her keeper by the arm like a child's doll, let go at last and somehow tumbled herself forward to snatch the ropes from Broz's neck. But Lethgro meant what he said, for as it happened he had been looking up when the first buffet of the wind struck, and had seen the shapes descending.

Afterwards he was glad enough that his first fear had melted him past speech or movement, so that he only gurgled a cry that was lost in the wind's noise; for he thought at the first sight that some great thunderbolt was falling upon them, or some pouncing god. But before he had had time to show himself a coward, what had seemed at first a huge and blazing meteor resolved itself into a lighted globe or egg that trailed a litter of lesser globes, and he recognized the Exile's pods, flying sweetly as thistledown. And like thistledown they settled earthward and then balanced in air, hovering still out of reach above their heads. But it was from the great pod that the merciless wind blew, rushing down and out, so that a little pool of calm lay straight beneath it, while all around was blasted by the gale. It was when the pod's belly opened and a knotted rope snaked down from it, just to the right of the Captain, that he understood and bellowed his 'Climb!' And seeing her otherwise occupied, and not liking to waste whatever time they had, he hobbled forward and grasped the rope. He was halfway up, climbing like a cripple because of his bonds, when he felt the sting of darts in his leg and haunch.

As the Exile told him later, with much apology and concern, that should not have happened. The wind was to have kept away the Quicksilvers and blown away their darts and their nets. But there was no wind straight under the pod where the rope hung, and it was there that Repnomar had dropped her keeper. So that for a little while it was not clear to any of them whether anyone would win up that rope. Broz, however, had definite opinions on that matter; and though the wind was such that he had to crouch and crawl against it, he reached the Quicksilver before the Captain did, and to such effect that she had to drag him off. 'Though I don't know why,' the Warden said, when he had heard all the story, 'you didn't let him eat the little beast.' He himself had finished his climb hunched half through the pod's hatch, his teeth ground hard together and his eyes glazed, having held off the poison from his brain by sheer stubbornness and the will to climb that rope, and the Exile had dragged him the rest of the way in, with no little difficulty.

But the Captain answered that the Quicksilver People were not beasts, and had done them little harm compared with what they might have done. 'And besides,' she added, 'we didn't have the time.' She had somehow worked Broz and herself up the rope by main force – not an easy chore, with her wrists still yoked to her ankles, and Broz's scrambling more a hindrance than a help – and the rope was drawn up and the hatch closed.

Then there was an awkward time, for though the pod was large, their four bodies packed it (as the Captain remarked) like a cargo of salt fish stamped down and with the hatches nailed shut. Lethgro was so much dead meat for the present, and awkward to handle; while Broz, who did not well understand where they were, was half frantic to get out, and all of them cramped into almost as tight a tangle as they might have been in a Quicksilver net. But the Exile, crawling over and under and between, got their bonds cut at last; and the Captain, laughing and swearing by turns, persuaded Broz that this strange vessel was a friendly one. So that when Lethgro came to himself, they were under way, though not comfortable.

If the Councils of Beng and Rotl had been able to see that vessel (so the Warden reflected) there would have been no more talk among them of the Exile being a god. Indeed it was all he could do to manage his peculiar craft, and he was full of apology for its clumsiness, regretting that he had not been able to contrive a better gangplank for them than that knotted rope, nor better quarters than this cramped cargo-hold. To which the Captain answered that she had climbed a rope before, though never before with her hands and feet tied together and a struggling dog between her elbows and her knees. 'And it's light here, and it's warm,' she added, 'which is more comfort than we've been used to lately.'

'But the best comfort,' said Lethgro, 'is that the walls are proof against poisoned darts.' And wondered, as soon as the words were out, whether that was true, for the walls of the pod were more like leather to the touch, supple and yielding, than like wood or stone.

Crouched with knees to chins, and their backs and heads pressed against that flexible hide, they had made room enough for the Exile to manage his steering. This he did very awkwardly, in the Captain's opinion, and yet as well as could be hoped; for he steered blind in that closed pod, only now and then opening a hatch for a quick peek outside, and otherwise judging their position by the marks and lights on the sides of a little box no bigger than his fist. The feel of the flying pod was somewhat like the feel of a boat, bobbing and swaying slightly. But as the Exile explained it, these pods were not meant to carry either passengers or crew, being cargo vessels only and intended to be steered from the outside – not meant for fighting, either, so that his attack on the Quicksilver troop, like his navigation, was all makeshift. There was little he could do, he said, except shine light and blow air, which he had accordingly done. And when they asked him what had so dismayed the Quicksilvers just before the wind struck, he answered that it was another kind of light, the kind the Quicksilvers saw with their great eyes, and so bright and sudden that it dazzled them. This the Warden found too unlikely to believe at first. 'But what could make more sense, Lethgro?' the Captain said. 'It's clear they can see where all's dark to us, and clear too that they can't see what we call light. Why shouldn't there be another kind of light on this side of the world?' Explained this way, it seemed reasonable enough; and when the Exile tried to tell them that the Quicksilvers' kind of light was also on the bright side of the world, being an invisible light that came from all warm things, they both refused to listen.

While they talked, the Exile had been anxiously steering the pod (which he did by touching certain buttons and levers set into the sides of his little box). Suddenly there was a rude jolt that jostled them all together, and the pod sat motionless, swaying no longer. The Exile cleared his throat and apologized for the rough landing. Another thing, he explained, that the pods were not meant for was much traveling, and he hoped they had come far enough for safety. So with some difficulty they crawled out through a little hatch in the side (smaller than the bottom hatch through which they had climbed the rope) and found themselves snug in a hollow of the bare rock.

Here they had good hopes of being untroubled by the Quicksilvers, who seemed to be people of the snowfields; and the sides of the hollow seemed high enough to shield them from the sight of any creatures that saw in darkness. The Exile brought out the stove with which he had warmed the pod (smaller and simpler than the one they had lost to the Quicksilvers, being only a little ball that gave out heat in all directions like a fire) and the torch with which he had kept it light, so that they stretched and eased themselves in great comfort, and ate very eagerly of the Exile's rations.

Meanwhile the Exile opened one of the smaller pods (that lay all tumbled now around the big one) and brought out the two crows. For he said that as he was searching for a place to put his precious things (here the Captain started to interrupt and then thought better of it, preferring to hear first about her shipcrows) the crow with Repnomar's message had found him; and though he had not been able to read a word of it, he had guessed it meant trouble, and the crow had showed him which way to go.

'We didn't know,' said the Captain, 'whether you'd

choose to come or not.' But at this the Exile appeared so hurt and sorry that the Warden felt constrained to take back the doubt, saying that they had only feared he would not get the message, and urging him to go on with his story.

They had been easy enough to find, he said, with the torchbeam flashing this way and that, and he had followed above them (where the Quicksilvers never looked, so that he thought there were no flying things in this country) till he was well assured of their situation. By that time, too, he had found the other crow, still following the troop and feeding on the leavings of the hunt. He had landed his pods briefly at the site of the butchering, where the crows had come to him trustingly enough, and he had stowed them in the small pod to prevent losing them, and again followed the Quicksilvers.

Here the Exile fell to begging their pardon for having left them so long in that danger and discomfort, and for having found no more graceful means of rescue. But the Captain broke in on this, asking roughly, 'What's this new place you're searching for?'

The Exile seemed unsure how to answer this, perhaps from not knowing the right words, but more likely (so Lethgro thought) from trying to hide his purposes. But when they pressed him, he told them frankly that he had remembered what he was to do in this world, and that it behooved him to send a message to his own people.

Now the Warden cursed himself heartily for having ever connived at the Exile's doings, considering that the nature of exiles is to trouble all around them till they can somehow win back to their own place. And considering also that they had gone far enough on this road, he stood up then and there, saying without ceremony, 'You'll send no message while you're my prisoner.'

17

Of a Dinner in Rotl

Broz was happy. That, so far as it went, pleased the Captain very well; but looked at in a different light, it was not all so good. 'We've got to move on,' she told the Warden fretfully, 'and Broz won't like it.'

'Neither Broz nor I,' said the Warden, taking a last stitch in his boot, which had been in sad need of mending; 'but it's high time to start. We have a long way to walk.'

'Walk!' cried the Captain. 'Wear out your own boots, Lethgro, if you choose – but I mean to fly.'

They had slept in turns, the Exile laying himself down very meekly, on the Warden's instructions, between Broz and the Captain. Indeed he had made no resistance at all, though clearly he had been taken much aback by Lethgro's pronouncement (not having considered himself, it seemed, a prisoner to anyone). But, 'The Sacred League of Beng and Rotl entrusted the warding of Sollet Castle to me,' said Lethgro, when the Exile undertook some timid argument, 'and you were given me as a prisoner to hold for the decision of the Councils. Till they decide, I have no choice but to hold you. I'll help you every way I can,' he added more kindly, 'but there are things I cannot do, and one of them is to stand by while you call down I don't know what outlandish nations from beyond the clouds.'

To this the Exile answered not a word, only blinking his eyes and screwing up his mouth in some distress. Indeed there was little he could have done, unarmed as he was, for the Warden and the Captain (and for that matter Broz) were each more than a match for him if it came to fighting; and they keeping carefully between him and his pods, there was no road open to him but out into the darkness and the cold.

The Warden, with some misgivings, had searched the Exile with his own hands, taking away his knife and one or two small items of dubious purpose; but he could not bring himself to bind him, having too keen a memory of his own bonds. Besides, he thought that the desolation of that unfriendly country was prison enough. 'Only,' he told the Captain privately, 'at all costs we'd best keep him away from the pods. There are too many outlandish things there that only he knows the use of.'

To this the Captain assented very laconically. She had stood back from all this matter between the Warden and the Exile; for though in general she was not one to shy away from a quarrel, neither did she like to plunge into one before she knew which side to take. She had no doubt that Lethgro was within his rights; what puzzled her was deciding whether there was more to be gained or lost by letting the Exile do as he pleased. There were several questions she would have liked to ask him, but she kept silent, judging by the wary look of his eyes that there was little truth to be gotten from him at present. But this temporizing did not well suit the Captain's nature, and had made her touchy and apt to veer to unforeseen courses; and it was thus that she declared without premeditation that she would fly and not walk.

Now, Lethgro (once he had made up his mind to act) had no doubt as to his course. Whatever the Councils of Beng and Rotl might inflict upon him could hardly be worse, he thought, than what the Exile might unleash with his message. It behooved them, therefore, to find their way back as promptly as possible to human countries and there make what peace they could. To the Warden, this clearly meant they would walk back in the direction they had come, taking what supplies seemed useful from the pods.

He was not eager to meet the Quicksilver People and their ropes again, but, as he told Repnomar, 'I think we know enough now to stay out of their way.' It was true he had no answer yet as to how they might win through all the hazards of the Dreeg and the Low Coast and the Soll; but he thought that once they were back in the light they could find a better road than they had come by. What he had seen of the dark side of the world had confirmed him more and more in the opinion that anything else was better, and he would have undertaken to face two Dreegs and two Low Coasts more willingly than go on into the untried dark in the blank hope of sometime coming out among the snow streams that fed his own Sollet.

So that when the Captain announced so hotly that she meant to fly, he undertook to reason with her. 'If you mean in a pod, Repnomar, as I suppose you do, you might as well give back his things to the Exile and tell him to take command. As soon as we're in that pod, we're at his mercy.'

'I've captained a ship at least as long as you've been Warden of Sollet Castle,' said Repnomar, 'and I watched him fly it with his little box. I may give us a rough ride at first, but I'll bet you a good dinner in Rotl that I get the hang of it before the first watch is half over. And if you're so afraid of the Exile, we can tie him up.'

This was unjust, and stung the Warden sharply, so that he answered with some heat, 'It's not him so much as you I'm afraid of, Rep. I don't doubt you can figure out part of it for yourself; but some things you'll surely have to take his word for, or risk worse shipwreck than any you've survived yet. And what's his word worth now – if it was ever worth anything? Whatever he tells us now may be a trick. And besides, where do you think you'll fly to?'

'To Sollet Castle,' Repnomar answered, throwing her arms wide, for the notion of such a voyage had put her quickly into better temper. 'Think of it, Lethgro! We'll come floating down from the Mountains like thistledown and land at Castle Wharf, and be rowed across the river in state to the Castle. Can't you picture the whole town running out to see us? And when they ask us where we've been, we'll say, "Around the world!" And then on to Beng and Rotl, and the Councils will be so flabbergasted they'll confirm you as Warden again and likely give you anything else you ask for. And after that, I've still got the *Mouse* to get off that waterfall, and – '

Here the Warden interrupted her. 'Didn't you hear him say these pods weren't made for long journeys? Likely the thing would fall like a spent arrow and leave us on foot in the very middle of the dark half of the world.'

But the Captain scoffed at this, saying, 'First you're afraid to listen to the Exile, and then you're afraid not to listen to him. For that matter, it's only his word that this darkness covers half the world.'

'And only his and yours,' Lethgro said hotly, 'that the world is round. If you happen to be wrong – and I think you've been wrong once or twice in your life, Repnomar – we'll have to turn back from the edge sooner or later, if we don't fall over it in the dark.'

The Exile had heard at least the latter part of this discussion, for he sat a few yards away, mending some clothes of his own and feeding tidbits to the crows, that sat at his feet. As the voices of the others rose, he kept his head modestly bent, tending very busily to his stitching. But now the Captain, tired of this pretense, swept her arm in his direction, saying loudly, 'There he sits. Why not ask him what he means to do? It may be this message you're so afraid of is harmless after all.'

This was the third time in as many minutes that Repnomar had called him afraid, and the Warden (having gotten his boot on his foot again) leaped up in great vexation. Still, he schooled himself to avoid a quarrel outright, saying only,

'There's no gag in his mouth. He can speak when he chooses.' And on this cue the Exile began to apologize once more for the trouble he had caused them both.

But the Captain cut him off before he had well started, declaring that she was tired of hearing what harm he had done, and only cared to hear what harm he was going to do. 'And mainly, what's this message, and what were you sent to do in this world?'

Clearly the Exile was embarrassed by such direct questions, and squirmed like a child caught in some foolish prank. But under the Captain's hammering, he swallowed and gave her a straight look at last and said solemnly that he had been sent to this world to see the weather.

'Weather!' Lethgro exploded; and the Captain, when she had made sure that this was indeed the word he meant, could not contain her laughter.

'You see, Lethgro, what a momentous matter of state you have here! And I suppose,' she added to the Exile, 'the message you want to send is how hard the wind blows?' And the Exile said yes.

By this time the Warden had forgotten his anger and was looking at the Exile very piercingly, for it seemed to him that both Exile and Captain might have spoken truth. 'Tell me this, Repnomar,' he said evenly; 'if you were taking a navy into waters you'd never sailed before, wouldn't you want to know how hard the wind blew?'

Now the Captain, who at that moment had been thinking eagerly of messages between worlds and voyages in flying pods, came about sharply, and she too looked hard at the Exile, who began to show signs of distress, knitting his crooked brows and squeezing his knotty fingers together. But he swore in a cracked voice that there was no navy preparing to fall upon them, nor any warlike intention among his people toward this world. And when the Warden inquired why then this monstrously secret mission, he said stoutly that the secrecy was a sign of his people's good will, not wishing to trouble or alarm any of the folk of this world, and he himself was to blame (though as it happened he could scarcely have helped it) for showing himself and so bringing disturbance to many and danger and death to some.

'Don't worry,' the Captain said harshly. 'You'll be blamed enough; there's no need to blame yourself besides, and wear out our ears with it.' For she still felt keenly the death of her two sailors, to say nothing of what might have happened to the rest of her crew by this time.

The Warden seated himself ponderously in front of the Exile, looking down at him with a face like an approaching storm. 'Let's have it all now,' he said.

So the Exile, not without hesitation, and proddings by both Warden and Captain, and with some difficulty at times in finding words for what he meant, told his latest story. This was that he was indeed no exile (or not yet so, as he added darkly) but one of a troop of searchers sent out to learn of other worlds, their lands and waters, mountains and rivers, and most specially their airs and winds and storms. For this purpose (he went on, warming to his subject) his people had already set certain devices to watch this world from above, looking down through the clouds; which caused Lethgro to look up uneasily and Repnomar to squint her eyes and stare into the black sky. But the Exile said that these devices could not be seen from here, being on the other side of the clouds.

'Then how can they see the world?' Lethgro asked reasonably.

The Exile was hard put to answer this, and could only say that it was a different kind of seeing (to which the Captain readily agreed, saying that if Quicksilver People could see in darkness, there was no reason why outlandish devices might not look through clouds). And he went on to say that though these far-off devices could by no means tell everything about this world, yet they had revealed the likeliest cause of the changing seasons.

'The seasons?' Lethgro repeated, and chuckled wryly; for it seemed to him a wry joke indeed if the Exile's folk had gone to such lengths for such a foolish purpose, fancying they had found an answer to a question that did not exist. 'Such things have no causes. Rains follow Windrise, Streamrise follows Rains, Windfall follows Streamrise, and so back to Windrise again. As well look for the cause of the Mountains or the Soll.'

But the Exile demurred shyly, saying that even mountains had causes, and that the Mountains themselves were the cause of the seasons, or part of it. For the dark side of the world, he said, was cold as well as dark ('We've already noticed that,' the Warden remarked'), and when it was coldest, and the Mountains darkest (for the world tilted slightly back and forth, so that the edge of the light was not always in the same place), cold air spilled over the Mountains, and this was called Windrise. Here the Warden nodded gravely, and said it was true that the light was very dim in the Mountains at that season.

Now Captain Repnomar, who lived by the winds, began to question the Exile keenly; but he excused himself, saying that there were many such questions that could not be answered from such a distant view. Therefore, he said, his people had sent a mission – himself and one companion – to set up devices that would measure wind and rain and heat and all such things and send word of them back to his own world, or more truly to a between-worlds ship, for his world was very far. But while they were looking for the likeliest place to set them up, they had fallen captive to the Quicksilver People, struck down by those same poisonous darts. And here the Exile was in much trouble, shaking his head and trying three or four times before he could get it out that it seemed this poison was more potent against his people than against other creatures; for though even the smallest beasts that the Quicksilvers hunted were only stunned by it or confused for a little time, his friend had died of the darts and his own memory had been washed so far down into the depths of his mind that only now were the last surges of it rising again to his knowledge.

'By all you've told us,' said the Captain, 'it's a long way from here to the Mountains. Or is this side of the world shorter than the other?' And when he said that it was not much shorter, though somewhat so, she asked him how he had come to where the Sollet loggers had found him.

This, however, he seemed still unsure of, only saying that he must have traveled a long way with the Quicksilvers, and that they had traded him to another people in the Mountains, from whom he had escaped and made his way to the Sollet, not knowing then who he was nor what he was to do.

It came out presently, however, that the message he had spoken of sending was no real message, and that he had merely meant to set up devices and let them send their word concerning the weather; for indeed (or so he claimed) he had no means of sending other messages. And he asked the Warden very prettily to consider letting him do this much, which he could well have done without hindrance, if he had not come back to save them from the Quicksilvers.

Now the Warden felt an itching at his throat, where the Quicksilver nooses had bruised it; but he kept his face stern, saying only, 'I'll consider anything,' and began at once to question the Exile about the flying of the pods and about the kind of place he sought for setting up his devices.

On these matters the Exile grew more voluble, telling them that it was very simple to fly the pods with his little box, steering only the great pod and letting the others trail behind on leash, and that the place he sought was simply any place in the open where the Quicksilver People were not likely to come. The setting up of the devices, he said, would not take long; and when that was done, the pods would be so lightened that they could well fly across what remained of the darkness, as the Captain hoped, and bring them at least to the Mountains, if not as far as Sollet Castle.

To all this the Warden listened closely, but without much faith. It emerged also, as the Exile talked on, that the place was already found, for he had unloaded some of his devices at a likely spot not far from here, and needed only a little time to set them working.

Now the Warden drew the Captain aside for consultation, saying softly, 'He may be telling part of the truth – ' ('I think he is,' said Repnomar) 'but for sure he's not telling all. I'd as soon let him set fire to Rotl as send his messages.'

The Captain had to agree that there was sense in this; but she held to it that they should fly the pods across the darkness, instead of turning back; claiming that even if they had to walk the last part of the way it would be easy going with the Exile's rations and torch and stove. 'And surely it's better,' she said, 'to steer for the Mountains and the Sollet than for the Dreeg and the Low Coast. Though if we got that far,' she added, and a speculative gleam kindled in her eyes, 'I wouldn't mind sailing back across the Soll in one of those Low Coast ships.'

The Warden looked at her with alarm. But the Captain added, 'To tell you the truth, Lethgro, I see no hope of getting the *Mouse* off that rock without another ship and a mighty lot of towing.' And she began to speak of the virtues of Low Coast ships and of the questions that itched her concerning their rigging and handling.

All this while Broz had been sleeping on the Exile's sheet, his old limbs stretched luxuriously in the warmth of the stove and his toes twitching from time to time in happy dreams. Now he woke with a yawn and began to sniff around the pods, and presently raised his leg to mark the big one.

At this Repnomar laughed triumphantly and said that Broz had given his approval to journeying in the pods. And Lethgro slapped his hands against his knees and stood up from the rock where he sat, saying, 'So be it!' For it seemed to him after all less hazardous to undertake that flight through desolation than to struggle with all the perils of the way they had come and on top of those the Low Coast pirates and their outlandish ships. 'And if it comes to walking,' he added grimly, 'we've done it before with less.' For the prospect of worse things had heartened him considerably toward the dark side of the world.

Repnomar too had leaped up, her face alight, for her hand itched for this new tiller. But the Exile's face, when he heard of it, was troubled. Still, he neither struggled nor tried to escape, and the Warden was glad of this. They discussed very calmly the difficulties of traveling far in such cramped quarters, but there was little they could agree to do about it. For the Warden would not have the Exile ride alone in one of the smaller pods (as he offered to do), and the Captain would not have Broz ride there (as the Warden suggested); and though the Captain, who was slenderer than Lethgro, might have managed to fold herself snugly into the second largest pod, she did not want to steer the great pod from there. 'For,' as she said, 'if I run it onto a reef, I should be there to take the shock.'

So in the end they did no more than move the last packets from the big pod into one of the others and then (a thing surprising at first sight but simple enough) change the shape of the big pod to fit them better. For all these vessels, as the Exile explained, were flexible and could be bent into different shapes by pressing them at certain spots (conveniently marked in yellow). The crows, much against their will, were tucked again into the pod where the Exile had first stowed them and – when Broz had been persuaded that there was no harm in the changed shape – all the others crept back into the largest, and (Lethgro and the Exile swallowing their anxiety as best they could) the Captain turned a knob and pressed a button, and they rose jerkily and floated in midair.

The Captain let out a whoop of triumph that was painful in that closed space; but immediately she bent herself to business, pressing the little box here and there very carefully, studying the lines and spots on its surface, which changed (so the Exile said) with the pod's movements. Closed in this windowless shell, they had no other means of knowing where they were or which way they were headed, unless by opening a hatch and shining a light out. This they would do, the Captain said, from time to time; but the Exile had convinced her that the pod would not fly well with a hatch open in its bow, and indeed she was eager to try steering a vessel with no glimpse of landmarks.

At first they paused often, to open the hatch and check their surroundings. But as the Captain learned to read her box more swiftly and handle it more surely, they all settled themselves a little, like birds shaking their feathers before they sleep, and began to talk peacefully.

'You'll have to admit, Lethgro,' the Captain said, 'that this is easier traveling than limping along down there on frozen feet. A good deal faster, too.'

'Cheerfully,' Lethgro answered. 'As long as it lasts.' And was struck at once by a pang of remorse for uttering words of such dubious omen, so that he added quickly, 'At this rate we'll see Sollet Castle again sooner than I ever dreamed.'

Here the Exile let slip a small but melancholy sigh, and the Warden felt another pang, for it was no happy fate to which he was returning the Exile. But that small person essayed a smile, and remarked that by his calculations this speed and this course would bring them out of the darkness in less than fifty watches if they sailed on constantly, or more if they stopped to sleep on the ground.

Lethgro reminded himself that the Exile had clearly lied about the flying ability of the pods (though which of his versions had been lie and which perhaps truth was not so clear) and that in all likelihood this last remark was made in hopes of getting the box into his own hands again while the Captain slept. But Repnomar required no cautioning on this point, for she shot a hard glance at the Exile before she answered, 'There's no need to drop anchor except when we want to stretch our legs. Two of us can keep this craft flying forever.' And she began to show Lethgro how to read the box, pointing out the dot that told how high the pod floated above the ground, and how the various-colored lines and their movements showed the wind and their own speed and the slope of the land ahead. To all which Lethgro attended closely but with a frown that grew deeper and deeper, for he found himself poorly suited to this sort of navigation. And it was while the Captain was saying, 'No, no, you get wind speed from the height of this line, and direction from the slant,' that they were all slammed against the front of the pod, that seemed slammed against them, and then pod and all settled downward with unpleasant scraping noises till in a minute's time they rested crumpled and gasping on what felt like solid ground.

The Exile, who had been sitting with his back against the pod's forward end, took the worst of the blow, and for a little while they feared that his spine had been snapped, for it seemed he could do nothing but croak feebly and spread out his stubby fingers, his eyes goggled and his whole ugly face stark with the violence of that shock. But when they had found a hatch that could still be opened, and dragged themselves out and brought him out as gently as might be, he was soon able to speak and move his arms and then to sit up and stare at the wreck of his pods. Meanwhile the Captain had first made sure that Broz was unhurt, and loosed the crows (much upset and with feathers all awry) from their small pod, which had taken a rough tumbling but seemed not broken, and now was trying the levers and buttons of the little box; but though the great pod quivered slightly, it did not rise.

'Well, Lethgro,' she said at last, 'I owe you a dinner in Rotl.'

18
The Red Wind

'And I mean to claim it, Rep,' the Warden answered grimly. He stood with the torch in his hand, looking up at the cliff wall into which they had crashed at full tilt, but what he was calculating in his mind was speed and distance, both of which looked discouraging. On foot they would have no choice but to stop for sleep; and since the pods traveled many times faster than a walking pace, those fifty watches the Exile had mentioned must be multiplied by some unknown number, and he thought he would be waiting a long time for that dinner in Rotl. But he was past despair now, and meant simply to go on so long as they had means, were it only by crawling. And not seeing any reason for delay, he turned again to the Exile, asking him if he thought he could walk.

This, when they had helped him up, the Exile managed in a painful hobble, and even observed deferentially that they were lucky the pods had been traveling so slow – a notion of slowness too outlandish to call for answer. At first he could not believe that his precious vessel was past flying, and insisted on opening hatches and creeping into and over it, tinkering with the little box and with certain devices lodged in the pod's walls, while the Warden stirred restlessly from foot to foot; but in the end he gave it up.

Both Warden and Captain were much relieved to find that he could travel on his own feet (for it would have made slow going indeed to carry him) and still more when he told them there was a packet of medicines among his supplies, one of which was good to dull pain and so should make his walking easier. This the Captain found and gave him, and then began to question him about the other packets. 'For,' she said, 'we want to carry everything that will help to get us through, but nothing that's not needed.'

But the Exile said there was no need to carry anything, for every one of the pods could fly by its own power, if only the little box had not suffered damage. And he showed the Captain how, by changing the setting of a knob, she could turn the box's force to one or another of the pods, or to all of them at once, making them swim in air like a school of fish in water, rising or turning all at the same instant and all the same way. This gave her much pleasure, especially as the largest remaining pod could carry either Broz or the Exile, if walking grew too wearisome for them. So it was with lighter hearts that they started off again, and the school of pods floated above them.

The first use the Captain found for the size of that largest pod was to make a shipcrow of the Exile, and this she did even before they started. For their first problem was how to pass the cliff where they had shipwrecked, whether by climbing it straight forward or by trying to find a way around. This was something the crows themselves could not well tell them, being not strong enough to carry a light, and besides not trained for such a kind of scouting. 'But,' the Captain told the Exile happily, 'I can send you up in that pod, and left and right, with an open hatch and the torch to see by, and you can tell me how high the cliff stands, and how far it runs each way.'

Now the Exile looked at her a little sickly, as one who faces a worse hazard than any he has passed; but he agreed cheerfully enough, saying only that with the Warden's permission he might contrive a means of signaling from the pod, and so lessen the chance of being smashed against the cliff, or some worse thing. And indeed there was sense in this, if he could do it; for Repnomar, staring blindly from below, could not well see where she was sending the pod.

The Warden did not much like to let the Exile fiddle with his devices (not knowing what indeed he might contrive) and wished heartily that he himself would fit into that pod; but in the end, weighing one risk with another, he told him to get on with it.

This the Exile eagerly did, opening a small device and poking into its entrails, explaining as he worked that this thing was meant to measure the heat of the air and send word of it; but by joining one part to another in its vitals, he could make it answer to the heat of his hand, so that when he touched it, it would send out its little word; and the Captain's box, when he had made another such adjustment in it, should hear that word and answer by lighting one of its dots, that was now dull and lifeless.

'And what answer,' asked the Warden, in a voice that made the Exile cringe slightly, 'will there be from that ship of your people?' But the Exile swore very earnestly that none of these devices could by themselves send a message so far, and that there was still another device – which he showed them, silent and motionless – that was meant to gather all their signals and send them out beyond the clouds, and he swore too that this device slept till certain things were done to it. And with this the Warden, biting the inside of his lips, was forced to content himself.

When it was done, they agreed that it had been worth doing. Whenever the signal dot had lit, the Captain had immediately stopped the pod, and then cautiously started it off again in another direction; and the crows had flown around it, as if jealous of this encroachment upon their profession. When she had brought him down at last (landing with only a small thump), the Exile had crawled out well pleased and greeting the Captain with a comradely grin, for it seemed that the pod had skimmed cleanly along the cliff, taking no hurt, and he had seen something of the country beyond it, as also how it sank and curved away from them on their left, so that he was for going left along it and thus rounding its flank.

This they did, in the course of that same watch. The Exile said no more of his mission and his messages, seeming now quite cheerfully bent on their journey, though the end of it did not promise well for him. They camped on a downward slope at the cliff's shoulder. This time the Warden, without a word spoken, bound the Exile's hands and feet and looped the end of the rope over his own arm before he lay down to sleep; and though the Exile looked grieved at this, he made no objection.

After that sleep, they went on with the feeling of a journey begun in earnest, as if all before now had been no more than sport. Their torch – their only torch, for the Exile said he had no other – did not penetrate far into that darkness, so that though they saw what lay before their feet, they had to guess by the slope and texture of the land, and the movements of the breezes, what awaited them farther ahead. In this their luck seemed good enough at first. 'For,' the Warden said with satisfaction, 'we're in a pass, and going down.'

Repnomar knew nothing of passes; but when this was explained to her as a channel or strait, she was pleased, for it seemed to mean they were coming down out of these snow mountains. And the Exile talked cheerily of the sights and creatures they had met on this journey, of slugs and snow-worms that fed on such slime as they had seen under the ice, and landkelp that fed on worms and snowfish that fed on landkelp, and the shoveler beasts that scooped up snow by the pailful in their broad jaws and ate whatever they found in it. Only Broz was dissatisfied, sniffing the air suspiciously and nosing at stones with a half-formed growl in his throat.

They found no game themselves (unless that term could stretch to cover a scrawny landkelp, dead and dried by the wind, which the Captain picked up from a bare rockside); but, as she rightly observed, 'We aren't hunting.' To all of them now, Broz included, it seemed that the one important thing was to push on without delay; and their rations, by the Exile's best calculation, were more than enough if they were not greedy. Snow was drifted in the depth of the pass, so that often they took to the slope on one side for better footing; but they traveled warmly enough, having the Exile's stove hung from one of the pods that floated docilely above them, shedding warmth upon them as they went.

'Your pass may be bringing us down,' the Captain said after a time (speaking indifferently to the Warden and the Exile, both of whom she held answerable for mountains) 'but it's taking us off our course.' The Exile looked worried at this, and began to say that it was difficult indeed to hold a course in the darkness, without landmarks, and that he had a little device for the purpose. But the Captain, exchanging glances with the Warden, said that she needed no device to hold a course, so long as she had her senses about her. So when they had slept again, at the bottom of the pass where it widened out into a plain or valley, they turned slantwise to the right at the Captain's direction.

Now the going was easy – or seemed so after what they had traveled before. The wind that had troubled them, gusting down the pass at their backs and making the pods bob and dance like floats in a mountain stream, had died away, and the rocks were smooth and bare of snow. So for some watches they made good time, trending always downward but sometimes crossing folds and rises of the rock. They were traveling now, for the most part, into a light headwind that the Captain swore was warmer than any wind they had felt before in this country. The Exile was for getting out his device again to measure its warmth, but this the Warden would not allow.

No one rode in the largest pod; for the Exile seemed to

have taken no lasting hurt from their wreck, so that after the second or third sleep he kept up the pace as well as ever, and without the help of medicine; and Broz, though not given to undignified gambols and dashes, was otherwise as eager for the journey as any young dog might have been. Repnomar too was in good humor, saying that it had taken this outlandish journey to show that she and Broz could walk as well as float, and making the pods turn and jog overhead, rising sometimes out of torchlight range or circling around their heads like giant bees.

They had neither seen nor heard anything of the Quicksilver People and their nets, but they kept up a guard, Repnomar and Lethgro taking it in turn during their stops for sleep, till the Exile offered to take his turn as well. For, as he said, it was not fair that he should have twice the sleep of the others, and though his hands and feet were tied, his eyes and ears were not. The Captain seconded him in this, saying that he had as good reason as any of them to keep honest guard; and the Warden, after a little thought, agreed that there was no likely harm in it, and considerable good.

But it was Broz who gave the alarm, and during the Exile's turn on guard. Repnomar sat up, demanding to know what was happening; but the Exile, much flustered to find his watch-keeping questioned, maintained that he had neither seen nor heard anything. The crows, too, were undisturbed, asleep with their heads under their wings; and all the Warden's casting of the torchbeam this way and that showed nothing but bare rock, dark and smooth as swells of the Soll transformed into stone.

'What makes you sure he noticed something, Rep?' he asked at last. 'I didn't hear him bark.'

But Repnomar thought this unworthy of any answer except a snort. It was true that Broz had not barked – indeed she would have been hard put to say exactly how he had waked her – but he stalked now warily at the edge of the torchlight, sniffing the wind and uttering low growls. Lethgro untied the Exile's bonds. But still no sound came to them out of the dark.

'One thing or the other,' Lethgro said after a time. 'We can go on as before, or we can look for another road. What we can't do is stay here forever.' It seemed to him there was no need now to add 'or turn back.'

'Right,' the Captain answered promptly. 'And we've no way of knowing that another road would be better. Let's hold our course and meet it head on.'

Lethgro did not like to consider too closely what that 'it' might be; but he took the torch in one hand and his knife in the other. Repnomar was fastening the Exile's folded sheet around Broz's back and sides, in case of darts. The Exile had found a loose stone the size of his fist, that might serve as a weapon for lack of a better, and the Warden did not object. So they started on cautiously, Broz a little in the lead.

Some hours later they had put away their weapons, for they knew now what had roused Broz; and though they did not well understand what it was they faced, it was clear that knives and rocks would be of little use against it. 'I should have known,' the Captain said sourly. 'Broz sees no better than we do; but he can smell ten miles farther.'

It was worse than a smell by now. It was like a redness in the air, that burned and bit, eating at the tender flesh of nostrils and throat, so that they drew every breath reluctantly and held it in pain. The Captain bent her head and plodded straight into the teeth of that evil breeze, with Broz sneezing at her heels. The Warden, with a seared sigh, had pulled the collar of his shirt across his mouth to breathe through, which eased his lungs a little. The Exile never faltered; indeed, he gave no sign of any discomfort, except for the wild grimaces into which he continually twisted his face. As for the crows, Repnomar had put them into a pod for safekeeping, not liking the sickly way they had hunched themselves in that unwholesome air.

They talked little, for the taste of the wind was like acid drizzled on the tongue. From time to time, Lethgro still swung the torch left and right, showing still the same blank swells of rock. A dim haze hung in the air and laid a powdery dust on their skin and clothing and all around them, softening that stony countryside a little to the sight, though not to the foot.

Presently the Captain, looking back and catching sight of the Exile's squinted eyes and puckered mouth, called for a halt and a drink of water all round.

'It's a nasty wind,' she said. 'Barely strong enough to lift a sail, but it has a red taste to it.'

The Exile ran his finger through the dust on his forehead and looked at it mournfully. He had long since given his opinion, which was that they should turn across the wind, either left or right, in hopes of getting out of its force before a worse thing came upon them. To this the others had not agreed, thinking it better to hold course as long as they could. But the Captain said now, 'It doesn't have to be either head-on or broadside. We can tack across the wind and still make headway.'

So they turned slantwise across that mild and bitter wind, moving now a little uphill along an easy slope. This cheered the Exile somewhat, for he maintained that the dust they walked through was the spitting of some angry mountain, and he feared sadly that it might change to a worse vomiting; so that it was well not to walk straight toward it, and better yet if they could put a rise of ground between it and themselves.

Some few hours later, by the Captain's estimation, they were all willing to acknowledge that he had been right, at least as to the desirability of shelter. The red wind had died; but they got little good from that. What had been a haze in the air had thickened to a steady snowing of fine, soft stuff like the powdery smoke of puffballs. They sat hunched together under the Exile's sheet and ate their rations, and the crows preened dust out of their feathers with all signs of disdain. The Exile was explaining, with ever greater urgency, what he hoped and what he feared.

The Warden put out a hand to still the Exile and raised his eyes to the Captain's. 'So, Rep,' he said. 'I'm not a gambler. But like it or not, we've got to lay our bets. Are we better off slogging through the dust around a mountain that's likely to burst any minute like a rotten egg, or flying through the air with those pods?' For this was what the Exile proposed.

'I'm ready to lay mine,' Repnomar answered, and stood up, shrugging off the sheet, so that for a few minutes they were all sneezing and coughing in a cloud of dust. By the time Lethgro was able to breathe again (and that only through a handkerchief held to his face) she had already got Broz into one pod and was stowing the crows into another.

The Exile, his eyes scrunched into slits, bustled about in the ruddy haze, taking gear from the pods. The light of the torch pierced only a little way into that slow rain of ashes, so that, as Repnomar observed, 'We might as well be ten feet down in murky water.'

There was no way of getting themselves into the pods, even if all the gear had been taken out; but what the Exile had now confessed, under the stress of imminent danger and long weariness, was that all this time they could have been flying, not in the pods but with them. 'Though these wings,' the Warden said doubtfully, 'look a little small for some of us.'

What he thought, in fact, was that the flying apparatus the Exile was spreading out in the dust might suffice to lift a dog in a high wind, but not a person of his size and gravity. But the Exile made haste to explain that these little wings ('fins,' the Captain suggested tersely) were only to keep them steady in the air while the pods towed them. The only danger, he assured them somewhat doubtfully, would be from the cold, for the pods could pull them at a great rate through the air, faster than an arrow. But when the Warden asked him why, with this safe and rapid means of travel at hand, they had trudged so long through the snow and the choking ash, the Exile admitted that the little wings were not meant for living things. He had not thought of them before, he said, because they were designed only for towing objects. And when the Warden wanted to know what kind of objects, the Exile seemed not to understand the question, but began to demonstrate how the fins could be attached to the Warden's legs and shoulders.

To make their flight warmer, the Exile proposed to hang the stove from the first pod in line, and cluster the others (to which they themselves would be tethered like lambs to a wool cart) close behind. This required considerable rearranging of the cables that connected all the pods, and led to a long discussion of cordage between the Exile and the Captain, so that the Warden had to speak severely to them both. 'For,' as he said a little testily, 'if it's not going to work, we'd better find out before we're too deep in ash to move.'

Certainly the powdery flakes were falling faster now. The Warden tied his handkerchief over his face, to keep the stuff out of his nose and mouth, and even the Captain had begun to move cautiously, not to stir up the ash. She too had made a mask of her handkerchief. But the Exile had no handkerchief; and the Warden, when he had seen enough of the Exile's grimaces, ripped still another piece from the tail of his own ragged shirt and handed it to the Exile, saying gruffly, 'We might as well all look like bandits.'

'Flying bandits,' the Captain said with a muffled laugh

through her handkerchief. 'We could pick a prisoner off the highest tower of Sollet Castle, Lethgro, once I get the hang of flying us.'

For the Warden still refused to put their lives altogether into the Exile's hands, insisting that if the Captain could fly the pods from the ground, she could fly them from the air. So, when they were all three fitted with fins and harnessed to pods with the Exile's ropes, Repnomar took the little box, and saying cheerfully, 'Here we go,' pressed a button; and they were hoisted like so many bales at a loading dock. The Captain let out a whoop of joy, and Lethgro gritted his teeth (which in truth were gritty enough, with the ash); but before he had time to mutter more than a scrap of prayer, they were streaming along like banners in a gale, or like birds borne down-Sollet on the wind. Except, as Lethgro reflected, that there was no wind to speak of but the wind of their own passage, so that the cold blast that tore at his ears and tossed his trailing legs like sticks in a torrent was only a measure of their speed through the dirty air.

That speed was enough to make him wince inwardly as well as outwardly, and he kept an anxious eye on the Captain, for he remembered how she had crashed the largest pod into the cliff. It seemed to him that they must be going even faster now; and in the rushing, ripping wind of their flight he felt as naked and helpless as an unfledged nestling tossed into the highest wind of the year. It was true that in the great pod they had been flying blind, whereas now there were no walls to block their view; but the Exile's torch cut only a short way into the falling ash – enough, the Warden thought darkly, to show how fast they were tearing across country, but not enough to keep them from breaking their necks if another cliff suddenly loomed in front of them. Flying into that ash was like facing into a wind-driven downpour of rain, blinding and stinging and stifling. Lethgro had sometimes the dizzy feeling that he was upside down, for the rocks and snowbanks below, misted with the reddish haze, seemed to fly past like clouds in storm-time. And though, in this desperate and undignified position, he was glad not to be at the Exile's mercy, he was not sure if it was much better to be at the mercy of the Captain, who had started them off with such an unseemly whoop and now seemed bent on shaking them to pieces if she could find no cliff to crash them against.

But in fact the Captain had settled very soberly to her task. She was glad to have the Exile's stove ahead of them, for it was better to be buffeted by a warm wind than a cold, and it meant she could push their speed higher without too much danger of freezing them all. This she did very determinedly, having made up her mind that her business was to get them through this ashy passage as quickly as possible and so come out into clear air again. Squint her eyes as she might, they burned sorely; and between that and the thick haze, she was hard put to see her course before her. But she pushed on mercilessly, thinking to herself that as long as her fingers were not too stiff to hold the box there was no need either to slow down or to stop, for the others had no work to do at all and could ride at their ease. Her hope was that they could fly like this for a full watch, or something near it, before they had to stop to thaw themselves. 'And if we're not out of the ash by then,' she thought grimly, 'we'll fly till we are.'

Long before that time, however, she began to think of changing her plans. Lethgro, in the tumult of the wind, could not clearly understand her shouting, and the Exile did no better, but her gestures with the torch showed them which way to look.

Ahead and to the left, there was a redness that could hardly be called light, for it lit up nothing. It was like the strange colors they had seen in the sky when they crossed the mountains into darkness – or, in the Warden's recollection, like the deadly glow of a burning forest seen through its smoke. But this redness seemed to come from a single spot, near (the Captain thought) to the horizon, if they had been able to see the horizon.

Careering through the air as they were, with the noise of their own flight in their ears and the Exile's little fins barely sufficing to keep them on an even keel, they were ill-placed for conversation. When Repnomar tried to consult with the Warden by gestures, she came near to flipping upside down, and thrashed wildly for a little before the fins set her straight again. So, thinking that she was captain here and could steer her vessel as she liked (though it was only a cluster of pods), she turned the leading pod in a great curve, and they swept like circling birds toward the redness.

19

Of the Indigestion of Mountains

Warden Lethgro was not an unreasonable man, nor, in general, an ill-tempered one; but to be dragged upside-down through the air in the direction of what might well be a bursting mountain (if it was not the maw of some uncouth and unfriendly god) seemed to him reason enough to feel surly. He had tried, when Repnomar first turned them toward the red glow, to express his disapproval by a vigorous waving of both arms. But that had only flipped him out of balance, and for a time he had spun and wobbled so violently that when his flight steadied again he did not know at first whether he was looking up or down. In the dark there was not much difference; but he saw in a little that the redness, which had been somewhat to his left, was now somewhat to his right. And it was when he had grasped the meaning of this (for his first thought was that there were two spots of redness, one on each side) that the Warden concluded he had a right to lose his temper.

He began to flap his arms again, as if he meant to fly under his own power. This set him spinning once more, twisting the cable that tethered him. But at last Repnomar took notice of his gyrations and slowed the pods until they hovered almost motionless in midair, with the three of them dangling like long-stemmed fruit.

'You'll never learn to fly straight, Lethgro,' the Captain said, 'if you keep spinning like a windmill.'

But the Warden answered with some heat that he hoped he would never learn to fly straight into an open fire, nor a devil's maw, nor the two together; and the Exile put in, with more fervor than was usual for him, that in this case he believed the Warden was right. 'And if this is the best course you can steer us, Repnomar,' the Warden finished, 'give me that box and let me do my own steering.'

The Captain made a gesture of indifference. 'You'd walk through Rotl Fair with your eyes closed, Lethgro, for fear of seeing something new. But I never sailed with a mutinous crew yet, and I don't mean to start now.' And without more ado she turned them back to their former course, and before the Warden could well get his breath they were streaming again through the murky air, slantwise away from the redness.

This, as they agreed later, was done in the nick of time, and Repnomar confessed very handsomely that she had come near to killing them all with her unseasonable curiosity. The Exile, who kept an anxious eye on the red glow as they flew, had been the first to notice; and by the time his squawking and flapping had drawn the attention of the others, that red glow had risen up like a column of flame, brighter by the moment, lighting the thick clouds that billowed from it. Repnomar took one look and began to press her buttons, slowing them to a smooth stop despite all Lethgro's bellows of protest. But it was only for a moment, and she started them off again at a new angle, shouting in explanation, 'I had to check the wind!'

Indeed they were downwind from that unwholesome light (faint though the wind was), and the Captain's one thought now was to get them out of the path of whatever would be blowing from it. She kept the torch clutched hard in one hand and the box in the other, thumbing its buttons, and soon they were tearing through the gritty air so fast that it screamed in their ears and stung their faces like sleet, and their legs trailed like wind-whipped signal flags.

At that speed, in that dry rain of bitter dust, it was not easy to see anything. The Warden kept one eye squeezed shut and the other squinted to a slit. He had found that as long as he held himself still (or as still as was possible for a large person being yanked along at high speed at the end of a towrope) the little wings kept him on an even keel. Now and again he snatched a one-eyed look toward the red light, and what he saw chilled him more than the cutting wind.

Like the plumes of some devil-bird tossing in an updraft from the underworld, thick tufts of smoke or cloud were rising in that crimson light, shaking their feathery heads and billowing outward into the darkness. And the redness was no longer only a distant glow; it was a tree of light, as if some subterranean god were waving a giant torch at the mouth of a pit. It was clear that whatever the Exile had feared – or something just as bad – was coming true.

The Captain's eyes, when she snatched a glance that way, were not on the flame of light but on the clouds that rolled from it. In her judgement, trouble was coming at them two layers deep; for the topmost plumes, flattened by the wind, streamed out toward them in fingers and sheets of smoke, raveling into haze, while denser clouds boiled along the ground below like racing storm waves. The flaring red light did not carry far, and from time to time she flicked the torchbeam in that direction, ready for the first sight of that approaching flood. When she saw it at last, she let out a whistle that nobody heard (the wind of their flight snatching it away) and thumbed a button of her box so that they were jerked upward like three fish on a line; for, having no way to gauge the distance of the flame, she had not realized till now the height of that furious cloudbank rolling toward them.

It was none too soon. As they rose, the cloud swept under them – not red, as they might have expected, but swelling blue-gray in the light of the torch. Repnomar let out a whoop of triumph or amazement, and the Warden, clutching his stomach, breathed a somewhat jumbled prayer. Beneath them, the ashcloud showed in the torchlight like Soll waters in turmoil. For a time, Repnomar kept her thumb on the button that hauled them ever higher; but when she judged them to be well out of reach of the highest billows, she leveled them off and steered straight across the cloud's path, thinking this the safest direction.

Now from this loftier lookout above the dust, they could better see the source of it, a boiling cauldron of red that glowed sometimes with raw white streaks. To Lethgro, it looked like the open forge of some blacksmith god, hammering out swords and knives that were most likely destined to no good purpose, while the smoke and steam of the forging rolled away in poisonous clouds. This seemed all the likelier to him from the comparative warmth of the air. To race at such a speed was like facing into the fiercest winds of the year; and yet at moments, shaken though he was by wind and worry, the Warden could not resist giving himself up like a baby to the pleasure of wiggling his fingers and toes, which were no longer stiff with cold. He had time enough to take note of such questionable blessings, for even at top speed they seemed to come no nearer to the edge of the cloud, that churned and roiled beneath them like a Soll of ash.

The Captain was glad of that warmth (for she reflected that Broz in his pod could be warming as well as resting his old bones) and gladder still that the course was so easy to set and hold. Blind as they were, they could not go wrong while she had the wind (much stronger now) and that red light to steer by. No matter how wide this ashcloud might stretch, it had an edge, and they must come to that edge sooner or later. The Captain was sure of this until the very moment when she saw the second light.

This one, too, was far to their left, but ahead – just such a pulsing red flame as the one they were slowly leaving behind. It was very small to the eye, whether from true size or distance, and at first glimpse the Captain turned her torch toward it for better view. But that made it still harder to see, and she shut off the torch altogether, so that the redness stood out clear against the dark. The Captain cursed. No question of it: there were two vomiting mountains – two at least.

Captain Repnomar was not one to hesitate for long. She paused only to light the torch again and sweep its beam as far in all directions as it would reach, lighting up the billows and levels of the ashcloud. Then she pressed the buttons of the little box, and they turned in a tight curve to the left.

In Warden Lethgro's opinion, this was too much. It was, he thought, a sad trait of the Captain's to run more often into danger than away from it; but as a rule she had at least some excuse for her folly. This time he could see no glimmer of sense in it, and he was weary of dangling like a puppet, without power or voice of his own. He therefore hesitated no more than the Captain herself, but seized his towline with both hands and uttered a roar that no beast in any wilderness they had passed through yet could have matched. He was prepared to drag himself forward along that towrope, hand over hand into the teeth of the wind, until he was far enough in front of Repnomar to catch her attention – or, if need be, to flap and wallow his way into her path and wrestle her for the box. But this proved unnecessary, for at his bellow Repnomar slowed the pods so precipitously that she heard a muffled yelp from Broz, and the three of them at the ends of their towropes were whipped forward by their own speed like cast fishbait. The lines pulled them up short with a jerk; and even while they swung backwards and forwards the Warden expressed himself loudly on the subject of the Captain's course-setting.

'What would you rather do, Lethgro?' the Captain

retorted with some asperity. 'Steer straight from one ash-cloud to another? I'd rather cut between them.' And so keen was she on this point that she set the pods in motion again, although slowly, so that they could travel as they argued.

They found little to agree on. The Captain's notion was that, for all they could tell, a line of flaming mountains might stretch from here to the far edge of the dark. 'And,' she said, 'we'll never be able to land so long as we're downwind of them, unless you want your mouth stuffed with ashes.' For she remembered how they had scraped midges out of her sailor's mouth on the Low Coast, and that put bitterness into her words.

To this the Warden answered that if a beast threatened to bite him, he would not thrust his hand into its mouth, and that if the Captain felt impelled to turn off-course she had better turn away from the burning mountains rather than toward them. As for the Exile, he held that the Captain might be right as to a line of mountains, or of something equally bad, but might as easily be wrong; and that the new course she had chosen might be the best and safest, if it did not bring them to utter destruction; so that he was hard put even to agree with himself, let alone anyone else.

All this while they were moving slowly through the air in the direction of the red flames, or more truly toward a spot midway between them. Even at this slow rate, they were considerably buffeted, for the wind blew strong into their faces. Repnomar, as she argued, did not forget to cast the torchbeam this way and that, about and below their line of flight. Now she cried out in triumph and pointed, and Lethgro felt a hollow space where his stomach should be.

Ahead and a little to the right, a rift or canyon opened in the ashcloud beneath them, and he saw for the first time how high they were flying. But in a moment he turned his eyes away and took a steadying breath, thinking that he would not get down any more surely be being sick in midair.

'Better go through a gap in a reef where you find it,' the Captain said, 'than hold your course and be broken in pieces on the rocks. Or smothered in ashes,' she added, to make her meaning clearer to landlubbers. And she pressed a button, increasing their speed till they were whistling through the air again, so that there was no more conversation for a time.

In fact, the Captain was relieved to have her course confirmed so quickly by that rift in the ashcloud. Though they seemed to be tearing along as fast as ever, that was by no means true, for she was steering them straight into a strong headwind, and it was very slowly that the two burning mountains drew nearer to view. The rift that had opened in the cloud closed again, but others opened and spread, until at last nothing showed beneath them but a faint reddish mist in which the torchbeam lost itself, and the red beacons of the mountains burned to their right and left. Now they all began to breathe easier – so far as they could breathe at all with the wind pounding their faces – for there were no more bursting mountains to be seen ahead of them, and the air below them was clearer by the minute. The Captain, accordingly, slowed the pods to an easier pace and began to bring them slowly downward. But not till the belching mountains were clearly behind them, impossible to be seen without twisting the neck and endangering the balance, did she stop all headway and lower them gently till their dangling feet (the Exile's last of all) found solid rock to stand on.

At first they stumbled and reeled, and the Captain laughed uproariously, saying they were all like landlubbers on their first voyage. But she brought the pods down neatly and lost no time getting Broz out to stretch his legs on honest ground, which he did with much snuffing and snorting and dashing about.

It was honest ground indeed, bare windswept rock with hardly a trace of snow. The first fire mountain was nearly lost to sight behind a swelling ridge and a jumble of other peaks. All they could see of it was an ominous red plume fading into the upper darkness. The other was clearer to view, nearer now and more brightly lit. 'But not much of a mountain,' the Warden pronounced, after consideration. They could see, by its own light, that it was not so much a peak as a long mound or rounded ridge like the one on whose slope they stood; and the baleful glow came not from a single pit but from half a dozen shifting spots along what the Exile said must be an open crack in the world. The Warden shivered, and looked down at his feet.

But they were all agreed now that the Captain's steering had proved good, for the air on this side of the mountains was clear and clean. The wind held strong and steady, carrying those unwholesome clouds straight away from them. It was colder on this side, too, so that they were glad of the stove, and Broz came back very cheerfully to its circle of warmth when Repnomar whistled him in. He had a different opinion when it came to thrusting him back into his pod. 'But in you go,' the Captain told him sternly, 'like it or not. We've no business strolling about in a country where the mountains vomit fire. And flying,' she added softly, 'is the next thing to sailing.'

It surprised Lethgro to hear what sounded like wistfulness in the Captain's voice, and made him no easier in his mind. He had long since resigned himself to pushing forward, by whatever means chance and the gods might allow them, to whatever end they might find, whether that was death or Sollet Castle; but it depressed him to think that Captain Repnomar could be reduced to a similar meekness. If the Captain was wistful, things must be even worse than he had thought.

With the exception of Broz, however, they were all content to fly until they were well clear of these unhealthy mountains. On the windward side they were safe enough for the moment, but in such an unstable country they all feared that the wind might veer round and blow the ash their way, or new cracks or peaks might spit at them. 'And the sooner we go on, the better,' the Captain summed up, 'for we won't make very good time.'

Lethgro wished that she had used words of better omen. Once aloft, it seemed to him that they must be making very good time, for he was as wind-buffeted as ever. But the Captain knew better. To fly crosswise to the wind, she must still steer almost into it, for it was stronger than the pods, and much of their force was spent in fighting against it. From time to time she gained forward speed for a little by running obliquely with the wind until her torchbeam picked out the first fringes of the ashcloud, and then slanting back windward to a more comfortable distance. From time to time, when her numb fingers threatened to let fall both box and torch, they settled to a landing on rock or snow and warmed themselves at the stove. For although on the Exile's suggestion, they shortened the towlines till the three of them were bunched awkwardly close together and just behind the stove, they could not keep really warm in flight. The wind, here where it was not warmed by any burning mountain, was colder than ever, and snatched away both heat and breath; so that flying, except perhaps for Broz, was more wearisome than walking.

It was, however, faster. Before that watch was ended (in the Captain's opinion, though Lethgro suspected that in the absence of any measurement but their own feelings the Captain's watches tended to be longer than other people's) they were well past all sight of ash or fire and had turned back to their original course, which was easier going. So they warmed themselves and slept, loosing both Broz and the crows, who had much to say about their long imprisonment. Before the Exile would sleep, he begged leave to examine his pods again, to make sure they were still fit for the journey; for they too had been sorely buffeted. The Warden saw no harm in this. So the Exile puttered briefly about the pods and announced that in his opinion they were strong enough to carry them to the end of the darkness, or almost, which cheered them all.

Indeed it seemed that their luck had turned for the better. That watch and the next, and for many watches afterward, they had no alarms and no delays. The wind held strong, so much on their own course now that they could fairly drift with it – the easiest style of traveling, the Captain said, that she had ever known, though so tedious that she had to sing songs to keep herself awake. The Exile, too, was pleased with it – especially as he now confessed that he had been perhaps over-optimistic as to the strength of the pods, which were steadily weakening. But with the help of this following wind, he thought, they could easily reach the light. And he ventured to offer a few songs of his own, or what he claimed were songs.

But for all his outward cheerfulness, it was clear that the Exile was troubled, and with good reason. The Warden still insisted that he must be bound securely whenever they slept. Indeed, the longer their luck held good, and the farther they journeyed without hindrance or obstacle, the more severe and wardenly did the Warden become. For he held it ever in mind that one of two things must be true: either they were coming to the light, the Mountains, and the Sollet, in which case his own fate depended on his bringing back the Exile as a prisoner, or else they were not approaching the light at all, in which case the Exile had lied to them from start to finish and must be thought of as an enemy.

If he was severe to the Exile, Warden Lethgro was no less severe to himself, for he thought the principal danger was that he would take pity on the Exile's helplessness; so the kindlier he felt, the more sternly he behaved, and knotted the Exile's bonds ever tighter when they prepared for sleep.

They slept sometimes on bare rock, sometimes on snow or ice, sometimes on drifts of what they took to be snow until it proved to be gritty ash, so fine and thick in places that the Exile sank into it hip-deep. But they saw no more ashclouds or belching mountains, and the fallen ash grew scantier and rarer, until at last they found no more of it.

They no longer spoke of the light, nor of rations, as if such topics were unseemly; but neither Captain nor Warden thought of much else (when they could be said to think at all), for the rations were running low and the darkness seemed to have no end. So that all of them, Broz and even the crows included, grew more and more silent, sunk in their own considerations. Their watches on the ground grew shorter, too, for none of them could sleep much – or rather they found less and less difference between sleep and waking, and thought their time better spent in moving than in lying still.

They were making camp at the base of a snowy slope when Lethgro, stamping out a flat place to spread the Exile's sheet, put his foot through a crust of ice into a stream of running water. He snatched his foot back as if he had put it naked into fire, and then went down on his hands and knees to scrape away snow and break away ice; for in this frozen darkness, running water seemed like something escaped from a forgotten world. 'Look at this, Repnomar,' he called a little hoarsely.

It was indeed a stream, tinkling sweetly under the snow;

and when, with the help of Broz, they had traced it a little way up the slope, the Captain and the Warden sat back on their heels and looked at each other. The Warden laughed a choking laugh. 'This whole watch past,' he said, 'I've thought the dark was getting a little lighter, and been afraid to mention it.'

Repnomar reached across the narrow rivulet and thumped him on the chest. 'I can see you, Lethgro!' she cried exultantly. 'Like a hulk in a fogbank, but I swear I can see you. Didn't I tell you the world was round? We're coming to the light.'

20
Coming Out

It was a good thing (so they all agreed) that the wind had helped them. For without its help, in the Exile's opinion, the pods would not have had strength left to carry them up the Mountains; and without the swiftness of the pods, they would have used up their rations before ever they reached the pass. This time there was no doubt that the Exile spoke the truth, for the pods were laboring badly by the time they reached the upper slopes, drooping so low, despite all Repnomar's pressing of buttons, that at times she felt her feet trail through the tops of the unwholesome vegetation that blotched the mountainside. It would not have been easy flying even with the pods at their best, for the mountain winds were gusty, veering and swooping so that often it was all the Captain could do to save them from wreck. Yet no one complained; for if flying was hard, walking would have been worse. For hours they had been moving upward through a dim landscape of ravines and rain squalls. The rocks below them were sometimes bare and streaming with water, sometimes sheathed in ice, but most often (so it seemed to Lethgro) thickly mantled with what was certainly an unfriendly mire of sodden snow.

This was of much interest to the Warden, and he strained his eyes to make out as much as he could, when he was not distracted by the wild swoops and jerks of their flight. He was searching for some shelter, where they might be able to rest, or for some sign of better footing, in case it came to walking. If these were the Mountains indeed (and he was willing to believe it now) they were no small barrier. When the pods died (and he was certain they would die) they would have a weary journey before they reached Sollet Castle. The Rains must be almost over now, so that Streamrise would be well begun by then, and the going wet. They had already traveled without rest for what the Warden believed to be almost a double watch; and if the pods failed altogether, or a downdraft smashed them against the slush-covered rocks, they would need (supposing they were still alive) a good rest before they began to climb. They were soaked through from the rain and well-nigh frozen, and the Warden's shoulders ached miserably from the tug of his harness and the little wings. But despite all this, and despite the giddy swerves and terrifying dives of their flight, the Warden's soul was at peace for the first time since they had left Beng harbor so long ago.

He had never really believed in the roundness of the world nor the likelihood of their finding an end to the dark, and all this while he had felt that the Captain and the Exile were dragging him against his will through countries he had no wish to understand. But now he felt, with a warm and unshakable confidence, that he was coming into his own land again. This faint light, that showed the snow-smeared slopes as a dim ghostliness beneath them, was the same light that shone so sweetly on the terraces of Sollet Castle; and these half-seen and unwelcoming mountains, on whose slippery rocks they were in instant danger of shipwreck, were in truth only the backside of the Mountains he knew well.

So that he was almost glad when the wreck came at last, though he would have been glad more truly if they had reached a pass first. It came with a shout from the Captain as two of the pods stalled at once and the wind slammed them straight toward a cliffside. The Warden closed his eyes and resigned himself to death, as he had done more than once already. But at the last moment they swept upward along the cliff face, and struck it almost gently, so that they were only bruised and half stunned, not shattered, though they took a little more damage as they slid down the icy cliff and collected in a tangle at its base.

The Exile, who had thudded into Lethgro's side and so escaped a worse blow, was the first to begin disengaging himself from the pile. The stove had given Repnomar a sharp rap on the knee; and though a great frenzy of yelping from one of the pods called her to action, she was too hurt and too entangled to do more at first than swear and thrash about in the wreckage.

But the Exile, with much presence of mind, turned first to the Warden, who lay with his face in the snow and a heavy pod on his back. It was not easy, for a person of the Exile's size, to get him free, but he managed to lift the Warden's face out of the slush and support it so while he rolled the pod off, with difficulty and the use of both his legs. By then the Captain had loosened herself enough from the towlines to reach the pod where Broz was voicing his muffled outcry; and after a time of confusion, they were all arranged more or less comfortably (if misery could be comfortable) at the cliff's foot. The Warden had not come to himself, but he was breathing, and the expression of his face – so far as the others could make it out in the half-light – was benign. Broz was limping with a sprained foot, the Captain's right knee (the same one that had been lamed before) painful and swelling, and the crows were badly ruffled in plumage and disposition. But the worst damage (pending the Warden's account of himself) seemed to have been taken by the pods. It had been hard work releasing Broz, for the hatch of his pod had been jammed shut by the impact and all the panels of the walls knocked out of kilter, so that the Exile could no longer adjust them; while one of the smaller pods had smashed open like a ripe fruit, scattering its contents across the snow. The stove, to the Exile's great relief, still functioned, and he ascribed this to its having struck Repnomar's knee instead of the cliff (which brought a wry laugh from Repnomar). He himself had not been so lucky; for though not as broken as his pods, he had (as he admitted under the Captain's prodding) a cracked bone in his left arm. The Captain bound it up firmly, and there was no more to do for any of them, for the Exile's packet of medications had disappeared in the crash. Another drizzle had begun, this time of snow, not rain, and they made what warmth and shelter they could against the cliff face with stove and sheet and the wreckage of the pods. 'And we could have had a worse landing,' the Captain said fretfully; 'but why doesn't Lethgro come round?'

Now, in fact Warden Lethgro had been at least partly conscious for some time, though to open his eyes had seemed to him an excessive and unnecessary labor. It was a great satisfaction to him to be lying motionless on solid ground, though it was a knobby rock covered with wet snow, and to know that when he did open his eyes he would be able to see, if only dimly. Bruised though he was, and still sodden from the icy rain, he was no longer ripped and tossed by the wind, and the heat of the stove was slowly penetrating his cold flesh. Most of all, he felt that he was almost home, being separated now from Sollet Castle only by the Mountains and the tempestuous course of the Upper Sollet; and he reflected peacefully that his notions of distance and of travel had changed since the long-ago time when he had dreaded a simple journey upriver from Beng.

Now, however, hearing Repnomar's complaint, he exerted himself to answer, though he did not go so far as to raise his eyelids. 'I'm tired, Rep,' he said comfortably. 'That was a long watch you put us through.'

Repnomar's face split with a grin, and she settled back against the rock wall and scratched Broz between the ears.

'We might as well have another long one now,' she said. 'Go to sleep. I'll take first guard.'

'Don't forget,' Lethgro said sleepily, 'to tie the Exile.' And after that he gave himself up to the warmth of the stove and the steadiness of the rock, and slept.

When he woke, his first thought was that he should have seen to the binding of the Exile himself, and he started up violently, upsetting the shelter and waking Broz and Repnomar, and had to lean against the cliff wall until his head cleared again. For a little he thought that his fears were realized, for he could not make out any sign of the Exile. 'Did you let him get away, Rep?' he asked bitterly. His head throbbed and his body ached, and he cursed himself for carelessness.

Repnomar snorted, and made a movement that in the half-darkness he could not follow. 'He's on leash,' she said, and put a rope into Lethgro's hand. 'Give that a pull if you want him.'

This was unnecessary, for the Exile was already clumping and clattering toward them through the wreckage. The Warden, however, did not apologize for his doubt till he had examined the Captain's leash arrangement. Then he did so very handsomely, for she had joined the Exile's elbows by a rope behind his back in such a way that he could use his hands but not get at the knots, and the other end of the rope she had tied to her own waist. Thus the Exile had been able to search for his scattered treasures while he kept guard; and though that in itself did not please the Warden, there seemed to have been no harm done, and the Exile was so childishly pleased to have collected a few of these objects unharmed, that the Warden could not bring himself to chide either him or Repnomar.

'And you've had your easy watch, Lethgro,' Repnomar added. 'The rest of us have had our fill of sleep, and you've had twice as much. Now put a little food in your stomach, and let's be moving on.'

Indeed the Warden was very hungry, for he had eaten nothing since the beginning of the previous watch, and the ration that he sternly doled out to himself now was not enough to placate his stomach; but it did stop his head from spinning, and he was at least as eager as the Captain to be on their way. He thought it likely that they were no great distance from the summits – for he did not suppose that the Mountains were much higher on this side than on the other, and they had flown steeply upslope a long way with the pods – and he therefore judged that their first business was to find a pass.

It was raining again, and their clothes, which had dried out somewhat with warmth and shelter, were quickly becoming sodden once more. The Warden turned his face upward into the rain and squared his shoulders. 'We'd best find a stream and follow it up,' he said.

Indeed this mountainside, though shrouded for the most part with snow and ice, was everywhere rustling and a-quiver with flowing water. The snow itself was soaked with it, collapsing underfoot into a frigid mush that got into shoes and caked between Broz's toes. The ice, where it sheathed the rocks closely, was wet and slick, and elsewhere apt to be rotten and undercut by rivulets. None of this made for pleasant traveling, but the rocks were carved by channels and broken by crosswise cracks, so that there were good holds to be found. The Exile was saddened by the loss of his pods, but he agreed that there was nothing for it but to leave them at the base of the cliff where they had wrecked. He packed them as securely as he could against its face, and they set soggily off, roped as they had been for their first climb at the other edge of the darkness, carrying stove, sheet, torch, rations, and not much else. And the crows flew above them.

On Lethgro's advice, they had not tried to climb the cliff, but searched along its base till they found the kind of stream he wanted, one that ran at the bottom of a deep gully or crevice, and worked their way up this. The Exile's teeth chattered. The wind boomed and whistled around the crags. After a time their gully petered out, and they made a reluctant traverse across a slippery slope to where the torch showed a rockfall that gave them better footing. Here they rested a little, for, as Repnomar said, 'We're out of practice for this, Lethgro' – though the truth was rather that they were all sadly weak from long cold and hunger, and still sore and shaken from the wreck.

But the Warden urged them on, and after a time of struggling over the loose and icy rocks they found a stream still more to his liking, for it was a regular little river (though nowhere so deep that they could not wade across it) with scrawny plants growing along its bed. Here they could walk, or in the worse stretches scramble, which was easier than climbing; but they did not unrope, for they did not know what lay still ahead, and the untying of wet knots with frozen fingers was not to be undertaken lightly.

From time to time the rain ceased, and began again. From time to time they gathered around the stove to warm themselves, for the wind so tore away the warmth that it did not carry far. The crows were often out of sight and hearing for longer than the Captain liked, for she feared they might be lost in the wind; but she had not been able to convince them that they were in no danger of being stuffed into some dark and dangerous pod if they stayed close at hand. 'And besides,' she said, stretching her hands to the stove, 'if we're as near to that pass of yours as you seem to think, Lethgro, they may sight it any time and give us a bearing.'

'Feel the wind,' the Warden answered, with such satisfaction in his voice that Repnomar looked at him keenly.

(Indeed the light was now enough to show faces.) Despite the Captain's words, he had no particular pass in mind, but he had felt sure for some time that they were nearing a pass of some sort; and at this moment, feeling the sweep and steadiness of the wind, he had concluded that it must be flowing straight on through a broad gap between mountain peaks.

And at this propitious time, one of the crows came squawking above them, beating hard against the wind, and whirled away again. The Captain laughed with satisfaction, being relieved to know both that her crow was safe and that it had found a passage for them. 'You were right, Lethgro,' she said. 'I'll buy you that dinner yet.'

The Warden swung the stove to his back (for they took it in turns to carry this comfortable burden) and they started on again. Yet even with these good omens, and the easing of the slope, and the dying away of the rain, they moved slowly. Repnomar's knee was now so stiff and sore that every step was a grim matter for her; Broz whimpered as he walked; and the Exile was in a sorry state, gasping as he trudged along on his short legs and cradling his wounded arm. The Warden himself was not much better off in body, but the nearness of his own country had lit a fire within him, and he strode on mercilessly, sometimes half dragging the others by the rope they still wore. So that at last the Captain was moved to complain that he seemed to think they must make the whole journey in one watch. 'Is your pass going to close up if we take a rest, Lethgro? I for one could use a little sleep.'

Now, in fact this jibe was not far from truth, for the Warden felt uneasily that it was important to reach the pass before they slept. If once they settled into camp, any number of calamities might strike them – the Captain's knee might stiffen so badly that she could not walk at all, the Exile might escape once more, or his people descend upon them from the clouds, another mountain might vomit and bury them in ash, or (more likely) a sudden storm bury them in snow. So long as they were awake and moving, and the omens were good, he felt very earnestly that they should press on until they were over the pass, or until they dropped.

But there was clearly much to be said for Repnomar's view, for they were piteously in need of rest, and even after the pass they would have a hard journey before them. Indeed, the Warden reflected, he could leave the others to rest in camp, if need be, while he scouted the pass and looked for game. In his opinion, nothing would restore their strength and spirits so rapidly as a good roast or stew of fresh meat.

But what settled him at last was the sight and sound of the Exile, swaying slightly on his feet and breathing heavily like an overloaded sheep. He did not seem much like a man plotting his escape, nor indeed capable of so much as taking his freedom if it were offered to him. So the Warden sighed, casting one more glance toward the unseen pass, and set down the stove. 'Call in your crows, Rep,' he said. 'Let's make camp.'

They slept soundly, taking turns as usual. Only one of the crows had come in to the Captain's hoot, which troubled her. 'But,' as she said, 'it's likely found a roost that suits it better, and we'll pick it up when we cross the pass.' And she curled up with Broz and the Exile, who had already made themselves comfortable, and the one dutiful crow settled beside them and tucked its head under its wing.

Tired as he was, the Warden was still restless, and spent his guard time setting snares in what seemed the least unlikely spots along the streambed and searching the vegetation and the waters of the stream for anything that looked edible. But in this he had little luck, finding not even such unsavory game as slugs or landkelp; and the plants were all sickly things with leaves like stiff leather and no fruits that he could find. Yet he did not despair, for there were creatures here – movements and rustlings that were not of the wind, small sounds and scents that made Broz stir in his sleep – and the plants looked to him like stunted and unfruitful versions of plants he knew from the light side of the Mountains. So in due time he woke the Exile and bound him, using Repnomar's system and being careful of his hurt arm, and lay down to sleep.

It was a noise of talking that woke him, not because it was loud, but rather because it was secretive and low. His hand went to his knife before his eyes were well open. Broz and the Captain were waking at almost the same moment, Broz with a growl in his throat.

In the half light, a circle of squat shapes showed whitish all around them, some with arms raised in what looked very much like threat, and others loomed in the dimness beyond. The Exile, seeing the others wake, cleared his throat apologetically and began to explain.

The Warden hesitated only long enough to hear him say that these ghostly forms were his friends, whom it would be better not to annoy. The tether rope still joined them, and Lethgro yanked at it hard with one hand while he drew his knife with the other. The Exile, jerked sprawling, cried out in pain; and at that, Broz and the Captain threw themselves forward. But the Captain's knee failed her, so that she too went down with a cry. The pallid shapes were all in motion, the raised arms lashing downward. Broz, like a shadow condensed to black solidity, had flung himself upon one of them, and Lethgro saw that at least two others had sprung to join that battle, strangely quiet except for Broz, who raged with throaty noises as he fought. By this time Lethgro himself was crouched over the Exile, with his knife at the Exile's neck. 'Call off your friends,' he ordered.

But the Exile answered painfully that he was sorry he did not know how to do that.

Repnomar had heaved her way into the melee around Broz, hacking grimly with her knife. White forms were surging toward them from all sides. 'Halt!' the Warden bellowed. Something cracked against his head.

21
White

When Lethgro began to think again, his thoughts were all regretful ones. He wished earnestly that the Sollet shippers had never delivered the Exile to him, or that he himself had never given the Exile those extra blankets with which he had made his first sail, or that Repnomar had never turned the *Mouse's* prow to the open Soll, or that neither of them had ever allowed the Exile to touch any of his devices. Through the ache and the throbbing (for his head hurt mercilessly) he could hear murmurs of low talk, and with great effort he opened one eye a little.

He thought at first that the blow to his head had blinded him; for though he heard voices that seemed to come from straight before him and nearby, he saw only a whitish blur. It was as if there were light of a sort, though not the clear light of the torchbeam, but nothing to see. Nevertheless, by squinting painfully, he began to make out pale shapes in the whiteness; and after a little further thought he concluded that what he saw was not altogether bad. 'For,' he reflected, closing his eye again, 'White People are a feeble-looking lot; and they must live close to the Sollet.'

He lay more on his side than on his back, dumped awkwardly against something cold and solid. So far as he could tell without moving (for he did not want to attract anyone's attention) he was not bound. In front of him, almost close enough to reach if he had cared to risk it, two people sat in conversation.

It was no wonder the Warden had called them White People in his thoughts, for they brought back to his memory the clumsy raft that had drifted down the Sollet one flood season with a crew of just such pallid folk huddled in their white furs. He had tried hard to talk to them, but without success; for though they had muttered and gabbled among themselves, they had refused to speak to anyone else and shown no interest in learning any other tongue. Two of them had died at Sollet Castle; and the others had seemed so pitiful, being both feeble and uncivilized, that in the end he had had them transported under guard back to the headwaters of the Sollet and there released. Repnomar, when she learned of it, had called him a fool for not finding out where they came from and how they lived and what they talked of in their strange tongue; but he had answered, 'They only went where the river took them. Why should I plague and pester them?'

Now Lethgro remembered all this and wondered if these were indeed folk of the same sort, and if White People were not so feeble as he had thought, or if these were unhuman creatures from beyond the clouds. On the next attempt he opened both eyes, very gingerly, and saw better. They were not, as he had supposed, in a snow cave like those of the Quicksilver People – or if they were, the snow was hidden under a covering, for the whiteness of the walls and floor and roof was the whiteness of fur. It was as if they were tucked into the armpit of some giant snow-white beast. The two people before him were clad in the same fur, which seemed to be garments rather than their own pelts; but their faces had hardly more color, so that, though their features were human enough, they were eerie to look at. He knew by the voices that there were others here whom he could not see, and that the Exile was one of them. The language they spoke was a soft squawking, meaningless to the Warden's ears. He moved his head, slowly and tenderly, in hopes of getting a glimpse of Repnomar or Broz; but that slight motion was enough both to send his senses reeling again and to attract the eyes of the White People. One of them stood up, lifting something that swung like a heavy fruit in a net, and the Warden's head twinged at the sight of it.

But the Exile came hurriedly foward and stooped beside the Warden, begging him to lie still and not distress himself, and then turned back to the others with a mouthful of gabble.

'Where's the Captain?' the Warden asked gruffly, and put a careful hand to his head. There was a large lump there, sticky with blood and painful to be touched.

The Exile squatted like a frog at his side, eyeing the White People with signs of uneasiness, and explained that he thought the Captain was well enough, though he was not so sure about Broz. At this, the Warden began to heave himself up, despite the Exile's protests, and two more White People came into his range of sight. Both carried objects that looked unpleasantly like weapons, and their pallid faces did not strike the Warden as friendly. He got no further than to his knees, and knelt there dizzily for a while, holding to the Exile's right arm, (for he had long since noticed that the Exile did everything by preference with his right hand and was clumsy as a baby with the left). It was not likely he could have stood upright in any case. The White People, though not as stumpy as the Exile, were nowhere near the Warden's height, and their white-furred roof hung low over his head.

He saw (once the spinning in his head had slowed) that he was near one end of an oblong shelter – or cave, or room; he did not know how to think of it. Farther down its length a lamp was burning, making a still light in the whiteness. It would have been dizzying enough, the Warden thought, even without a broken head; for the featureless soft white, above, around, below, gave the eye nothing to grasp, and the white-clad White People moved like transparent fish in water. So that his gaze came back to the Exile in search of steadiness, and he asked again and more fiercely where the Captain was and what had happened to her.

But as the Exile was twisting up his mouth to answer, a door opened in the whiteness close beside them, and the Captain herself entered, stooped almost double to negotiate that low passage. 'High time you were awake, Lethgro,' she greeted him. 'That head of yours seems to get tenderer every time it takes a knock. And you might as well let go of his arm; he's as much a prisoner as we are.'

Indeed the Captain had been sorely worried over Lethgro's tender head, for she thought that at this rate he would not survive many more sharp knocks; but she had had more urgent worries. She herself had not been sure of surviving the fight, and had come out of it with a wrenched and broken arm to balance her damaged knee on the other side. The weapons of the White People were stones, variously tethered with thongs and nets and bags of leather, so that they could be hurled or swung and retrieved. It was one of these devices – two stones joined by a thong – that had wrapped itself around Repnomar's lifted forearm so violently that the bone had snapped, and others that had brought Broz down. She herself had not been able to do much damage, for the thick furs of the Whites had shielded them against her knife. But Broz had done better. By the time he was put out of the fight, choking and gagging with a cluster of stones around his neck, two Whites lay dead.

That, it appeared, was the problem. The White People – so the Captain optimistically believed – were not so savage as to slaughter travelers without reason. But they had hauled Broz down to the stream and thrust his head into the icy water, and only the violent yells and struggles of the Captain (whom half a dozen Whites barely sufficed to hold back) and the pleadings of the Exile in their own language had deterred them for a time. Broz now lay tightly bound in another shelter nearby, and the White People, so the

Exile said, were preparing to consider his case judicially, for they had strong laws against murder. Having settled that much, the Exile had come to this shelter to see to the Warden, and after a time the Captain had been allowed to follow.

When the Warden asked how the Exile had come to know these people and to speak their language, he answered frankly that it was they, or rather another party of them, who had received him from a roaming band of Quicksilvers in the dark and brought him to the edge of the light, where his memory first began to return to him; and that he must have spent many watches with them, for he found that he understood them passably well.

'And the good of that,' Repnomar added, 'is that we'll have an interpreter at the trial.' For Broz, it appeared, was to be tried in a court of law, or what passed for such among these savages.

Now certain of the White People began to crowd around them with signs of impatience, and the Exile said apologetically that it was time for the trial to begin. So Lethgro, with some help from the Captain, got himself to his feet, and they went out. And though the Warden, after stooping to get through the low door, straightened himself very carefully, he staggered nevertheless and jostled the Captain's wounded arm so roughly that she bit her lip to hold back a curse. They were in poor shape for fighting, she thought, if it should come to that.

They stood here (so the Warden concluded slowly, as his head steadied and he gazed around) in a city of the White People. The light was still very dim, and yet he saw well enough, for that dim light was everywhere reflected from whiteness: a sweep of level snow (for they seemed here to be in a tranquil valley, protected from the wind) and the white walls of the low buildings – furred outside, it seemed, as well as in. The Warden shivered in the chill air (it had been much warmer inside) and let himself be guided to another of the furry houses. White People were crowding into its doors from every direction, gabbling excitedly, but they made room for the Warden and the Captain (though they jostled the Exile without compunction). The Captain's face was tight with grimness and with pain. 'Come on, Lethgro,' she said, and ducked her head to enter.

This house was even longer than the one in which Lethgro had awakened, though no wider, and lit here and there down its length by the little white-flamed lamps, so that it was like a tunnel of fur. There seemed to be a door in the other end as well, and from both ends the place was filling up fast with more white fur, as people shoved and elbowed their way in. The Captain and the Warden, who could only keep their heads from rubbing the ceiling pelts by stooping, had a better view than anyone else, and could see where Broz lay like a pool of blackness midway down the room. Repnomar plowed her way through the crowd like a ship cutting through rough water, and Lethgro followed in her wake with the Exile bobbing behind him.

But when she reached the front rank, the Captain found herself blocked by a solid cordon of armed Whites, who lifted their netted stones and weighted thongs menacingly. It went against the Captain's grain to be commanded by force; but she thought it prudent for Broz's sake to make no disturbance, and stopped with as much show of docility as she could manage.

The hall was now so crowded that (the Warden guessed) there must have been more than fifty people squeezed into it, and most of the lamps were now put out – to lessen the danger of fire, the Exile said. Broz lay motionless; but his eyes were wild, and a growl rose over and over again in his throat. The Captain spoke to him, but her voice was sunk and lost in the hubbub of talk. Yet even with such a crowd, all of them yammering and excited, and packed into that low-roofed space, there was an unnatural softness to all sounds, that were as if wrapped and muffled in furry whiteness.

Now certain White People stood forward into the open space that had so far been left around Broz, and the hubbub died away. The Exile slipped under Repnomar's arm and put himself also forward, saying something in the White tongue.

'You know law, Lethgro,' the Captain said anxiously. 'What can we do?' But the Warden only grunted, being still unconvinced that any folk so uncivilized as these could have law worth mentioning.

The Whites who had stepped forward began to gabble and yammer one after the other, waving their arms and turning back and forth to address both ends of the room; and Broz, alarmed by this hullabaloo so close to him, began to struggle and rage. This in turn alarmed the speakers and the Whites of the first rows, so that some cringed backward away from him, and others raised their weapons and threatened him with cries. Things might have gone badly then and there, but the Captain by shouts and whistles was able to quiet Broz, and the Exile by much gabbling to reassure the Whites, and the proceedings continued.

These proceedings were such as to confirm the Warden in his opinion, for there seemed to be no rule of order except that whoever shouted loudest would be heard. Many of the Whites took it in turn to shove their way forward and shake their weapons over Broz, who could not be restrained from growling and snapping. The Captain stood stony, only speaking now and then to calm Broz; and this somewhat relieved Lethgro, who had feared she might precipitate a battle.

Such a suspicion was unfair, for the Captain was prepared to endure any barbarous folderol if it would get Broz free. But seeing the Whites wax hotter and hotter against Broz, and considering that she had as good a right to shout as any of them, she called out for silence in her most captainly tones, to such effect that the whole white turmoil was quiet in an instant, and Broz turned his eyes up to her hopefully.

'Tell them,' the Captain directed the Exile, 'they can listen to our side of it now.' And she began (pausing from time to time for the Exile to interpret her remarks) to explain very reasonably that Broz had only defended himself and his friends when they were set upon by strangers in their sleep, a thing any decent dog or human would do, unless lacking means or courage; and that furthermore he could not be held fully responsible in a human law court (for she thought it wise to flatter the Whites a little here), being only a dumb animal and ignorant of law.

These arguments seemed to baffle the White People for a little, and the Captain began to take heart. But after some muttered conversation the Exile reported that the Whites did not understand why she mentioned these things, which in their opinion had no bearing on the case. Broz had killed two of their people; how and why did not matter. Human, animal, or rock, he must die. And since he had killed twice, he must die twice.

At this point the Exile excused himself, saying that he was a poor interpreter, since he knew one language little and the other less, but that he truly believed he had translated correctly, and the Whites indeed meant to execute Broz not once but twice. To which the Captain replied hotly that once might be harder than they thought; and the Warden suggested in some haste that instead of translating this remark, the Exile should call for a recess.

This took some time to explain, first to the Exile and then (through him) to the White People. But this was lucky, for during the explanations the Warden had time to think of reasons for his request (which had been at first only a desperate try at postponing disaster); and the Captain, quickly seeing a new hope, joined in with vigor. The Warden asserted that it would be contrary to all law, decency, and common sense to execute a prisoner in the very place of judgement, and that the interested parties had a right to confer and to prepare a statement before final sentence was pronounced, let alone executed; while the Captain claimed her right to commune with her dog one last time – and, as she insisted, 'without all this fur in our noses.' For she felt that if they could get outside into the open air, they might find some chance of escape. Neither of them mentioned the impossibility of executing Broz twice, thinking that once would be more than sufficient. And when the Exile had conveyed these arguments at considerable length, some of the Whites began to move, opening a path through their ranks toward the far door. The Captain scooped up Broz with her one good arm and strode grim-mouthed down this narrow lane, limping badly but wasting no time. The Warden put his hand firmly on the Exile's shoulder and steered him after her; for he was determined that if he came home alive from this journey, he would come home with the Exile as his prisoner.

The outside air struck them like a plunge into river water, for it had been warm in that furred and populous hall, and even in this sheltered valley the wind was up. They had come out at the opposite end from where they went in, and the Captain stared about her eagerly, hopeful for some kind of cover. She had been feeling out Broz's bonds as she carried him, and had her fingers already into one of the knots.

This, clearly, was the edge of the little fur city. The valley opened before them, a level paleness between the bulks of the mountainsides. For a moment Repnomar thought that she was watching snow stirring in the wind; then she realized that the moving whiteness before them was alive. As far as she could see in the dimness, white forms milled like seething surf viewed through a haze. Low sounds came from them.

Some of the White People who had followed the prisoners out or gone ahead were massing around them now, swinging their stones sugggestively. But the Captain's step never faltered (except for her limp); she took three unhesitating strides to a little rise behind the door, and put Broz down on its far side, telling him to be still. Lethgro hustled the Exile forward, and they all crouched over Broz like doctors around a patient. 'What are those things?' the Captain demanded, jerking her head toward the field of moving forms.

'Sheep, maybe,' the Warden hazarded. 'Whatever they get their furs from.' And the Exile confirmed this, saying he did not know whether they could be called sheep, but that the White People reared them for food and fur; and he added that the creatures were fierce and difficult to handle, so that Whites were sometimes injured or even killed in the milking or tending of them. Every city of the Whites, he believed, had a great flock of hundreds of such beasts, penned behind fences that were made of the bones of their own kind.

Now the Warden asked him how he knew all this; and he answered that the tribe of White People he had first known had set him to tending such a flock, and it was only when he had proved inept at this that they had decided to pass him on over the Mountains. For, as he confessed in an eager whisper, he had once left a gate unfastened, so that the beasts ran loose and caused much uproar and damage.

At this, the Captain and Warden exchanged looks, and the Captain said brusquely, 'Good. You'll do it again,' before the Warden had time to inquire if he *could* do it again. But the Exile only asked when he was to do it. And the Captain answered, 'Now.'

This surprised Lethgro slightly; for with a dozen Whites gaping at them within arm's reach, he was sure she had had no chance yet to loosen Broz's bonds. But the Captain thought she was not likely to have that chance without a diversion to busy the Whites; and she thought that she could carry Broz a long way and in a considerable hurry if that was what it took to keep him alive. Besides, she had loosened one knot already.

Now the Exile suggested meekly that if the others made as if to go back to the long house, he might slip away to the gate of the sheep pen before the Whites noticed him; and this they agreed to do. After that, they would simply try to get away in the disturbance. The Warden was not happy with this, for he feared losing the Exile; but he did not argue, reflecting that there were things more important than bringing back a prisoner to the Councils of Beng and Rotl.

So they stood up again, Repnomar draping Broz over one shoulder so as to have her good hand ready to seize a weapon if the chance arose. 'What will you have for your dinner in Rotl, Lethgro?' she asked loudly, and they began to discuss this with some vigor, turning back toward the door, so as to lead off the Whites' attention from the Exile.

But no sooner had the Exile begun to edge away toward the penned beasts than four or five of the White People closed up around him, nudging him back toward the house door, and one of them gripped him by the arm and threatened him with a stone. The Warden's heart sank.

But the Captain wheeled suddenly, with a whistle that made everyone within yards of her jerk and Broz almost bounce from her shoulder, and waved her free arm with a violent downward motion. Lethgro, not waiting to find out what the result of this behavior might be, turned back and struck the White who held the Exile, a good round-armed blow to the face, and with his other hand snatched the White's thonged stone as it fell.

Before the Captain's whistle had died away a flash of blackness burst like a lightning stroke upon the Whites around the Exile. The Exile ducked away; shrill cries went up from the Whites; and the Warden, pausing only to use his stone on a convenient head, leaped to the end wall of the long house and set his back against its door. He looped the thong of the stone around his hand, and prepared to swing it whenever the Whites outside should recover enough to follow him.

It was one of Repnomar's crows that had plunged to the attack, and clearly it was an uncanny thing to the White People, for they scattered from it, flailing wildly with arms and weapons and shrieking in panic. Repnomar herself took advantage of this diversion to work at Broz's bonds, and got his front legs free quickly enough. But before she could finish with the knot that held his hind legs (not much helped in her work by Broz, for in his impatience he was lunging and scrabbling in the snow) one of the Whites took note of what she was doing and rushed at her, swinging a heavy stone in a net.

A roar burst from the Warden's throat, and he hurled his stone, thong and all; for he knew that Repnomar, with one bad arm and one bad knee, would be at grave disadvantage in a fight. He was not skilled in the throwing of such weapons, but he had a strong arm and an archer's eye, and his throw was good enough to tangle the White's legs. The Captain lunged forward to wrestle the sprawling White for either or both weapons; but before that contest had lasted long, Broz by much kicking had gotten himself free from the last of his bonds and joined in, so that Repnomar had all she could do to prevent him from killing a third White and so making himself liable to three deaths.

Meanwhile the Warden was having his own difficulties,

for two of the outside Whites had turned their attention to him (unarmed as he now was) and those within were pushing and pounding against the door. He was a good deal bigger than either of his assailants, but the stones they whirled were formidable weapons, and he could not move from the door without letting loose a horde of others. He could only duck and dodge, trying to protect his head and to grab at the whistling thongs. Indeed, nothing saved him but the crow, which left the White it had been chasing to fly in the faces of these two; and that might not have saved him for long, but for the new uproar that now burst out. The Warden lowered his arms and straightened his back against the bulging door. 'Not sheep,' he said decidedly.

The beasts stampeding toward them were not clear to see in the dimness, but it was clear enough that they were like no sheep he knew. These were not docile pack animals but uncouth and dangerous-looking brutes, rearing and bellowing as they came, tossing their pointed horns and showing great broad teeth like carpenter's chisels. One blessing, as the Warden had time to note, was that they were not very big – rather less than the size of packsheep and probably no higher than his knee. Another was that unless they were truly bloodthirsty, they might not pause in their wild rush to attack a large person plastered tightly against the end of a building. With this in mind he called loudly, 'Over here, Repnomar!'

The Captain, with a firm grip on the back of Broz's neck, was already hobbling toward him, for she had had the same thought. The crow, seeming to think it had done its duty, settled with a squawk on her shoulder. Indeed all the Whites within sight had turned to meet the onrushing beasts. 'Move over, Lethgro,' the Captain said, 'and give me a share of that door.'

This the Warden was glad to do. The door of the long house – like the rest of it, so far as they could tell – was only a framework between two layers of skins; and under the shoving of the crowd within, not only the door but the whole end wall was bowed and bulging like a sail. They leaned hard against it, bracing their legs (a painful business for the Captain).

The Whites, who had cowered and fled from a single flapping bird, were less dismayed by a herd of rampaging brutes. Indeed, they went to meet them, hooting loudly and waving their arms. But the beasts hooted more loudly still, and rolled on like a storm, sweeping around the Whites as a storm sweeps around rocks in shoal waters. Broz burst into wild barking, and the Captain raised the stone she had wrested from the White.

Now the beasts were upon them. One after another, the oncoming brutes feinted at them with their horns and veered away to race along one side or the other of the long house – many to the left and more to the right, so that the house was an island in a river of galloping animals. But a few charged straight at them, aiming their horns maliciously. The Captain swung her weapon; the Warden, taking his cue from the Whites, waved his arms and yelled; Broz dodged and lunged; and the crow flew shrieking above them. Perhaps all this blackness (for in the dim light and the surrounding whiteness, the clothes and faces of Warden and Captain showed very dark) looked dauntingly strange to the beasts. However it was, without exception they swerved at the last possible moment, tossing up their heads with wild hoots, and merged again into the stampede.

The Whites in the midst of that moving mass were striving to steer it, edging the current of beasts away from the houses. One of them grasped an animal's horns, throwing it down with a twist, and the whole stampede skewed away, farther to the right. But another beast, with larger horns and a crest of long hair between them, gored a White in passing, so that blood ran dark on white fur.

Now two or three things happened at once. The Warden caught sight of a dark spot on the white field before them, which he recognized as the Exile escaping behind the beasts. The Captain became aware that Whites were emerging from the other end of the long house (though the door at her back still bulged and shook with pummeling and pushing), where they seemed to be turning the tide of the stampede. And on that, she stepped aside, almost into the path of the beasts, and jerked at the Warden's arm, saying, 'Let them out, Lethgro. Quick!'

Lethgro, with these inducements, did not hesitate. He yanked the door broad open by the thong handle that had been cutting into his back. The door brought with it a furry tumble of Whites, those ahead stumbling or sprawling into the path of the beasts, and those behind rushing into them before they could stop themselves.

But neither the Warden nor the Captain stayed to witness this confusion. As if with one mind they plunged into the lesser stream of animals on their left, which by now had thinned to a scatter of galloping beasts. There they were able to dodge their way between the horns, spreading confusion of their own, and reach the open snow beyond.

This was none too soon. The flood of beasts had almost spent itself. The Warden pointed, and they ran with long strides through the snow, circling behind the herd, the Captain cursing silently at every jolt to her knee. Where the animals had run, the snow was trampled hard, and in short time they caught up with the panting Exile.

There was little need for conversation. Before them, the land rose steeply, mounting ever darker out of sight, while still farther above there was a lightness in the sky – not the redness of sick mountains, but the wholesome light of clouds. Without a word, they set their course upward. In a little while the Exile's foot splashed into a stream, and they followed this gladly, thinking it would bring them by the swiftest route to some nearby pass. But it brought them first into dense thickets of thorny low brush, so that to travel at all they must wade along in the stream.

From below them in the valley came a distant hubbub – the Whites dealing with their flock. It seemed to the Captain that these people, barbarous though they might be, were not a very savage lot. In the dim whiteness of the valley, the fugitives must have shown like normal crows on a white sand beach. Stampede or no stampede, some pursuers could surely have followed them. And whatever lead they had, the Captain reflected, was likely to lessen fast. The White People were at home in this country; no doubt they hunted these thickets and streams, and could make better time here than any stranger, let alone a limping one. So that it was some comfort to think that if they had been dead set on punishing Broz, they could have been close on his heels by now.

The stream brought them presently to the end of the thickets, but only to offer them a worse problem, for it poured here in cold sheets down a sheer cliff face. Now the crow showed itself useful, flying back and forth above the cliff while they groped along its base in the wet, and calling them hastily to an easier slope where another stream ran through a gully. This too was overgrown with brush, by which they helped themselves along in the steepest places, grunting and swearing as they grasped the thorny stems. Between their own noises they heard what seemed like a dainty music, for the mountain tinkled everywhere with the flowing of streams; and from below still came, distant and soft, the cries of the White People and their beasts. A fine rain began, noiseless itself and yet muffling all sounds. They climbed steadily, favoring their wounds as well as they could, until they came out on a saddle of flat rock between heights. The Warden took a deep breath and nodded toward what lay before them. 'Home,' he said.

22
Down

Home was perhaps an exaggeration. But it was clear to the Warden (if to no one else) that from here onward they would be moving down the light side of the Mountains, and in their lightest season. He was so warmed by this knowledge that a great smile spread across his face, and kept bursting out again when he had forced his features into a dignified expression. He had not much considered his dignity in the dark; but now that he had traveled one side of the world and more than half the other, the distance from the top of the Mountains to Sollet Castle seemed scarcely more than a step, and he felt his office about him like a familiar garment.

Before them, the mountain fell away in dark folds and dimly lit ridges. The rocks where they stood were crusted with mossy growths, some hard and some spongy, and low brush clung to the slopes below. Right and left in front of them, other mountains rose, shutting out the view; but straight ahead they could see into a landscape of misty light. Here in the pass, the rain had changed to soft snow that melted on their faces, and the wind chilled them through; so in a little while they limped down a slope littered with broken rock, in search of shelter. But before they had gone far, a loud squawking stopped them, and the second crow (which they had not seen since before they met the White People in the dark) came with stately steps around a boulder. The Captain greeted it with a whoop of joy, whereupon it turned and paced back the way it had come, still calling.

So they followed, and the crow (to the Captain's great

pride and pleasure) led them to a spot where huge flakes and blocks cracked from the mountain's face lay tumbled together. Three or four of these, leaning heavily against each other, made a shelter large enough for all of them to creep into, with a raised floor that was even dry, though frosty. Here they settled themselves with so many groans that the Captain threw back her head and laughed. 'A fine crew we are, Lethgro! I with a bad arm and a bad leg, you with a broken head, and Broz with a hornet's nest of White People after him! But at least the crows are fit enough to keep us on course.'

Indeed they were a wretched lot, soaked through, shivering with cold, unsteady from their wounds, and weak from hunger. But they took much comfort from the light before them, and some warmth from huddling together in the shelter. And now the Exile brought forth a great chunk of cheese from under his shirt, confessing that he had got it from the White People (though it was not clear whether this was by gift or by theft). So they ate and made merry, and the Captain was only restrained from singing by the reminder that there might be Whites on their trail. This, however, none of them believed likely, so that they agreed to sleep where they were, for they sorely needed rest, and thought they were not likely to find better shelter. But they no longer had any rope with which to bind the Exile, and on this account the Warden would not allow him to stand watch, and insisted that he must be crowded into the back of the shelter, farthest from the entrance.

The Warden himself took the first turn on guard. He was glad of a little time alone, for he had a trouble he did not want to share with the others. This was the state of his head, which was alarmingly liable to fail him at odd moments. More than once in their climb by the gully he had found himself grasping a thornbush as a drowning swimmer might blindly grasp a stalk of kelp, with no least notion of up or down, left or right, and unsure if he had clung there for an hour or a split second. He counted on the light to steady him; for it seemed to him that he had been dark-sick, as ship passengers were sometimes Soll-sick. But he moved his head very cautiously, trying out different positions, of which some gave him unpleasant pangs; and after a time he leaned his head upon his hands and began to pray very earnestly to the gods of healing.

Whether it was by the action of gods or of sleep (when his turn came for that) he felt much steadier when he woke again, and glad that he had not confessed his weakness to the others. Now they strengthened themselves with a little more of the cheese (of which enough still remained for two or three more meals if they were frugal) and set about choosing their route through the Mountains. The crows were less useful for this than Repnomar had hoped, for they did not well understand the difficulties of land travelers, and would have led them across chasms and down sheer cliffs. Without a rope, they had to choose their path circumspectly; and without weapons or other hunting gear, their most urgent need was for food. So for the first few watches they made only slow progress, husbanding their cheese and feeling their way from one easy slope to another, backtracking often, but always drinking the light as if it were bodily nourishment. Then in their third traveling watch, the Warden at last found dry tinder, and when they camped he contrived to light a fire at which they warmed themselves luxuriously, and the Exile wept with relief. That same watch they caught fish in a pool, and so feasted.

Now the Exile, though grateful for the warmth and the food, grew ever more despondent; and once when the Captain had gone ahead with Broz to scout out the shape of the land, he began to plead frankly with the Warden to let him go. For he claimed that unless he could get back to his lost devices and send a message to his people, the world was in grave danger.

This made the Warden's head ache painfully; for it confirmed his worst fears and yet left him in cruel uncertainty. It seemed likelier to him that the Exile's message would call down danger upon them from the clouds rather than fend it off; but the little man's ugly, earnest face was so pitiful that it was hard to call him a liar out and out. The Warden told himself that in all his years of experience he had never found there was more profit in listening to wild tales and fancies than in following clear duty and common sense. But he was not easy in his mind, and asked the Exile repeatedly what this danger was. And since the Exile seemed unable or unwilling to explain this, saying often that his people meant no harm to this world but were yet a danger to it, they made little headway.

All this was heavily on Lethgro's mind when he took his turn on guard at their next camp. He had built his fire in the arrowhead-shaped cleft between two boulders, laying a roof of brush across the top of the cleft for protection against the weather. Repnomar and Broz slept beside him at the broad end, and the Exile in a doleful heap on the other side of the fire.

It came to the Warden, as he sat brooding, that what he should have asked the Exile was, 'What message would you send?' and he stood up suddenly, with those words on his lips.

When he came to himself, after what seemed a long time of blackness, he felt as if he had drifted back to a past hour, one he would have liked to forget. Nearby he heard a soft gabbling and the growls of Broz; and when he opened one eye he saw white fur, so that he shut it again promptly. But in a few moments he had braced himself, so that he opened both eyes a little way and saw all the worst of what was happening.

As before, white-furred figures crowded near, some with weapons at the ready. At the mouth of the shelter, Repnomar stood over Broz, stooping to hold him back from hasty action. But from where he lay just outside, the Warden could neither see nor hear the Exile. He sat up cautiously (causing two or three Whites to draw back their arms for a swing) and moved his head slowly to take in the scene; then he lunged to his feet, bellowing a shout, for he had caught sight of the Exile already some yards up the slope from them and moving away as fast as his short legs could carry him.

It would not have surprised Lethgro if another stone had cracked against his skull (and this time likely cracked it open for good). Indeed, he had already lifted his arms to protect his head as he staggered after the Exile, with no better hope than that Repnomar and Broz and the crows might make good use of whatever time his noisiness had bought them. He heard the whistling flight of a flung weapon and jumped aside, clumsily enough; but almost before he could realize that he had not been hit, he saw the flying thongs wrap themselves around the Exile's legs, so that he stumbled and fell heavily. The Warden did not hesitate, but raced on up the slope, getting his hand on the Exile's shoulder before the little man had gotten to his knees. 'Are these your friends, too?' he asked sternly.

The Exile managed a smile of sorts and said nothing, having the breath well knocked out of him by the sudden fall. The Warden untangled the weapon from his legs as quickly as he could, feeling for broken bones and finding none. All the while he shot glances downslope to see what the Whites were doing. But they only stood watching, talking among themselves; while the Captain, with one hand still on Broz, seemed trying to join in their discussion. So the Warden shepherded the Exile back toward them, hefting the weapon in his hand. This was not a single thong but a fan of half a dozen, knotted together at the center and weighted with stones at all the ends; and Lethgro thought somewhat wistfully that if they came through the present trouble it would be a good weapon for hunting.

He noticed now that several dark bundles lay scattered behind the Whites, and for the first time it occurred to him that these people might be hunters or traders who had chanced upon them, rather than pursuers. Certainly they showed no special interest in Broz, other than to keep well clear of him. They squinted their pale eyes and screwed up their pale faces, so that they looked mildly displeased by everything they saw, and they gabbled incessantly to each other and swung their weapons casually from hand to hand.

When the Warden and the Exile approached, one White stepped forward with outstretched hands. The Warden took this as a welcoming gesture, and nodded and smiled graciously in response, as he might have done at Sollet Castle. But the White muttered restively and waved one hand up and down, and the Exile whispered that this was the owner of the weapon that had felled him. So the Warden, though it pained him, gave back the weapon with a good grace; for he thought he would rather make friends with these people than fight them.

'If they want something from us, Lethgro,' the Captain greeted him, 'I can't tell what it is.' She had feared at first, when Broz had waked her with an urgent snarl and she had seen Lethgro lying fallen and still and the Whites muttering over him, that what they wanted was Broz at least, and perhaps more. But they had seemed only curious, pointing and snuffling and making questioning noises; and when the Exile, after some quiet conversation with them (and ignoring the Captain's questions) had hurried off, they had watched with interest but with no show of excitement. Now they clustered around him, laughing cheerfully, and the one whose weapon had struck him down patted him on the head like a puppy or a child. Others gestured toward the cleft between the boulders, and soon they had all settled themselves there. The Whites, far from taking up position at the mouth of the cleft where they could keep the others penned within, crowded as far back under the Warden's thatching as they could manage, and the Exile explained that the bright light tired their eyes.

The Captain was glad to hear this, for in fact the light was very dim, and she thought that if they could once leave this set of Whites behind, they were not likely to encounter more where the light was brighter. 'Find out what they're doing here and what they want of us,' she told the Exile peremptorily

To this he answered at once that they were gathering fodder for their animals, and that it was the custom of the White People to visit this side of the Mountains for that purpose, since otherwise they would not be able to raise such large flocks; adding that he thought these Whites had not heard of Broz and his killings, whether because they came from a different tribe or because they had been here at their gathering when it happened.

Meanwhile some of the Whites reached into their furs and brought out chunks of cheese and what seemed to be dried meat, offering this fare very sociably; so that the Warden got out what bits of fish remained from their last meal, and they shared alike. The Exile, after more gabbling, and considerable merriment from the Whites, reported that this crew of gatherers had been following them for some few watches, curious to see such uncouth strangers on their mountainside; and when they saw the Warden fall, they had naturally come near to learn what was the matter. And he admitted ruefully that he had begged them to look after his friends (meaning the Warden and the Captain) and taken to his heels. This they had let him do without argument. But when the Warden had revived and shown himself so sternly bent on retrieving the Exile, they had obligingly struck him down – and done so, as the Exile himself pointed out, gently enough; for he knew their skill with these weapons, and was certain they could have struck him dead.

Indeed these Whites seemed a jolly lot and without sign of malice; and though they were shy of Broz, they were content to share their rations with him, so that after a little he ceased to snarl, and lay down peaceably at the Captain's feet. Now the Exile tried (so he said) to learn if these people were from the same city of the Whites where they had been held prisoner; but they could only tell him they were from a place with many fur houses and many beasts on the dark side of the Mountains, and he could not make out from their description of its bearings whether it was the same place or a different one. And after a little more conversation, during which the Whites spoke with some vehemence, the Exile reported that when he asked if there had ever been a double killing in their city they had answered yes, years ago; and the murderer had been first drowned and then beheaded, so as to satisfy the spirits of both victims, who might otherwise have made trouble. So that it was clear that if these folk came from the city where Broz had so nearly suffered the same punishment, they had left beforehand and not yet heard the news.

'It's too bad we don't know for certain,' the Captain said thoughtfully. 'But in case it *is* the same town, I think we'd better send them a message.'

'Better not,' the Warden said uneasily. 'What we want now is to slip away with no fuss.'

'Right!' the Captain agreed. 'And whichever way we slip, let them think we went a different way. I'll leave it to you, Lethgro; you know the Mountains.'

Now, the Warden saw the sense of this; and seeing also that the Exile was about to begin gabbling again, he stood up as quickly as he dared move his head, suggesting loudly that Repnomar and Broz and the Exile should go look for fish. At the same time he invited the Whites, with a friendly gesture, to come with him.

This they did, as soon as they understood; and while Repnomar, with a cheerful whistle, hustled Broz, the Exile, and both crows off toward a stream on their left, the Warden led the White People to the right where the brow of a cliff gave a clear view of the Mountains ahead. Here by much pointing and motions of his hands he tried to show the course they might follow into the light. The Whites squinted and gabbled and pointed in their turn, seeming to suggest other routes, all of which the Warden rejected with vehemence (though in fact he noted them well). But presently they tired of this and turned away, blinking and rubbing their eyes, to pick up their faggots of twigs and leaves and mosses. The Warden walked with them to the stream where the others were splashing with sticks in the cold water, trying to drive fish into the shallows; and after helping with this sport for a little, the Whites headed upslope along the stream, pausing often to pick twigs from the low brush or gather handfuls of moss.

So the Warden stirred up his fire and they cooked their fish, watching the Whites until they were out of sight among the crags (for even in the dimness their white furs showed for a long distance). Only the crows were inclined to resume their interrupted sleep; all the others were too much aroused by this encounter, and Warden Lethgro in particular had unfinished business. 'Now,' he said sternly, licking the last crumbs of fish from his fingers and fixing the Exile with a steady glare; 'what message would you send?'

The Exile's eyes opened wide for a moment at this direct question; but he answered modestly that he only meant to report to his people that he was alive and that all was well here. This struck the Warden as unlikely, and he asked why this message should be so urgently needed to save the world from harm. To which the Exile answered even more meekly and even more earnestly that unless his people received such a report, they would come to investigate. And though he repeated that they would not come in war or in anger, he seemed strangely doleful concerning the consequences of such a visit.

Here the Captain demanded an explanation, and had to be told of the Exile's plea that he be allowed to send his message. At which she laughed, saying to the Exile, with what the Warden considered unseemly levity, 'If you were so eager, what stopped you from sending it under our noses? The Warden and I could no more tell what you were doing with your devices than Broz could read a letter.' And the Exile confessed that he would gladly have done so, but said that it was not so easy as she seemed to think. For since no one could know how long it would take him and his friend to perform their mission, it had been agreed that they would stay in touch with their ship by sending various signals at various times. So long as those signals were sent often enough, the ship would stay away, considering that all was well and the mission proceeding. But if there were no signal for a certain time, the ship would come to search for them, landing at the place where he and his friend had first been set down – unless (and here the Exile's face knotted grimly) he had sent a message naming another time and place of meeting. Such a message, he said, must be in his own voice, not simply a signal that some other might have given. And while it was true that he had already sent off a few of the signals ('I should have known it!' muttered the Warden), yet, being so closely watched, he had not found opportunity to send a message in his own voice. This had not troubled him too much till very recently, when there came back to him one more of the memories that the Quicksilver poison had washed so long ago from his mind.

'And that was – ?' urged the Warden, for the Exile had fallen silent.

And the Exile raised his eyes with a melancholy look and said that he remembered now that if he did not send a voice message very soon, his ship would come to look for him, no matter how many signals it received. And when the Captain asked what prevented him now from doing so, he answered that he had only one device that could send such a message, and it lay somewhere in the snow at the foot of the cliff where they had crashed. The Captain had listened with such interest that now the Warden stood up hastily, saying, 'Come here, Repnomar,' and drew her aside, leaving the Exile crouched by the fire with Broz and the crows. 'We're not going back,' he said firmly. 'And we're not letting him go.'

'You're right, Lethgro,' the Captain said. 'Though if we were in better shape you'd be wrong. I wouldn't bet a turnip on our chances of coming through another season in the dark alive – even without a tribe of White People looking for Broz's head. But once we've mended our bones and put some meat back on them, we'd be fools if we didn't go back with him to this meeting place of his and see what comes out of the clouds.'

Now the Warden, who at first had been pleasantly surprised by her ready agreement, was perturbed by her notion of foolishness. But neither of them had strength or inclination for arguments that could be put off till later; and after scanning the upper slopes without catching a glimpse of white fur anywhere, they called the others, bundled up their firewood (for dry wood was scarce in this season) and started down the mountain. They took a far different route from the one the Warden had pointed out to the White People.

The light grew ever brighter, and the landscape more wholesome to view; but only Broz and the crows took much pleasure in this, for the others were sick with pain and weariness and long hunger, and consumed by their own worries. Only now and again Repnomar tried to speak of what a great thing it would be to talk with people from beyond the clouds, and how they and their giant flying pods might help to rescue the *Mouse* and her crew from the waterfall of the Dreeg, and of what cargoes might be carried in such pods. But the Warden would not hear such talk; and the Exile, with a sickly smile, told her that such things were never as simple as they seemed – which somewhat ruffled her, for it was like being scolded for ignorance by a child.

In spite of the light, it was not easy going, with frequent rains that swelled the streams to torrents and built and tore away dams of mud and rubble. More often than not, they could build no fire. Their course was a limping zigzag, down one slope and up another, often turning back to find an easier route. But Broz and the crows fattened on frogs and fish and small game of many sorts, and frolicked in the growing light. And after a time the land eased; and the Warden, his chest heaving in a sigh, pronounced that he knew this country. For they had come to the headwaters of the Sollet.

23
Home

It was (so they told each other afterwards, with grim laughter) a marvel how quickly they could all agree together when the need was on them. What they had to decide, and swiftly, was whether to make themselves known to the people of this country – the loggers and shippers who harvested the forests of the Upper Sollet – or to try to reach Sollet Castle unobserved. In favor of the first was that they were in sad condition bodily, needing food and rest and doctoring; but against it was that they knew nothing of what had been going on in all the time since they had sailed out of Beng harbor with an inspector for the Council of Beng in pursuit, and natural prudence made them uneager to step forward before they knew how the land lay. Besides, now that they were coming into the great woods, living would be easier, for the Warden was no mean forester, and there was plenty of food and fuel and shelter for those who knew how to take them. As for the Exile, he clearly hoped for anything rather than to be returned to the power of the League. So with little argument they determined to keep their distance from the towns and logging camps along the river, and to work their way through the woods and so downstream until they came to Sollet Castle, where they could be assured of a welcome from the Warden's own people.

The rain fell, the wind blew, and every slope tinkled and gurgled with flowing water; for this was the season of Streamrise, when the melting snows filled and overfilled all the tributary streams that fed into the Sollet. But if the going was no more comfortable, it was far healthier, for with snares and deadfalls and woven wicker fishtraps they caught all the game they could eat, pausing for a few watches at a time to hunt and cook and then moving on at a stiff pace until they needed meat again. The forest was bursting with life, all abloom in the light and the wet. There were lush herbs and bulbs in plenty, and the early fruits, and in the dense woodland the Warden could usually find something dry enough for a fire to kindle on, so that they ate well; but their clothes were no more than wet and filthy rags. The Captain was for filching a few items from some of the logging camps they passed; but this the Warden would not allow. When the rain ceased, they began to be in better temper, all except the Exile, and the Captain spoke longingly of the speed they could have been making on the Sollet with any decent boat and sail. But the Warden told her that at this season the Sollet was too wild for any but the ships built specially for it, and that even they came to grief often enough.

They no longer allowed the Exile to take a turn on guard, for he was clearly too restless to trust. He tried privately to tell sometimes the Captain, sometimes the Warden, the alarming things that would happen if his people came; but the Warden did not believe him, and the Captain, far from being alarmed, listened eagerly and said that she would be glad to meet his shipmates. So he gave it up and trudged in silence.

As storm waves sink slowly into a level calm, so the wooded hills died away to the rolling forest land of the Middle Sollet. The trees and underbrush changed, and with them the birds and beasts and the very feel of the wind; and the Warden, who hour by hour grew easier with the world and walked with a more commanding step, now felt himself so much at home that he threw aside all concealment and led them boldly down a forest path. For, though trees still hid the castle, they had come into its very grounds, and anyone they met here would be of his own household.

But they met no one till the trail brought them to a thinning of the woods, and they saw the towers of the castle, and the lawns around it, and a sentry strolling along the path that circled the lawns. The Warden strode forward into the open and hailed the sentry, who whipped out an arrow from her quiver as she turned, and had it well nocked to the bowstring before she recognized who it was that had hailed her (and that only by his wardenly bearing, for the people of Sollet Castle were not accustomed to see their Warden disheveled and dirty and in rags). But she lowered her bow and came to him hastily, exclaiming in a low voice that he had best hide himself again among the trees. 'For,' she said, 'you and that Exile and Captain Repnomar of the *Mouse* are all declared outlaws, and a reward offered by the Councils of Beng and Rotl for your heads.'

The Second Turn

Windfall was a short season. And Windfall ended with Windrise, when once more the Sollet Mountains tilted out of daylight into darkness, and this world ranged farthest from the sun that its peoples had never seen. Cold air would pour over the barrier of the mountains, and people of the light side (you could not call it bright) would smile at each other and say, 'The winds are rising.' The winds of the year: *it was a graceful phrase, as so much else in this world was graceful – and most of all, its swift, strong, generous, stubborn peoples.*

Windfall was a short season; it would be over soon. And when the winds rose on the Sollet, they would be rising also on the Dreeg. Not so strong nor so steady, nor with such an abrupt onset; for when Sollet Mountains were darkest, the nameless mountains beyond the Dreeg were most nearly light, and there was no sudden spilling of the cold air dammed behind them. But that air was at its coldest – aphelion was the chillest season everywhere on this chill and temperate world – and the mountains of that limb were lower. Currents of darkside air would begin to flow through the low passes into the relative warmth of the marsh country, and the ponderous wheel of air would roll again.

And soon it would be too late. That was the thought that would drive you, rousing you out of sleep or mixing your sleep with sad and ugly dreams, so that again and again you lifted the mats that hid you and lay watching the banks creep by, willing the boat to go faster. It would be too late – how soon? You could not know. It might be too late already. It might be there had never been a chance.

24
Decisions of the Council of Rotl

The Council of Beng, as usual, was in less than full agreement with the Council of Rotl. The question was raised, as it often was, whether the benefits of the League were truly greater than the disadvantages, certain councilors protesting that the will of Rotl must not be allowed to outweigh the good of Beng. But the consensus, as always, was that prosperity depended on doing what had brought prosperity heretofore, and that to break the League after so many years would risk irritating the gods of Rotl and all the Coast beyond. Besides, in this particular instance Rotl was very reluctantly agreeing to follow the suggestion of Beng, so that some might claim (for once) that the shoe was on the other foot.

But others retorted that Rotl's reluctance was only another sign of Rotl's pride, seeing that ex-Warden Lethgro happened to be a native of Rotl.

In truth the Council of Rotl had been most unwilling to believe that Lethgro had so far betrayed their trust as to abet the flight and escape of that sinister Exile from a land unknown. Long after the evidence was clear before them, several councilors maintained he had been a victim of that Captain Repnomar whose impiety was notorious up and down the Coast. But at last they had been brought to sign the decree of outlawry, only insisting that a larger reward be offered for Lethgro alive than for his head, and adjoining a proclamation that invited him to give himself up and implied a hope of pardon. Naturally there were no such concessions for Repnomar, who enjoyed the protection of no god and had assaulted the representative of a Council.

Something that weighed with both Councils, and pushed the Council of Rotl to issue its tardy decree at last, was that the past year's weather had been decidedly poor. Windrise had been early and fierce; the Rains had been longer than usual; Streamrise had been disastrous, with such heavy snowmelt in the Mountains that there had been flooding all along the Sollet and the web of canals that spread out from the river on each side through the Lower Sollet country; and Windfall, far from bringing relief, had brought drought to the streaming fields. Elderly folk claimed that it was the worst year since the Great Floods they remembered from ninety years ago. Which had required much anxious negotiation with the gods and extensive rebuilding of the canal system, whence the League had had its beginnings. It seemed clear that the gods were displeased again; and the likeliest cause was the escape of the Exile, with the clear assistance of Captain Repnomar and the probable connivance of ex-Warden Lethgro.

Now that Windrise was once more approaching, most people agreed that the weather had returned to normal. And the new Warden of Sollet Castle, a person of gravity and with excellent contacts among the Sollet shippers, reported good progress toward a revised agreement on the ever-vexed question of log tolls.

So that all in all, this year promised to be better than last. But there was annoyance here and there along the Coast, among people who had been accustomed to do business with Captain Repnomar of the *Mouse* (who, they said, must be a skillful captain indeed to have succeeded so long without the help of any god). And there was regret in Rotl and along the Middle and Upper Sollet, for Warden Lethgro had been well liked and well respected, while the new warden was respected at most.

It was generally supposed in all these places, except by those who knew Repnomar, that Captain, Warden, and

Exile alike were long since drowned in the Soll. No one between the Soll and the Mountains (with the exception of three or four people at Sollet Castle) would have expected to find them floating down the Sollet in a high-boarded dinghy with a load of nuts and treenails.

There was little likelihood of anyone recognizing Lethgro, shaggy and weatherbeaten as he was now, and dressed in the rough garments of a Sollet drifter. Repnomar's transformation was not so striking, for a ship's captain is weatherbeaten enough in the first place, and on the Lower Sollet there was more chance of encountering folk who knew her. Therefore she wore a scarf that muffled most of her face, and lay low whenever they found themselves in heavy traffic. Broz, who was as well known as the Captain, had had his tail dipped in black dye, hiding the white tip, and so was free to show himself. But there was no disguising the Exile, who must therefore lie hidden under the mats that covered the cargo, bedded among the nuts and pegs.

They tied up, when they could, under the banks of islands and sandbars to give themselves (and especially the Exile) a little relief, for they could not risk landing elsewhere – least of all near the canal mouths, where there was always much business, with Sollet ships anchored close inshore and unloading their goods into canal boats that would carry them left and right through the flat countryside. The crows fared worst of all, being stowed inside a basket and never released. Lethgro had suggested leaving the crows behind, as a hindrance and a hazard (for he feared they might draw attention by their squawking) but the Captain had answered shortly, 'I may have to sail somebody else's ship, but I'll have my own crows to work with.'

For what they planned was to hire a ship in either Beng or Rotl and take to the Soll again. Warden Lethgro, by virtue of his office, had been a wealthy man; and it proved lucky for him now in more ways than one that he had been a good master to his household, for not only did some of them bring clothes and other needful things to the fugitives and contrive to find them a boat, but one of his former guards, on Lethgro's own instructions, found and brought to him the secret money-box to which he still carried the key.

They had debated deeply in the woods. Perhaps, Lethgro thought later, he would have argued differently if he had known the full text of the Council of Rotl's decree. But, believing that they were all condemned without appeal, it was easy for the three of them to agree that their only hope was to keep themselves secret till they could get beyond the reach of the Councils. They might have turned back upstream and sought safety among the loggers and woodworkers of the Upper Sollet; but Lethgro held that the power of the League ran too strong even there. As he put it, 'We were wise enough not to show ourselves there before, and we'd be utter fools to do it now.'

Here the Exile had begun to speak with all the stunted eloquence he could command, begging them, since they were outlawed by their own people, to help him with his mission. For he said that if he could find his gear and send his message, he would ask for help for them too.

'Help?' Lethgro retorted. 'Not long ago you were trying to scare us with this ship of yours and all the harm your people would do unless you kept them away. And now you want us to believe that they can help us?'

The Exile answered yes, that was what he wanted them to believe, explaining that the harm would come if his people arrived without knowing his whereabouts and set off to search for him; and that no such danger was likely if he was able to talk to them first in his own voice.

Here the Captain asked if his people could help her take

the *Mouse* off the waterfall of the Dreeg; and when he said yes, her mind was made up. And Lethgro, who a few seasons past would have turned away in horror from such a proposition, nodded his head brusquely and said that this time they would know what supplies to take on their journey.

First they had talked of going back the way they had come, up the Sollet and over the Mountains. But the Castle sentry they had first seen, who brought them news and food and what else she could, told them that the new Warden had sent armed parties upriver to search for them, offering rewards through all the villages and logging camps; and then there would be the White People to deal with. Besides, the Exile's devices lay scattered in the snow where they had fallen (if they had not been picked up by Whites or other savages); and he now told them that it would be much easier to find the gear he had left in a safe place in the country of the Quicksilvers. For, as he confessed with some embarrassment, he had already performed a good part of his mission, leaving devices ready to send word of such matters as wind and snow, and a speaking device with them; when he first flew away from the others in his pods. The Captain was pleased at this, saying they had better follow the route they had taken the first time, and visit the *Mouse* on their way. Indeed she grew very cheerful, for, as she said, 'If we can't get the *Mouse* off, this time around, we may at least find a way to bring off the crew, and we can use their help for the rest of the journey.'

Thus it was that before many watches had passed they were drifting down the Sollet in a dinghy, like many another crew of small traders carrying enough forest products to pay their way back with a load of cloth or leather goods. Such people Lethgro hailed affably, exchanging small talk while the Captain slept under mats or sculled with an oar in the bows, her scarf around her face. This was how he heard the details of the Council of Rotl's decree, and learned that there might be a pardon waiting for him, at least in Rotl. But he did not see how he could save his own head except at the expense of Repnomar's and the Exile's, unless he was to hide himself till they were safely gone; and neither of these prospects suited him. For if there must be talking to these people from beyond the clouds, he did not mean to leave it to the Exile and Repnomar alone.

Next to being recognized, the worst hazard on this voyage was being run down by the great Sollet ships and lografts. It was for this reason that small boats like the dinghy generally stuck close to shore (except at certain bends, where the current could trap a boat between a ship's side and the bank). For this reason, too – among others – the many-oared patrol ships of the League moved here and there through the river traffic, warning captains and log drivers and sometimes assessing fines for unsafe navigation. These vessels, of course, they did their best to stay well clear of.

It was strange to Lethgro to be seeing the Lower Sollet from this level rather than from the deck of a great ship, with farms and pasturelands sweeping by on either side like the pictures in a book; and hardly less strange to Repnomar, who had not been upriver from Beng for years and had all but forgotten the world of the Sollet. The result of this was that she enjoyed her voyage mightily, and said with a laugh that if she had known there was so much to see on this side of the Soll, she might never have been tempted to cross to the other. At which Lethgro laughed more heavily and said it was late in the game for prudence.

But it was a short voyage. Windfall was perhaps the best traveling season for small rivercraft; for the current was at its swiftest and the light breezes strong enough for their little sails. So the dinghy clipped along at a rate that pleased them all.

But when the wooden towers of Beng came in sight, with their carved and painted balconies looking over the water, Lethgro's heart smote against his ribs, for here they must risk their lives more openly by trying to buy or hire a ship under the noses of the Council of Beng. He waked Repnomar, and she sat up and gazed very soberly at the city. 'Better me than you, Lethgro,' she said.

'They'll know you on the waterfront,' Lethgro objected.

'And they'll know you anywhere,' Repnomar answered. 'You can pass on the Sollet, Lethgro, but not face to face in a town where you've been famous for years. And yes, they'll know me on the waterfront; they'll know I'm not a public enemy, whatever the Councils say, and they'll do business with me. Besides, I know ships, and I know sailors.'

This was a point worth making, for a ship would be of little use to them without a crew to sail it. 'And no matter how many lies we tell them,' as the Captain said, 'they'll find out soon enough that they're set to cross the Soll, not just cruise down the Coast; and that means we'd better pick them well. A mutinous crew's worse than none.'

So at last Lethgro agreed to stay in the dinghy with the Exile while the Captain looked for a ship and crew, she having vowed not to approach any skipper whose friendship she was not sure of. They tied up before they reached the main city, above the basin on whose broad beaches Sollet ships were being broken up and sold for timber. Here there were only market gardens and a few houses and boats, and the inlet where they moored was sluggish and grown with weeds both on the banks and in the water, so that it was not very noticeable from the river or the basin. The Captain preferred to go the rest of the way on foot, for they were not likely to find any other mooring so inconspicuous between here and the outer harbor itself, and the dinghy in the harbor would be a slow minnow in a pool full of sharks, if trouble arose. There was some difficulty when she left the boat, for Broz was not accustomed to be left behind, and the Captain had to speak to him severely before he would consent to stay. It went to her heart to do so; but even with her scarf and his dyed tail, she feared that the two of them together would be too familiar a sight in the streets of Beng.

So Broz, Lethgro, and the Exile settled themselves uneasily to wait; and this they did, to their great discomfort, for several hours. They had made no agreement on what to do if Repnomar did not come back; for, as she had said, 'You'll do what you think best, and I'll do what I have to do, and there's no telling how it will come out. Just take care of Broz.' Lethgro would have felt better if she had not added that last remark. And worse still was that, already on the path, she had turned back with a grimace, saying, 'No. Take care of yourself,' and turned again, striding away at a great pace. Time and again since then, Lethgro had stood up, grasping one of the swords with which his people at the castle had supplied them, and more than once he had stepped out onto the path. But he could not get past the obstacle of the Exile.

The Exile did nothing, except now and again to look out despondently from under his mats. But the weight of him was heavy on Lethgro's mind – him, and his pods, and his devices, and his people lurking beyond the clouds. If those were not dealt with, it might make little difference what became of a coastal ship's captain and the former Warden of Sollet Castle. So he would sit down again in the dinghy and turn back one of the mats and question the Exile.

Thus the Exile told him, in interrupted segments, of another world (in many ways not too different, he said, from this one) which his people had visited. They had set up their devices, and they had traveled about the world, observing its weather and many other things of interest, and trying not to trouble the folk they met. But the people of that world had much admired their powers and their gear, the pods with which they flew through the air and the boxes with which they threw voices and pictures around the world, their evident wealth and ease and many other things. And like a stain spreading suddenly on wet cloth, trouble had spread from the Exile's people. They had meant no harm, but they had overthrown the gods of that world. Some folk had taken them for gods in their own right, though they had not wanted that honor. Others had concluded that if those who were not gods could be so powerful, then gods were useless, and their teachers had lied to them; which made them disorderly and discontented. Yet others had proclaimed new gods of their own, or new versions of old gods, declaring that these would make their worshippers as rich and powerful as the Exile's people and destroy all those who would not follow them. And there were some who cared little for gods but cared much for those powers and devices. So that all the countries of that world were soon in turmoil. And the Exile's people, wishing to help, had gone about teaching and giving gifts and freeing those folk from many afflictions and perils that had long troubled them. But these good things were overshadowed by bad; for, while some folk prospered as none had ever prospered till then, others were reduced to a degree of misery heretofore unknown. And new afflictions arose, and the governments were overturned, and decency confounded, and new decencies imposed by force, and the world so dirtied by the making and using of devices that beasts and plants and people sickened, and the weather itself (which was what the Exile's people had come to learn about in the first place) was altered, and grew worse.

It was such troubles that the Exile feared for this world. Lethgro, who had expected perils of another sort, was puzzled at first what to make of these; but they stuck in his mind, and the weight of them grew heavier and heavier, tying him down like stout cables to the dinghy. Though he was a prudent man by nature, prudence before now had never stopped him from going to the aid of a friend. But if he took Broz and went in search of Repnomar, it was all too likely that none of them would return, and that the Exile would never be able to send his message, and that his people would come looking for him. The consequences of that, in Lethgro's opinion, would be still more disastrous than the Exile feared; for (despite what the Exile said) they were likely to come in anger, and he did not relish the thought of what weapons such people might have. So he stayed with the dinghy in the inlet, grimly resolving that if Repnomar did not return soon, he would raise the sail and head for Rotl, there to try his own luck at hiring whatever ship he could get. But as he was vainly trying to reckon how many hours she had been gone, Repnomar herself came striding along the path at a great rate. Broz ran to meet her, with Lethgro not far behind, and the Exile peeped anxiously from under the mats.

'No good, Lethgro,' she greeted him. 'We'll have to try Rotl. And we'd best be on our way right now.'

Indeed she had been sadly disappointed by her reception on the waterfront, and it was a relief to her to have come safe again to the dinghy. The rewards and threats of the Council of Beng, no doubt, had had their effect; but worse, as she told Lethgro, had been her own honesty. 'They asked me where I've been,' she said ruefully, 'and I told them across the Soll and around the world. Some of them didn't believe me, and some of them did. Either way, nobody is willing to hire out a ship to me; and the prices they're asking for an outright purchase would take all your money and leave us nothing to pay a crew with.'

She had told lies enough on other points, claiming that she had left the Warden and the Exile on a desolate stretch of the Coast before she had crossed the Soll; and no one had argued with her on this. Many people had warned her that she was in danger, but none had threatened her or tried to apprehend her, and she did not believe she had been followed. 'But people will be thinking about the reward,' she added, untying the mooring rope, 'and likely enough somebody's reported me to the Council by now. Can you steer a boat through harbor traffic, Lethgro?'

For they must pass the mouth of Beng harbor, and Repnomar thought best to pass it under the mats, leaving only Lethgro and Broz to manage the boat. And Lethgro, seeing her look, answered that he had learned a bit on the voyage downstream and thought he could find his way without bumping into anything.

'Especially patrol ships,' Repnomar said, settling herself among the treenails, and pulled a mat over her face.

That was the last talk they had for some time, for traffic in and out of the harbor was heavy indeed, and Lethgro did not dare to speak to the Captain where others might notice the conversation. So, with several near misses but no collisions, and with a few grunts from the Exile and stifled curses from the Captain when he stepped on them in his hasty movements, he got the boat past the harbor and headed downcoast.

Now he called the Captain out from her nest, and they rowed out from the cliffs to catch the wind, and set sail for Rotl. Here they had elbowroom, with only a few sails in sight. So they let out the crows, who had much to say about their long confinement, and even the Exile was able to stand up and stretch and take his turn at the oars.

This was a pleasant enough voyage. Lethgro, feeling the rhythms of the wind and the waves and the boat, fancied that he was beginning to get the knack of being a sailor; and the Captain so far agreed with this that she was content to let him handle the business alone from time to time. Traffic between Beng and Rotl was steady, so that they met and were passed by vessels large and small, under sail and oars; but it was nothing like the crowding rushing traffic of the Sollet. They felt they could relax at last, seeing no likelihood of their being recognized and arrested. So that it was a grave surprise to Lethgro when he was hailed by a passing ship and ordered to come on board.

It happened that he alone was upright in the dinghy just then, Broz being curled in the bow and the others asleep under the mats. For a moment, he thought it was a pirate vessel that had hailed him. But he saw the insignia of the Council of Rotl hung on the rail, and groaned. With the ship on one side of him and the cliffs on the other, with their few weapons under the mats, and a row of archers at the ship's rail training their bows on him, there was no hope in either flight or resistance. So he trod on Repnomar, saying loudly at the same time that he was alone and unarmed and there was no need to threaten him with arrows. The Captain jerked convulsively under his foot, but any noise she made was covered by his voice and by the growls of Broz, who had sprung up bristling. They flung him two ropes from the ship, one to make fast the dinghy (which he did very loosely, whispering to Repnomar all the while) and one to haul him aboard. So he lowered the little sail and was pulled up the ship's side and over the rail, and the dinghy trailed behind, with Broz snarling in the bows. The crows circled high above, seeming to withhold judgement till they saw the outcome of this affair.

Bad luck, as Lethgro reflected later, was a prickly fruit that might have good luck under its skin. It was bad luck that a member of the Council of Rotl had been homeward bound and leaning over the ship's rail at that particular hour. But it was good luck that Repnomar and the Exile had been out of sight, and that the councilor had been an old friend, who looked at him with such a mixture of disbelief and gladness and reproof that for a few minutes neither of them could speak. Afterwards they had much talk in the ship's cabin.

They were hard at it when a sailor came to report that the dinghy had come loose and was drifting toward the cliffs. The councilor merely waved one hand in dismissal, saying, 'Let it go,' and Lethgro took a drink of ale to hide his relief. 'So you think,' he said gruffly, 'I may be able to keep my head on my shoulders. But will the Council give me a ship to chase the Exile?'

Meanwhile the Captain and the Exile were having their own discussion. Lethgro had not had time to tell them anything except that he was being taken on board a ship that bore the Council of Rotl's insignia, and that if he survived he would look for them, and for a ship, on the waterfront of Rotl. The Captain had waited till all was calm, no sound but the rowing song from the ship and the sounds of the water and the oars, before she stretched out a cautious hand to undo the towrope. They must lie hidden, unable to steer, for it was likely they would be seen from the ship, and all their hope was that no one would think it worth while to retrieve what seemed only a shabby dinghy and a dog.

But they could talk. The cliffs here were not greatly dangerous, as coastal cliffs went, and the Captain thought they had good chances of getting safe inside one of the wave-eaten grottoes at their base, though the dinghy might take some damage. After that, the first question was how to reach Rotl. The Exile could not pass as a child, because of his beard; so he must stay out of sight, whether in the grottoes (while Repnomar made her way on foot to Rotl) or under the mats in the dinghy (while she sailed them there). The Exile was for sailing, since it would likely get them there sooner and no one would need to return for him. The Captain, though she agreed in her heart, said it must depend on what happened when they struck the cliffs, which by the sound would occur at any moment; and just then they struck.

The dinghy was thudded and pounded as the waves sloshed and sluiced between the great knobs of rock that stood in the water, and its port bow stove in just above the waterline before they had been half a minute in the surf. The Exile had to scramble hard, not to be buried in nuts and pegs (for the cargo hammered from side to side in the boat) and the Captain shouted to him to dump them overboard as fast as he could. She herself had snatched an oar with which to fend off from the rocks, and before they had shipped enough water to settle them below the hole in the bow, she had got them pointed into an opening between two rocks, and with the next wavethrust they slid into a cave. Here the water, its force broken by the rocks outside, ran mildly back to a little curve of beach less than a yard wide. And here in the wavering half-dark, lit by ripples of light from the moving water, they dragged the dinghy up onto the gravel. And with the waves sloshing about their feet and lifting and nudging the boat and threatening to pull it off again, they jettisoned most of what was left of their cargo, though not the money-box; and contrived to patch the bow with a few mats. Their weapons (two swords, with Lethgro's bow and arrows, and a short pike for the Exile's use) were undamaged though tossed about, the arrows being secure in a stoutly-made quiver; but their food, along with the basket for the crows, had gone overboard. At this the Captain laughed shortly, saying that people who had crossed the backside of the world on a few handfuls of moss and rations like dry leather could probably make it as far as Rotl, and the Exile agreed very cheerfully. Most important, the mast and sail and one of the oars were safe, and they could see the second oar dashing among the rocks at the mouth of the cave.

So with much labor and not a little danger they worked

the dinghy out into the surf once more, rough-housing it along from rock to rock, and caught the floating oar (which had its blade split but not shattered) and in that tumult, with their side against a cliff and every wave smashing against them like a waterfall, they raised the little mast and set sail. Next they shoved off as violently as they could with a receding wave, and plied the oars with all their strength. And though they were thrown back more than once, with much striving they got the boat out far enough at last to catch a breeze. Repnomar gave the Exile the warmest smile she had yet bestowed on him. 'Keep it up and you might do for a sailor someday,' she said cordially. And the Exile grinned.

It was an easy enough voyage to Rotl, but the Captain was weary by the time they came in sight of the harbor; for she had not been able to sleep except in brief snatches. The Exile maintained that he could handle the boat alone, at least in the easy stretches; but the Captain pointed out that it was not safe to be *seen* handling the boat alone. So she took her sleep sitting upright, with her head propped on her hand or sunk on her chest, while the Exile peered from under the mats, ready to rouse her when the boat needed her attention.

What came next seemed to the Captain as hard as anything she had ever done. It began with doing nothing. The councilor's ship would have reached Rotl long before the dinghy, and the whole town would know by now that ex-Warden Lethgro had been taken. Repnomar was as ready as the next captain to take risks, and readier than some; but with their lives and all else at stake, it would have been foolhardy to venture onto a waterfront buzzing with talk of them. On the other hand, if Lethgro got free he would look for them, so that they should be where he could find them. And if Lethgro did not get free . . . 'I've never done business with pirates,' the Captain said grimly; 'but I can learn.'

With these things in mind, they skirted Rotl harbor and tied up near the point of the long island at the harbor mouth. Here the dinghy could be seen from the waterfront by an eye that knew what to look for, but it was not likely to attract anyone else's notice. And, 'If it comes to it,' the Captain said, 'we'll be ready to drop down the Coast.' For the Coast below Rotl was a warren of pirates.

Here the Captain bought food from the shore fishers who lived on the island, and slept for a solid watch on the rocky ground beside their mooring, while Broz and the crows stood guard. But she slept restlessly, and not only because of rocks. When she woke she saw the Exile's eyes peering over the side of the dinghy from beneath his mat, and he asked her very wistfully how long she meant to stay here.

This was hard. It was against all Repnomar's inclinations and habits to sit still when she could be moving, and she knew that in the Exile's opinion there was a desperate need to move. But she was not willing yet to leave Lethgro boxed up in Rotl. He might have been executed already, or his case might be haggled over in Council for many watches to come. And the end of that haggling would be one of two things; either he would lose his head or he would gain his freedom, and the Captain saw nothing she could do to make one likelier than the other. So with a sigh she stood up, saying, 'Not much longer,' and sauntered over to the little wharf where a few loafers lounged around a fishing boat, idly laying bets on two dogs that were fighting over a pile of fish heads.

Presently she returned and untied the dinghy's mooring rope; for, she told the Exile softly, 'If they'd chopped off the Warden's head, the news would be all over the harbor. He's not dead; but he's not free, either, or he would have found us. It's time for a little excursion down the Coast.'

What made this part of the Coast a pirates' nest, in spite of its nearness to Rotl, was that here the shore curved like the inside of a bowl and the cliffs sank to a rocky jumble, and the curve of the bowl was filled with islands, some of them no more than rocks and some big enough to raise sheep on, and all of them full of inlets and waterline caves. From time to time the Council of Rotl, and sometimes the Council of Beng, sent ships and soldiers to clean out the pirates; but there was no denying that there were still pirates here.

Into this stew of trouble the Captain steered. As she explained it to the Exile, 'We'll be the safest boat in these waters. Nothing to steal – as far as anybody can see – and no way to do harm.' She was not quite so confident in her thoughts, for some of the pirates might take her for a Council spy, and some might recognize her as an old enemy (for she had fought pirates more than once).

There seemed no need now for the Exile to hide himself; and when he saw the Captain lay a sword where it would not show from outside and would yet be convenient to her hand, he did the same with his little pike. Once they were well among the islands, they lowered the sail and sculled gently with the oars. And the Captain watched narrow-eyed as two boats came swiftly to meet them, one from each side and closing in.

When Lethgro sailed out of Rotl harbor, the first order he gave was to take down the Council's insignia from the rail. He had none of his own to put in their place, and so the ship moved unmarked out into the Soll and turned upcoast toward Beng. The Council had accepted his story (how much they believed it was another question) of chasing the Exile through strange countries. He had searched Rotl and its surroundings for any trace of Repnomar (claiming that his search was for the Exile) and found none. It seemed likely, then, that the dinghy had never reached Rotl, and he was sorely afraid of what wreckage he might find.

But the wind was rising, and the skipper told him somewhat testily that even with the use of oars they could not hold close enough to see every floating plank that might be knocking about among the rocks. So Lethgro sent two boats to comb the surf line, looking for any sign either of a wreck or of a landing. The skipper made a sullen face, for he did not approve of so many sailors gone from the ship with an early Windrise threatening, and he did not like to risk the boats; but Lethgro carried a certificate from the Council of Rotl and was not to be disobeyed lightly.

It was while they were thus occupied, the ship standing far out and the boats busy along the foot of the cliffs, that they sighted another vessel bearing down on them from the open Soll. It carried no sail and moved fast under oars; so that the skipper, without bothering to consult Lethgro, immediately began to signal to his boats to come in. At this, Lethgro had the Council insignia put back again; for while he had not wanted to scare off Repnomar or the Exile, he wanted decidedly to scare off pirates.

There were no other vessels in sight except a distant sail upcoast and a pair of fishing boats out by the edge of the Current. But the skipper raised all piracy signals and steered straight away from the approaching ship, so as not to take the impact broadside when it came; for many of these pirate vessels were beaked and could stave in a slower ship with one blow. Now weapons were made ready, though there were few enough to use them, for what sailors remained on board were almost all busy with the handling of the ship, and the boats did not look likely to reach them in time to be of much help. But now as Lethgro was pulling back his bowstring till his fingers brushed his ear and taking aim at the pilot of the pirate ship, a flicker of blackness caught his eye, and at the same moment he heard a familiar yell; and there in the pirate's bow were Broz and Repnomar.

'Heave to, Lethgro!' the Captain was shouting. 'I've got a ship for you!'

Lethgro lowered his bow, with a great breath of relief that swelled his chest. 'And I've got one for you!' he shouted, and turned to give orders to the skipper.

When all was calm again and the signals taken down, they gathered on the foredeck of the Council ship: Repnomar, Lethgro, the Council's skipper, and the pirate captain, with Broz sniffing about their legs. It had not been hard to persuade the Council skipper not to fight, for he was glad enough to keep his crew safe (at least till they could all be brought on board and armed) and his ship undamaged; but he was less willing to join forces with a pirate. His commission was to search for the Exile, under Lethgro's command; but Lethgro had been an outlaw a few watches back, and this meeting on the Soll smelled of conspiracy. What made the skipper most dubious was that Lethgro had commanded the ship's boats to stand off a little way, and the pirates had promptly put a boat of their own between them and the ship.

Lethgro, for his part, felt like a juggler with too many balls in the air. It had been a fine stroke of Repnomar's to keep the Exile under cover, so that even now the Council skipper did not know he was on board the pirate ship (though Repnomar had whispered that news quickly to Lethgro). But sooner or later the skipper and his crew would learn that the supposed object of their search was already found – indeed, the pirates might let it slip at any moment, and in that moment Lethgro would find himself an outlaw again.

It was Repnomar's idea that two ships, both with well-armed crews, would more than double their chances of coming through the hazards ahead of them. She had not expected to find Lethgro in command of a Council ship; she had only hoped to capture this one while its boats were away and enlist the crew for a voyage across the Soll. But when she had spotted Lethgro on the deck she had given a cry of jubilation and shoved the Exile hard, so that he fell at her feet. The pirates (none of whom had altogether grasped what enterprise they had embarked on when they undertook to do business with Repnomar) took this as a quarrel among friends; but the Exile himself had quickly understood, and crept to a hiding place behind the forward anchor.

Now her hope, like Lethgro's, was to arrange all without fighting, so that they could begin their voyage with two full crews and with clean hands. But if the Council skipper could get his sailors back on board, within reach of their weapons, he might well decide to fight, for clearly a shipmaster commissioned by the Council of Rotl should have no truck with pirates. Considering these things in her mind, Repnomar proposed a choice to the skipper: either he could swear to sail with them wherever Lethgro commanded, or he could be put ashore here and now, and make his own way back to Rotl.

The skipper (who was a meager, sour-faced man) looked narrowly from Repnomar to Lethgro to the pirate captain and said that there was no need to swear anything, since he was already under Lethgro's command; at which the pirate, smelling treachery to come, loudly agreed that oaths were useless, and suggested that the best solution would be to weight the Council skipper with a ballast stone or spare anchor and drop him overboard, so as not to excite the Soll gods with blood, which sometimes led to storms. This argument had a strong effect on the skipper, who after a little more discussion agreed to be put ashore in a cove where the cliffs were lower and not undercut by the waves.

The sailors in the boats, who at first were much disturbed to see their skipper put into a pirate's dinghy, were soon reconciled, for Lethgro shouted to them the cheering news that they were not to be either marooned or murdered. They were still more comforted when he promised that all who sailed with him would be well paid. So that in the end only two decided to be put ashore with their skipper, and the others rejoined their crewmates on the Council ship. And the Exile came out from his hiding place and greeted Lethgro warmly, thanking him for all the risks he had run.

Now they steered slantwise away from the Coast, hoping to pick up the Current before they passed Beng, and so be making good speed in the event that anyone gave chase. But they expected no pursuit, for it would be some time before the skipper's news could stir up any action. Repnomar had taken over as captain of the Council ship and was busy learning its ways, while the crew learned hers. Lethgro had decreed that the Council insignia should remain on the rail so long as they were likely to be seen; while the pirate ship, unable to look so respectable, kept on their Sollward side, like a gaunt pickpocket skulking in the shadow of a pompous councilor. The Current had shifted since they last came this way, but they found it a little beyond Beng (no one having challenged or followed them) and let it carry them in a long graceful curve into the heart of the Soll.

25

Of the Difference between Meadow and Desert

When the long smudges of the Low Coast came in sight, the pirate captain (whose name was Brask) would not at first believe it. She was a stout, choleric person, with little patience for what she took to be nonsense; and what Repnomar called Low Coast, she said was only the darkness of the clouds on the horizon. Most of the sailors on both ships were inclined to accept this opinion. Repnomar scoffed at their disbelief, saying they should never have agreed to cross the Soll if they could not recognize the far side of it when they saw it. The pirates for the most part did not care which side of the Soll they were on, nor whether they would ever come home again; but the sailors of the Council ship (which was called the *Blue Crow*) were anxious, and some of them said openly that they hoped what they saw would not prove to be land; since if it was not, there would soon be no choice but to turn and sail homeward.

But Lethgro reminded them that the longer their voyage, and the more countries they passed through, the more they would be paid at the end of it; so that there was only a little grumbling when it became clear to all that what lay before them was land indeed.

Repnomar and Lethgro and the Exile had all been straining their eyes in the glare (by which the Exile was least troubled), trying to decide if the Current and the winds had brought them to the same part of the Low Coast as before. But presently the Captain declared that she recognized the dismal point of land near which they had first met and fought the Low Coasters. This time they saw no sails; but as the current carried them near the shore, they saw something stranger.

'I was wrong, Lethgro,' the Captain said, shading her eyes. 'This can't be the same coast we saw before. Look at it.'

'If it's not the same,' Lethgro answered, 'it has at least the same shape to it.'

It had the same shape, low and marshy, without a landmark; but whereas the first time they had seen only bare dunes and lifeless pools, now the land spread before them like a bright garden, all fresh green and flower colors, and birds danced above it. Lethgro clicked his tongue as he caught sight of what seemed a distant herd of animals moving slowly across the rolling meadows, with flocks of birds rising and settling again about their feet like a many-colored mist.

All this was so inviting that they turned shoreward out of the Current; for though they had begun this voyage well supplied, they were ready for fresh food, and ready for solid land beneath their feet. So they anchored along a curving shore where the waves ran gently to a sandy beach, and sent in boats, the sailors having cast lots to decide who should be of the shore party.

Even the beach was flushed with the colors of tender grasses and bright flowers, scattered over the sand to the water's edge, so that the last fingers of the waves ran among their stems and stirred them; and dainty insects hummed about them. But strangely they saw no midges, nor any other hurtful thing. There was game to be had for the taking; small creatures, some furry and some naked, that bounded or slithered through the grass, or stood with lifted heads to watch them approach, and seemed not to know what arrows were.

Repnomar, seeing this bounty, could not believe that they had come to the same section of Low Coast as before, and talked of changes in the Current's path; but Lethgro stooped to run his hand through the lush grasses and feel the naked sand beneath, saying in puzzlement, 'This is all new growth.' And not long after that, the Captain stumbled over something in the grass beside a winding creek, and went down on her knees to bend aside the flowers and stems. But at once she jumped up, calling for Lethgro and the Exile to see what she had found. For there in the rich grass lay all that was left of their first camp on the Low Coast: the blackened sticks and ashes of a burned-out fire, and a leather cup that someone had dropped in their flight from the midges.

So they walked marveling through this paradise that last year had been a desolation. And when the hunters had brought in meat enough to supply their present needs, some of the sailors ran races and played games in the meadow, while others prepared a feast on the shore. The Exile was much interested in how the land had changed, and went about plucking up plants to look at their roots and trying to get close to the flocks of birds. In this pursuit he wandered off across the meadows, and Lethgro followed him, for he had vowed that henceforth he would know everything the Exile did.

There was a herd of beasts grazing on what last year had been the barren dunes inland from the creek. They were larger than any animals between the Mountains and the Soll, for a sheep's head, or a dog's, would only have reached to their withers. The birds, busily pecking about their feet, seemed to be feasting on insects stirred up by their passing. Lethgro and the Exile neared them slowly, stopping and moving as the herd did, so as not to alarm them.

All at once, the grazing beasts flung up their heads, poised for a moment, and began to run – not away from Lethgro and the Exile, but across their path and close in front of them. Lethgro, who carried his bow in his hand, snatched out an arrow, for one of these creatures would feed many a hungry sailor. But they fled so fast on their long and slender legs that half the herd was past before he could shoot, and his first arrow missed. The second struck the throat of a racing beast but did not bring it down, and he got off a third as quickly as he could, that caught the same beast in the flank, so that it began to stumble and slow. Before he could do more, the Exile tugged at his sleeve and pointed.

Lethgro's neck prickled. Bits of the meadow itself seemed to be rising up to chase the herd – green things, spotted with red and blue and yellow and shades of violet, invisible against the flower-spotted grass except that they were in swift motion, following with a leaping gait on the flying heels of the herd. It was hard to grasp their size or shape (except that they were large) or even the number of them, though they seemed much fewer than the animals they pursued.

All this was what Lethgro saw in the first moments. Then one of the flowery beasts passed close in front of him, and with a great spring it struck the haunches of the animal he had shot, knocking it down in the grass, and Lethgro ran forward to defend his quarry and his arrows.

That was a mistake. He had pulled out his knife as he ran, ready to cut the herdbeast's throat if it was still alive. But before he was close enough to make sure of that, the green thing burst at him out of the grass, slashing and shrieking, so that he stumbled back, flinging his arms over his face. In another moment, a second green monster shot past him like a breath of hot wind, and the two began to raven at the fallen beast, while Lethgro staggered hastily away. He was streaming blood from arm and side, where the creature had cut him with claws or teeth – it had happened so swiftly that he did not know which. The Exile, much distressed, helped him back toward the shore, and others came running and eased him into the boat.

Repnomar, when she returned (for she and Broz had gone off in another direction to scout the land) inspected Lethgro's bandages very severely, and redid some of them to her better liking. 'Well, Rep,' Lethgro said wryly, as she was finishing one of these, 'I thought I knew how to hunt.' Indeed he had half expected her to chide him for his ineptness, of which he was badly ashamed; for he had lost both his game and his arrows, and made a casualty of himself into the bargain.

'And I thought I knew how to navigate,' said Repnomar, tightening a knot. 'But what's the use of finding the same place if it's changed to a different one?'

'It's a better place now than it was then,' Lethgro said with a grimace (for his wounds were tender). 'The midges were worse than any meadow monsters. And since when have you been sorry to see a change, Repnomar?'

So they laughed, and agreed that if all the countries they were to travel through were as much altered as this one, and in similar ways, it would be a good journey. 'For,' said Repnomar, 'we can stay out of the way of a few monsters.' And the pirates and the other sailors made offerings to various gods on the shore.

Now for some watches they voyaged along the Low Coast – not uneventfully, for in the second watch after their first landfall they met a Low Coast vessel, which tried unwisely to grapple the pirate ship, and ended fleeing before it. But the Low Coasters, to Brask's disgust, were too swift to be caught. After that they saw sails often enough, but had no more meetings. The land continued green and flowery, and from time to time they went ashore to hunt, very cautiously and without accident. The Exile marveled at what he called the rapid healing of Lethgro's wounds, though to Lethgro it seemed tediously slow.

In a while they came to the islands where the Low Coasters moored their ships, and there saw two or three of the family ships on which the women lived with their children. Captain Brask had to be restrained from attacking one of these; but if she cared for nothing else, she cared for the pay and pardon that Lethgro had (perhaps rashly) promised her, and did not want to lose them before she had enjoyed them. Besides, she was easily convinced, from the look of them, that these ships held no booty worth taking.

They sailed close under the brow of one of the larger islands, and there saw the first sign that Low Coasters could work on land, as well as fight on water. 'If I saw that in a civilized country,' Repnomar said, 'I'd call it a wooden god.'

Indeed it seemed to be a painted statue, larger than human size and not human in form, bright green and spotted with other colors, its hands or forepaws raised to threaten across the water toward the Low Coast. Quarreling birds and a drifting smell told of dead fish heaped around its feet. So they sailed on, glad to be past it.

Beyond these islands the Current turned away from shore. But here Captain Repnomar proved stubborn, saying that they no longer needed the Current, and should stick to the shore till it led them to the Outlet (or, as they called it now, the Dreeg). For she wanted to know more about the neighborhood of that great gateway into the land – whether there was good anchorage there or anything that might be called a harbor, or if on the contrary there were shoals or sandbanks or other hazards. And when Lethgro pointed out that such things were of little interest, since no one was likely to make this voyage again, she only snorted and said he should speak for himself, not for others; which made him uneasy.

As for Brask, she cared little which way they went, and said that coasts and currents alike were fields, that could be reaped. But the Exile was anxious, urging them to choose the swifter route, which he judged to be the Current. This, however, Repnomar disputed, claiming that with sails and oars, and the comparative shortness of the coast route, they could be in the Dreeg as quickly as the Current could have brought them there. So that Lethgro, who always felt his ignorance in matters of ships and sailing, agreed to follow the shore. Besides, he wanted to try his luck in another meadow hunt; for his wounds were nearly healed now, and the crew were eyeing the greenness ashore and talking of fresh meat.

So they left the Current, and anchored both ships under a rocky headland (having come to that part of the Low Coast which was not so low). This gave them shelter from waves and wind gusts, so that the most part of them could go ashore, climbing an easy slope from a broad shingle beach to the top of the headland. Repnomar and Lethgro led the way eagerly.

But at the top they stood speechless, gazing at what spread before them, till Captain Repnomar let out a long, low whistle. 'Ask your gods what happened here, Lethgro,' she said coarsely. 'Themselves never made such a desolation.'

Indeed it was still more desolate than their first Low Coast landing a year ago. There they had seen at least some sickly grass, weeds in the pools, and no lack of midges. Here there seemed no living thing at all, and the naked earth was more obscene than bare rock and sand, for it should have been clothed with life. It was strange to see the raw soil gullied and wind-worn, after those lush and flowering meadows full of game; and strangest of all for Repnomar and Lethgro and the Exile, who remembered barren and dreary dunes where now those meadows flourished.

'It's not as if everything died here,' the Captain said. 'It's as if nothing ever lived.' Indeed they saw not so much as a bone, nor the dried or rotting stalk of any plant. But the Exile, whose point of view was nearer to the ground, stooped over a shallow puddle that had formed in the hollow of a rock, fingering the silt at its bottom, and reported that there were certain scraps there of what had once been living things – scales and stony fibers of certain plants. And when they had walked on for a little, the Captain, stooping in her turn, lifted a handful of something like fluffy dirt, saying, 'Look at this, Lethgro. What do you make of it?'

'The wind has piled them behind this rock,' Lethgro said, when he had held up a pinch of the stuff, and dug the toe of his boot into the little drift of it caught by a boulder. For the stuff was not dirt, but the dead bodies of little wormlike things, soft and shriveled, the biggest hardly half the length of the Exile's middle finger (which was his longest).

Now the Exile, studying these things closely and slicing several of them open with the tip of his knife, said that because of their dried condition it was not easy to be sure, but that they seemed to have no mouths or stomachs, and asked the others if such creatures were common in this world. And when they told him they had never heard of such (for all creatures must eat), he grew excited, saying that in some worlds there were animals that took it turn and turn about, either to eat or to breed, and could not do the one when they were fit to do the other. But while they were discussing what he meant by this, some of the pirates, who had wandered off to the right, began to make a racket, calling boisterously on Lethgro to bring his arrows; for here, they said, was game he could safely shoot.

This, Lethgro felt when he had reached them, was a bad joke; for not even the crows cared for such game as the pirates had found, and he was not accustomed to be mocked by thieves and murderers. Yet it was a sight worth seeing; and gradually, by twos and threes, the whole shore party gathered till all stood side by side, looking down at the ground before them and now and then moving forward a step.

That very ground seemed moving, a steady shallow churning as if the skin of the world had loosened and were creeping slowly forward. Yet it was only a patch, a few yards each way, and it was not the ground that moved, but the worms that covered it. These, as the Exile declared with excitement, were clearly the same sort of creatures as those they had found dead. They moved as if held together by strings, side by side and nose to tail, all the same way and at the same pace, hunching their little bodies along over whatever obstacles the ground offered, for they could climb straight up the side of a rock as if it were level pavement. In this way, however, sections of the mass must fall behind, when they had to climb over boulders while their mates were advancing on flat ground; and the Exile suggested that perhaps this whole patch had been separated from a still larger mass in just such a way.

Repnomar, squinting ahead for any sign of such a crawling troop, saw something more attractive instead; for before them the land was as green as it had been behind them. So with Lethgro and Brask and a few others she went forward to investigate; and the Exile (who had been eagerly occupied with the crawlers, trying what happened when two or three were separated from the mass) came trotting after them at Lethgro's call.

There was no sharp line between the desert and the green, for as they walked they came upon solitary clumps of grass and forlorn flowers, and these grew more and more common till ahead they merged into a lush cover that seemed to Repnomar like that of the meadows where Lethgro had been wounded. In the uncertain zone between lifelessness and plenty they saw more dead crawlers, gathered by the wind at the base of grass clumps or rocks, and one smaller mass of live ones, doggedly humping over the ground.

'There's your chance, if you want to try again, Lethgro,' the Captain said cheerfully.

Lethgro, who had been stooping among the plants of this new field, looked up with no pleased expression, for he thought that even Repnomar had begun to mock him. But she was pointing inland; and when he straightened to look he saw another grazing herd moving placidly toward them.

He took out an arrow slowly. If the herd continued its present course and he timed his shots well, he thought, he might bring down a beast near at hand and so have a good chance of getting it on board without interruption by monsters; for he hoped that those green and flowery brutes would not venture into the desert country, where their coats would show like signal flags. But he scanned the field closely, for he did not intend to quarrel with such creatures again.

It was well that he did so. Gazing very earnestly downwind (for if meadow monsters were about, they would most likely be coming from that direction) he saw a patch of flowering grass that seemed to move the wrong way in the breeze; and after a little study, he saw that it was not quite following the herd. At this, he fitted arrow to bowstring, saying in a quiet voice, 'Don't run, and don't act excited. But the sooner we get back to the boats, the likelier we are to die in bed.'

Now, Captain Repnomar was not entirely sure that she wanted to die in bed, and Captain Brask had never even considered the possibility (for it was an option that pirates seldom had); but both of them were fond of living, and they did not hesitate to take Lethgro's advice. Broz, feeling something wrong but not certain what he should do about it, growled softly, and Repnomar silenced him with a sharp word.

What Lethgro had realized at first sight and what was soon clear to the rest of them (except perhaps Brask, who could not make out the monsters at all and had to take the others' word for them) was that it was not grazing beasts that were being hunted – it was themselves. Lethgro kept one eye on a certain pattern of blossoms that moved closer in slow undulations and sudden, silent bounds; yet even so he could not trace the outlines of the beast. Sometimes a green shape showed briefly against a boulder or one of the scrub trees that grew in scattered clumps, and disappeared again into the grass. They walked, keeping close together, at a good pace back toward the barren ground. The Exile carried a tuft of grass in his hand, so that he looked foolishly like a child just called home from play. Repnomar had drawn her knife, and Brask the sword she always wore.

They were well into the barren ground, and breathing easier, when Broz spun around with a roar of fury. They faced about, lifting their weapons, and Lethgro drew his bowstring and loosed an arrow faster than he had ever done before in his life, but there was not one of them who was not daunted in heart by what burst upon them now as a storm wave bursts upon a rock.

There were three of the monsters, huge to see as they came forward in great leaps, and hideous to hear, for they shrieked as they came with voices that cut the ear as their fellow's claws had cut Lethgro's flesh. Their grass-green coats stood out against the bare earth in discordant brilliance. The first of the three had taken Lethgro's arrow full in its chest, but it came on, and he had no time to shoot again. Broz sprang forward bravely, and Repnomar sprang with him; and for a moment it seemed that they might have the best of this encounter, for they took the wounded monster one on each side, striking for its throat with teeth and knife. But it lashed out left and right with its great forepaws, lightning-fast and screaming like a devil, and plunged past, leaving them both struck to earth.

Brask, who had not become captain of a pirate vessel by holding back from fights (though a fight like this one was new to her), held her sword low and forward-pointing; and when one of the monsters leaped upon her with its shriek, she drove the whole length of the blade into its chest. But its rush was not to be broken by one blow, however deep, and they went down together in a thrashing mass.

Lethgro had his chance now to try his knife on the beast that already carried his arrow. But while he was occupied with this (and indeed it was a business that left him little leisure, for though the beast was wounded, it might as well have been a wounded whirlwind) he was still aware that the third monster had stopped short to busy itself with Repnomar.

Now was an ugly time on the barren ground. All this affair had happened so swiftly that none of the sailors from either crew had had time to come to their aid, though many were running toward them. The Exile, with more pluck than good sense, had seized the stubby tail of the beast that was worrying Repnomar (being the easiest part to get hold of) and yanked hard. At that moment the creature had crunched Repnomar's knife arm in its jaws; but she, with great determination, took the knife in her right hand and drove it into the beast's throat, thus perhaps saving the Exile as well as herself. Lethgro had managed to stay out from under his monster, at the price of a terrible wound to one arm, and was now more or less astride it, with his teeth buried in the thick green fur of its neck (for with one arm dangling useless and the other occupied with his knife, he used what means he could to hang on). The monster curled itself, digging at his legs with its claws and sinking its teeth through his boot into the flesh of his foot, so that for the present it ceased its shrieks.

Indeed there was now a kind of silence that pounded in their ears, though none of them was conscious of it; for all the screeching had stopped. There was only the sound of Broz snarling as he dragged at the beast whose throat Repnomar had cut, and the yells of the approaching sailors, and the Exile's anxious queries as he tried to help first one and then another. Brask heaved herself from under the beast that had borne her down, pulling her dripping sword behind her; and they all straightened themselves as best they might and looked about them. The three monsters were dead.

'Well, Rep,' Lethgro said wearily. And she answered with a ghastly grin, 'We may die in bed sooner than we thought.' For they were both sorely hurt. By now some of the *Blue Crow*'s sailors had come up, marveling at the dead monsters, and these helped them along, though neither Repnomar nor Lethgro would consent to be carried outright. And the Exile scampered about, looking for the clump of grass he had dropped and picking up the arrows that had spilled from Lethgro's quiver.

So they hunted no more that watch. A few of the pirates had begun hastily to skin one of the monsters, Captain Brask telling them coarsely that if they were killed by the monster's mates it would be their own fault, and that she for one would say no prayers for them. But they were not interrupted, and finished the job so expeditiously that they caught up with the others before they reached the landing place (for Lethgro's progress, with his bitten foot, was very slow, and Repnomar's little better, going with her hands clasped to her belly).

By then the whole landing party had crowded around

them, all talking at a great rate, telling each other what had happened and making much of the wounds and skill and courage of the monster-killers. These three themselves were less noisy, sunk each in their own thoughts; for to fight a meadow monster to the death was not a thing to be shrugged off lightly. So they only blinked their eyes and answered curtly when they were questioned, and Brask was exceedingly rude, offering to stick her sword into anyone who might be curious about how it felt.

When they had come to the landing place, one of the pirates who had skinned the monster unrolled its hide, thinking to make a soft seat for Captain Brask in her boat (for Brask too was hurt, though not so much as Repnomar or Lethgro); and all stared at it in surprise. Its brilliant colors had faded – the rich green to a dingy gray with only a tinge of greenness left in it, the beautiful reds and blues and yellows of the flowerlike spots to dull black. This seemed so bad an omen that the pirates, and others as well, began to mutter prayers and make signs against evil, and Brask waved the skin away violently, saying she would not have such a thing on her ship or boat. Now the Exile begged for the hide, calling it harmless and interesting, and Captain Repnomar would have let him take it; but the sailors of the *Blue Crow* objected strenuously, and Lethgro thought best to command that the hide be left on shore.

So when they were on board their ships, and all wounds dressed, they raised sail and followed along the Low Coast, determined not to land again till they were in the Dreeg.

26
Downstream

It would have been an easy voyage, all in all, but for the trouble that hung over them. Lethgro (whom Captain Repnomar always referred to as the Warden, in spite of his demotion) was more severely wounded than he had been willing to admit, and for a time there was talk of his likely death. Repnomar herself was not much better off; but, as she observed brusquely, she was too busy to die, what with managing the *Blue Crow* and tending the Warden and keeping an eye on Brask.

For the pirate captain, disgruntled by her first experience of the Low Coast and seeing little promise of plunder, was thinking of breaking her agreement. Repnomar knew this from one of the *Blue Crow*'s sailors who had made friends among the pirates (for the two captains had grown very chatty, and not only communicated by signals and message crows but sent boats between the ships every few watches, exchanging news and consulting on their course; so that there was much coming and going of sailors).

This was a worry, but no crisis; for the pirates could not well turn back across the Soll, against the wind and without the help of the Current, unless after much replenishing of supplies. For this reason, Repnomar kept the *Blue Crow* close to the pirate ship and discouraged all talk of shore parties, saying that meadow monsters were nothing to the monsters of the Dreeg; which impressed the sailors.

The Exile grieved that he had lost his medicines; for with them, he said, he could quickly have healed the Warden and both captains, and he might even have saved Broz's eye. To which Repnomar replied philosophically, 'It's the next one that counts.' But in fact she was much moved by the injury to Broz. The first stroke of the monster's forepaw had raked a claw through the ball of his left eye; and though he had later fought gallantly, taking several lesser wounds without complaint, he was from that moment blind on one side. This puzzled him badly, so that he kept turning in circles, trying to see where he could not. But none of his other wounds was severe, and the Captain was pleased, all things considered, that he had gotten off so easily.

She herself had been slashed about the face, her left arm mangled in the monster's jaws, and, worst of all, the brute's hind claws had sliced into her belly, so that the entrails showed. This was what gave the Exile the most anxiety; but by good luck nothing inside had been opened, and in due time the wound healed, leaving a scar that, as Repnomar said, would be a good argument if anybody disbelieved her story.

But Lethgro was in worse case. He had lost much blood, and some of his wounds turned bad, so that for a long while he had a fever and was sometimes out of his head, talking restlessly of the affairs of Sollet Castle and arguing with the Councils of Beng and Rotl. And when the burning and the oozing subsided and it seemed clear that he would live, they found that he had lost the use of his right arm. No bones had been broken in it, but the muscles and sinews had been so torn that it was all he could do to move his fingers, and he could not lift the arm at all. This was awkward, and depressed him more than he liked to admit; for, he felt, it did not well become the Warden of Sollet Castle to carry a uselessly flapping fin, and he took it as an omen that he would never get back his post.

By this time they were well into the Dreeg, and bowling swiftly downstream. Repnomar thought it safe now to anchor where a rocky outthrust of the bank made a little cove, and send out hunters and foragers, telling them that they were past the worst of the monsters. Nevertheless, they went in large parties and well armed. The Captain trusted that Brask, having no experience of rivers, would not be likely to turn upstream without some assurance of profit. 'Otherwise,' as Repnomar put it to Lethgro, 'she's thief enough to try it.' And when he objected that ships could no more float upstream on the Dreeg than on the Sollet, the Captain answered with a strange glint of triumph in her eye, 'Not float, Lethgro – sail! On the Dreeg, the winds blow upstream,' which gave Lethgro new cause for worry. But if the same thought had occurred to Brask, she kept it to herself (or to her own crew) and the foraging parties returned successful. Monsters were heard, but not surely seen; and afterwards they went on with stomachs and larders well stocked, and the crews cheerful.

The Exile, for all his anxiousness and trouble, was pleased by the things he had learned on this voyage. He was very proud when a cluster of tiny eggs (attached to the stems of the grass clump he had gathered on shore just before they met the meadow monsters, and had kept carefully ever since) hatched out into what were certainly midges. This confirmed him in an idea he had already propounded: that when the midges, by smothering and choking every other living thing and eating the remains, had reduced one tract of land to desert, they moved on to another. It was his belief that the wormlike creatures they had seen, so doggedly trudging over the barren ground, were another form of midge, competent to crawl straight ahead and to lay eggs in a good place when they came to one, but for nothing else.

'I don't know about that,' Lethgro said. (He was well enough now to sit at the *Blue Crow*'s rail and watch the passing banks.) 'But I know there was a difference between the two places where we met monsters. That meadow before the desert was all new growth, like a fresh-planted garden. But the high ground on this side has been overgrown for years.'

'How do you know?' Repnomar asked; and he answered, 'I know land, Rep, if you know water. I knew by the look and feel and smell of the plants, and the roots and matted stems between the grass stalks.' And he added thoughtfully, 'And the monsters there were a different shade of green, to match the difference.'

'And *I* know why those Low Coasters worshipped Broz,' the Captain put in, laughing. 'They didn't take him for a god; they took him for a meadow monster.'

The Exile eagerly agreed with these remarks, and for some time they talked of the Low Coast and its curiosities. The Exile wondered why even plants died out where the midges came, guessing that perhaps their seeds would not grow till they had passed through the gut of some animal. And Lethgro asked gloomily what the midges would do when they reached the Dreeg, and whether they would turn back and round the Soll, desolating as they went till at last they reached Sollet mouth.

But the Captain soon lost interest in all this, answering absently, with her eyes fixed on the river bank. In a little while she sprang up, calling for a signal flag and a boat; for, she said, 'It's time to talk to Captain Brask. We're almost there.'

They had come to a bend that she recognized; and, as she said presently, when they were anchored alongside the bank, 'I came to get my ship back, not lose another one.' And she sent crows down the river, to make sure of where the waterfall lay. These were the same two birds that had been already once around the world with her; and to the leg of one of them she attached a message, instructing that crow to carry it to the *Mouse*. 'But if the bird doesn't come back,' she said sternly to all within hearing, 'that won't mean anything.' For she was determined not to jump to conclusions about what had happened to her *Mouse* and her crew, when a few more hours would bring sure knowledge.

Now they held council on the shore. They were well prepared, for Captain Repnomar had made her plans and laid in her supplies before ever she left the pirates' nest below Rotl (pirates having generally good stocks of many things). There were stout cables coiled in the holds of both ships, and plenty of muscle in both crews, and it was with these that the Captain proposed to take off the *Mouse*. 'And if that fails,' she said, 'we'll see then what help we can get from beyond the clouds.'

This was assuming, of course, that the *Mouse* was still there, and worth taking off. The closer they came, the more uneasy the Captain was for her crew, and the more she thought of the sailors who had already died in her service. But she did not speak of this, and when Brask inquired coarsely what she meant to do if the crew of the *Mouse* were all dead, she merely answered that a good ship was worth something even without a crew.

They were still checking their cables and testing their capstans (for everything must be strong and sure) when the first crow returned, very pleased with itself and calling so loudly that they heard it before it came around the bend. Repnomar gave a brusque signal with her hand for all to go on with their work, and waited somewhat tensely for the crow to come in. And when she had satisfied herself that it carried no message (and indeed was not the crow she had sent to the *Mouse*, but the other) she gave only one more glance to the sky and turned back to the work in hand, shouting out roughly that it shouldn't take a whole watch to look at two cables – though a minute later she added that if one weak strand showed up when the pull came, she would use it to tow whoever had let it get through across the Soll. The Exile offered to go scouting down the bank in hopes of seeing the falls and the island and the *Mouse*, but she told him there was no point in this, for they would soon be under way again. 'And if it hasn't moved yet, it's not likely to move in the next half hour.'

The truth was that Repnomar did not like the notion of anyone else seeing that island before she did. By now everyone was ill-tempered – even Broz and the Exile, neither of whom was usually snappish. When all preparations were finished, they weighed anchor and moved on downstream, with oars at the ready and no sails set, keeping close to the left bank.

This time – whether because there was little wind to carry the sound, or because all eyes were straining and eager – they saw before they heard. Above the smooth edge of nothing, where the river swept downward out of sight, white mist hovered, and dark specks of birds. The wooded island sat as if poised to plunge over the precipice, and at its near end they could already see the *Mouse*.

Now boats were lowered: one from the pirate ship and one from the *Blue Crow*, with Captain Repnomar herself in the latter. She had insisted on this, declaring that the *Mouse* was her ship and that there was nothing to do at this end of the cable except heave, which any fool could do. The boats moved out into midstream, rowing hard across the current, so that they were borne steadily toward the island and the *Mouse*; and the cables they carried hung from the ships' decks behind them and drooped into the water. The ships themselves kept well inshore, to be sure of firm anchorage. Lethgro, standing in the bow of the *Blue Crow*, watched the boats make their sidling way, swiftly downstream and slowly crosswise. His eyes were so glued to this sight that he saw nothing on the island, and it was one of the *Crow*'s sailors who cried out, 'They're alive!'

Figures were swarming on the island's rocky tip, beside

the *Mouse*'s anchorage. They seemed to be waving their arms, jumping up and down, and giving other signs of excitement; but any sounds they might be making were lost, for now the voice of the waterfall made itself heard, a throaty rumble full of threat for those who had heard it before.

In the boats, they were straining hard; but the weight and drag of the cables, that now trailed almost their whole length in the water, held them back. Repnomar had had floats tied here and there along the cables, and this somewhat eased the burden on the boats. Nevertheless, they were heeled far over by the pull; and presently Lethgro, unable to bear the sight longer, sent out the last boat (for the pirates had only the one) to row hastily along between the cables and lift them as much as possible. This meant that most of the sailors were in the three boats and in no little danger of being swept over the waterfall. Now Lethgro gave orders to drop anchor and to stand by at the capstan, ready to haul in the *Blue Crow*'s cable; and Brask, at his signal, did the same on her own ship.

It was a good thing that Repnomar had started the boats so early; otherwise (as everyone agreed later) they would never have reached the island. As it was, the pirates' boat barely managed to make land far down the island's side, and the sailors in the third boat only saved themselves by a firm grip on one of the cables. But the Captain's own boat reached the point of the island, just as she had planned it; and when she sprang ashore, such a shout went up from the *Mouse*'s crew that they heard it on the ships through the rumbling of the cataract. Presently both cables were made fast to the *Mouse*'s bow, and the third boat's crew worked their vessel back to the *Blue Crow*, hand over hand along her cable, for they were needed at the capstan.

Then came the haul. The *Mouse* which had been pointing downstream, had to be headed around into the current, pivoting on her stern anchor. When that was done, the anchor was raised, and on all three ships all hands began to heave. The capstans went round swiftly enough at first, but when the *Mouse* came well into the current, the strain threatened to be too much for the gear. The pirate ship (which was lighter than the *Crow*) began to drag its anchors, and Brask was kept busy throwing grapples to catch at trees or solid rock on shore. This she did with her own hand, for all her crew that were not on the *Mouse* were busy at the capstan. Luckily she had a powerful arm and a sure eye, and enough of her grapples held so that the dragging slowed and stopped.

Lethgro, meanwhile, saw with a sinking heart that the *Crow*'s capstan could not much longer take the strain; for the pawls that held it from moving backward, and thus unwinding all the cable they had laboriously wound up, were cracking one by one. So with the Exile's help (for he was one-armed, and all the sailors were straining at the spikes of the capstan) he rigged a spare winch to take a little of the stress. And although, as Repnomar later explained to him, this could not have helped much, it helped enough; for the capstan held.

But the *Mouse* was far from a dead weight. Captain Repnomar on her part made such good use of rudder, oars, and jibsail that in the end the cables needed only to hold the ship from being swept over the falls while she worked it shoreward, not to pull it upstream against the current, and from time to time she could even let out a little of the cable they had already hauled in, so as to ease their way. This brought them once so close to the edge of the cataract that all other sound was lost in its roaring, and two sailors swore later that from the deck they could see down the face of the falls; while Lethgro watched stricken, and threw his weight so hard against the handle of the winch that it broke. But at last the *Mouse*'s anchor caught and held in the shallows under the bank, and sailors swarmed ashore with ropes to make fast to anything possible, so that, as the Captain said, 'If the *Mouse* goes over, half the bank goes with her.'

Now there was celebration beside the Dreeg. The *Mouse*'s crew declared noisily that they had never doubted the Captain would return and bring them off (though by and by Anscrop and some of the others began to speak regretfully of the gardens and cottages they had left on the island). They were all in good health, though somewhat hard of hearing, and had prospered so well on the island that at least two of them were now pregnant. They reported proudly that during their year in the wilderness they had hauled the *Mouse* out for cleaning and repair, so that now all was in the best condition; and they apologized for Repnomar's message crow, which, finding itself on board the *Mouse* after so long a time and such a perilous and unseemly journey, had flatly refused to leave again, and was even now preening its feathers in its own nest box beside the Captain's cabin. And though the Captain was usually rather stern with her crows, she forgave this fault readily, saying that she felt much the same herself and did not mean to be soon parted from the *Mouse*. Indeed she was in a mood of jubilation that worried Lethgro, saying openly that if there had been time to wait for Windrise, she could have sailed the *Mouse* off without the need for cables. And they built fires, and danced, and made merry all the remainder of that watch. 'For,' as the Captain pointed out, 'after this we begin the hard part.'

The next step of their plan (which no one else embraced as wholeheartedly as the Captain) was certainly not easy; for it was to haul out the ships, carry them past the waterfall of the Dreeg, and set them afloat again. Even the Exile was doubtful whether this would save time, considering the labor that would be needed. But the Captain told him that humans could work as fast as gods when put to it, and promised they would waste no time. And she herself left the celebration to scout out the riverbank with Broz. Lethgro went with them; for, he said, for once Brask could watch the Exile.

Afterwards, when they were sailing comfortably down the river, they agreed – at least Lethgro, Repnomar, and the Exile agreed – that it had been well worth the labor. Certainly it had saved them many watches of traveling time; for the whole operation had been performed in two watches of dogged and sometimes frantic effort: one to prepare the trail for the ships and haul them out of the water, and the other to drag them down the slope. There had been vigorous discussion on some points. They had ended by leaving the *Blue Crow* anchored above the falls, with a skeleton crew that included the pregnant sailors, for all agreed that the journey to come would not be a good time to give birth.

All was not well, however. Lethgro's arm was no better, and neither was Brask's temper. The Exile was doubly anxious, first from his haste to find his message device and second because he had lost his midges. This, indeed, had happened somewhere upstream; but he had not spoken of it before – not wishing, he said, to add trouble to trouble when the Captain, the Warden, and Captain Brask were all suffering from wounds. To such remarks Repnomar answered, with a grimace of laughter, that she did not think the news of a few midges mislaid would have much increased her pain.

But Lethgro listened more soberly, for the Exile explained that if by chance the midges (which, it seemed, had eaten their way through the cloth he had used to cover their box) found their way to the opposite bank of the Dreeg, they might there begin to make desert of a new country that had heretofore been safe from them, with results unforeseeable. On the one hand, it might be of no consequence – indeed, there might have been midges on the far bank from time immemorial; or the midges might die out quickly in the new land; or at least they might be no worse than on the left bank, where it seemed the land was accustomed to heal itself, and no doubt the midges were a necessary part in the life of many creatures there. On the other hand, in a country not inured to them they might wreak unheard-of havoc, wiping out some breeds of creatures altogether, changing the very weather by their depredations, and sweeping along the coast till they reached human habitations. Lethgro shuddered at this, and sternly asked the Exile why, if he had such fears, he had brought the eggs on board in the first place. To this he had no good answer, saying only that he had wanted to know, and had thought he could keep them secure. And seeing that his words had troubled Lethgro, he tried to cheer him again, saying that the likelihood of these ill things happening was very scant. Then too, if he did not send his message in time, the worst the midges could do might go unnoticed in the greater troubles that were coming upon the world. Lethgro did not take much comfort from this.

But he had other worries besides midges and devils from beyond the clouds. 'I don't know about you, Repnomar,' he observed in a private conversation, 'but I'd prefer not to have my throat cut.'

'Brask is no fool,' Repnomar answered. 'If it were only me and the *Mouse*, she might think of cutting throats. But she knows you're on a mission for the Council of Rotl. She has everything to gain by sticking with us – good pay and a pardon from the Council. And if she *did* decide to pull out, what's to stop her from just turning back?'

'You're the one who claims she would have done that above the waterfall if she were going to do it,' Lethgro said morosely. 'And I wish you hadn't talked about sailing up-Dreeg, Repnomar. She may imagine she could really do it.'

'I don't doubt she could,' Repnomar answered, with no sign of repentance. 'But the wind's not strong enough yet. And the farther she goes with us, the longer the way back. I think she'll stick to her bargain – at least till the going gets rougher.'

Lethgro blinked his eyes dubiously. 'She's surlier watch by watch, Rep. I wouldn't bet much on her not turning, and I'd bet even less on her not thinking it safer to finish us off before she turned. Besides, she'd want the *Mouse*, and the *Blue Crow*, and any booty she could find on them. In spite of the lies we've told her, I suspect she suspects that we're carrying all our money.' (Which indeed they were.)

To this the Captain could only answer, 'We keep good watch on the *Mouse*. And we have all the swords we need.'

But if Brask meant to turn her ship upstream (whether with or without the *Mouse*) she would have to do it soon, for they were coming to that Reed Soll where they must leave their ships and take to the land. Brask had been warned of this, and had agreed to a journey that was to be half on land and in the dark; but it appeared now that she had not really believed what they told her. For as they came among the reeds and the light began to fade, she called for a conference on board her own vessel; and when Repnomar would not agree to this, shouting from the *Mouse*'s stern that any business they had could be conducted in boats between the ships, or by calling from one to the other ('for your lungs are as good as mine, Brask') or by crows, Brask lost her temper altogether, demanding with indignation what they were taking her into.

To which Repnomar answered loudly, 'If you can't stand this, Brask, you'd better leave now – because it's going to get worse.'

This conversation, conducted between the stern of the

Mouse and the bow of the pirate ship as they plowed through the reeds, and in the hearing of both crews, struck Lethgro as dangerous, and he tried to draw Repnomar aside for a few prudent words in private. The Captain, however, was not to be bullied on her own ship, and she stood her ground, shouting out to Brask, 'If you want to turn around now, turn! – and you'll get half the pay you bargained for, as soon as we get back to Rotl. But if you want it all, you'll have to stay the course!'

'I'm not leaving my ship in a swamp!' Brask thundered.

'Then turn around now! Or you can carry your ship on your backs while you climb the mountains, and try how it sails on ice rivers.' Here the Captain cupped her hands around her mouth to make her shout carry more clearly. '*We* went the whole way, Brask! But maybe you're not good enough.'

Now there were sounds of dissatisfaction from the pirates, while those of the *Blue Crow*'s crew who were on the pirate ship looked at each other uneasily; and Brask roared, 'We'll show you what we can do!' and stalked away from the rail.

'Now you've done it, Repnomar!' Lethgro said. 'She won't be satisfied till she sees you dead in your blood.'

'Then she'll wait a long time for satisfaction,' Repnomar said cheerfully. 'But you're wrong, Lethgro. We're better friends now than we've ever been before. Not,' she added, with a laugh, 'that we've ever been friends.'

Under oars, the ships plowed their way smoothly through the reeds, with a sound like sickles cutting through grass; and though it was tedious rowing, and the oars were hung with broken reeds like the coarse green hair of some god, it was easier than Repnomar had expected. For from the masthead she could see those channels that her crows had not been able to find, their first time through this country. 'And no wonder,' she said to herself; for the channels showed not as clear water but as winding stripes of a lighter green. Here the reeds were softer and slighter, leaning with the flow of the water and every breath of the air. At the bow of the *Mouse*, a sailor with a long pole kept prodding for bottom.

'And how will we keep from getting mired in the muck, Repnomar?' Lethgro asked gloomily.

'We walked on those reeds, remember,' the Captain answered. 'I think we can slide a ship on them.'

Lethgro, who remembered all too well what it had been like to walk on and among those reeds, sighed deeply. But when, a few hours later, the sailor with the sounding pole shouted out that they were into the mud, and their path of pale reeds narrowed to an end, the Captain at once sent out a boat to beat down the stiffer reeds ahead, bending them sideways across the *Mouse*'s course, and called for Brask to do the same. But before the pirates' boat had come up, Repnomar herself had leaped from the *Mouse*'s bow ('to show the crew how easy it was,' she explained afterward) and thrashed her way forward to stand chest-deep beside the boat, to the astonishment of its crew. Here she waved her arm and shouted, calling sailors by name to follow her; then pulled out her knife and stooped into the water.

And it was thus that they managed the business, bending all the nearby reeds flat across the path of the ships and cutting or breaking armfuls from farther away to lay on top of these. Over this smooth and springy cushion they dragged and shoved both ships; and, as the Captain said, 'They had a rougher road around the waterfall.' To which Brask replied, panting heavily, that at least it had been downhill there.

But when at last both ships lay canted on the spongy ground beyond the reedbeds, in that unwholesome dimness below the mountain peaks that stood like fangs against the dark, the Captain ordered two full watches of rest and sleep and preparation, and even the Exile did not object to this delay. 'I don't want anybody beginning the trek already worn out,' Repnomar said. And Brask stood with her arms akimbo, looking up at those teeth of light, and said nothing.

27
Of the Truthfulness of Exiles

It was a very different business this time. With two full ship's crews and half another, all warmly clad and loaded with supplies, it was, in Repnomar's words, 'like coasting downwind on an easy reach.' Probably, however, only she and Lethgro and the Exile and Broz appreciated the ease of it, for to the others it seemed hard work indeed. The *Mouse*'s sailors, who had weathered a full year in the wilderness, and were besides overjoyed to have come off so neatly from the waterfall and very pleased with their Captain, were merry enough, in spite of the dark and the cold and the hard climbing; for they thought that if Captain Repnomar had been this way before, it was a safe course for them to follow. But apprehension weighed heavier on the others with every step they took into the darkness. When they looked back from the peaks and saw the far clouds red where their journeying had sunk the light behind them, there were many who called it the evilest omen they had ever seen.

But they went on, and in due time came upon the ice river and the snowfields beyond. Here the Captain led them with a torch, one of the long-burning sort soaked in sheep's tallow, which in the darkness gave a light of surprising brilliance, though it did not reach far. Once they had got the hang of walking in snow they made good time, for no one was willing to be left behind in that swallowing darkness. Brask proved herself useful, too, in rousing the laggards, convincing them that they were not so tired as they had thought; for she explained with vigor that all who were weary could put down the packs they carried, but that no one without a pack would eat.

They were on the lookout now for any sign of Quicksilver People. Lethgro's hope was that the Quicksilvers, seeing them so numerous and well equipped, would leave them alone and let them pass unmolested to where the Exile had stowed his gear. Brask and Repnomar had quarreled about the matter of weapons, Brask saying that she would not let her people walk defenseless into the dark, and Repnomar that swords were defense enough, for she wanted to confiscate all bows and arrows and the light javelins that some of the pirates carried. But Lethgro had pointed out that since both arrows and javelins were useless in the dark, it mattered very little whether they carried them or not; and the pirates kept their weapons.

'What I'm afraid of, Lethgro,' the Captain confided, as they strode together at the head of the column, 'is that some fool will hear a noise and try a shot at it, and we'll be in a battle before we can blink. Don't forget the Quicksilvers can see in this country, and we can't.'

'I don't forget that, nor their poisoned darts either,' Lethgro said. 'I only hope they're prudent enough to keep their distance. They can't be used to dealing with such a troop as this.'

'Broz can help us,' Repnomar said, stooping in her step to pat the old dog's head. 'He may have lost an eye, but his nose is as good as ever. If he smells Quicksilver, he'll let us know.'

As if that had been a signal, Broz stopped in his tracks, lifting his muzzle. Repnomar hesitated, but only for a moment. Then she strode on, clucking her tongue to call Broz alongside her. 'Unless he growls,' she explained to Lethgro, 'it's not worth stopping for. He's caught a little whiff of something, but it can't be very near. No use making the whole crew jittery.' Still, she pulled out her knife, to have it ready in her hand, and Lethgro did the same.

'Or perhaps,' Lethgro added after a minute, 'what he got a whiff of was a red wind from a belching mountain.'

'Maybe so,' the Captain said shortly, and marched on.

Now began an uneasy time. Broz was more and more restive, sniffing at the air and the snow, whining in his throat, and now and again giving one of those growls that Repnomar had said would stop them but which she now seemed to ignore. And it was not only Broz who sensed something outside the torchlight. Lethgro, straining his ears to listen through the sounds of their feet crushing the snow, through the breathing and rustling and low voices of so many people on the move, caught now and then (or thought he did) a faint chirping or whistling. Repnomar, staring into the dimness beyond her torchlight, saw too clearly for doubt the flash of silver-gray that she had been waiting for. And once they crossed the tracks of many little paws in the snow.

Lethgro, who had only one good hand, put away his knife and drew his sword; and the sailors, seeing this, began to bring out their own weapons and to look about them suspiciously. Lethgro turned and shouted an order that no one should shoot or strike except on command; and the sailors of the *Mouse* and the *Crow*, who were accustomed to obey him, passed the word along till all were sure of it. And those in the rear crowded on the heels of those before them, for it was very dark.

The Exile, somewhat short of breath from trotting beside Lethgro, declared that in his opinion there were Quick-silvers on both sides of them, keeping pace as they moved. Captain Brask now came up from the rear, puffing worse than the Exile (for she was stout and short-limbed), and they held council as they marched. Brask was for kindling more torches and staging a sudden rush to one side, that would scatter the Quicksilvers and teach them a wholesome respect; but the others, who knew better what they were dealing with, all spoke so vigorously against this proposal that in the end she was persuaded. The wisest course, they agreed, was to keep on as they were, making the best time they could manage and taking no hostile action. Sooner or later the Quicksilvers might conclude that there was no profit to be had and no danger to be feared from these travelers, and so leave them in peace. 'And even if they followed us all the way, there's no harm in it,' the Captain said. 'Except – '

'Except that we have to sleep,' Lethgro finished. (For the Exile had told them his things were still several watches distant.) 'And who knows what they may decide when they see us stop, or when they see half of us asleep and helpless?'

'But it doesn't have to be half of us,' Repnomar said quickly. 'We can make do with a little less sleep for a few watches. If three quarters of us are awake and armed at any one time, we'll still make a pretty good show.' There was more confidence in her voice than in her thoughts, for such a halfway measure did not well suit her nature; but she could think of nothing better. And they began to talk of camping in a circle, with only five or six of them at a time sleeping in the middle, and the rest on guard around them.

'But better go on as far as we can, and give them a chance to lose interest first,' Lethgro said. 'And with the snow as smooth as it is here' (for they had come to a level plain of firm snow without crevices or ridges worth mentioning) 'it's easier going to drag our packs than to carry them.' Indeed some of the sailors had already begun this, tossing down their packs behind them and leading them along by a strap or rope so that they glided over the smooth snow like well-trained puppies on leash. 'That way we can go on longer before we have to stop.'

'Except that we don't have to stop at all,' Repnomar

cried, and promptly stopped dead, waving her sword arm with such enthusiasm that the Exile shied away and Brask raised her own sword. 'If we can drag packs, we can drag each other! Let's try it.' And she stuck her torch in the snow and her sword beside it, and began to pull out a blanket from her pack.

It worked better than Lethgro would have thought possible. Indeed it would not have worked at all, in his opinion, with any sort of people except sailors. But sailors were accustomed to sleep on swaying, moving devices, with strange sounds of swishing and thumping and creaking in their ears. It took them a little while to rig litters of a sort from blankets and ropes and a few javelin shafts; but once that was done, there were more than enough volunteers to ride them, and much swearing and merriment as to who must pull them. They rode very smoothly (by nautical standards) over the snow, and one or two of the riders were soon snoring peacefully. So they tramped on, some of the sailors singing as they went, and all somehow cheered.

But, as Repnomar observed inauspiciously, this was too easy. They might have gone on thus as long as needed, taking it in turn to sleep on the litters and eating as they walked, with the Quicksilvers flitting like ghosts beyond the torchlight on each side of them; or the Quicksilvers might have made up their minds to attack them with a shower of poisoned darts, or perhaps to turn away from them altogether. But none of these things happened. For when Repnomar decided to take her turn on a litter (having offered the chance first to Lethgro, who said that with such a vehicle he would sooner pull than ride) and Lethgro was stooping over the awkward business of getting his one good arm into a loop of rope, Brask suddenly yelled out, 'Stop the toad!' and they all looked up to see the Exile disappearing into the dark.

There was a burst of whistles and trills, quickly drowned

by shouts from the column of sailors, and someone hurled a javelin haphazardly into the dark; but Lethgro roared out for silence and order, and a strained quiet followed. The Captain had sprung up again, grabbing back the torch she had handed to Anscrop (for she would not entrust it to Brask); and now she raised it slowly, shedding light a little farther into the darkness.

'Do you see anything, Lethgro?' she demanded.

And Lethgro, who saw only that the Exile had betrayed him once again, and that once again he had invited that betrayal by too much trust and kindness, blinked his eyes in answer.

Broz, who before this had done no more than growl, began to bark fiercely, and for a minute the Captain was hard put to hold him back. But presently he ceased; and though she strained her ears hard, she could hear no sound from the darkness. After a little, 'Do you hear me, Exile?' she shouted. 'We're going on!'

Here Lethgro protested that the whole purpose of this journey (aside from saving the *Mouse*) had been to help the Exile send his message. 'But if he's told us nothing but lies, then there's no message to send, and no point in going further. He's taken what help he wanted from us, and scorned the rest. We don't know where those precious things of his are now, nor what to do with them if we found them. Why should we go on?'

But the Captain declared ominously that there was always point in going further, and that they could send messages without the Exile. For the thought had come to her (indeed, it had been churning secretly in her mind for some time, like the undertow that churns below the surf) that if they could find the Exile's devices, they might contrive to work them.

'And if his shipmates don't speak our language, at least they'll find out that we're here, and that we *can* speak,' she was saying a few hours later (for this was not an argument to be resolved quickly).

They had gone not one step farther, Lethgro declaring he would not allow it till this matter was settled. They had made a kind of half camp, those who were weary sleeping on their blankets around the torches, but most of the sailors huddled in little groups and talking low. Repnomar, Lethgro, and Brask still sat on their packs beside Repnomar's torch at one end of the column. Whether it was head or tail of that column remained to be decided.

Lethgro, clearing his throat to reply, broke off suddenly. Two figures stepped into the torchlight.

One was the Exile, his hands stretched out appeasingly. The other was large, for a Quicksilver, with great deep-blue eyes like saucers of ink. The Exile began to say something in his usual way, like a child who hopes not to be punished, but Lethgro cut him short. 'Are these your friends too?' he asked bitterly. And the Exile said that he hoped they were, for they had his devices.

Now other Quicksilvers began to appear in the fringes of the light, prancing forward and back like dancers or skittish sheep. And the Exile explained (standing with open hands in the torchlight while Lethgro and Repnomar glared at him, and Brask and several of her crew rose up with weapons in their hands) that he had learned a little of the Quicksilver language when he was their prisoner; and though he had forgotten it for a time, it had come back to him, with other things. He was glad that the Quicksilvers remembered him and bore him no ill will, for they had the devices he had set up, or at least knew where they were. And he apologized for not having been entirely frank, since he had never mentioned before that he had already set up a station, which had been sending messages to his people all this time.

Most of the Quicksilvers that the Captain could see had

their little blowpipes in their paws, or even cocked upright from one corner of their mouths; and she looked askance at Brask, who had never felt a Quicksilver dart and so might not appreciate the value of peace. 'What do you mean to do now?' the Captain demanded, fixing the Exile with a look more curious than unfriendly.

But Lethgro interrupted, saying harshly, 'Why ask, Repnomar? Is he any likelier to tell the truth now than ever before?'

Here the Exile protested that he had told as much of the truth as he knew and thought they could understand, or almost as much; and that he was indeed likelier to tell the full truth now, since he had learned to use their language better – learned, too, to consider them more deeply his friends. As for what he meant to do now, it was first to make peace between Quicksilvers and humans, so that no one should be hurt or wronged, and then to hurry to his gear and send his message.

'Go talk to your friends, then,' Lethgro said, 'and let me talk to mine.' For he was bitterly angry, at himself as well as the Exile.

The Exile bent his head and withdrew into the dark; and the big Quicksilver, after sweeping them all with a wide blue stare, gave a shrill whistle and bounded after him. The flitting shapes of silvery gray faded back from the light like dissolving shadows, and a twittering rose and died away.

So they took counsel, Repnomar and Brask sitting on a blanket in the snow, and Lethgro pacing around them; for his anger would not let him rest. 'He has us where he wants us,' Lethgro said, 'which is at his mercy. He's lied to us from beginning to end, and there's no way now we can know which is worse, to stop him or to help him. If his message were as harmless as he claims, he wouldn't have run away from us to send it. No, he's gone to call down a devil-war on our heads. And yet – '

'And how *can* we stop him,' Repnomar asked, 'even if we should want to? Think of this, Lethgro: once he was loose in the dark with the Quicksilvers, he could have gone about his message-sending without our help. Why should he come back to lie to us?'

'Unless these Quicksilvers forced him,' Brask said; 'either to make peace for them, or to get us to drop our guard. And if *I* were trying to stop him, I'd light all the torches we have and make a rush.'

'We don't even know if sending messages is what he really means to do,' Lethgro said with exasperation. 'I grant you he may have told us some truth, but we don't know what. And rushing around in the snow with torches will get us nothing but a hailstorm of poisoned darts. The only good I can see is to get our hands on the Exile, and this time – ' (he squeezed both his fists tight, though that was not easy to do with his wounded arm) 'make him feel it.'

'And wouldn't that bring another hailstorm on us?' retorted Repnomar. 'And how do you propose to catch him, anyway?'

'The question is,' Lethgro said, halting in front of them, 'how close is this friendship of his with the Quicksilvers?'

They discussed this (for Brask, it seemed, was not unwilling to give an opinion on matters about which she knew little) and all thought it likely that his friendship with the Quicksilvers was no more solid than his friendship with the White People, or indeed with themselves. But, as Repnomar pointed out, they could not be sure; and if they snatched the Exile under the Quicksilvers' blue eyes, they might be very promptly in battle.

'And when did you learn counsel prudence, Rep?' Lethgro said, with a laugh of sorts. 'Where we stand now, doing nothing is as much a risk as doing all we can. And the Quicksilvers don't seem to have weapons worth mentioning besides their darts. We're too many for them to knock down with one whiff; and it's a good bet that once they see what swords can do, they'll leave us alone. I say let's grab him when we can.'

So at last they agreed to this, and all stood up, facing into the dark, while Repnomar waved her torch to signal to the Exile (for, as they remembered, Quicksilvers did not see light, or not the same light as other peoples). And almost at once they saw the shadowy form of the Exile, with gray gleams dancing around him, who stepped forward and became solid and clear in the torchlight.

So Lethgro (moving to have the Exile between himself and the two captains) said firmly that the humans would make no move against the Quicksilvers unless they were first attacked, but that they reserved the right to march peacefully through the country of the Quicksilvers, doing no harm to them or their possessions.

To this the Exile answered mildly that in his experience it was harder than might be thought to pass through an alien country and do no harm; but that he welcomed Lethgro's words and would explain them as best he could to the Quicksilvers. And turning to the Quicksilver beside him (who, Lethgro thought, was likely the same one as before) he began to squeak and twitter.

Some of the sailors standing near could not contain their laughter at these uncouth sounds, and the Quicksilvers too seemed to find them strange; for while some bobbed about in the shadows, chirping among themselves, others addressed the Exile earnestly, upright on their haunches and gesturing with their little hands. But he spoke always to the large Quicksilver, who seemed to understand him best; and presently this one turned toward the darkness, whistling a high, sweet note. There followed a musical discussion among Quicksilvers, while Brask, showing signs of impatience, made signals to Lethgro that he ignored. For he wanted the Quicksilvers to understand, when he seized the Exile (as he meant presently to do) that it was not an attack on them but a private quarrel among humans (for he still found it hard not to think of the Exile as human).

Fortunately for his hopes, there was not time enough for Brask to resort to violence of her own before the Exile, turning back to them with a wan smile, announced that the Quicksilvers agreed to let the humans pass peacefully through their land, so long as they kept together and did no damage.

At this Lethgro stepped forward and took him hard by the right arm, a little above the hand, saying very grimly, 'Now tell them that you stay with us.'

He was prepared to wrench that arm as cruelly as need might be (since he himself did not have two arms to grapple with). But the Exile, turning up his face to him with a look of such earnestness that it shook Lethgro to the heart, said very clearly, 'I stay with you,' and then screwed his mouth into a strange shape and chirped out something in the Quicksilver tongue.

Now the one who had been the Exile's companion and interpreter came nearer, laying a paw on the Exile's other arm and twittering softly. Lethgro looked over their heads to catch Repnomar's eye, for he thought that if they could get through this minute without fighting, they would have a good chance of keeping the peace thereafter; and Repnomar gave Brask a warning look.

But the squeakings of the Exile seemed to reassure the Quicksilver, who turned and bounded away, whistling; and the others followed, as least so far as the light showed. Now Lethgro was tempted to loosen his hold, for the Exile made no resistance and looked up at him like a sad child; but he hardened himself and said roughly, 'You've lied your way to the bottom of a hole. The one certain thing we know is that you're a liar; and if we let you play with those toys of yours, what's to stop you from calling down on us a worse curse than any you've threatened yet? The best and safest thing we can do is to cut off your head and take it back to the Council of Rotl.'

But the Exile made no real answer to this, for he began to talk of the comrade who had been with him when he first came to this world, and who had died from the darts of the Quicksilvers. He could not blame them for that, he said, since they had not meant to kill and had had no way of knowing that their poison could have so grave an effect on strangers. But he had just learned what had happened to his friend's body, something he had not known before this hour: the Quicksilvers had eaten it.

Here he stopped, and they waited in some puzzlement for him to go on. Repnomar remarked (as he kept silent) that if he had stayed with the Quicksilvers long enough to learn their language, it was odd that he had not heard this news before.

To this he answered that he knew very little of the language, and that he supposed they had not told him because they saw that he was distressed and did not want to distress him more by speaking of his friend. And here his voice broke, and he said chokingly that he wished he had heard it then, so that he would not have had to learn it now.

From this they could only conclude that he was troubled not only by his friend's death but by the Quicksilvers' very reasonable use of the body; which seemed so curious that no one knew how to respond. But Lethgro, who had not been Warden of Sollet Castle for nothing, was not to be distracted by this show of piteousness, and he shook the Exile's arm, asking him if he had anything more important to say before he died; and Brask fingered her sword-edge and called for a bag to carry the head in.

At this the Exile roused himself and said that indeed he had something very urgent to tell them, and that someone had better write it down. This sounded promising, and Repnomar (who could generally be relied on to have the wherewithal for sending messages) sat down on her blanket and got out pencil and paper. But something caught her eye, and she pointed up into the darkness, saying, 'Look at that!'

Like a spark thrown from some giant torch, a speck of light glided across the sky, trailing lesser sparks, and descended out of sight to their left. The Exile drew a long breath like a sigh. 'It's too late,' he said.

28

Of Gods and Quicksilver

In Captain Repnomar's opinion, Quicksilver People were more civilized than half the population of Rotl, still more of Beng. 'And they manage without castles and councils, Lethgro,' she observed, waving a slice of her dinner (whatever it was) for emphasis.

'Maybe so,' Lethgro said glumly. 'But humans are human.' For he had been thinking of differences and likenesses between humans and other peoples, ever since he had met the Exile's folk. And Brask grunted and licked her fingers.

It was Lethgro himself who – when the Exile told them that the spark across the sky was a ship or boat of his people, sailing downstream from the clouds to moor beside the station he had set up – had turned to the others and announced, in a voice that brooked no argument, 'Then we'll meet them now and get it over with.' For, though this was the very thing he had dreaded from the beginning, he thought it would be worse to skulk in the shadows when such strangers were loose in the world than to confront them straight and learn what the worst was likely to be. Repnomar had jumped up eagerly, and Brask (as Lethgro thought with some condescension) had not known enough to object. So he had squeezed the Exile's wrist a little tighter, and the Exile had nodded wordlessly and led them across the snow, with the whole column following.

After a minute the Exile spoke, saying quietly that what he had meant to tell them was where to find his devices and how to send a message, with certain words they could have used that might have mollified his people. And he added that for him to tell them such things was against the law and the regulations of his people, and could have caused great trouble for him. But he had seen no other hope of forestalling worse trouble for a whole world.

The flying light had gone down behind a line of hills on their left, so that it was some little while before they reached the spot. But they knew their course much sooner, for the shape of the hills began to show, outlined against a light that glowed softly from behind them. For a time the sailors talked noisily among themselves; but as they climbed and the light grew brighter, bit by bit they quieted, and they came to the crest all silent, with only the crunching of the snow under their feet and the noise of their breath sounding louder by the minute. Lethgro still held the Exile firmly; but as they reached the crest the Captain took him by the other wrist, saying, 'You may need your arm for something else, Lethgro.' So the three of them together, with Brask and Broz close behind, took the last steps that brought them over the rise, and stood looking down.

The light in the valley before them was so bright that Repnomar and Lethgro squinted their eyes against it, trying to make out the shapes that moved within it. But the Exile lifted his free arm (for Lethgro had released his hold) and called out something; and as more of the sailors came over the ridge and gathered behind them, he called again and again. Neither Repnomar nor Lethgro tried to silence him, thinking that what he shouted might be needful for their survival. But Repnomar asked him what he was doing; and he answered that he was telling his people they had no need to rescue him, for he was among friends.

This struck Lethgro, who had so recently offered to cut off the Exile's head, as unlikely. But likely or not, the figures in the valley did not seem to be taking warlike action. They were gathered close around something which Lethgro took at first for a house, but which Repnomar had guessed instantly to be their ship. In fact it was somewhat like the Exile's pods, at least in its outward look, but so large that it was easy to believe the whole troop of strangers (though there seemed to be as many as half a dozen) could be packed inside it.

So they came down the slope into the light. The rocky ground was running with slush and water where the snow had been melted as by some great heat; and in places snow and slush alike had been driven into drifts and ridges as by a stormwind. Two or three of the strangers held devices in their hands – weapons, perhaps, as Lethgro darkly imagined. The great ship shone behind them in the light.

That golden light was very warm. Some of the strangers (though none of those with the devices) advanced to meet them, calling out to the Exile as they came, and the Exile answered; so that by the time they met in the open ground before the strange ship, there had already been considerable conversation in their inhuman tongue. The Captain and Lethgro had exchanged many glances but spoken little. Now Lethgro with all the dignity becoming to a former Warden and an agent of the Council of Rotl, said (speaking to the Exile, but with his head up and his eyes on the nearest strangers), 'Tell them that we mean them no evil. Tell them they can take you and leave in peace. But we want no devices left in this world that can do harm.'

Here the Captain, seeing a great opportunity about to be lost, would have liked to add that harmless devices were another thing altogether, and that there was no need to leave just yet. But she thought best not to contradict the Warden before these outlanders; and in very truth there was something about the strangers that awed even her. So she kept silent, and heard the Exile speak, and one of the strangers answer. It was clear that the Exile did not confine himself to translating Lethgro's words, for the exchange went on until Repnomar (with a glance at Lethgro) jerked a little at the Exile's arm. So he turned to Lethgro and answered very courteously that his captain was well pleased with this arrangement, and that with their permission he would go now.

But Repnomar, who could no longer restrain herself at this, snapped out, 'Not yet!' at the very moment that Lethgro uttered the same words; and the Exile, feeling her grip tighten, looked up at her with signs of apprehension.

That was the beginning. After a while the strangers had brought out sheets like the one the Exile had carried, spreading some of these to sit on and offering more to any sailors who wanted to use them. Some had preferred their own packs and blankets; but because of the melting of the snow, there was much wetness, and many had taken the sheets to save their things from soaking it up. The Exile had hastened to explain that these were not gifts, but only to be used (by his captain's generosity) during this conference and then returned, for they would be unwholesome and dangerous if kept longer; which had caused a few sailors to give them back at once.

'Not,' Lethgro observed now, shifting his back against the wall of the snow cave where they sat at their meal, 'that we know what they were really saying; and not that they necessarily know what we said.' For he was still brooding on the unreliableness of the Exile, who had been their interpreter.

'Nor what the Quicksilvers said,' Repnomar added.

For after they had spent an hour or two in argument and discussion – the strangers (by the Exile's translation) wishing not only to leave devices both here and elsewhere in this world, but to spend some time observing and studying it, and to inquire into what had happened to the Exile's companion – one of the strangers had suddenly started and looked about, and then two others. The Exile cried out in horror, and Repnomar and Lethgro ducked their heads behind their arms.

The outlanders were leaping up, knocking darts from their necks and hands and faces. Broz growled, and the Captain tried to shelter him with her arms. One of the strangers nearly reached their ship before he fell. Another snatched up a device and swung it toward the darkness in a half circle, making a curious humming sound that hurt the ears. But before it had well begun, the affair was over, the strangers lying slumped on the wet ground (except the one that the Exile was dragging toward the ship), Lethgro and the Captain still shielding their faces, and Broz (who scorned such defenses) bristling and barking at the surrounding dark.

The Captain, seeing that only outlanders had been struck, shouted out that the sailors should keep their weapons handy but not use them unless forced to it; and Lethgro, thinking that the Exile might have been spared by more than oversight, lunged after him and wrestled him away from the body he was dragging. This was awkward with one arm, for the Exile was determined, and Lethgro had regretfully to fall upon him in order to hold him down. The next thing, Lethgro thought, would be nets.

He was right, but the nets were only for the dart-struck strangers. Quicksilvers poured into the golden light, and Repnomar let out a whistle of admiration that blended with their own whistles and chirps. They darted forward two together, each with one paw lifted to hold the net gathered between them while they ran on the other three; then rose high on their hind legs and flung the net, that spread itself like the opening fingers of a hand and settled unerringly over its target. Before it was well down, the Quicksilvers were upon it, tightening and knotting it about their prey; so that in a very few minutes they had each of the fallen outlanders bundled in a separate cocoon.

Meanwhile the Exile, with shrill squeaks, bustled among the darting forms of the Quicksilvers; for Lethgro, pitying his distress, had let him up again. But they took little notice of him, except to avoid him with sidewise leaps. Soon, however, the large Quicksilver who had seemed to be his friend or keeper came at a more dignified pace out of the darkness, and seemed to listen gravely to the Exile's desperate twitterings. Now Lethgro and the Captain (who had quieted Broz at last) put themselves forward, asking what the Quicksilvers intended. But the Exile turned on them angrily, crying out that he wanted to know why they had led him and his people into this trap and what harm they meant to do next, and threatening them incoherently with menaces they did not understand; all of which surprised them, for till now they had seen him only mild and kindly.

But now the cocoons began to stir, for the strangers were already awakening – much to the excitement of the Exile, who ran from one to another, speaking to each one anxiously till he got answers that satisfied him. Meanwhile the Quicksilvers, who seemed uncomfortable in the warmth, were attaching ropes and beginning to haul the bundled outlanders up the rocky hillside.

Now again the Exile was distressed, and (forgetting his recent anger) appealed to Lethgro and the Captain, begging them to help him persuade the Quicksilvers to release his friends, or at least not to drag them over the rocks like bales of cargo. This they tried to do; but the Quicksilvers would not be persuaded, and showed signs of restiveness at this interruption, fingering their blow-guns when the Captain set sailors to block their path.

'Tell them we'll help, then,' Repnomar said to the Exile. And they settled for this compromise, pairs of sailors swinging the netted strangers between them while the

Quicksilvers led the way and the Exile trotted between, consoling his friends.

So it was that they ended that watch crouched in a Quicksilver snow cave, eating a generous (if mostly unidentifiable) meal and discussing Quicksilver civilization. 'It's a camp, not a city,' Repnomar observed. 'They make these things as they need them, where they need them.' For on the slopes of the hills at the edge of the level ground, where the snow lay deep and firm, they had found Quicksilvers digging such caves, throwing out great showers of snow with their hind feet so that the scene showed in the torchlight like a blizzard. Into one of these new holes the netted outlanders were stowed.

But there was already a warren of interconnecting snow caves in one of the hillsides – as the humans learned only gradually, for the Quicksilvers would not allow them to bring torches inside (no doubt for fear of melting) and it was by groping their way through passages, often on hands and knees, and bumping into each other in the dark that they found it out. So for a while the hillside was a-throb with muffled noises – oaths and thumps and laughter and panicky cries. But the Quicksilvers were good hosts, and soon had all the humans settled comfortably enough, and served them with strange foods, some of which could be recognized as raw meat.

This was done with much chirping and chirruping, and friendly pats of little paws (though the Quicksilvers soon learned to stay away from Broz, who did not care for these attentions). Repnomar had ordered torches to be planted outside the mouths of some of the caves, so that they could have at least a little light. And Lethgro, by much talking and gesturing, at last prevailed upon one of the Quicksilvers to bring the Exile. They needed an interpreter; and besides, as Lethgro said, 'The closer he is to hand, the less mischief he's likely to be doing.'

In a while the Exile came, still in lively discussion with the large Quicksilver (whom Brask had dubbed Whistle, though that name would have done as well for any of them) and they all sat down to talk in the torchlight just inside the cave mouth. It was not easy talking, for it was clear that the Exile had not lied about one thing, namely that he understood little of the Quicksilver language – or at least that the Quicksilvers understood little of his attempts to speak it. Then too, he was so earnest in his argument that he often forgot to translate what Whistle had said till Lethgro jogged his arm, or Repnomar or Brask swore at him impatiently.

Nevertheless they learned that (according to Whistle, according to the Exile) the Quicksilvers had seen the landing of the strange ship and decided that such potent visitors were better netted and caged than wandering at will in their country. They meant them no harm (so the Exile said that Whistle insisted) as was shown by their having used the mildest possible poison on their darts, for they remembered the unfortunate death of the Exile's comrade. (Here the Exile reported on his own account that to his great relief the poison had not much clouded the minds of his people nor wiped away their memories, and he thought that the Quicksilvers had used not simply a lesser dose but a different sort of poison; for which, at least, he was grateful.)

'And what do they mean to do with your people?' Lethgro asked.

The Exile replied grimly that this was what he was trying to find out, and went back to his twittering and squeaking. But all he could report, after earnest discussion, was that this was still to be decided by someone or something – who or what, he could not make out, except that it was the one authority to which all Quicksilvers deferred.

At this, Repnomar sprang up (so far as she could, an action which stirred a shower of snow from the roof of the cave), saying, 'Well, if they can't tell us, let them show us.' And when the Exile had explained this as well as he could, Whistle patted her leg and bounded past her into the torchlight outside.

They followed, to see a crowd of Quicksilvers already beginning to collect in the open. 'I told you that was the right name,' Brask remarked, for Whistle was uttering whistles so piercing that Broz laid back his ears and whined pitifully. In a little, all the open ground (as far as the torches showed) was flowing with silver gray; and Whistle reached up to take the Captain's hand, gesturing around them.

The Captain made a sound of understanding. 'I was partly wrong, Lethgro,' she said. 'This is their council.'

'Not a council,' Lethgro objected. 'This must be their whole tribe.'

'And why shouldn't their whole tribe *be* their council?' the Captain asked. To which Lethgro answered nothing, for the notion tumbled his idea of councils upside down.

In a little, however, he had to admit that she was right, for what took place then on the open ground was not far different from council meetings he had attended in Rotl and Beng. There was much discussion, with all signs of oratorical flourishes, and a fair amount of what seemed to be vigorous argument. Brask found this shilly-shallying hard to understand. 'You mean they haven't killed them yet?' was her only comment; after which she went back into the snow cave to finish her meal.

As Lethgro saw it, there was something to be said for that brutal approach. 'It won't be easy for them to make friends after this beginning,' he observed to the Captain. 'And I wouldn't want to have the Exile's people for live enemies.' Nevertheless, he hoped for some peaceable solution; for to kill a delegation of folk so potent that their ships could sail through the clouds was surely to invite more danger.

This seemed to be also the conclusion of the Quicksilvers. For though the Exile could not follow the heat of the debate, Whistle turned to him from time to time with reports on its progress, and some of these he was able to understand well enough to pass on to the others.

But just as the Exile was telling them, with more hopefulness than he had shown yet, that his people were to be fetched from their prison cave to join the discussion, a disturbance arose on the edge of the Quicksilver crowd. First there was nothing but a stir of gray like a shudder; in the next instant a wave of whistling swept across them like a scream. Involuntarily Lethgro made a sign against evil, and Repnomar put her hand on Broz's bristling neck.

Destruction showed before the destroyers. Quicksilvers were falling, cut down like ripe grass by an unseen reaper. Then the things themselves advanced into the torchlight, glinting dully; short and squat, so that for a wild instant Repnomar thought they were some of the Exile's people, broken loose and armed with invisible scythes that cut swathes of desolation before them as they came. The snow was covered with Quicksilvers crushed down like the lodged stalks of a grainfield after a tempest. Lethgro beside her doubled over with a grunt, and then the battering struck her too and she forgot all else.

'I don't doubt they're gods,' Captain Repnomar said; 'but that doesn't mean I'll bow down to them.'

'Gods or not gods,' said Lethgro, who had his doubts, 'we have to deal with them.'

Indeed on this point it seemed that Lethgro and Repnomar had almost traded places; for the Captain, who before now had scarcely admitted the existence of gods, and scoffed at every divine manifestation pointed out to her, was convinced that if godhood meant anything, it meant such powers as the Exile's people possessed; while Lethgro, who felt he knew the Exile too well for such notions, ascribed it all to devices, which anyone might learn to use. And whereas Repnomar had long been eager to meet the Exile's people and hold friendly talk with them, while Lethgro had feared that very thing, now he found himself arguing against her that they should make friends as far as they were able.

'I'm as willing to deal as anybody they'll find,' the Captain said now. 'But not while they treat me like some sort of animal. Not,' she added, 'that they know how to treat animals.' She had already remarked that she gave the crows (not to mention Broz) more respect than these people gave her.

'It's no worse than what the Quicksilvers did to them,' Lethgro said mildly. And the Captain snorted.

They were penned like animals indeed in the open ground before the snow caves – held not by any visible fence but by a line they did not dare to cross, while the creatures of the strangers prowled unceasingly around them. The torches lay tumbled and half buried in the snow, their flames all extinguished, but the prisoners were brightly lit, for one of the golden lights shone upon them from the top of a pole set just outside their circle. In its hot brilliance the snow was melting, so that they stood or sat or crouched miserably in deep slush, watching their dead turn sodden.

There were not many dead, considering the number of wounded. What had cut them down, Lethgro and Repnomar believed now, had been no ordinary weapon but a flat blast of wind, narrow as a swordblade, swung like a scythe, indeed by those unholy reapers. It stunned, it bruised, it snapped bones, and sometimes it did worse. The humans were only battered and sore; but Quicksilvers, it seemed, were frailer. Besides their broken bones, which were many, they had taken hurts inside, and most of the dead and the worst wounded had blood at mouth or nose or ears. There were some newly dead, for the prisoners had learned by cruel experience the boundaries of their prison.

There were only three of the creatures, but they were enough. They moved relentlessly around and around the circle, insectlike with their many little legs and their blank, unchanging eyes; ever busy and yet missing nothing, for every Quicksilver who crossed the unmarked boundary line was felled by one stroke of an unseen blade.

Those in the snow caves (for some of the Quicksilvers had managed to take refuge there from the first attack, and most of the sailors had never bothered to come out for the Quicksilver Council) were not pursued; but when any showed themselves at a cave mouth, they too were cut down, in a great swirl of blown snow. This had happened often at first, so that now most of the cave mouths were sealed with fallen snow, with here and there the gray limbs of a Quicksilver showing at an odd angle through it, lifeless and unwholesome. Round and round the creatures trundled, armless, headless, their eyes (or what might be eyes) set in a circle around their top edge, their stout dark-gleaming forms spotted with knobs and slots.

'And our whole crew buried in there,' the Captain said bitterly, with a jerk of her head toward the caves. 'And Brask.' She laughed without mirth. 'It's a safe bet that's not the way she expected to die.'

'They may be alive,' Lethgro said, 'and better off than we are. Those caves are deep, and we don't know how far back they've collapsed.'

'No, we don't know,' the Captain repeated. Her mouth was grim. She had come near to sending a crow (for the crows, who had flown upward when the attack came, were unhurt) with a message for the *Mouse*; but she had decided against it, since, as she rhetorically asked, 'What can I tell them, except that we're in trouble and they should stay away?' For she would not call the rest of her crew into the reach of these murderers. Several times she had stood up, on the verge of yelling out a challenge or a demand to the strangers who must be lurking somewhere in the darkness behind their creatures, but prudence and Lethgro's hand had held her back. Those invisible blades could kill very swiftly. Lethgro, who had been giving the matter some thought, believed that in the first attack the creatures had not meant to kill at all, only to strike down, whereas now they were ready to give more deadly thrusts.

He also believed, sadly, that it had been a grave mistake ever to entertain kindly feelings toward the Exile. It was clear now that for all the little man's professions of friendship, he had abandoned them as soon as he was able to rejoin his own folk – abandoned them like beasts penned for the slaughter. It was true, of course, that Lethgro had threatened the Exile with death not long before, but that had been under extreme provocation; and, Lethgro told himself, in the unlikely event that he had been forced to make good his threat, he would at least have done it with dignity and humanity. He would not have condemned the Exile to this misery in the snow.

Whistle, who had survived the attack with no worse damage (or at least none visible) than a broken forearm, showed ever more clearly as a person of importance among the Quicksilvers, restraining those who wanted to run for it and arranging some care and comfort for the wounded. Lethgro and Repnomar had tried to help, but there was little they could do. The Quicksilvers were very wretched, crowding as far from the hot light as they could safely get, shaking their wet paws and covering their eyes (for strangely enough it seemed that they too could see this light) and grooming slush out of their fur.

'But they haven't killed us all outright,' the Captain said. 'They must see some use for us.'

'And that may not be good,' Lethgro answered.

They had come to this dreary point in their talking and, having no more to say, looked away from each other, when suddenly they both stiffened. Lethgro stood up, saying grimly, 'Here he comes,' as the Exile advanced into the light; while at the same moment Repnomar, facing the other way, saw a net flying through the air toward one of the creatures. She cut off her whistle of surprise in mid-breath; but the creature took no notice, and the net settled over it.

For a moment it trundled forward as if nothing had happened, till the meshes began to hamper its movement. Now Repnomar could make out dim forms on the ill-lit hillside beyond, Quicksilvers and humans together hauling on the ropes of the net. The creature pressed doggedly forward against the pull, its little legs tangling in the meshes, till it was tilted at a steep angle. Its leg churned. Snow burst from the ground in one spot after another between the thing and where Repnomar stood among the other captives – the invisible sword striking wildly and askew.

The Exile, on the other side of the circle, shouted out something in a voice of anguish and ran forward at his clumsy gait. Lethgro saw that he carried something in his hands. Meanwhile, the other two creatures continued their mindless rounds, and one of them was now approaching its snared fellow. On the shadowy hillside there was movement, and Repnomar had no doubt that another net was being readied for its prey. A whining sound rose from the netted thing, and it began to tilt back toward an even keel. The bursts of flying snow that marked its swordstrokes leaped closer. The meshes were tearing.

29
Conferences in the Snow

They had, the Captain saw, only a few moments before the creature would be free enough of its net to turn its killing blast on her and the other prisoners. There was no shelter; but there was a gap of sorts in the circle of their unwalled prison, since two of the creatures were now close together on one side. She stooped to pull at Whistle's good arm, pointing and gesturing with her other hand, and shouting at Lethgro and Broz all the while.

But the Exile was shouting too, one word that cut through the Captain's cries and the whistling of the Quick-silvers: 'Wait!' At the same moment all three creatures stopped dead, the pull of the netted one ceasing so abruptly that it was yanked bodily toward the hill and lay motionless, tumbled on its side. A confused cheer went up from the hillside, and a second net descended on the second creature, which made no move and let itself be overturned like its fellow.

Now the Exile had arrived panting within the circle, and began to plead for calm. He carried a small device in his hands, which, he said, gave him power over the creatures (though he asserted they were not creatures, but themselves devices, no more alive than his flying pods). It was urgent now, he said, to call off whoever was on the hillside, so that negotiations could begin in earnest and in peace.

The Captain cupped her hands around her mouth and hallooed in that direction, calling out that any sailor under her command, and anyone else of good sense, would be well advised to stop all hostilities immediately and wait for orders.

The Exile had been staring about him at the carnage of the Quicksilvers' camp, the wounded and the dead, the wrecked caves and the blue eyes glazed with misery, and he began to speak in a broken voice, saying that he was sorry for the damage, which might have been avoided with more patience. But the Captain interrupted him. 'If you mean to do the Quicksilvers any good,' she said, 'you'll let them get out of this muck and this heat. Is that boundary safe to cross?'

The Exile swore that it was, so long as he held the control device, and explained this as best he could to Whistle; and in a very few minutes the living Quicksilvers had disappeared into the darkness, the ablest carrying the worst hurt on their shoulders. Only Whistle perched within sight, above the sealed mouth of a snow cave.

Meanwhile one of Repnomar's sailors – Anscrop, as they saw when he reached the light – had come down the hill, reporting that (with all due respect to the Captain's orders) there was something that needed doing at once, for there were still people trapped in those collapsed caves, Captain Brask among them.

'What are you waiting for, then?' Repnomar snapped. 'Get to it!' And Anscrop, pausing only to say that they were hard at it already, turned and scrambled back up the snowy slope. 'So they dug their way out,' the Captain observed with satisfaction.

Lethgro and the Exile were gazing at each other with looks of grim appraisal. It was Lethgro who spoke: 'Well, friend, am I your prisoner, or are you mine?'

The Exile answered mildly that he hoped there was no need for either to hold the other prisoner, especially if they were friends indeed, as he trusted they were. But he did not fail to point out that he and his people had powers that could destroy everything within sight in a moment, though they did not like to use them for such purposes. Here

Lethgro cast a look of much eloquence at the ugliness around them, the clean snow changed to dirty swill, and the bodies of Quicksilvers, no longer silver and no longer quick, soaking in the slop. And the Exile added, still more mildly, that unless some agreement could be reached, his people would have no choice but to destroy all who had witnessed this affair.

This seemed excessive to both Lethgro and the Captain, and they said so with vigor. 'But never mind that now,' the Captain finished, with a stroke of her hand through the air as if to wipe it all away. 'For there's nothing we want more than an agreement. Let's put away the weapons and talk.'

The Exile agreed heartily with this, and would have led them back to his people's ship at once; but Repnomar wanted first to see to the welfare of her crew (not to mention Brask) and Lethgro insisted that the meeting must be on neutral ground and that the Quicksilvers must be in it. So that with one thing and another it was some little while before they were settled at last on a nearby hilltop. By general consent, all sides had taken time to eat and refresh themselves and lay their plans before they came to conference.

Captain Repnomar was in high good humor, for none of the sailors had been killed, or even much hurt, in the collapsing of the snow caves, nor any of the Quicksilvers except those who had been cut down at the entrances. The sailors who had been trapped inside, while their comrades had been attacking the creatures with nets, had much to say about this uncivil neglect; and Brask, snorting like a walrus and beating snow from her clothes with both hands, assured anyone within earshot that she could have handled the whole affair better.

Another reason for Repnomar's cheerfulness was that (though she agreed with Lethgro that it would be foolish, as things stood, to trust themselves on board the alien ship or even too close to it) she hoped sooner or later to have a view of that ship and all the wonders it must contain. Indeed the Exile had hinted that he might be able to arrange such a tour if once an agreement were reached. It tickled her fancy mightily to be conferring with gods, and she meant to strike a good bargain with them. All her bitterness of a little while ago was, though not forgotten, at least set aside for present purposes.

Whistle and a number of other Quicksilvers were there, and all but one (so the Exile claimed) of the strangers, that one being left with the ship. On the human side, Repnomar and Lethgro took the lead, supported by Brask and Broz, while the sailors crowded behind them for a view of the strangers.

These, indeed, were not much to see, except for their outlandish clothing, for they all looked a good deal like the Exile. But they conducted themselves with some dignity. In deference to the Quicksilvers, they had not set up one of their fiery lights, but a much cooler one. First the Exile's captain (whose name was as unmanageable as his own) made a short speech, which the Exile, with apologies to the humans, translated first into Quicksilver chirps; for, as he said, it was addressed mostly to them. The Quicksilvers listened gravely, sometimes interrupting him with a few sharp whistles. Then they conferred among themselves while the Exile repeated the speech more briefly to the humans. The gist of it was that the strangers, having been attacked and imprisoned without provocation, had very naturally called their devices (by means of smaller devices which they prudently carried) to rescue them and defend them; but that in spite of this inhospitable reception, they meant no harm to any of the peoples of this world. They were prepared to make restitution in the form of medical care for the wounded. And the Exile added that this offer was not only for Quicksilvers, and that he had good hope that even Broz's eye and the Warden's arm might be healed.

Now Whistle (with occasional additions from other Quicksilvers) delivered a spirited reply, to the effect (as the Exile eventually explained it) that they would allow the strangers to try their healing on a few of the wounded who were thought to be past help, so long as it was done in the open away from the ship. And on this, two of the strangers withdrew to fetch their medicines and gear, with a Quicksilver to guide them to the patients.

And the conference proceeded – slowly, since everything must be translated twice, and the Exile was sometimes at a loss for proper words in one language or another. They were all seated, the strangers on their sheets, the humans (except for some of the sailors, who were still craning to see) on their blankets and packs, the Quicksilvers very comfortably on their haunches in the snow. But in the midst of one of the Exile's translations Lethgro stood up, rising to his full dignity, and the Exile fell silent.

'We've heard enough lies,' Lethgro said, and his voice boomed across the snowy hillside, 'and enough smooth speeches. Let's have straight talk. Why are you here?'

The Exile cast a glance at his captain, but to Lethgro's surprise he did not at once translate those words. Instead, he answered softly, 'I'll tell you.' And he began to tell.

'You know there are many worlds,' he said. 'I've told you so. Most have no peoples, no beasts, only rocks and clouds. In some worlds, the people are trees or grass.' (Brask, who was still not accustomed to the Exile's strange statements, gave a great guffaw of laughter at this, but he went on.) 'My own people were born in a world very far from here – "Earth", we call it – but we have been coming nearer for a long time, visiting many worlds, settling in some; meeting other peoples, which is good for us, and sometimes good for them. Now, there are agreements among the peoples of these different worlds – not all of them, but the ones who know how to sail from world to world. There is a league, like the league between the Councils of Beng and Rotl. The league of worlds is a good thing, because it makes for peace between worlds. But there are other agreements, more important.'

Here the Exile, though he had been speaking with unaccustomed fluency, seemed hard put to find the next words; and his captain took advantage of this faltering to speak sharply to him. The Exile answered; and after a short exchange he turned back to Lethgro, saying mildly, 'If I've made trouble for you, I've made trouble for myself, too.'

'What other agreements?' Repnomar demanded.

Now the Exile answered that in many worlds there were folk whose pleasure and business was always to learn new things; and from this came not only their own livelihood and satisfaction, but all those powers and devices that had so amazed and troubled other worlds. 'And we have a league of our own,' the Exile said. (From which they took it that he and his comrades were among these curious folk.) 'And there is a league of traders, too. And these leagues are more powerful than the league of – of councils.'

'And what does your league want with this world?' Lethgro asked, for at last he began to see a kind of sense in all this.

But the Exile thought best to refer this to his captain, who made another speech. It was not clear, however, if the Exile translated it or not; for what he said was, 'I was sent here – I and my friend who is dead and eaten – to set up devices for reporting the weather, as I told you. If there was anything I did not tell you, it was only that there are many such missions, each to a different world. We take the reports of all these devices and put them together to learn as much as we can about the making of weathers, why one world is different from another, how peoples can use their weathers – all this and much more. But one other thing we have learned – ' (here the Exile's face squeezed up ruefully into an expression of pain) 'one thing we've learned is that it's dangerous to touch a world. It's not like a little rock you drop into the Soll; it's like a knife you stick into a sail, and when the wind blows, the cut tears wider and wider. Everything changes, before we can find out what it is. Everything changes, and we've set somebody else's ship adrift. Now we try not to touch a world too hard. We send two alone with the devices, to set them up secretly. (Also,' he added, 'this way is cheaper.) But now – ' He gestured helplessly. 'I had to tell my captain that the Quicksilvers killed my friend.'

'And what comes of that?' asked Lethgro; for he thought that if these people's idea of justice resembled the White People's, there was trouble ahead.

'An investigation,' said the Exile. 'There always has to be an investigation. But only a small investigation, because I have already explained what happened. It's too bad – ' He stopped, and started again with a different thought: 'Then my captain will decide what to recommend.'

Now Repnomar inquired sharply what the stranger captain would be recommending to whom about what; and the Exile answered that there were three possible recommendations: to leave this world unexamined, hoping that not much damage had been done to it; or to plant the devices as secretly as could now be done and try to cover their traces; or (and here the Exile hesitated, as if he disliked what he had to say) to call for another ship.

'Another ship to do what?' Repnomar snapped, ignoring for the moment the fact that he had not answered all of her first question.

'To make the survey,' said the Exile, using a word that he must have learned at Sollet Castle, for it was ordinarily used of the Warden's periodic progresses through the

Upper and Middle Sollet country, observing the countryside and dealing with its problems. So there was a little confusion till the Exile explained that by 'survey' he meant the studying of a world, the gathering of all those reports that the devices were meant to send; 'except,' he said, 'that a survey crew can learn more than the devices alone, and do more damage.'

'And to whom,' Lethgro put in, 'does your captain make his recommendation?'

'To certain officers of our league,' he answered. 'And they decide, though usually they follow whatever recommendation is made to them. And all this may take several watches to settle.'

'And if a survey crew comes,' said Repnomar, 'how long does it take to do its work?'

But the Exile said dolefully, 'When the survey crew comes, your world begins to die.'

This chilled Lethgro. But he said, looking curiously at the Exile, 'That makes you sad?'

And the Exile answered, 'Yes.'

Here the conference was interrupted by those wounded Quicksilvers that the strangers had been treating. These bounded into the light with musical trills, dancing about their comrades, who petted and patted them eagerly with their swift paws and joined in the trilling. And they opened the flaps of their chests to each other, which the Exile said was a kind of greeting. Lethgro waggled the fingers of his useless arm painfully, and Repnomar ran her hand over Broz's head; but they said nothing, for there were other things still to settle.

30
A Dinner in Rotl

'We know we could have done worse,' the Warden said feelingly. 'But we won't know for a while whether we've done well.'

'Knowing is one thing, and being sure is another,' the Captain answered. 'And I'm as sure as I need to be that we've done very well, Lethgro.'

The Warden filled his plate again. 'May you be right this time, Repnomar,' he said devoutly.

Repnomar waved a juicy drumstick, scattering gravy. 'We've got the *Mouse* home safe,' she said, citing first the point closest to her heart. 'And you got the League a treaty with the White People, if the Councils decide to sign it when they're through with their yammering. And you're Warden of Sollet Castle again, in spite of not bringing back the Exile – which shows that a Council's threats aren't worth much more than a god's.'

'Drink your ale,' said Lethgro, who did not much approve of such imprudent and irreverent remarks, even in private. He poured her another cup, pleased to be able to do it with his right arm. 'If we hadn't been able to prove he was dead, we would have had a different welcome.'

'That's true,' the Captain agreed cheerfully. It had been chancy enough as it was, for though the Council of Rotl had accepted their story after only six or seven hours of deliberation, the Council of Beng had been harder to convince, citing a lack of material evidence. Only a long procession of sailors, one by one deposing under oath that they had seen the Exile plunge from the top of the Dreeg waterfall and disappear into the roiling waters, had persuaded the councilors not only to revoke the sentence of outlawry but to concur in restoring Lethgro to his former office (to the general pleasure of the folk of Sollet Castle, Castle Wharf, and all the Middle Sollet, for with some exceptions they had missed Warden Lethgro). That had been a nervous time for Lethgro and Repnomar on two counts. Not only were their necks in danger, but there was the chance that one sailor or another would testify too much – though they had all taken awesome oaths in the frozen darkness of Quicksilver country, and more recently (in case they had forgotten) outside Beng harbor, never to mention what they had seen and heard of the strangers from beyond the clouds. ('They'll tell their families, of course,' Repnomar had observed philosophically, 'and bit by bit stories will get around. But it won't hurt if these are a few more gods worshipped. And these at least are real ones.')

But not a sailor had said too much or too little. They had all been notably well paid; for Lethgro had received a fat bonus from the Council of Rotl, which he had promptly divided among the sailors, on top of the pay they had already had from his own money-box.

'I know you're worried,' the Captain added, setting down her cup, 'and so you should be, Lethgro, because it's your job to worry. But the only thing that worries me is Brask over there on her own. If I don't get back there soon, she and that cutthroat crew of hers will have finished work on the Dreeg portage and headed upstream to see what they can steal from the Low Coasters.' She chuckled. 'That should be a fair match.'

'It will surprise me,' the Warden said gloomily, 'if they've been working on the portage at all.'

'They know they won't get their pay, let alone their pardons from the League, till they've finished that job and I've checked their work,' Repnomar said. 'We'll have a portage that's as easy going up as going down, and easier both ways than you and I have seen it.' This was said with some feeling, for it had been a rough haul up the rugged slope beside the waterfall, and the *Mouse*'s planking, as well as the temper and limbs of all three crews, had been sorely strained. 'What we really need,' the Captain added musingly, 'is a canal, if it could be made somehow in steps . . . And you know, Lethgro, if we could do that on the Dreeg, we could do it easier on the Sollet. There's no reason why you shouldn't be able to sail a canal upriver all the way to Sollet Castle and beyond, given a few more years. With what we know now – ' She broke off with a laugh. 'With what we knew all along, Lethgro – there's the joke of it! I've been sailing against the wind for more years than I like to count; but it never occurred to me or anyone else to try sailing against a current – not till I learned from watching outlanders that there are more ways than one to travel, and to think, too.'

This was a topic that interested the Warden personally, and he leaned across the table. 'I thought you said you'd undertake to sail a ship up the Sollet anytime,' he said a little anxiously, for he was weary to the very bones of uncomfortable and hazardous journeyings, and he longed to be back at Sollet Castle.

'Yes, if I had the ship for it. A step-canal would be easier going, with no current to speak of, but I'd sail you upriver right now if the *Mouse* weren't hauled out for repair. A Sollet ship doesn't have the rigging for the job, nor the hull either. Besides, as soon as the *Mouse* is ready and loaded, I'll be off with my first cargo for the Quicksilvers. Give me another year, Lethgro.'

The Warden chuckled ruefully. 'It's been a long time already, Rep, and another year or so won't matter. If it happens in my lifetime, that will surprise me enough.'

'And I have to send my report,' the Captain said with

relish. This was the finest plum that she had plucked from the whole adventure, and she was mightily proud of it. There had been some difficulty when the Exile first proposed this compromise, for, as he had regretfully admitted, regulations did not provide for such an arrangement. It was not thought proper, he explained, to leave the reporting devices at the mercy of natives of the world under study. Those devices should be either well hidden, or protected by a crew of his own people. Nor was it thought right for such a native ('meaning me,' as Repnomar had observed with some indignation) to gather and send such information as his league desired. But the Exile had explained at some length to his captain that Repnomar, who had already flown his pods, was well able to work the message devices, and was moreover an experienced ship's captain and therefore much at home with weather and skilled at noting its changes. And after some further conversation, the Exile had reported with shining eyes that there were precedents of a sort, at least for the gathering of information by natives, and that something might be worked out.

In fact it had taken many watches to work out everything: peace with the Quicksilvers (for there was evidently some inclination among the strangers to regard them as enemies to be fought), the oaths of secrecy (which the strangers did not seem to value highly, being more moved by the consideration that, as Lethgro, put it, 'Whatever we say will be taken for lies or madness, or else the doings of gods'), the placing of the devices and the agreement with Repnomar (whereby she was to watch over them and make her own reports each year with one of their talking boxes, giving them such news of the weather as their devices could not collect alone). This last agreement was provisional, and reached after the stranger captain had received what the Exile admitted was a grudging approval from the officers of their league.

The placing of the devices had been in itself a matter of some delicacy. The Exile's captain insisted that no one but his own people and Repnomar should know their exact locations, which was sensible. But when he proposed to take Repnomar in his ship to set them up, and the Exile hinted that this would be somewhere near the far edge of the darkness, Lethgro had swallowed once and demanded to be taken along. This was partly because he doubted that he could face the sight of Captain Repnomar getting into that outlandish ship with none but a passel of alien godlings and flying off to an unknown destination; and partly because he wanted to talk to the White People, if indeed they were going to that part of the world. So in the end Lethgro and Repnomar and Broz had climbed into that ship together, leaving Brask in charge of the remaining humans (with firm orders not to harass the Quicksilvers). And while Repnomar and Broz went with the strangers to view the setting up of the devices and note bearings and landmarks, Lethgro had gone off with the Exile to negotiate with whatever White People they could find. They had all returned well satisfied to Quicksilver country, and found things there still peaceful. 'More thanks to Whistle,' as Repnomar remarked, 'than to Brask.'

But during all these momentous and historic doings, there had been a weight upon Lethgro that grew heavier and heavier. He had watched the Exile plead the humans' case with his own people, and the Quicksilvers' case as well (though they had killed his friend). He remembered how the Exile had rescued them once from the Quicksilvers, and many times stood by them sturdily in time of trouble (though there were times enough, too, when he had deceived and abandoned them). Most recently, the Exile had labored along with him to make peace with the White People (and of those dealings, Lethgro had saved up many good stories to tell Repnomar, and especially how the spirits of Broz's victims had been pacified by the slaughtering of two of those savage sheep, which had provided a considerable banquet). That labor had been to such effect that Lethgro now carried the draft of a treaty and a trade agreement in his pocket to be submitted to the League.

He was, in short, fonder than ever of the Exile, in spite of all his efforts to think of him as nothing but a dangerous and unreliable alien. And though it was possible that the Councils might be persuaded to a pardon, that hope seemed to Lethgro still more dangerous and unreliable. Nevertheless, the Councils had entrusted him with a responsibility, and it was not his own liking that he must consider.

So when the time for good-byes had come, and all were listening politely while the stranger captain made one last speech, Lethgro composed a short speech of his own, clearly explaining that he could not return to civilization without the Exile, or proof of the Exile's death; so that, if the Exile sailed off beyond the clouds with his comrades (as he seemed about to do), Lethgro himself would be an exile and disgraced forever. When his turn came, he drew himself up very stiffly and delivered this speech word for word as he had thought it out, not trusting himself to speak his feelings freely. But the Exile, with that childlike look of his, said simply, 'Yes, I know.' And then cleared his throat and added. 'I think we can arrange it.'

They had arranged it, the Warden thought, rather well. 'And it was no easy thing he did,' he said now, pensively cutting himself another slice of mutton, 'devices or no devices. You couldn't have paid me to jump off the top of that waterfall.'

'We both did it once,' Repnomar reminded him, dipping her bread in the gravy.

'With a proper sail, yes – and I'm not sure I'd do *that* again. But all he had for a sail this time was that little bit of a thing that barely carried him away from the rocks. And then the weights in his pockets to drag him under, and not knowing surely if he could clap that thing to his face soon enough to breathe with – ' ('There was plenty of time on the way down,' Repnomar said,) ' – or if he could swim safe to shore underwater against the current.' ('He had that device to drive him through the water,' Repnomar said.) And Lethgro drew a long, whistling breath at the thought of that maelstrom under the falls.

But the Captain, who saw no need for regrets where all had ended happily, poured out more ale for both of them, saying, 'We know his ship was waiting for him a little way downstream. And we know he got there, because the crow came back to us.' This had been her own idea, to leave one of the crows secretly with the outlander captain, to be released when the Exile returned to his ship.

'We don't know it for certain,' the Warden said with stubborn gloom. 'That captain may have turned it loose just to keep us from tramping up and down the riverbank looking for the Exile, and maybe seeing his ship sail off again. Or just to get rid of the noisy thing.' For the crow had not liked being left with such peculiar strangers.

Now the Captain laughed at him outright, but fondly. 'Drink your ale, Lethgro. What's done is done. And we have other things to do now: you to make your deals with the White People, and I to take the *Mouse* across to the Low Coast again.' She squinted her eyes thoughtfully. 'And I'll bet you a better dinner than this one' ('It's a very good dinner,' Lethgro said,) 'that once I have it worked out properly, and know my courses and my times, I'll be visiting you in Sollet Castle every year. Or at least every other.'

'You mean to make the whole circle of the world every year?' Lethgro asked, with a bit of a shudder, for he remembered vividly those dreary and desperate watches among the ice rivers and snowfields and belching mountains of the dark side.

'Why not?' Repnomar retorted. 'It didn't kill us the first time. But I'd rather take it the easy way, and that's by water. There's Broz to think of, too.' (Here Broz, who was lying at her feet, rolled his eyes upward to look at her and thumped his tail comfortably once or twice on the floor.) 'He's done enough trekking through the dark for a while. So first we'll sail across the Soll and down the Dreeg to trade with Whistle's people and check the devices there; then back the same way with a cargo for Beng and Rotl. Then up the Sollet – *up* the Sollet, Lethgro! and that's when I'll visit you – and into the Mountains to check the second set of devices and send my messages and trade with the White People; and back down the Sollet again.'

Now the Warden chuckled deeply. 'And my job, Rep – aside from taking care of matters on the Upper and Middle Sollet, which till now I thought was job enough – is to keep you from making a mess of things with your voyaging and your trading.' For he had taken the Exile's stories much to heart.

'And I'll know in half a year or less,' the Captain added optimistically, 'if he's all right.' For half her mind, like Lethgro's, was on the Exile. 'Don't forget he promised to answer my messages, and maybe come back now and again for a visit.'

'Which is a sign,' Lethgro agreed, 'that these outlanders are fairly sensible beings; for the Exile is the only one of them who knows this world, and it's only right he should be the one to deal with us.'

'Fairly sensible for gods,' Repnomar said, with a snort of laughter.

'But they're not gods,' the Warden corrected her. 'You've seen for yourself the Exile has no special powers without his outlandish gear, and I don't doubt that's true for all of them.'

'Which is what I mean exactly,' the Captain insisted. 'I say that's what gods are – and what most people call gods are bad dreams and indigestion.'

And they began to argue with such vigor, and went on for so long, that the innkeeper looked in on them three times, wiping her hands on her apron, for she would have liked to close her dining room and get some rest. But she did not disturb them, for they were notable personages, and likely to leave good tips.